FROM THE DUST . . .

They had found the tomb of a king. But what king? What king was executed by the Romans? The Romans didn't execute Jewish kings. The Romans didn't execute any kings, at least not in the provinces. Kings were brought back to Rome.

Unless of course this wasn't a king, wasn't a king at all. The disk had been put there to mock him, to mock a claim, to show he wasn't a king, but a helpless criminal. It was in Aramaic because that was the common language of the Jews at that time, and authorities wanted to emphasize he was not the real King of the Jews.

And suddenly there was not enough air in the cave or the world for Sharon's lungs. Her mouth opened and she could not move . . .

THE BODY

Richard Ben Sapir

PINNACLE BOOKS NEW YORK

THE BODY

Pinnacle Books edition, published by special arrangement with
Doubleday & Co., Inc.

Doubleday edition published 1983
Pinnacle edition/December 1984

ISBN:0-523-42249-0
Can. ISBN: 0-523-43241-0

Printed in the United States of America

PINNACLE BOOKS, INC.
1430 Broadway
New York, New York 10018

9 8 7 6 5 4 3 2 1

For
Patricia Kathleen Chute:
My love, my wife, my friend—
a special and gracious woman

ACKNOWLEDGMENTS

This book had the help of many people, researchers, and editorial critics. They are:

Judith Netzer, Lisa Drew, Will Murray, Shira Nahari, Joseph McCormick, S.J., Dr. Joseph Feger, Joan Poulin, Dr. James Morris, Richard Senier, Linda Sloss, Betsy John, Reid Boates, P. K. Chute, Elizabeth Coffey Chute, Rosaleen Regan, Jay Acton, Dr. Joseph Sapir, Martha Feinstein Sapir, Mary Chute Brownell, Ken Rosen.

Two Israelis asked that their names not be used.

CONTENTS

THE BODY

1

Beyond the Limits

The young American spotted it first.

No bigger than a knuckle it was, appearing after another monotonous stroke of a straw whisk in a morning of monotonous strokes of the straw whisk. He stopped.

It was the same yellow-brown limestone from which much of Jerusalem was built, giving the city a golden presence under the sun.

But that was three stories above, in modern Jerusalem, where the group had started at the end of June in a spot north of Damascus Gate in the Old City walls, 11.6 carefully measured meters above where now there was the late summer heat, and car honking and fumes and tourists and food and all the sense rattling of a living city.

Down at the bottom of the archaeological dig it was cool beyond the seasons, a minimum of fifteen hundred years down into the sediments of civilizations.

Down here more limestone was supposed to mean the end of man because it was supposed to be more bedrock.

They had been told that when they had exposed all four corners of this dig to bedrock, they could be assured that everything there was to find of man in this scholarly hole had been found.

By then everything would have been sketched, photographed, locused, and cataloged, hopefully adding another precise shade of history to the place. Done for others to refer to as data.

But this small exposure of limestone was just slightly different from the bedrock the young American had been seeing for the last two days. It had a smoothness. He whisked away more hard-packed earth. The fragment became larger, the size of his palm.

He tucked the straw whisk into his belt next to his hand pick and withdrew the camel's-hair brush, a finer, gentler tool that would scratch nothing.

He cleaned to the edge of the fragment, dusting away dry centuries. All of it was as smooth as the first knuckle-sized piece.

His feet rested on the downward slope of bedrock, but this smooth piece did not slope. And staring close, he knew what he had seen. The smoothness meant worked stone. Chisel blades had worked that stone. He could spot that now.

He was a volunteer and he had come a long way this summer. He could sit on his haunches for hours now without pain, and he knew when the presiding archaeologist should be called and when she should not.

He thought about her as he looked at the stone. His name was Mark, and he played Frisbee and went to the University of Michigan, and he believed in Jesus Christ, Son of the Almighty God, Messiah of all men, Jews included, whose time would come only when the entire world was saved.

He had wondered when he arrived in Israel for the dig whether Jesus would come when he was there. He was sure the Second Coming was going to happen in Israel, where the first had happened.

And he was sure it was soon. The Bible said the Jews would return to Israel just before the Second Coming, and here they were, according to the Bible. Here was everything according to the Bible, although Sharon, Dr. Golban, had warned him specifically that the best way to prove the Bible was to be a proper archaeologist first.

Sharon was a Jew, an Israeli, and her family had come from Persia and had been there since Nebuchadnezzar, and that was in the Bible, too. She was right about the Bible: it was all around here and true. Not like true in Flint, Michigan, where it was a story, where you had to believe it or not; but it was right here in your face, all around in the rocks and places and people.

You could see the stones of Herod. It wasn't a story. It had all happened.

Which in a way took some of the wonder out of it. But as Dr. Golban had said at thĕ beginning of the dig:

"A known fact, a pottery shard which we have discovered, and how and when it was fired, is greater than all the imaginary universes that ever were."

"Do you believe the Bible, then, is a fairy tale?"

"No. I don't."

"Do you believe the Bible is one hundred percent true?"

"I believe what you call the Bible, which is really Greek for book, *biblion*, or what you call the book, is a collection of books."

"And that means what?"

"That they are documents."

"I know you don't believe in Jesus. Do you believe in Moses?"

"I believe Moses existed. That God talked to him, well, who knows?"

"Is it 'cause you can't get married?"

"Who told you that?"

"Everyone on the dig knows. They say you were married, and even though everything wasn't your fault, you still can't get married in Israel because it's against religious law."

"That's right."

"If you were a Christian you could get married again. I'd marry you."

"If I were a Christian?" She had said that, laughing. She was beautiful. She was thirty-two, twelve years older than Mark, and she was beautiful, with eyes as dark as midnight dreams, golden skin and rich black hair, and a beautiful body with trim legs, which, when she wore shorts, and she did that a lot, made Mark think how he would like to stroke her thighs. And he didn't like to think those thoughts. When she wore a shirt, sometimes it would be unbuttoned and he would try to stop himself from looking down and seeing how healthy and tan the breasts were where they met the sharp white-cloth bra line. He tried to stop himself from looking, and that meant he was always looking.

She was the chief archaeologist on the dig, and he was sure

he loved her. He didn't care what she believed. He could always save her soul later.

"I'd marry you, period. I think you're beautiful," he had said.

"Now, Mark, lying is a sin."

"You are beautiful."

"Come, come, Mark." And she laughed and kissed him on the cheek, and he wasn't sure he should kiss back. That she didn't for some reason believe she was beautiful was just part of her beauty.

But she was beautiful, even if she wouldn't let him say it to her, and even if he couldn't talk God to her. She had taught him when something was important and when it was not.

And looking at the stone, Mark, the young American, had little doubt that this was important enough to call her down to take a look. He dared not go farther alone.

He looked up to Haneviim Street and the twentieth century and called out:

"Something. Sharon, I think we have something."

There was no answer.

"Something," yelled Mark again, standing up on his feet, straddling what was now the platter-sized top of the stone. It was definitely not bedrock.

"You know enough now," came the voice of Dr. Sharon Golban from above. The people at the dig spoke English because it was the most common language of the volunteers. "Label it. You're at Locus II B."

"I think you'd better come down."

"I'll be down in a minute, Mark," Sharon called down into the dig without peering in.

"A serious delay?" asked the Arab businessman she had been talking to. There was worry in his eyes. He spoke in Hebrew, although they had often conversed in Arabic. She answered in the same tongue. It was not her first language.

Farsi was that and Hebrew was her daily tongue while English was the universal language. She had taken Arabic as her one elective language in school while others studied French, not only because she thought Arabic was more beautiful than French but because she thought ultimately her country should look to that part of the world.

Like her languages, she was between worlds. A Persian beauty fit for a tapestry, yet she dressed in the hard practical clothes of the West, shorts, blouse, sandals, and sometimes sunglasses.

She thought Western, yet often felt Eastern. She smoked too much and was too direct, yet with Mr. Hamid she understood his concerns. She was quite precise in shaking her head and making sure she explained the situation thoroughly. He deserved that.

"No. No. *No*. There are delays and delays. If it's a stone fragment, we'll have it labeled and sketched and photographed and then go on," she said in Arabic.

"And if it's not?" asked the businessman.

"It probably is. We have been at bedrock for a day. It should all be over soon. We are just following the slope, as I have told you."

"And I was just digging a basement," he said with a pained smile.

Sharon took a deep pull on her cigarette, holding the sharp, burning smoke in her lungs, trying to get filled with it before she went down again. She would not smoke at the bottom of any dig for fear of grinding an ash accidentally into an object with a foot, and then when the object was unearthed fully and if it were carbon-dated it would come back reading not 200 B.C.E., or so, but last Thursday, plus or minus a century.

Mr. Hamid was right. Both of them were trapped here because he had wanted to build a basement for his new appliance store. He could not build it until the Department of Antiquities was assured he was not pouring any new cement over any old historical treasures, and Sharon was the one who had to do the assuring, when she would rather have spent a summer on digs inside the Old City walls. That was where important work was being done.

It had been a sequence of bad luck for Mr. Hamid, or inevitability if one knew how things worked in modern Jerusalem.

He was successfully overseeing the preparation of the foundation when a bulldozer cracked out part of a blue and gold mosaic floor two meters down.

One of the laborers knew where he could secretly sell a melon-wide piece of the tile floor. He took it to an antiquities dealer off Via Dolorosa, in the Old City, named Zareh Tabinian, and this would not have been so bad, except this dealer was suspected of selling an especially proscribed antiquity, which meant he was in danger of losing his "grapes."

And this fear of losing "grapes" ultimately would lead to a basement becoming an archaeological site.

"The grapes," as they were called, was a decal of two ancients carrying an oversized bunch of blue grapes, which the Ministry of Tourism granted businesses that met government standards. To be without one's "grapes" meant a merchant virtually had to give up the influx of American dollars, because Americans, in a blizzard of oriental strangeness, trusted only those official decals on shop windows.

For an antiquities dealer to give up the American tourist dollar meant doom. Israelis just did not have the kind of extra moneys that would pay for antiquities. When they did have money, they didn't buy oil lamps from the hallowed rebellion of their hero Bar Kochba, or ancient shekels or lustrous Roman glass. They bought television sets.

So to protect his livelihood, Zareh Tabinian righteously took the piece of tile to the Department of Antiquities and announced that he would forgo this piece, even though he had paid for it with his own money, money he knew he stood to lose by submitting the tile.

"No, no," said the woman at the Department of Antiquities. "This is a common Byzantine floor. You know yourself better than anyone that what you sold, Mr. Tabinian, was not just a proscribed antiquity, but the most proscribed."

And he did know. For while all antiquities were legally proscribed for sale, the authorities, for the sake of tourism, would overlook small infractions if they were pieces of pottery or mosaics or oil lamps, especially since most antiquities sold throughout Israel were imported by the many shops from Jordan, Egypt, Greece, and Cyprus. They were not Judaean at all.

But never would the authorities allow the sale of something with the written word on it found in the land of Israel. More valuable than gold or statuary was the word, in clay or stone or papyrus.

And Tabinian had sold an ostracon with Hebrew on it to a German professor who had more experience in annotation than subterfuge. For while he had promised to disguise whom he had bought it from, when his article appeared in print, everyone who knew antiquities and who sold what, and what things tended to be found where, knew the shop had to be Tabinian's, off Via Dolorosa.

And while there was no legal evidence for this, nothing that would survive an Israeli court, there was, in the daily business of all antiquities shops, so much against the law that the Department of Antiquities could get Tabinian convicted on a dozen provable counts, and thus get the Ministry of Tourism to yank his grapes.

"You've got to give us more, Mr. Tabinian," said the woman in the antiquities department. "Where was this found?"

"I don't know where. He was just a laborer," said Tabinian, whereupon the woman suddenly noticed a corner of a cross on the piece of mosaic tile.

"A cross. This floor had to be before 430 A.D.," said the woman.

Both of them knew that any floor with a cross on it anywhere in the eastern Mediterranean had to have been laid before that date, because that was when the Byzantine Emperor Theodosius decreed the cross was too holy to be walked on.

"Why is it," said Tabinian, "that when I surrendered this paid-for fragment of a floor, it was considered to be valueless. But when I tell you I am not sure of where it was found, then it becomes valuable?"

"You have a good point, Mr. Tabinian," said the woman, smiling, the woman who could get his grapes removed.

"Haneviim Street," said Tabinian, with a shrug. "Nasir Hamid is building a basement to an appliance store."

And with those words, Zareh Tabinian made an enemy of an old Jerusalem family, which he didn't want to do, stopped the basement on Haneviim Street, gave Nasir Hamid a new partner and Sharon Golban a summer dig.

For no work could be continued until the Department of Antiquities made sure that nothing remained under that sign that could be of historical value. An archaeologist had to supervise a registered dig to bedrock.

"When will you start?" were the first words Nasir Hamid had asked of Dr. Golban.

"I am sorry, but we have to wait for the beginning of summer. Then there is less chance of destructive rains, and then we have the use of so many volunteers."

He begged her to be swift. She assured him she would. When he tried to press money into her hands, she refused in such a way as not to demean his dignity, always showing the utmost respect.

She kept him informed of daily progress and gave him estimates of how long they would be at the site. She worked with good speed, mostly because she didn't want to have to spend another summer at this site. She wanted to get back with one of the major digs, inside the walls of Jerusalem.

But so grateful was Mr. Hamid for her courtesy that he gave her a fine necklace with several glistening opals. This was too personal a gift to refuse. She had to take it, and she did, saying in Arabic, which she knew well:

"This is such a beautiful gift, please do not shame me by anything more because I can never repay such generosity."

Legally it was a bribe, and her story would have been laughed at by most Ashkenazi, Israeli Jews descended from those who came from Europe. But she knew she had done right, and she made certain he saw her wear it, even though it was too pretty a thing, she felt, for her.

Nor would she give it away ever, because it was not given as a bribe, but as a very fine gesture.

Mr. Hamid, too, had learned a bit about archaeology during this summer, and when the American, Mark, called up that he had found something, Mr. Hamid saw himself paying full city taxes on a vacant lot for another year.

Sharon put out her cigarette.

"I will be back soon."

"You have my prayers," said Mr. Hamid.

"As God wills," she answered in Arabic, which she said only as a courtesy.

She descended by ladder through the recent British occupation, the Turkish rule, down beyond the Mamluks, the brief Crusader kings, the Arab rule, and the Byzantine level, where an entire floor had been removed by covering it with gauze to bind it, and then carefully sawing it into numbered squares, and then carefully carting it to a warehouse to wait for a university somewhere to ask for it, if one ever did, because there was already an overabundance of these floors, and every time another one was discovered it was preserved in the same way.

The descent, like the dig, was vertical. City space was too valuable to allow leisurely ramping for a dig of this minor importance. It went straight down, like an excavation for a slender skyscraper, and so did Dr. Sharon Golban until she was on bedrock, which she had labeled II B.

Everything down to the Byzantine floor was Locus I, and everything beneath it, Locus II. Nothing significant enough had been found to warrant establishing another level until she walked up to Mark, who stepped back into the small group of volunteers that was now waiting around Mark's find.

Sharon lowered herself to her knees. She looked at the exposed portion of the stone. Not only had chisels smoothed it, she didn't think it was even part of the bedrock, or even attached to it. She looked up to the far wall. There were roughly three meters of packed horizontal earth to go to reach it. It might be quite deep to bedrock beneath that area, enough to trench down, exposing what was underneath.

"You're right. I think it is something," said Sharon.

"I thought so," said Mark, and put a whisk in her hand.

She brushed toward herself, and the stone ended in a sharp line. She brushed at the line. The stone dropped vertically.

She leaned forward and brushed away from her, and reached another sharp vertical drop. Between the two lines was roughly a meter. Apparently it was the width of this stone. She whisked to her right and there was a curving downward. There was an identical downward curve to the left.

They could be working the top of a massive stone circle, thought Sharon.

She brushed between stone and slope, deeper now, until she saw where they touched, the smooth stone apparently set against bedrock, very tight.

"All right," said Sharon to the crew. "We'll trench down the far side of the stone with picks. But we will maintain thoroughness. Everything found is to be handled as to form. No rushing."

Before evening they had cleared a solid trench down behind the stone and then along both sides. The stone was perfectly round, roughly 1.3 meters in diameter. The height of most sternums. It was set firmly against the slope, which was formed to accept it. Sharp chisel marks from rough hewing were visible. Probably the stone covered an opening to something, possibly a cave.

On the way down they had gotten good dating for Locus III. It was a Pilatus coin just at the lower level of bedrock, where the stone rested. The big P on the coin signified the cognomen of the Roman governor at the time, P. Pilatus.

The coin was the two hundred and twelfth object found, and was cataloged 212, Locus III.

A meter rod of white and black markings was set in front of the stone. Then it was photographed. Whoever saw the photo would know the size of the stone from the meter rod.

The stone was labeled 213, III, the two hundred and thirteenth object found at Locus III.

"Could this be a tomb?" asked Mark.

"I don't think so," said Sharon. "This is not a burial ground, and while this sort of stone was used often to seal worked-stone mausoleums, it wasn't used to seal caves."

"Why not?" asked a British volunteer.

"For the same reason you wouldn't use a fine oak door as a garden bench. They just didn't do it."

"Boy, it would be great if it were a tomb," said a volunteer.

Sharon reached out a hand and one of the volunteers placed a whisk in it. She worked at where the round stone touched the hewn rock. Packed dirt fell away into darkness. She peered in. And she recognized what she saw.

"I guess we should get on with it, eh?" said the British student, suddenly and strangely subdued. She had been cheery all summer during the drone and grit of the dig.

Up on Haneviim Street, amid the diesel cough of Jerusalem taxis, an Arab merchant let out a groan. All he needed to see was the excitement. He did not wait to be told by the Israeli woman. His appliance store was not going to be built this season.

What she did not tell the volunteers, and hoped they might not realize, was that stairs could now mean a tomb. It was not that she did not want them guessing, or even hoping.

If it were a tomb, there would be talking, and that talk might get to the Mea Shearim religious quarter nearby. Some fanatic ultra-Orthodox might attack them if he heard they were disturbing a body.

Whether it was a three-thousand-year-old Jacobite soldier or the chief rabbi of their sect made no difference to them. They thought all bodies were Jews until proved otherwise, and therefore had to remain undisturbed.

"Let's clear a trench to the right, where we have some space, and tomorrow morning, first thing, we will take a look at our cave. Now, I don't want a great audience, so until we know what's inside, let's not start celebrations among friends. Let us keep our find to ourselves."

She climbed up through the centuries to Haneviim Street and had a cigarette. Mr. Hamid was gone. Down the streets the lights went on, illuminating the Old City walls for the tourists.

She felt light-headed and realized she had not eaten.

But she did not want food. She wanted to put up big floodlights, get a crane to lift the stone like a loose tooth, and then dive right into that cave, like the rankest amateur.

If it were a tomb, here where no tombs had ever been unearthed, then it was a hell of a find, possibly.

She lit another cigarette from the stub of her cigarette, and smoked several more without a match. Finally, the crew was climbing up. Someone volunteered to spend the night.

"No, the stone has been there for a couple of millennia. I think it will safely seal the cave for one more night," said Sharon.

The next day was dry and clear and everyone was at the site early. Sharon had a breakfast of green grapes and Arab sesame bread, two cups of thick black coffee with extra sugar, and three cigarettes.

Then, with cameras and notebooks, and leaving the new garbage in modern Jerusalem, they all went down to the stone.

"It hasn't been moved," said Mark, peering closely at the bottom of the stone.

"Did you think it would?" said Sharon.

"I put a match fragment under the stone. If anyone had moved it, the fragment would have been ground into the earth."

"Well, good for you, Mark. I never thought of that, but precautions never hurt," said Sharon.

She checked her top blouse button. It was closed.

"We know this stone was placed here before 430 C.E. or Common Era because of the mosaic floor above us, or Mr. Hamid's great tragedy. We know, because of the Pilatus coin, that this Locus III was not B.C.E. or Before Common Era. The Pilatus coin gives us at least 20 C.E."

"Maybe the coin was carried around for a long time and then lost," said the Dutch girl.

"Possibly, but probably not. Usually when a coin is found, unless it is part of a deep-buried hoard, and this was not, it gives us a good dating as to time of use."

She also gave them a reference point in time:

"Pilatus was before the governor Glaucus, who was responsible for innumerable troubles, which gave us all those wonderful disasters that preserve the past so well."

And then came the moving of the stone. Mark stood on top of it, his back pressed against one earthen wall, creating pressure on his feet for the rock to roll. The Dutch girl put her shoulder behind his feet, and Sharon and the British girl each got their hands on the stone, and when Sharon announced, "Push," the stone moved, almost tumbling Mark down on his back. There was space for him to get down behind the stone now, but its mass was much harder to move without the backing of the wall. They needed another man. Three women and one man could not move it. Then Mark got part of the ladder wedged under the stone, and with all of them pushing up on the ladder, the stone rolled with a great heavy groan along limestone bedrock.

The cave was open, probably for the first time in two thousand years.

Sharon saw immediately that the cave was carved out by chisel. The steps were even, and relatively smooth. The opening went to a carved floor.

The volunteers looked to Sharon. They were waiting for her to enter.

"We photograph the entrance," she said. "If any of you thought we should just walk in, I would have been a failure as director of this dig."

After the proper photographs were taken and notations made

for them, Sharon took a flashlight and got down on her knees. She leaned in and shone the light about. The floor was a simple hewn stone, without pattern and rough. She suspected that the ceiling was higher beyond the steps.

They photographed the steps before Sharon lowered herself to enter. With a whisk in one hand and a flashlight in the other, she lowered herself feetfirst into the opening.

It smelled like an old basement. She had been told that by other archaeologists who set foot in tombs or buildings or tunnels where men had not been for centuries. A month or a millennium, they all smelled like old musty basements.

The cave was over two meters high beyond the entrance, and went back three meters to a smooth wall, of lighter color than the limestone. The floor and ceiling were hewn stone, as were the walls.

"No objects at first glance," she called back. "The inside is a little over two meters high. Nobody will have to bend down in here."

The camera and lights were brought in, and the inside of the cave photographed in a light that numbed Sharon's eyes even when she faced away. It was as though the cave had exploded in light.

"Nothing?" asked Mark.

"It might well have been some form of a storehouse, and people came in and stole the goods."

For the rest of the morning the floor was whisked and brushed and photographed centimeter by centimeter. There were no inscriptions. The direction of the central axis was written down, and Mark made a good observation about the chisel marks on the cave interior being much rougher than those of the stone that sealed the cave.

"I think they may have transported the stone from elsewhere," he said, quite professionally. "Scavenged it from the formal tombs of the Kidron Valley."

"That's a good supposition," said Sharon, "because the Kidron tombs were before the Roman occupation and our Pilatus coin. And you can scavenge only from what is there."

"Could well be the Romans," said Maria, the Dutch girl.

"They did a lot of that during their occupation," said Mark. "Cut right through many tombs to get building material."

"Excellent," said Sharon.

They all climbed up to the honk and fuel exhaust of Jerusalem in a hot noon, and went to a small shop to have salad for lunch, and enjoyed the discussions of their cave. Now they all had a right to conjecture because they were talking about what they had labeled, sketched, and photographed.

Now also there was no danger of some religious fanatic attacking them for disturbing a body. Sharon talked about occupations of the city, and some of the hallmarks of the conquerors. She thought the cave was an unexpectedly good find, and another confirmation that it was not a burial area because the cave would have been a fine site for just such a purpose.

She talked at length of the Assyrians, who were for a long while a greater influence on the people of the area than the Greeks, but she could tell that, while she was steeped in the culture of the East, her volunteers, raised in the West, thought the East was just some kind of footnote to their history.

At least they learned not to think of everything in terms of religion. Perhaps they did think that, but no one was going to mention it in front of her anymore, and that was enough.

Jerusalem was not just the focal point for religious sects, it was a midpoint of great cultures, and if there was one thing she wanted to give her volunteers it was an appreciation that all things did not happen in the West.

She also had some good news for them.

"This afternoon I want to look at that rear wall. Did any of you notice the different colors and indentations?"

There were yeses.

"Those are probably unfired clay. Irregular brick just thrown up by the owner, probably. I don't want to conjecture, but I think there might have been some other entrances."

"That far down?" said a volunteer.

"It wasn't that far down two thousand years ago," said Sharon. "It was their street level then and maybe the stone sealed one entrance and the brick the other, although why they used clay brick, I don't know, because anyone could go through it with a knife."

"Maybe it was not sealing an entrance, but another room," said Mark.

"Maybe, but why seal it up?" said Sharon. "Who or what are you sealing another room from?"

"I'm excited," said Maria.

"So am I," said Sharon. "I was saving it for dessert."

"Do you think we'll find something significant?" asked Mark.

"We will find whatever there is to find," said Sharon, and she had her last cigarette going to the site. They had left someone at the ladder because she didn't want people poking around down there if they saw an opening. Someone could climb down and lose something that might throw them all off. It wouldn't be so bad if it were a modern key or something, but what if they had an artifact in their pocket?

Sharon entered the cave first again, and already it had lost that basement smell. It was no longer historically virgin, she thought.

Sharon went to the rear of the cave, and when everyone was ready behind her, including the Dutch girl, who would take notes, and another volunteer who would photograph, and Mark, who would sketch, she ran a finger against one clay brick. It cut.

"Unfired," she said.

Then, easily with a pick, she made an indentation. The pick went through. There was space behind the bricks.

Carefully she picked out a bowl-sized piece of brick. She had a photograph made of the hole. She measured its height, then, with her discipline bursting, she shone a light inside. "Bones," she said. "Human bones."

"How many?" asked Maria. "How many bodies?"

"I think one," said Sharon. She shone the light at different angles through the hole. The body rested on an empty ledge. The ceiling above it was rounded. This was a niche. She reached in with the pick. The back of the niche was less than a meter away. Solid rock.

The bones were brown, indicating age, lying there without a visible shred of connecting ligament or tendon, gone with the centuries, leaving the limbs and spinal column where they had once been part of a body but separate now as dice. They looked as though they had been laid in order, waiting to be attached by some model-maker.

The skull faced upward, and with nothing to hold its jaw in place, it rested on the spinal disks of what had once been a neck.

"Compass," said Sharon, and she determined that the spinal column was on an east/west axis, which meant the face could not have been facing east. While Islam came seven hundred years after the believed date of this cave use, Sharon, like all archaeologists in the area, automatically determined the direction of the face of the skull because Muslims in this part of the world were always buried facing east.

"Spinal column axis east/west, forearms across rib cage," said Sharon. This was unusual for this time period. A fetal position was more normal. It was possible the body had been laid down like this and no one had returned to put the bones in an ossuary.

A disk the size of a modern license plate rested on the spinal column above the pelvis. It appeared to be kiln-fired clay. The body would have been roughly a meter and a half tall.

"One point six five, one point six five meters tall," she said

"The skeleton or the body?" asked Mark.

"The body, the body. You've got to add three or four inches for flesh and skin and cartilage, which makes the body taller than the bones."

"That comes to five feet five inches tall," said Mark. "A woman?"

"No, that's about the normal height of a man at that time, maybe a little taller, but not much. Five feet four was normal. I don't think it was a woman, looking at the pelvis. But we will know for sure."

She noticed some orange discoloration on the right tibia. It was in a line, with the same form of orange discoloration on the left tibia, placed beneath the right. Both leg bones had it.

Sharon had seen that orange color before in Jerusalem digs. Orange was oxidized iron. There had been a spike there. The man had been crucified, a common form of criminal execution for the Romans.

But this seemed rather an elaborate tomb for a criminal, unless, of course, he had been part of one of the rebellions against Rome, and had come from a good family who had carefully hidden him here.

She widened the hole in the unfired clay brick.

"I want a photograph, especially the position of the clay disk resting on the vertebrae. It looks like a slave disk of some sort, but a bit heavy for that. It's wider than his chest, but it has a hole in it. That's what makes me think it's a slave disk."

Maria moved to the hole with the Zensa Bronica and flash.

"Get several angles. I'm going to turn over the disk," said Sharon.

"I can't get too many angles, it's just a hole."

"Get what you can."

The clay-sealed niche muted the explosion of light.

"Were there many slaves in this area?" asked Mark.

"Mark, there were slaves everywhere. This recent period of nonslavery in countries is rather brief."

"We haven't had slaves in America for a hundred years," said Mark, "and Europe for three hundred."

"That's what I said," said Sharon. She could see the afternoon light coming in down the hewn stairs, very white, very precious, and two thousand years ago the street was right out there. Perhaps the body had been stolen from a cross.

Perhaps the Romans, in one of their mass executions after a rebellion, had decreed the bodies would rot. The Romans liked to display their executions. Roadsides were the usual crucifixion sites; thousands would be killed this way. And a traveler could go for days on a Roman road after a rebellion and not be out of sight of a body.

Perhaps it was too much for a family to see, and they stole the body from the execution cross and hid it, not in burial ground, but in a storeroom. And perhaps they had planned to properly remove the body and clean the bones and place them in an ossuary a year later for proper burial in a proper place. And perhaps they were killed or some other misfortune prevented this.

"Done," said Maria, lowering the camera and backing away from the hole.

"All right. I have good news. I think the disk has writing on it," said Sharon.

Maria let out a little shriek.

"All right," said Mark, looking for a hand to slap. One of the other volunteers asked what Dr. Golban had said.

"The disk has writing on it, Dr. Golban believes," she was told.

"Oh, that's wonderful. You know, I thought, I really did, that we were just going to dig and clean and dig and clean and make sure it was all right for an Arab's basement. I really did. Oh, this is wonderful. This is wonderful."

Maria moved aside and Sharon went to the hole. Her right hand held a white powerlight. Murky yellow flashlights were virtually useless in a place like this.

With the tip of her finger she raised one edge of the disk.

Immediately she recognized the first distinctive lines in the clay. It was Aramaic or Hebrew, similar languages. She lifted the disk higher at her end, reading downward right to left, which was the proper way to read Aramaic. The inscription was two words, single line:

Melek Yehudayai.

It was not Hebrew. Hebrew would have been *Melek Yehudim.* Both meant "Jewish King."

They had found the tomb of a king. But what king? What king was executed by the Romans? The Romans didn't execute Jewish kings. The Romans didn't execute any kings, at least not in the provinces. Kings were brought back to Rome.

The Assyrians. They had executed kings. Yes. The Assyrians had executed a Jewish king. But what king was it? But the Assyrians didn't crucify. Assyrians impaled prisoners on a spike, pushing the victim down a long metal spike entering the anus and letting the weight of the body carry it downward until the spike reached the heart. The special cruelty was in the amount of time they took to let the spike reach the heart.

Assyrians also desecrated the body after death. Crucifixion was actually benign compared to Assyrian execution.

What Jewish king? What Jewish king?

"What does it say?" someone asked, startling her.

"Shh."

Royalty would explain why an entire single tomb would have only one body. But why the disk? Why not inscribe it on the rock, such as in the tomb believed to be that of the last Hasmonaean prince, the prince hastily buried as Herod assumed the throne. That, too, was during the Roman occupation.

The disk had a hole in it, which was why she had assumed it was a slave disk, meant to be hung somewhere. If it hung somewhere, it was to give other people information. They would not kiln-fire a disk unless they had time. It was not a sudden execution.

And if this were a king, why would anyone have to be told he was a king? Wouldn't everyone know it?

If some revolution overtook King Hussein in Jordan, would the body hanging on a wall need a sign saying "Jordanian King"?

No.

Sharon felt tugging at her arm. She ignored it.

Unless of course this wasn't a king, wasn't a king at all. The disk had been put there to mock him, to mock a claim, to show he wasn't a king, but a helpless criminal. It was in Aramaic because that was the common language of the Jews at that time, and authorities wanted to emphasize he was not the real King of the Jews.

And suddenly there was not enough air in the cave or the world for Sharon's lungs. Her mouth opened and she could not move.

She understood. Finally she understood. If she had not been raised in a Muslim land she would have known right away, thought of it right away. If she had been raised in the West, she would have known right away. It would have been the first thing she thought of, instead of the last.

She knew now what she was looking at, lying there with its forearms across its chest, skull to the roof of the niche in the back of the cave, unopened for two thousand years.

She was looking at the God of the Western world.

She was looking at Jesus, the Nazarene. Jesus, the Christ. Jesus Christ.

People were tugging at her now.

"Nothing," said Sharon, turning from the hole and blocking it with her body.

"Are you all right?" asked someone.

"Yes, yes," said Dr. Golban.

"Do you want to sit down?"

"What?"

"There is no place here to sit."

"Yes," said Dr. Golban. "There is no place here to sit."

The students helped her to the outside, where she breathed the air of the deep pit trench. She lit a cigarette there. Eventually everyone climbed up to Haneviim Street.

The next day, four Israeli soldiers rolled back the stone, and were not told why they were doing it.

2

Chosen

"Why the hell haven't you phoned back, Jim?" said the caller, and Father James Folan, S.J., knew he had another priest on the phone.

Laymen, especially Protestants and Jews, always made a special point of calling priests "Father." Only another priest would talk to him like that.

"That you, Joe?" said Father Folan.

"Yes, unless, of course, you have a whole list of people you rudely and routinely ignore."

"What do you want, Joe?" said Father Folan to the deputy provincial of the New England Province of Jesuits, Joseph Wingren, S.J., the man who had been leaving notes with the rector of Jim's formation house on Newbury Street for a day now.

"Why haven't you returned my call?"

"Because I know what it's about," said Father Folan.

It was lunchtime, and his secretary was out, and he was preparing his own files on the upcoming freshman class at Boston College. He was Dean of Students, and if he left these particular files to others he would spend the first semester trying to remember names instead of his real job of getting to know the people, and helping them, if possible. He had been Dean of Students here for only two years but knew already almost anything one did with an eighteen-year-old would more than likely cause harm instead of good, unless it was carefully thought out. And to do that, one had to know the people.

And that took time. And that meant he couldn't waste time on other things, especially not during dorm assignments. There were always at least half a dozen freshmen at this Catholic college who suddenly discovered to their absolute surprise that they were not allowed to share rooms with the opposite sex.

One girl with a lovely ruby and gold cross asked quite angrily how long this had been going on.

"About two thousand years for us, and you can add on another few millennia for the Jews."

"Jews do it all the time, Father."

"You're an authority?"

"Barbi Adler, who is an absolutely perfect Jew, has been doing it since fifteen. And she is my best friend, Father."

"Have you heard of the Babylonian Talmud and why it is different from the Palestinian Talmud, or the Mishnah, and why it became almost a second Pentateuch?"

"What?" said the girl.

"What I'm saying is, you couldn't tell whether your friend is a perfect Jew, but let me assure you, it is the same for them as it is for us. It's no."

And to explain things like this took time, and Father Wingren should have known he didn't have that time, not just before fall semester.

"The provincial is looking for archaeologists and ancient historians, right? Am I right, Joe?" said Jim Folan.

"Yes."

"Well, I happen to have only a master's. I teach a course in Roman history, only because B.C. can save money by not hiring a doctorate for that course. I'm Dean of Students. I'm an administrator. I personally can name half a dozen Jesuits in this very area with better credentials for ancient history than I."

"So could I. But you're going."

"I can't go over to Commonwealth Avenue now. We're beginning a semester."

"You're not going to Comm. Ave., Jim. You're going to Rome."

As a Jesuit, Jim Folan was under a vow of obedience but he

did not interpret this as obsequiousness. He was going to argue this one.

He was thirty-five years old and felt much younger than that, sometimes like a freshman himself, with all the bounce of life, and all the joy that only autumn in New England could bring.

He was strongly built, with a light complexion and blue eyes and a handsomeness that came more out of his honestly happy smile than his square pug features. He combed his sandy blond hair as he had since he was four, with pompadour in the middle and part on the left, and a cowlick that had remained triumphant over time and tonic. He wore chinos, a checkered shirt, and a sweater because if they got dirty no one would be able to point to a slovenly priest.

He wore black and a collar only when he had to sit on podiums or for formal occasions, which were blessedly rare.

He was not bothered by women making advances while he was out of collar because he never knew they were coming on. Friends would sometimes ask him how he felt about a woman showing him some attention somewhere, and he would always be puzzled at how the friends might see it and he didn't. He called it God's safety net for weak priests, although since his vows he had never violated chastity.

He took a bus to the deputy provincial's office because, even if Rome were calling, he still had to live on $800 a year. And besides, he was sure this call was some form of clerical error.

Father Folan arrived at the deputy provincial's office talking.

"Joe, Boston College is going to have a mess if I leave now. You don't fully understand the mess."

"I take your word for it," said Father Joseph Wingren, S.J.

"If you were choosing a scholar in archaeology or ancient history, would you choose me?"

"If I had no one else, yes. But compared to what's available, no."

"Then does it make sense to send me to Rome? I mean I wouldn't mind seeing Rome, I've never been there. Does it make sense?"

"Not to me," said Father Wingren.

"Then would you tell that to the provincial?"

"I did."

"And what did he say?"

"He said you're going."

"Did he have any reasons?"

"I think he was told they want you."

"They? Who's they?"

"You're going to Rome and you're asking who they are?" said Father Wingren. "The Kirov Ballet, of course. Mikhail Baryshnikov has defected, and they have sent out a call to the Society of Jesus for a replacement. The Jesuit Curia, of course. The Black Pope."

"Am I going to meet him?"

"I don't know. It's not just American Jesuits. From what I gather, and I am not supposed to gather this, it's a call to Jesuits all over the world."

"Why so many?"

"I shouldn't say. I know all of this is supposed to be secret."

"It's your conscience and my life," said Father Folan.

"I think they're looking for one man."

"Then I definitely wouldn't be that man."

"You're going, Jim. You can draw money here. And Jim . . ."

"Yeah?"

"God bless you."

"And you, Joe."

Father Wingren had promised to take care of everything with B.C. until Jim got back. All Jim had to do was pack and make airline reservations. Jim carefully folded a black suit and collar into a Georgetown University polyester overnight bag, and added one set of underdrawers and undershirts, one toothbrush, one razor, and the most used toothpaste tube in the bathroom of the Jesuit formation house, wrapping the toothpaste several times in plastic lest his fresh, black official priestly suit suffer a gruesome white smear.

There was a Jesuit cassock in the formation house, but no one ever used them anymore. He borrowed a tweed jacket almost his size to cover the sweater, and took a cab to Logan Airport, which would have cost his entire weekly expenses if he hadn't had traveling funds. He took a shuttle to New York City and by nightfall he was on an Alitalia jet, first class because that was

the only seat they had available immediately. He ordered an
orange juice, and looked back down the aisle.

A white-haired priest motioned for Jim to sit. He recognized
an old teacher of his in the rear. Since Jim Folan did not drink,
he offered his first-class seat to the older Jesuit. The old man
refused.

"We took vows of poverty, not stupidity," said Jim. "Why
waste free booze?"

The old man smiled.

"Do you know what this is about?" asked Jim. The older
man was from another formation.

The older man shook his head. "I believe that they are looking for one man."

"I know. I got a round-trip ticket," said Jim.

"So did I," said the older man. "Do you know who's on this
plane?"

"No," said Jim to the man who had given him two years of
Hebrew and Talmudic studies, a Semitic-language scholar at
Georgetown University.

"Some very important people in archaeology," said his
former teacher, and he mentioned their names as though Jim
should know them immediately, and as in the classroom when
he wanted the teacher to pass by and not dwell on a subject he
was not familiar with, Jim Folan kept a very blank face.

"You never heard of them?" asked the teacher.

"I think I heard of one. I just teach a course in Roman history. I'm an administrator."

"Oh, that's a cross."

"As a matter of fact, it seems to be kind of easy. Everything
is reasonable," said Jim.

"Oh, to have you for a week in my office."

"The key to administration is knowing what is most important and that decides everything else. It really does. It lets you
know what you shouldn't bother with. Even phone calls."

"I try to do everything well."

"That's why you're a scholar, Father," said Jim, reverting
to the way he had always addressed the older man when he was
a student.

"You weren't a bad student, Jim."

"Thank you," said Jim, knowing that was the old man's

kind way of saying his student wasn't good enough to make teaching his job. Every Jesuit had a job, even though the order was famous for scholars. There were surgeons and lawyers and, like Jim Folan, sometimes administrators.

He went back to his seat and along the way he heard some other priests he assumed to be Jesuits talking about *nauraghi* in Sardinia. He asked what they were, out of curiosity, and one man gave a detailed explanation of *nauraghi* formations, which could have been fortresses or storerooms at one time. What Jim heard was that they were huge piles of rocks found in Sardinia, at least three thousand years old. He listened politely, sorry he asked, and then went back to his seat alone.

He had never been to Rome before and had flown out of America only once, and then across the Pacific. He had been nineteen years old going, and twenty-one coming back. He had served in Vietnam for one tour as a Marine, and stayed one more year, going into Laos for the government, spending a year with one group of villagers, setting up a system to find out what people were talking about when they came back from markets. Someone had rightly figured that the best rough information came from general gossip. He had for one year organized that flow of gossip.

When he came home he was a hero of sorts, because in Portland, Maine, the Vietnam War was still believed in at that time. It was the year his father had died in the state hospital, screaming that rats were going to eat him alive.

His father was an alcoholic, and almost all the wine that passed Jim's lips thereafter came in later years during the Mass.

There was an incident at the funeral home. They didn't know the Folans were on state assistance. The funeral director had been talking in all these warm, caring phrases until he found out the Folan financial situation, and then he didn't want the body. It was horrifying to hear the same warmth come from the man's lips as he referred to "an appropriate home for your father."

"That's not my father, that's his body," Jim had told the funeral director. "And this is not a home, and you're not sending him to a home. He left a home when he had to go to the hospital, and he's going to one when he goes back to God. You're not a home. You're a fucking greedy way station."

The family was poor at that time and he was worried about his mother needing financial help, but she had said:

"Jimmy, if that's what's keeping you from the priesthood, let me share your poverty. Let it be mine too, if that's the only thing."

She lived to see him ordained and hear him say of his poverty, "Well, at least now it's on purpose."

There had been sadness in his life, and horror, but nothing that didn't strengthen the faith more.

And he had come to believe, in his thirty-fifth year of life, that his God was never really going to test him spiritually. Perhaps rough him up a bit from time to time, but never open those great troughs of despair that so often afflicted holy men and saints.

He was quite happy not to be even remotely a saint. Unless of course God decided that. Which was not Jim Folan's job. As a good administrator, he knew what not to worry about.

He got two hours' sleep on the flight. At Leonardo da Vinci Airport there was some confusion with the cabs. The taxi drivers wanted to make single fares out of the Jesuits, who had now become a group of nine, milling about in some confusion, trying to get the right pairings for two cab rides and falling all over each other with politeness and a willingness to go along with whatever anyone else wanted.

In the midst of this, two Jesuits got into a discussion over the proper conjugation of an Italian verb when one was addressing a taxi driver, and were trying to get one of the drivers to act as a final arbitrating source of knowledge. All this while the driver was trying to split them up into separate, more profitable fares.

Jim Folan sent four Jesuits into one cab, and got in the other, which took five.

"That was rather good," said the Semitic scholar. "You really handled that well."

"Yes, that was rather good," said another Jesuit.

The average IQ in the group came in at genius, and here he was getting compliments for dividing nine into four and five.

The Jesuit Curia was just off Via della Conciliazione, on an ill-dressed street of vulgar lighting and souvenir shops in Rome. It stood out by its grayness and mass. The simple address plate read "Borgo Santo Spirito 8."

The door had just the address, and no other sign that it controlled twenty-six thousand Jesuits around the world.

Unlike other orders, there was no formal religious greeting at the door, but a check of names. Behind the Jesuit at the entrance was a large switchboard for the phones.

Somewhere in the building was the new computer complex, which Jim had thought might have made a mistake in calling for him. Going onto a computer system always created problems. It was like translating something into an entirely new language.

His name was correct, even at the door, and then the Jesuit there stepped aside, and a priest in long black robes, and with very formal pronunciations of English, speaking in an Italian accent, announced that the Americans should follow him.

They rode up in a small, creaky elevator in groups of three. The priest guided them to a sparse, white-walled room with a giant black crucifix. There were folding chairs before a lectern.

The priest took the lectern, and immediately shot down Jim's theories of a computer foul-up.

"All of your histories have been thoroughly studied. We are not going to need all of you. We are looking for one. We have, through the most helpful cooperation of your father general, been given access to all the current histories of Jesuits. I can only tell you I am from the office of Almeto Cardinal Pesci himself."

"He is the Secretary of State of the Vatican, right?" asked one of the Jesuits, with a Texas twang in his voice.

The Italian priest smiled nervously, as though the man had to verify the most obvious fact of civilization. Did one ask "Jesus Christ?" when Christ was mentioned?

"Yes, yes. Of course," he said.

"Are we going to meet our father general, Pedro Arupe?" asked Jim.

"Please, please," said the priest for the Secretary of State.

"If we are not selected, can we meet him anyway?" asked Jim. The man was a hero of his and of many other Jesuits. A Basque, Father Arupe was in Nagasaki the day the atomic bomb was dropped there. He had brought change to the Jesuit order, the first in centuries. Jim was one of the new Jesuits.

"I don't know. Please, no more questions," said the priest.

"Now, are any of you in any state of emotional turmoil? Is anything bothering you?"

"I don't see how it's possible not to be," said the Jesuit with the Texas twang. He was identified as Dr. Robert Griffiths, of Stanford University, a Biblical archaeologist.

"You may go downstairs now," said the Italian priest.

"That's it?" said Dr. Griffiths.

"Yes, you may go home," said the Italian priest. He had a dark face, with even darker lips, and his skin looked so smooth, and his voice so soft, once Jim had to remind himself the man had just axed his first Jesuit.

"Any others bothered in any way?"

"I don't like the way you just got rid of that guy," said Jim.

"And you are?"

"Jim Folan, Boston College, New England Assistancy."

"Uh huh, and do any of you," said the priest from the Secretary of State, looking at the entire group, "have current physical ailments that bother you, or any ailments that might act up again under severe pressure?"

There were no answers.

"I have been informed that you Jesuits have a discipline where you once a year confront each other on whether you can, as you call it, *make it on the outside.*' And in this you explore some of your worst possible motives for becoming priests. Your wrong reasons. If any of you would be too embarrassed to disclose them now to me, or the scrutiny of others, in writing, please go."

There was hesitation. No one moved. Then Jim's old teacher from Georgetown got up and left the room.

The six remaining Americans were given sheets of paper and notebooks to put them in.

"In detail, please explain those reasons, those wrong reasons why you may have become a Jesuit."

Jim Folan clicked the cheap little yellow ball-point pen and, in the building that was the headquarters of his order, began with one simple sentence. It didn't even need a verb.

"Premature ejaculation," he wrote, and then went on into his fears, and into what it was like for him before he entered the order.

He had wanted to be a Jesuit for a long time, since he had

gone to a Jesuit high school. But he didn't feel he could make it. So he had volunteered for the Marines because at that time he had felt that second only to serving his God was serving his country.

Many people later wouldn't understand that, but he had been raised that way, even with a portion in the back of his Catholic Bible for military service, along with marriages, births, confirmations, first communions, and extreme unction of the family members.

Only when he had been in the killing did he begin to question that. And yet after the war, seeing what happened when America lost, he still questioned. He had taken so many different positions on that war in his own beliefs that he had to come to the conclusion he just didn't know, and neither did anyone else.

And when he came back from the Marines he wanted the Jesuits even more, because after the pain, after the deaths, the only thing that made sense in this world was Jesus Christ. There weren't any other answers after you saw an eight-year-old boy hand a bottle of poison soda pop to your buddy, and then watch your sergeant make the boy drink it himself under the threat of shooting off his testicles.

Jim Folan had gone into the Marines believing that Jesus Christ was the only salvation of mankind. He left the corps knowing it.

He had also gone in a virgin. He did not leave that way.

A Saigon whore had taken that prize when Jim was so drunk he couldn't even remember her face. He only remembered his buddies cheering him on, and him thinking he wanted to get it over with because he was not going to like remembering it.

They had thought they were doing him a favor because no one should die a virgin. Even with the taste of rum and lemonade still in his mouth the next day Jim had gone to confession because he knew he shouldn't die in a state of sin.

At the cost of betraying his God, however, he had gotten his fighting brothers off his back. After the Marine Corps was a period of deciding.

It was also a period of waiting. His veteran's benefits and the bonus he had gotten for his extra work in Laos had put him through Georgetown, as the Jesuits had advised. They wouldn't take him as a novice until he had his bachelor's degree. This was the new way of Jesuits, no more seventeen-year-olds. He was talking to the Jesuits, he was talking to Western Electric, and he was also talking to Ginny Spaduto.

She was a secretary with the Agriculture Department, and said she didn't want to get married. She wanted her own life, she said. That was all right with him, he wasn't planning to get married either.

"I may become a priest," he said.

"You're full of shit," she said.

"No. I am," he said. "I'm taking philosophy, Greek, Latin, and some Hebrew."

"C'mon," said Ginny. They were in her apartment, a small box of a place with some good white light from the windows, and plants drinking in all of it. She had one bedroom, which was the living room also. Two of them could not fit into the kitchen simultaneously. He was on her couch-bed. She was making hamburgers. He had brought a large bottle of red wine.

"I am. I'm thinking about it, really."

"Wanna fuck?" she said sprightly.

"Sure," he said.

"And you're gonna be a priest?"

"Yeah. Maybe."

"You're full of shit."

"I'm not a priest yet."

"You're full of shit, Jim Folan. You just want to get into my pants."

"It's not a 'just,' Ginny. That's one of the priorities of our relationship."

"Jim Folan," she said, pointing an accusing spatula, "you're full of shit. I swear to God Almighty, you are full of shit."

He had laughed. It was a good dinner, and the wine was good because there was a lot of it, and while they were watching television he felt her lean into him, and she noticed he wanted her very much. He was hard. He had been like that through supper.

What he didn't tell her was that for most of their two dates he had been like that. She had those dark features that seemed so organically right for joining with him.

He was burning as he sucked her lips, and then kissed her breasts, and when she pushed off her white panties he felt the intense moisture between her legs, and knew she was ready too. He entered, smooth as oil through a valve, and then he exploded. It was over.

"That's all right," she said. "It's all right."

"I'm sorry," he said.

"That's all right," she said.

But the next time was the same, and so was the next. He even tried masturbating once before he took her out, but it only took him longer to get erect with her and when he came it was just as immediate as before, and had to be just as unsatisfying for her.

The last time she didn't tell him "That's all right." She asked him if he wanted a soda.

She was the second woman he had had sex with.

In Georgetown he had been meeting irregularly at a Jesuit formation house with a novitiate rector, and he told him about both women.

"Are you sorry for it?" asked the rector.

"The sex?"

"Yes."

"I am."

"Do you intend not to do it again because it is an offense against God, a separation between you and God, a mortal sin?"

"Yes."

"Then you are forgiven. Go in peace. What is your problem?"

The problem was, and it came up at the end of his first year, at the long retreat, the suspicion that he may have chosen the priesthood because he couldn't make it as a sexually active man.

In the Jesuit Curia, with the notebook in front of him and only two hours of sleep, he organized and set down his reasoning for his doubts.

"I had wanted to be a priest, but the above-mentioned problems may have been the deciding factor, that last mite on a balanced scale. It certainly was not the major factor. But it has lingered within me as a suspicious deciding factor in that very vulnerable time of decision."

And then he added one more necessary thought:

"Since I have become a Jesuit and grown spiritually, that is not, to my deepest belief, a factor anymore."

A bell rang, and his group was led to an eating hall, but it was not the great hall he had heard about where Jesuits here ate their meals. It was like dining in a bowl of wisdom.

Some men wore sports jackets like Jim, one wore a suit, most wore black suits with collars, but two wore the cassock. There were at least a half-dozen languages being spoken as they discussed exhaustive minutiae of archaeology, which Jim would not have understood in English, either.

They seemed so monumentally concerned with trivia. Jim wondered if he dropped a plate here, would other men centuries later be as involved as his brother Jesuits in discussing the fragments?

The luncheon meal was salad beans, lots of bread, chicken, and a white Chianti. They were served by priests Jim believed to be Jesuits. They had all been told not to discuss what was going on even among themselves, should they suspect what was going on.

Half the seats in this eating hall were empty, with place settings sparkling clean in front of them. Jim estimated those were the ones who had already been sent home, thirty out of forty-eight. Might have been bad planning.

There were eighteen men left from around the world.

They lingered over their lunch, with no one coming for them. Finally, priests Jim assumed to be from the Secretariat came in with armfuls of the notebooks the Jesuits had written on.

The priest who had conducted the first test returned also. He gave one notebook to a Jesuit and told him he could keep it or destroy it. He was free to leave. Only two Americans were left out of ten.

He took Jim up to the small room where the testing had first begun.

"Father Folan," he said, "you are not engaged in any sexual affairs now, are you?"

"No."

"Is that a weakness of yours?"

"Since I became a novice, I have not had an affair with a woman, nor do I intend to."

"I see. Do you have homosexual affairs?"

"No."

"Is there anything anyone could use to sully your name in

any way? Anything? You do not have to tell us. But we must know.''

"Nothing to my knowledge."

The priest smiled. "You know, in your case, perhaps God was working through your special problem to bring you to the Church."

"That's theologically impossible, since fornication outside marriage is a sin, and whereas God will use the result of sin for good purposes, he does not use sin itself. You see, theologically that's impossible."

The Italian priest fluttered his hands as though Jim Folan were talking trivial nonsense.

"That's basic theology. It's the law of God," said Jim.

"Yes, yes. Thank you. Would you please send up the other Jesuit who was in our little group?" The priest pointed to his watch; apparently he felt this was a waste of time.

Jim went downstairs to the dining room and sent up the other Jesuit and sat down to another cup of coffee. He had assumed in Italy the coffee would have to be good. It wasn't. He had a glass of water.

There were now seven men in the room. The other American Jesuit didn't come back.

The seven men were taken to a single room, where they were all given glossy lined papers and pens.

"You have until dinnertime. Answer this question as thoroughly as you can within the time limit," said the priest. "Why do you believe Jesus Christ is God?"

Jim Folan clicked the cheap little yellow ball-point pen and made a scratch on the glossy lined paper. The pen worked. He thought of stating Thomas Aquinas' five proofs of God, and then going on to establish the proofs that Christ was God, begotten, not made, of one substance with the Father. There was scripture and tradition and supportive evidence for both. It would be neatly organized, easy to finish by supper, and would take roughly ten good essay pages.

And it would be the wrong answer. The question was, why he believed Jesus Christ was God.

And he wrote down his answer. It was brief:

"I believe Jesus Christ is God because I spoke to Him this morning in my prayers and have known He was God since childhood. I cannot ever remember not believing Jesus was God, and not knowing He was my best friend, even though I have not always been His.'' Jim Folan handed in his paper and left as six other men simultaneously looked up from their papers.

''Is there nothing you wish to add?'' asked the priest from the Vatican Secretariat.

''Nope. That's it,'' said Father James Folan, S.J. It was all there. The rest of his life, and all his studies, had only been an embellishment.

He was taken back down to the dining room, where he waited, and dozed off to sleep, hoping that in his lifetime he might find out what this was all about. There was no guarantee that whatever transpired here would be made known in his lifetime, or anyone's lifetime, or even if the result of whatever this mission was for came to light internationally whether he would recognize his little part in it as being one of those considered.

Through the centuries, especially during those times when the Catholicism of nations was threatened, the Church had called upon its Jesuits for crucial, often desperate missions.

Most people thought of Jesuits only as great scholars, but their first calling was as soldiers of Christ.

They were the Pope's men for times of crisis.

Some countries even banned the order. Often Jesuits would be killed, with the Church so careful of its privacy of motive that never a word was spoken from Rome to protest or even acknowledge the deaths.

During the early 1960s scores of oriental scholars disappeared from the order without a word ever being mentioned publicly, where they went or where they died. The order itself did not speak of it, but J's knew they were just no longer among them, and word inside the order was they would never come back.

Jim was sure the Church was now looking for something in the Middle East, something ancient. This would explain the archaeologists and the Semitic scholars.

But it would not explain him. What was he doing here?

Jim did not think about this long. He was tired and the chair was soft, and he wanted to give himself up to sleep. He was sure the next round of clerical cuts would eliminate him. He shouldn't have gotten even this far. Unless, of course, this mission was something beyond anything he could imagine.

And if that were so, he wasn't going to waste one moment awake imagining. The chair was soft. The room was warm and he went to sleep with all the comfort of a warm bath in a familiar tub.

Suddenly someone was tugging on his arm. Jim woke. It was a man. He spoke in a British accent.

"Yes?" said Jim Folan.

"Dinner," said the man.

"Are you serving?" asked Jim.

"No, my good man. I am dining. With you."

Jim looked around the large room. They were alone. Only two plates were set out.

"The others have gone home," said the British Jesuit, and then he introduced himself, and when Jim said who he was, the man confessed he had never heard of Jim Folan.

"I'm not known for archaeology or ancient history. I don't think I belonged in this group. I'm waiting to go home."

"And I'm waiting to be called," said the British Jesuit. "Frightful, I just knew it would be me. I don't think it's pride, do you, if you know the level at which you operate? The only question I had was whether these fellows would know. They're from the Secretariat. All Italian, you know."

"Peter should have thought of that before he moved the shop here," said Jim.

The British Jesuit laughed. Supper was lentils and little bits of ham followed by a custard dessert that had a promise of sweetness that kept Jim eating. The promise was never kept, and Jim didn't know why he finished it.

"I guess we're going to sleep here," said Jim.

And then one of the priests from the Secretariat rushed into the room in a flurry of yellow paper. He was followed by another priest in a black cassock, trying to keep his yellow papers in order. There was fine red piping to his cassock. He was a monsignor.

Romans, thought Jim, used red to show rank too, and he wondered if the thin piping of the monsignor had come from the Roman rank of knight or horseman, with the large amounts of red going to cardinals, just as the Roman pagans had used larger amounts of red to show the higher rank of senator.

"Excuse me, excuse me. Excuse me," said the monsignor. "I must ask this question even at the dinner table. Yes?"

Both Jesuits nodded.

"It must be done tonight," said the monsignor. He glanced at a yellow sheet of paper.

"Either one of you may answer first. Suppose someone finds a . . . I can't read this word," said the monsignor, turning to one of the assisting priests.

"Ancient. It is bad handwriting. It is not Cardinal Pesci's handwriting. I know his," said the priest.

And the monsignor lowered a disdainful glance at the priest for mentioning something he didn't have to, and continued:

"Suppose someone found an ancient object in the ground, and came to you with it. How would you verify its authenticity?"

"Jim," said the British Jesuit, offering Folan first chance.

"After you, Father."

And then the British Jesuit gave a short course in carbon dating, stratification, and the general instrumentations of dating old objects. It could have been an advanced course in archaeology. One of the monsignor's assistants held a microphone to the British Jesuit's mouth. The line went into a black briefcase, where obviously there was a recorder. The monsignor wiped his brow and tidied his appearance.

Jim realized he was just a courier, as was every priest who had come here from the Secretariat. Undoubtedly they had certain key clearing questions to which they had the right answers. But the questions that required writing went to someone else to read, just as the tape recording would go to someone else.

If anyone interrupted this line of communication between the interviewees and the real interviewer, whom Jim knew none of the Jesuits had met yet, there would be nothing that would let some enemy or foreign power know what the Vatican was doing. Only those who had to know, knew.

It reminded Jim of Laos. Ah well, he thought, the Church was part of the world too.

And then the microphone was in his face.

"First, I probably would hire my British colleague," said

Jim, and everyone laughed except the monsignor. He wasn't even listening. "This is not a joke, or as much of one as it may seem. Expertise can be hired, and certainly my colleague has demonstrated his talents and disciplines. But there is something else. I would ask who brought this thing to me and why. Why did he bring it to me? And then, besides the mechanics, I would look into the natures of the people, the motives of the people, and then one more thing that I believe is perhaps one of the most useful tools in finding out what is really going on. Gossip, the weather, the very smallest things are often the best corroborating or disputing evidence. What I mean is this. If someone comes to you with a story of a great purple building down the road, you don't ask him about the purple or the building so much as what the people were eating when they built it, and what did the trucks look like that carried the cement, and would he perchance know the person who sold the cement. Because if that building is really there, those are the things that will be known and accurately known. But if he's making it up, he is not going to slip up on the fact that the building is purple, or how big it is, but on the trivia. The weather, the gossip, what people are eating, and who does what."

Jim paused to think, to add one more clarifying statement.

"Are you done?" asked the monsignor.

"Yeah. I guess. Sure, that's my best."

He was awakened that night, and told to pack. He was sleeping in his underwear, and he dumped everything into a small bag and put on the suit and collar because he knew he would be flying only one way and he could get it cleaned at home.

It was 1 A.M., and he dozed in the car, having said a little prayer for the British Jesuit, who was now going to meet his calling.

Jim felt a nudge, and the car door was open, and someone was helping him out into a drizzle that had come upon Rome. He tasted the custard he had had for dinner. Now it had taste. Hours later.

"Come, come," said the priest. With a courtly flourish, he was led into the building. Ornate tapestries hung everywhere. Chairs were covered with gilt. The floor was covered with impeccably intricate marble designs, and was immaculate. Soft, yellow lights illuminated the ceiling. There was an elegant hush to the place, almost a sense of perfume in the air.

Behind an elegant, dark-wood door was an elevator, so rickety Jim would not inflict it on a Boston prison. It chugged up to the second floor.

Here the tapestries were rich yellows with coats of arms, and men in helmets and pantaloons stiffly holding pikes. He didn't have to see St. Peter's Square outside as he walked along the hall. He knew now where he was. He was in the Vatican.

Two guards raised their pikes in salute, and one, holding a pike in his left hand, opened the door with his right.

An elderly cardinal with a soft, fleshy face worked at an ornate gilt desk, looking up only briefly from what was in front of him. When he saw Father Folan, he dismissed his aides.

Jim bent a knee to kiss his ring as a sign of respect. The cardinal accepted it briefly, and raised his hand, signifying he wanted to get on with business.

"Sit. I am Almeto Cardinal Pesci, Secretary of State, as you may know. You have never been to Jerusalem, correct?"

"Yes. Correct."

"Good. We didn't think so. I had thought that the British scholar might have been the one, but I guess your answer to the last question made the difference. We have a standing archaeological commission, but it never had the strength of the Jesuits, you know. And in the end, the third floor decided absolutely in favor of the broad range of investigative abilities."

The third floor meant the Pope himself, the floor he lived on in this building. The final arbiter, the man whose handwriting the priests could not read too easily back in the Jesuit house, was His Holiness.

And broad range could mean only one thing. The Pope had chosen Jim from among all the other Jesuits because of Jim's year in Laos, because of that year in the CIA. In that case His Holiness might be a bit wrong.

His Eminence did not give Jim a chance to discuss this, but started pushing to Jim's side of the desk pictures of what appeared to be some very old settled bones, data on strata which he didn't understand, background on a Dominican archaeologist who was the first Catholic on the scene, the difficulties of the Church's position in the Middle East, and the significance of Aramaic on a kiln-fired disk.

"How do you know it's Aramaic?" asked Jim.

"Don't you know?" said Cardinal Pesci, looking at the black and white photograph of a piece of pottery with strange sticklike drawings on it.

"No," said Jim. "I thought it was supposed to be like Hebrew."

"They say it was," said Pesci, looking at the notes in front of him.

"I can't make out one letter," said Jim. "What does it say? And why are these bones important?"

3

The Romans Are Coming

Sharon Golban was furious, and she did not like to be furious on a Friday night because that began Shabbat, and while she did not believe in the Shabbat prayers, she did believe in her older brother's family, and in being with them every Friday night to share events of the week.

But the last week's events were so disheartening she did not want to share them with anyone, least of all her family. And besides, officials had asked her to keep everything about the dig on Haneviim Street to herself unless otherwise instructed.

It started with her doing what she considered her responsibility. Recognizing how the body had conformed significantly to Christian Gospels, she reported it to the Department of Antiquities. She thought there would be some religious implications, some possible difficulties that could well be avoided before they became massive.

But before nightfall things started to become ugly. She was told to dismiss her crew.

"What am I supposed to tell my volunteers? They're a good crew. They deserve better."

"Tell them that the dig has been closed because of Religious Party opposition."

"Is that so?"

"Tell them that."

"It's not so," Sharon had angrily replied, "and I will not do it."

41

The next day she found out it had been rudely done for her, and she would be working with a Dominican priest, showing him all her data.

"What does a priest have to do with this? Our holy men, their holy men. The worst thing you can bring into a dig is . . . is religion. You might as well lower your pants and defecate. The difference is you can clean that up. What holy men do, nobody can clean up. It lasts for centuries, forever."

"His name is Pierre Lavelle," she was told.

"Dr. Lavelle?"

"Yes."

"Why didn't you say so? Dr. Lavelle. Pierre. He's an archaeologist. He's a good one. He's a solid man. A priest, you say? Well, he'll be fine. I never knew he was a priest."

She did not bring up the fact of Dr. Lavelle's priesthood while she worked with him, but was sure the priesthood was some form of juvenile passion he had never bothered to resolve on his way to becoming a respected archaeologist.

At the dig Sharon watched his face to see who was doing the observing, the priest or the archaeologist. He asked more right questions. He seemed perhaps too calm for such a historically significant find.

But on leaving, as he got down on his knees to get through the small hole at the top of the carved stairs, he paused before he moved on. Sharon saw moisture there, quite dark and clear in the dry, yellow-brown stone. She thought he had spilled something on the steps until she realized they were his tears.

And then he was gone.

At noon on Friday, just before the Shabbat Eve, Sharon got a very good idea as to how sticky everything was going to be.

She was asked to see a man called Mendel Hirsch, Deputy Director for Jerusalem in the Ministry of Religious Affairs, on the third floor of a drab, sandy-colored building opposite the glorious domes of the Russian Church of the Holy Trinity.

As he explained it, his job entailed smoothing things out when different religions bumped into each other, keeping things out of the courts and news.

Naturally, Sharon understood, he explained, every religion had its own courts for its marriages and intrareligious disputes. Mendel was a sort of friendly referee. He smiled a lot. He had a healthy tan, and two white tufts of hair over his ears. Otherwise, he was bald. He knew every bishop and patriarch in Jerusalem. There were many pictures in his office of him posing smilingly with all manner of holy men. There were also pictures of Mendel with Israeli politicians. She judged he was with the right-wing Likud block, and, by his age, he just may have been a member of the extremist Irgun before independence.

"Sharon," he said, "there is no good way to break bad news, so I won't try."

But he had been trying, lapsing into Yiddish phrases to show warmth. Ashkenazis did that. Why Yiddish was still a language of warmth for them, she could not understand. It was based on German, and considering what the Germans did to the Jews, she would not think any Jew would want to use that language again. Besides, it was not beautiful like Farsi, or graceful as Arabic. It was far too guttural for her, an ugly sound. But then she didn't like the sound of most European languages.

"Sharon, you cannot return to Hebrew University. You are assigned indefinitely to this dig. You will work under my direction."

"And what do you know about archaeology?" asked Sharon.

"Only what you tell me, Sharon."

"If you must know, Christianity is not one of my strengths, although I am familiar, of course, with the Byzantine period. But there are better than me for this dig."

"We are not bringing in another archaeologist at this point. Too many people know about this already. What we want now is fewer people knowing. That's part of my job."

"When will Lavelle return?" asked Sharon.

"Oh, that," said Mendel. "Dr. Lavelle will not be returning. You are to meet in a few days a Mr. James Folan, at Ben Gurion Airport."

"Who's James Folan?"

"I presume an archaeologist."

"Not in this area."

"One you haven't heard of, perhaps," said Hirsch.

"No. Everybody knows everybody else. There are only seventy or eighty solid ones. Is there a member of the Knesset you don't know?"

"There are some I would like not to know."

"Yes, but you know everyone. This man James Folan may not have any serious qualifications."

"That's all right," said Mendel.

"How is it all right?" asked Sharon, outraged.

"It's all right. All right?"

"No."

"I am sorry. He is the one we have been informed the Vatican is sending."

"What in a pound of celery does the Vatican have to do with this?"

"The Vatican is very important," said Mendel. "It's Roman Catholicism, the largest single Christian sect."

"So?"

"You don't understand how touchy this whole thing is. It is a basic Christian tenet that Christ rose again from the dead. Resurrection. It is basic. You don't know how this city gets turned upside down at Easter."

"I know that. He is their Messiah. Ours is yet to come. Of course, no rational person is holding his breath for either of them."

"To have the State of Israel involved in any way with something so damaging to an essential element of their faith could have serious repercussions. Very serious," said Mendel Hirsch, with his gravest and most authoritarian voice.

"What repercussions? We haven't done anything," answered Sharon. She had little respect for this politician, bureaucrat, Deputy Director Ashkenazi, who obviously knew how to keep himself in a job if he knew nothing else.

Mendel Hirsch leaned forward as though to whisper. But he spoke loudly, his hands flying out in exasperation.

"Who needs this? Right now, the last thing we need with everything happening everywhere, and very little of it to our good, is a big fight with the Christian community. Yes. That's it. What we want out of this is *no trouble*."

"Then, why didn't you blow up the body the day I found it?"

"There was some talk of that, too, Dr. Archaeologist. What happened was, no one knew what to do. At the highest levels, they didn't know what to do. You don't understand what this means in the Western world."

"How did you get to the Vatican? What was your thought process for that?"

"Aha," said Mendel. "It was decided that we should get a Christian sect involved, to participate in everything going on so there could be no fingers pointing and saying, 'Look what the Jews are doing to our God.' "

"They are always pointing fingers. If you're worried all the time what people say you wouldn't get out of bed."

"There are pointing fingers and pointing fingers. With the Catholic Church now involved, we are, as you say, covered."

"But Dr. Folan may not even be an archaeologist," said Sharon. "Complications or no, you don't operate with a bread knife. You use a scalpel."

"Dr. Folan is not our problem, Sharon. He is our solution. And by the way, how did you find out he had a doctorate?"

"He doesn't?" asked Sharon.

"They didn't say," said Mendel Hirsch, with a shrug of a shoulder and the exclamation of an upturned hand.

Sharon got the spelling of Folan's name in English letters and went to the library, but the only Folan who might remotely have any sort of related discipline was a Brendan Folan who was an authority on Sumerian architecture. And he had died five years before in Leeds, England. James Folan was no one.

And, on that realization, Sharon headed to her brother's apartment, which was behind Hebrew University, on Naveshanan Street. He was a doctor and had both an apartment he owned as well as a car, something beyond ordinary Israelis. Sharon herself had chosen to rent her apartment and buy a car.

Her brother was the physician to much of the Persian community in Jerusalem because he knew the "old cures" as well as the Western ones. He also, through that, had a large Arab clientele.

The apartment was convenient to the university, and many a night she would have liked to have slept there, but there was no space. Avrahim's bedroom was his study, and daughter Mari's bedroom was little more than a closet, and the older son's bedroom was also the living room. His wife, Paula, raised in America, said doctors had big houses in America, if all one wanted out of life was a big house.

The one reason she sometimes talked of taking the whole

family to America was to give them a good Jewish education, which she loudly proclaimed was getting more impossible every day in Israel. Just the other day, Rani, fifteen, had gotten into a fight. With fists. And hitting in the head, no less. This was no way to get a decent Jewish education. Paula warned Rani that if he kept on getting into fistfights, he would never be accepted into the paratroopers. That was his ambition. His sister Mari's ambition was getting breasts, she often confided to Sharon. She was twelve and did not have them yet, while others had them. And her mother didn't like her looking in the mirror so much, watching for them to bud.

It was her only family. Avrahim said the prayers as Paula lit the candles. The whole ceremony was pure Ashkenazi, like Paula, down to the meal of boiled beef and ground potatoes, fried, no less, called latkes.

"In America, we call it Jewish cooking," said Paula, who seemed to direct the gastronomy with a wooden spoon.

"In Israel I call it indigestion," joked Avrahim, and immediately assured everyone he was joking. Everyone wanted to know why Sharon had not dropped in once during the week, since it was the end of digging season and she should be resuming her job across the street at the university.

"Things. We found something on the dig, and it's hush-hush."

"A bomb," said Rani, excited.

"Hush, hush," said Avrahim, and on that there was no more discussion. "When things are not to be spoken, they are not to be spoken, especially if it is a bomb." And Rani, who would be a soldier, understood.

"Sharon has found someone?" said Mari, excited. "A beautiful man." Mari had the dark skin of the Golbans and the blue eyes of her mother.

"Hush, hush," said Paula, banging the table with the wooden serving spoon. "She's married. And until her husband can be found to get a proper divorce, she is still married."

"I'd go to Cyprus and get married if I were *aguna* like Aunt Sharon," said Mari. "I would."

"No," said Paula, "that is not the lesson. The lesson is to be careful and choose the right man, not getting married whenever you feel like."

"How could we have known he would have disappeared for ten years? How?" said Avrahim.

"You know when you see the character of a man. You know when he talks about nothing but money he is no good. You see, Mari, that is what you should be thinking. A good man."

"Why did you bring this up?" asked Sharon.

"I thought maybe you had met someone," said Mari.

"She's married. How can she meet someone?" said Paula. "Would you like me to meet someone?"

"You're really married, Mom."

"So is Sharon."

"From what country would the name Folan be?" said Sharon, putting the accent on the last syllable and getting off her marital status.

"How do you spell it? It sounds French," said Paula.

"It's definitely French," said Avrahim.

"F—O—L—A—N," spelled Sharon, using the English letters. The children did not understand.

"What's the first name?"

"James."

"Folan!" said Paula, putting the accent on the first syllable where it belonged. "It's not French. It's Irish."

"It sounded French," said Avrahim.

"It's Irish."

"From Ireland?" asked Mari.

"Where else, silly?" said Rani.

"No. No," said Paula. "It could be from anywhere, practically. America, Canada, Australia, England. The Irish are like us, from all over."

"I thought they fought the English," said Rani.

"I wonder if he's married?" said Mari. "That's a handsome name."

Sharon smiled at Mari. She wanted to tell her this man Folan with the beautiful name was being sent from Rome for all the wrong reasons.

She wanted to tell Mari there was something precious in a chiseled stone left a thousand years or so ago. A person had to be quiet to hear what it said, because the past talked in whispers of truth so random and fragile any preconceived opinion would blow it away before the opinion's organized and determined noise.

Dr. Folan was bringing the best-organized full orchestra of opinion in all history, the theology of the Roman Catholic Church. Rabbis and mullahs were but little nettlesome guerrilla bands compared to this grand army coming out of the West to do battle for its God.

"Aunt Sharon is daydreaming," said Mari, and Sharon smiled.

"Folan is a beautiful name," said Sharon.

"I bet he's beautiful, too, and Aunt Sharon and the man Folan will be married," said Mari, giggling wildly because she knew her mother would hate that.

Paula answered with a severe banging of the wooden spoon.

"You're letting her tease you," said Avrahim to his wife.

"Even in tease it's not allowed," said Paula.

"And live happily ever after with a big American car and a stereo television," said Mari.

"Hut," screamed Paula.

"And have affairs in bars," shrieked Mari, the wildest American thing she could think of.

And that was too much. Mari was sent away from the table for such talk on Shabbat Eve. Later, Sharon took her some food and did tell her that handsome men could be dangerous. This she could share.

"Did he hurt you, Aunt Sharon?"

"No, precious. I hurt me."

"Mama was wrong about him."

'No, Mari. Unfortunately, as is often the case, Paula was so very right."

"Then why did you marry him?"

"Later I will tell you that, I think."

"How much later?"

"Three years, precious," said Sharon, kissing the girl on the forehead.

"Oh, I want to know now. I know about everything. You can tell me. Oh, you can. I know who is kissing in school."

"Good night, precious," said Sharon.

What could she tell her, that no one brought her to orgasm like Dubi Halafi? What could she say, that just thinking of his organ made her moist with want, that she knew what he was even when she married him.

And if he were outside this very Shabbat Eve, she would whisk him over to her apartment so fast the candles would go out from the breeze. What could she tell her niece, that she tried to find other men, but none could work her body, or do so much with so much?

Could she tell her niece that she overlooked everything because he was a sexual technician, that this man could not carry on a civilized conversation?

Could she repeat to the girl what an Ashkenazi friend told her, that really great lays, the super-sexual men, were all bastards?

"You screw them, you don't marry them," her friend had said.

"I'm afraid he'll leave," Sharon had answered.

So she had married Dubi Halafi, and two months later he left with her bank account and every bit of folding money in the house as well as her self-respect.

There had been other men. But the only thing she could ever trust was her archaeology. She could invest everything in that, and it would return in kind. She had found in her life that her science was something she could truly love.

When a colleague told you you did solid work, that you could trust that from him, that meant something. When a man told you how beautiful your breasts were, it meant he either wanted to get into your body or your purse.

She wondered briefly that night if Dr. Folan, who would be arriving soon, would make some sexual overture. She already hated him for what he was going to try to do to a perfectly innocent dig.

4

Diaspora

They never failed to let Warris Abouf know how lucky he was, how even Russians did not have the car he had, or the apartment in Moscow that he had, or the amount of certificate rubles he had which enabled him to shop at the Beryozka, where the quality goods were, namely, the imported goods.

And when they stressed to Warris Abouf how lucky he was, they did not mean in comparison to other Palestinians like himself, or Africans, or Asians, they meant compared to Russians, real Russians, Caucasian Russians.

And when they made this comparison, they did not even refer to the ordinary White Russian. They meant even Caucasian members of the KGB who did not have the blat of Warris Abouf.

Blat was the single word the affluent Russian lived by. It meant influence and that translated into luxury goods, restaurants, off-limits cinema, apartments in Moscow, and a personal car.

And the one thing Warris Abouf never let them think for one moment was that he was not deliriously happy in Moscow, and not for one moment eternally grateful to the only real friend he had in the world.

Warris Abouf was very careful about that.

Even this day at 2 Dzerszhinsky Square, sitting across from the KGB major, he had to show how grateful he was for sharing the "sensitive" information on Soviet long-range policy in the

Middle East, even though he knew it was neither sensitive nor policy because it was just too benevolent.

It could have been delivered to an open assembly of Third World students at Patrice Lumumba University.

Warris Abouf interjected with gratitude to the Russians on behalf of all Palestinians. He reminded the major that he understood what good friends the Russians were and how much they trusted him.

He better than others understood all the peoples who had betrayed the Palestinian cause. But never, never the Russians.

And for some reason this day the major mentioned how the Roman Catholic Church might someday prove to be a prime enemy of the Palestinian struggle and then he moved quickly on to enumerating other Palestinian enemies. But Warris Abouf had seen too much.

The dark eyes in Major Vakunin's bone-white face had wandered around the room, and that always meant a crucial point even though the major never wanted Warris to know exactly what was important and what was not.

The Russians were like that. They even tried to hide innocent things, as though some ancient tribal superstition dictated what you knew about them could be used for bad magic. In this respect they were often more African than Africans.

Finally, when Major Vakunin put his red box of cigarettes on the standard green-felt tabletop of these KGB offices in front of Lubyanka Prison, central Moscow, Warris knew he would find out what he was summoned for. Vakunin always placed something or rearranged something on the desk when he came to his purpose.

"We are looking for someone. Not just an Arab. We want a Palestinian," said Major Vakunin. He lit a cigarette for himself and dwelled on the smoke for a moment.

"He must speak Hebrew. And he must have a knowledge of the Roman Catholic Church, especially in the Middle East. Not chaff. Definitely not chaff."

Warris nodded. There were kernels and there was chaff. Chaff were those people of low intelligence or of unstable violent temperament who would be guided toward guerrilla training, where they could be lost.

But the kernels were those people of higher intelligence and greater emotional balance and selectivity who were most of all prone to being loyal to Moscow as the one true center of world socialism.

These people would prove invaluable in the struggle to come, which would begin when the Palestinian state was formed. They would be the cadres to fight the Peking-backed socialists, the Islamists, the pan-Arab nationalists, and the multitude of other liberation groups not allied to Moscow.

It was Warris' job, and the great rewards for it, to select those kernels from the students at Patrice Lumumba University. It was he who, having judged a young man or woman as worthy, would befriend them and show them through his own life-style how well the Russians loved and respected their Arab brothers.

And he would move them off to their destinies, the kernels for further education and luxuries, and the chaff to wherever they ended up, either on some plane they hijacked, or shooting up some Israeli schoolroom, or unfortunately, as was too often the case, some other Palestinian faction.

In this sort of separation, Warris could not have agreed more, for just these sorts of hotheads were the most disruptive to any organization or project, so ready to accuse even the closest compatriots of being traitors. It was these sorts, as much as the Israelis, who had landed Warris in Russia in his twenty-eighth year of life, facing another abysmal Russian winter, made more miserable by the Russians' enjoyment of it.

"Not chaff," Warris repeated.

"Definitely not chaff," said the mayor.

"So it could be a woman?"

"Yes."

"And how soon would this person be needed?"

"Not this afternoon, but not next year either," said the major.

"There have been several I have been looking at," said Warris. "But I sense there is something more that's wanted. What about the Catholic Church? Should the person be aware of the liturgy?"

"The Vatican," said the major. "Someone knowledgeable about the nuances of the Vatican."

"Diplomacy?"

"The Vatican," said the major, giving no more.

Warris nodded. "I myself come from a Melchite Catholic family. I do not, of course, believe, but I am aware of many of our Vatican's attitudes in the Middle East. I would imagine any other Melchite would be just as aware. Do you know what 'Melchite,' the word, comes from?"

The major lit a cigarette and Warris asked for one now.

"Melchite comes from the old Hebrew *'Melek,'* which is the same as the Hebrew for 'King.' When the Israeli fascists who support the fascist Begin wanted to cheer him on they would yell, 'Melek Yisroel,' which means 'King of Israel,' " said Warris.

And seeing the major was uninterested, Warris added:

"I was just offering something that might have been useful to you."

"Of course," said the major.

"Of course," said Warris, and gave a little bow as he rose from his seat in the windowless office. "This will require careful thought and thoroughness."

He could have named three candidates for the job immediately, all students at Patrice Lumumba, but he had learned never to make anything look easy or to propose a candidate for a special school or assignment right away because there was nothing like ease or speed to make a Russian suspicious. Besides, he wanted to think about what had really happened. Undoubtedly, something had happened between the Vatican and America or more likely the Vatican and Israel.

It could have been a meeting between two diplomats, a report from some agent inside Israel, or even a minute change in radio traffic between Israel and the Vatican. Warris knew the Russians had gotten computers from America that could monitor patterns of vast radio traffic to determine if something extraordinary was going on between two points.

He knew they were American computers because the Russians did not stress they were Russian computers and the Russians would never have missed that kind of opportunity if they had built them.

It could have been anything that had caused this sudden need for someone for something special. And somehow the Roman Catholic Church had to be involved. Offhand, Warris guessed that the person would be sent somewhere, somewhere where he

knew the land and could blend in, somewhere where it was
warm and the sun baked the earth and the people on it, where
courtesy and nuances of words were appreciated, in that part of
the world which he had left so long ago.

He had only a Volga car, but this day he used the center lane
reserved for emergencies or the cars of the more important people who drove Chaikas and Zils.

Warris could get away with this because he was almost always mistaken for a diplomat, given his swarthy skin and
prominent nose, especially when he spoke Russian with his
lilting Arabic accent at which little children sometimes
laughed.

He taught in Russian and ordered food in Russian and made
love to his wife speaking Russian. But for his son, in little quiet
moments, he would speak Arabic, caressing the words as he ca-
ressed his son. Each word he gave with something pleasant,
like candy, so that the son would not think the words were
funny or unappealing.

He would do this when his wife, Tomarah, was not around,
lest she mock it, as she often did Arabic things, his wife with
the so white skin and pink cheeks and blond hair that their son,
Arkady, did not have.

But Tomarah dared not mock Arabic when he spoke it with
students he brought home from Patrice Lumumba University,
where he taught international policy studies.

She dared not mock then because if it were not for those students whom he recruited, Warris would not have a propiscka,
that crucial resident's permit that let him live in Moscow, the
real reason Tomarah had married him.

Of course, he never let her know he knew. One never let a
Russian know you were onto them, especially if the Russian
was your wife.

Warris had always treated her with loving respect. She, on
the other hand, could go into rages at his customs, accusing him
of that lowest Russian word, being a "zhid," which meant Jew
in slang.

She would say of all Arabs at times of extreme anger, "You
are all zhids. All of you."

This was not an uncommon thought for Russians. At some
"confidential" briefings on international events, Warris would

hear the officer point out Russian heritage of some Israeli general if they were a success, and the Israeli, it was understood, was successful because of some possible Russian blood. Failures of the Zionist enemy were of course done by zhids.

Yet, unmistakably, the tone was the same as for the failures of Arab allies. And if there was anything Warris Abouf could read like a street sign it was the tone in a man's voice, or the squint in the eye, or the gesture, or where a man sat on a chair, or how the lips smiled in relationship to the eyes.

He thought about these things as he drove along Ordynka Ulitsa and out into the less-populated areas where, on Ordzhonikidze Street, Patrice Lumumba Friendship University stood like a massive artificial insult against the gentle woodlands behind it.

But even as he reminded himself how much he would miss the apartment, car, and blat if ever he had to give it up, he wondered what the Galilee, where his father was born, looked like in autumn.

He wondered if someday he would take his son to the Galilee and show him his father's house and say, "Here were the olive groves." He did not know whether his father had olive groves, but he had told that to his son. A place one had never seen could be anything, and it did not hurt to make it grand to let the boy know he had come from important people.

Warris' own father never talked of the Galilee because the old man knew he could have stayed, knew he had made one inaccurate decision after the other that had landed him and his family penniless in a refugee camp outside Beirut, and his oldest son, Warris, with nothing but his wits for survival.

Still, Warris had done well for himself. Quite well. The Russians trusted him. Someday they might let him leave with his family for a visit, if the political situation were right. Especially if a Palestinian state were established, in which they would see to it that Warris held an important position.

After all, why shouldn't they trust him? They gave him everything.

As Warris pulled into a narrow driveway hidden by a ten-foot wall surrounding the compound of his apartment building, he found himself humming a tune he had thought he had forgotten.

It was a simple melody and it was Arabic, and he loved the sound of his voice in the language he loved.

And when he brought his grand Volga automobile to a stop in his own reserved spot that was supposed to be so valuable because there were so few of them that even White Russians didn't have them, he realized how much he wanted to go home. He realized how much this was not his home.

He waited a mon ent until it passed. These feelings always passed when he reasoned with himself.

But this day it would not pass. Even if he had wanted to let it pass, it could not, not after what would happen to him in his three-room apartment with the new television and washer and stereophonic phonograph from Czechoslovakia.

He found his son standing in the corner with his face to the wall. Arkady was seven, slightly short for his age, but nothing that would cause him embarrassment. Arkady, however, this day looked small because his head was shoved into the corner of the living room. He would not move.

Warris came up behind him, and kissed the back of his hair. His beautiful, full, rich black hair.

"Arkady, Arkady. What is the matter?"

"Leave me alone. Leave me alone."

"Why are you not out playing?"

"I don't want to play."

"Arkady, Arkady. Come now. You are a man. I know you are a man. Why are you crying? You always love to play."

"They laugh at me. They laugh. They laugh now. They call me girl. They call me girl-boy."

"Who? How dare they? Do they know who I am? They dare call you that? Who?"

"Everyone."

"Why?"

Warris watched little Arkady lift his head from the corner, and when he turned around, Warris gasped. There on the cheeks of his only son was the faint pink coloring of woman's rouge.

"Take that off now," said Warris.

"I can't."

"You will. Soap and water will do it."

"I tried. Mama spanked me. She says I must wear it."

"But why?"

"Because if I don't wear it, I look too sickly. I look sallow."

"But I look sallow, Arkady. You have my complexion."

Arkady did not answer. And Warris watched his only son turn his head and put it back into the corner of the wall.

And all Warris could do was stifle an apology to his son for giving him his coloring in a land where it was not welcome.

It was then, at that moment, that Warris knew no stereo from Czechoslovakia or any meal, no matter how rich with meats, could make this land his home.

Somehow he was going home, and now he knew for sure where home was. It was a place where little boys were not ashamed of looking like Warris Abouf, Warris Abouf who was about to find for the first time in his career that no one currently available for a mission to the Middle East was quite acceptable. There would be something wrong with every Catholic-Palestinian-fluent Hebrew until he himself was chosen.

He had learned in the bitterest way possible that an old saying was wrong. The enemy of your enemy was not your friend. He was just the enemy of your enemy. Warris Abouf was going home.

5

Let This Cup Pass

Jim Folan awoke in a sparse room with a large crucifix on a painfully white wall, and he couldn't remember falling asleep. He looked over at the small, brown wooden desk with the stacks of gray cardboard folders.

"Oh, God, no," he said. "No. No. No."

He shook his head and kept repeating, "No." He went to the desk. He remembered where the photograph was, that harsh, flash-lit black and white picture of a find in Jerusalem. It was the third folder down, under the label "Golban, Dr. Sharon."

He unsnapped the rubber band and opened it. He just wanted to see what he had seen the night before when all these folders had been given to him by the Vatican Secretary of State.

There were the skull and the bones resting on that rocky altar, with a dark streak on the tibia. Jim knew it was the tibia only because he read the notes that said the dark mark was oxidized iron on the tibia, and there was that big leg bone with the mark.

So that had to be the tibia. And here he was, selected by the Church itself, to defend a challenge to the very foundation of Christianity when he had learned only just now from notes for certain that the big leg bone was the tibia.

And there was some archaeologist who, for some sophisticated reasons he did not altogether understand, claimed the possibility that those were the bones of the unrisen Christ.

Not for one second did he entertain the remotest idea that

those dark bones could be those of Jesus lain hidden for two thousand years.

But the very contention was so awesome that he felt numbed by its magnitude.

If Jesus did not rise, then He could not be God. If He did not rise bodily, then how could mankind itself believe in its resurrection? If He did not rise, death won for all time for a Christian.

His resurrection proved His divinity and His sermons. His resurrection was the great fact of Christianity. It made a Christian a Christian, and not a Jew or Muslim.

And there was death in the picture of the bones, very quiet, with the eyes and brains out of that helplessly grinning skull. Some scientist was claiming that could be the Christ, the Light of the World gone out forever long ago, never really coming back from death to show the way. There in those disconnected bones.

Impossible. What an assumption. The Romans once crucified three thousand people in Galilee alone after a rebellion.

And that particular body was supposed to be what was left of the Hope of Heaven lying there in Locus III, whatever that was. Ridiculous. The Church knew that. And they would prove it.

But what so drained Jim Folan numb to the marrow that morning was that the "they" was him.

The Church that he had always looked to to protect him from such things was now Jim Folan himself.

It was impossible. He had taken the notes the night before, making memos to himself, and had tried to establish who Father Lavelle was (Dominican archaeologist unsuitable for this situation), as well as Dr. Golban (Israeli archaeologist, finder of body), Mendel Hirsch (Jerusalem Director of Christian Affairs, a proper diplomat and main contact).

There was a coin that somehow established a probable date. There were tests to be done for a sure date. There was the axis of the spine, whatever that was for. And the Hebrew he couldn't read because it was handwritten, and the only Hebrew he knew was the printed kind with the bowl letters, the kind he had used to study Jewish Thought and Liturgy 204. The kind he would see on a kosher butcher shop in Boston. Not the line writing he had to read in the gray folders, similar to the disk, of which special note was made that it was kiln-fired. Why that was important he didn't know, either.

But he did know one thing that morning. He would make an appointment with His Eminence Almeto Cardinal Pesci to explain that the Church had chosen the wrong man.

Surprisingly, Cardinal Pesci saw him the same day. Father Folan was told to enter through a special passage because His Eminence was cutting five minutes from each of four meetings to give Father Folan twenty minutes and His Eminence did not want any of his audience seeing him and suspecting they were losing something.

In daylight the office of the Vatican Secretary of State was even more impressive, with incredibly ornate and rich tapestries and furniture that looked as though they should be in a museum.

The chair Jim had sat on the night before was probably worth more than his priestly allowance would amount to in a lifetime. Cardinal Pesci's rich red robes seemed to glisten with opulence. The room smelled somehow of old wax.

"Sit, sit," said Cardinal Pesci, waving his ring in a gesture signifying the ring was kissed by a unilateral outward thrust and didn't need Jim's lips. "You have found something. What is it?"

"I am the wrong man," said Jim.

"That is too late. Too late now. Arrangements have been made. Positions have been clarified. No. No. Too late."

"I can't do this thing. I am just not qualified."

"Nonsense. We went through a whole procedure."

"Well, for one thing, I have never been anything special. I was in the CIA, but it was only for a year in Laos. I gathered information. We must have someone better in the Church than that."

"As a matter of fact, there was a man who had been an officer in the Deuxième. The Deuxième," Cardinal Pesci repeated, to let Jim know the French secret arm was a respected one.

"And why wasn't he chosen?" asked Jim.

Cardinal Pesci went into a silk-covered book with loose papers inside. He took one out, and Jim recognized the papal seal atop.

"He was rejected because of too intellectual a faith."

"Archaeologists. We must have many archaeologists."

"Yes. Oh, yes. There were twelve. Eight were eliminated because they had been involved in that area."

"But wouldn't that recommend them, Your Eminence?"

"Unfortunately, that is a part of the world where political passions often cloud loyalties."

"Yes, but that is politics. This is scientific and religious."

"Father Folan, nothing that happens in that part of the world is not political. Nothing."

Father Folan could have disputed that point for an hour and not begun to fully bury a statement so broad as to be untenable past junior high school. It was just the sort of statement a person immersed in politics would make. It was the lazy man's way to explain away the vast and incomprehensible multitude of what went on.

But Father Folan was not here to win an argument but to save the Church from a very serious mistake.

"What about the other archaeologists?"

"Not broad enough. There was one, the last one, who seemed to have everything. But your answer on how to approach this problem showed we could get both his expertise and the expertise of others, and without the prejudice of a narrow archaeological discipline."

"There must be someone better than me."

"You are an administrator by training, a man of professionally trained suspicion, high intelligence, impeccable loyalties. And you are a Jesuit. You can bring to bear a multitude of skills and discipline on this thing."

"I cannot be the best man in the Roman Catholic Church to face this."

"Why not?" asked Cardinal Pesci quite pleasantly. He had gone on to his papers and was answering Jim now as he read and signed them.

"Because it is so important."

"Do you refuse?"

"I can't."

"Would you like an audience with the man who selected you? Would you tell that to your Pope?"

Jim hesitated. "Yes," he said finally. "I would do that. I would have to do that."

He had always thought that perhaps someday he would have an audience with a Pope, undoubtedly among hundreds of priests, and probably to hear His Holiness address them on some special subject for some special occasion.

Jim Folan never thought it would be to tell his spiritual sovereign that the man had made a mistake. And he never thought it would be alone face to face, in what had to be one of the starkest papal apartments on the third floor. Unlike the Secretary of State, His Holiness had no rich tapestries, damasks, or ornate furniture. The room was lit by harsh fluorescent lights, and twenty chairs that could have been used for a Boston College assembly were set against a far wall.

Jim waited by himself for almost an hour, and then His Holiness entered quickly and alone. He was a large man, with kind Slavic features and eyes Jim remembered always smiling in pictures. There were no smiles this day. Jim paid the proper respect, falling to his knees and kissing the papal ring. This was his sovereign on earth. His Holiness spoke in English.

"Well, Father Folan. We hear you think we made a mistake."

"Yes, Your Holiness."

"Why?"

And there was no place left not to tell the truth.

"Because," said Father Folan, lowering his eyes, his palms turning up in helplessness, even his voice so weak it took the force of a yell to get a whisper. "I'm just Jim Folan from South Portland. My father worked at Pourtous Mitchell Department Store as a floor manager, when he could hold the job, and my mother's name was Elizabeth Mary and her maiden name was Coffey, and she did part-time work most of her life. Their grandparents came from Ireland, I went to Georgetown University, and I was not a great student. Nowhere, anywhere, Holy Father, is there anything in my life that has shown I am supposed to do a great thing. This is too big for me . . . I'm just Jim Folan."

"James, let us sit a minute," said His Holiness.

Jim felt the Pontiff take his hand and guide him to the chairs against the wall.

"Sit. Sit," said His Holiness.

Jim could not look at his Pope, and he felt most uncomfortable sitting next to him, as though this were wrong. He stared at his hands.

"James, I too think this is a great thing that has come against us. Not for one moment do we think it is true, of course, and neither do you. Our good Secretary of State in his duty thinks of the diplomatic situation. He suspects intrigue. He thinks we should treat this whole thing as though it is a diplomatic maneuver. Now why, when I know, personally know, they have found the body of some poor man who suffered crucifixion like our Lord, am I concerned? Why do I want every scientific and logical process borne out to show this cannot be whom we know it is not?"

Jim looked up from his hands. The question was not to be answered by him. There was concern on the Pontiff's face, but not worry. A decision had been made for the care of the Church, and now its pastor was laying out the course safest in this world for his church at this time.

"I am not concerned about what it is. I am concerned about what it can do to the faith of many, and not just the least intelligent or the least faithful. Have you met our Father Lavelle?"

Lavelle, thought Jim. He remembered the name from last night's briefing. That was the Dominican archaeologist who had returned to Rome with the report of the body, the one Cardinal Pesci had pointed out had been selected by the Israelis themselves. Cardinal Pesci had repeated that twice. Lavelle was in Rome within the Vatican under instructions not to leave.

"I have not met him. I have been informed of him," said Jim.

"Father Lavelle, James, is a good man. He was good in his faith. It was not based as strongly as yours, perhaps, but it was a faith strong enough for him to leave great wealth, sever with close ones, and follow the Lord. I spoke with him. His good mind, which had helped him with his faith, had wounded that faith with the same intellectual lance. That is the danger we face."

"Your Holiness," said Jim, "that still does not make me adequate for this task."

"Father Folan," said the Supreme Pontiff, "you may be inadequate for this task. But that is your perception and not ours. You are the best from what is available to us in this world for a multitude of factors, which I hope you are aware of. But I personally feel good that you are here, that we have you. You are who we want. And that you feel inadequate to the task is only another sign that we are fortunate to have you. Son of Mary Elizabeth Coffey Folan."

The Pope gestured with a sweep of his right hand to the walls.

"The Church is not these buildings. It is not one stone of one of these buildings or any building anywhere, or diplomatic covenant. It is the people who are the Church, and their faith that makes them part of it. This is the most direct assault on that faith which the Church has suffered. And the ones who will suffer the most are the ones who think the most."

"Holy Father, you are not making me feel more adequate to the task," said Jim.

"There is no reason you should feel adequate, James. But you always have our best friend. Go. And remember, above all, in every way, protect knowledge of this from loosing its poisons until you have made it harmless."

And from this Jim realized his Supreme Earthly Sovereign had not only read but remembered that essay on why Jim Folan believed Christ was God. He was left alone in the room again, as the Pontiff went off toward other people of the world. Jim took a moment to do a Jesuit spiritual exercise, going through how he felt about the day, and how that related to God.

It took him less than two full seconds to get to what he felt. He was scared. He went to the drapes and pulled back a corner. Outside was St. Peter's Square. When St. Peter had come here from Galilee, he could have gone up to anyone in the street and talked of God and they would have answered him, "Which god?"

That was two thousand years ago. And he probably would have answered them at that time, "The god who rose from the dead."

Now, Jim would be going in the opposite direction. He wondered if he would see Galilee. And then the force of his examen hit him. But it was too late, even as the prayer came again:

"God, let this pass from me."

And then Jim dropped the curtain back. God had answered him. The answer was "No." Jim had things to do.

He was to work through Cardinal Pesci's office exclusively, which would report to the Pope. The first thing Jim asked for was an appointment with any expert on the physical evidence of Jesus Christ extant in the twentieth century. He wanted one man who could be trusted.

"Are you going to tell what you are working on?" asked His Eminence.

"No," said Jim. "No one who does not already know will know. Too many people know already."

"Do you think word might leak out, so to speak?"

"I would be surprised if somebody somewhere hasn't been noticing something."

"Yes," said His Eminence.

"Nevertheless, as you know, I must in no way investigate this thing so that I expose it."

"Yes. I know his orders," Cardinal Pesci had said. "Before you go to Jerusalem, you must understand what is going on in that part of the world."

"I am sure you will prepare me well."

"No," said Cardinal Pesci. "I will spend only an afternoon with you."

Father Lavelle had a small two-room apartment in the second-floor state complex. A young priest sat at a table before the door to the apartment. He was Pesci's man and checked Jim out by phone before he let him enter.

Father Lavelle sat on his bed, his back against a wall, his feet drawn up beneath him, his shoes still on, soiling white sheets. He was in his middle fifties, with tufts of whitening hair above his ears and a deep tan on his bald forehead. He had sad round eyes and the sort of tender face many small men seem to have, perhaps through buffeting up against a larger world.

He wore a white polo shirt, so wrinkled that Jim assumed he had slept in it for the last few days, yet Jim knew cleaning was available through the ever-present bustling nuns who serviced the Vatican. There was no match for someone who thought she was serving her God when she ironed a shirt.

The most significant fact about Father Lavelle was that he was doing nothing when Jim entered. There was no book in front of him. No radio on, no form of entertainment or any other visible occupation, such as prayer.

"Hi, I'm Jim Folan, I'd like to talk to you," said Jim in English.

"So you are the one," said Father Lavelle. His English was accented but not burdened by his native French. The English was good enough so that Jim did not have to concentrate on deciphering the words through the French-slurred consonants.

"I assume you mean that I am the one chosen to investigate this thing. Are you hurt about that?"

"In the hierarchy of my pain, that is not even a novitiate."

Jim nodded. Even a despairing witticism was better than none in the man's condition.

"May I sit down?" asked Jim, and when he got permission he put a manila folder on a small bare table and sat three feet from Father Lavelle.

Only Father Lavelle's eyes moved.

"Father Lavelle, from what I gather you have been a Communist once?"

Lavelle nodded. "It is so."

"And you changed, and became a Dominican late in life."

"Yes. Yes. That is so."

"I was wondering why you became a Communist?"

"So you can explain away things as a Communist plot, no?" A weak, pitiful smile crossed his delicate face.

"No," said Jim. "I want to know why you believe things, and then Why you don't. There is something that happened in that cave on . . . ." Jim reached for the folder, careful not to let the contents be seen by Father Lavelle because it had a short dossier on his life. "Haneviim Street."

"That is pronounced Hanava . . . eem," said Father Laville. "I became a Communist because they seemed like the only ones willing to stand up against the Nazis."

"And how long did you believe that?"

"Until they got into bed with the Nazis. The invasion of

Poland and the peace treaty between the two ended that. They are not all that different, you know, they just have different classes of *Untermenschen*, 'subhumans.' Those who are to be hated.''

"And being anti-Nazi was important to you?''

"Certainly you have in that file, Jesuit, that my mother was Jewish.''

"And then you became a Catholic. Why?''

"Because I came to believe that Christ was the answer. He was the answer to the wars, to the hate, to the despair of the world. It was a world of sin that I saw so clearly and Jesus was the only answer to that.''

"And the Talmud lacked the answers,'' said Jim, referring to what could best be described as the guide to a good Jewish life.

"I was not raised as a Jew, or even as a Catholic, for that matter. Of course, having a Jewish mother was enough for Nazis. A Jesuit should know that, yes?''

"How did you know first that I was a sole investigator, the one, and then that I am Jesuit?''

"You are, aren't you?''

Jim nodded.

"It was not that hard to reason through,'' said Father Lavelle. "There was such a concern for secrecy. Who did I tell? Who told me? These things the Pope himself asked. So I knew that when this was looked into it would not be a commission, it would be a single man.''

"And the Jesuit?'' asked Jim.

"It would have to be from the Jesuits.'' There was that smile again.

"Why?'' said Jim, remembering Cardinal Pesci making a point that he himself, not the Pope, chose the Jesuits.

"You don't know about taint, and blemished blood?'' asked Father Lavelle.

"I think I know what you are talking about,'' said Jim.

"Jewish blood is considered tainted. How many generations back can your Church be sure you have no Jewish blood? How many, Father? Five, ten, sixteen? Eh? What is the fear there? That some distant blood relative of Mary sneak into your order. The Vatican would have to have a Jesuit to be safe.''

"Father Lavelle, you are referring to a sixteenth-century law made by frightened and foolish people in Spain because of a fear of Moorish and Jewish influence in the Jesuit order. It is a fact that Jewish converts played an early and prominent part in the Jesuits. There was resentment. There was the Inquisition. There were Marranos, Jews who ostensibly converted on the outside but remained Jews. Some of them were Jesuits. In a foolish act during a horrid time, a law was passed that prohibited anyone who had Jewish blood up to ten generations back from becoming a Jesuit. Even at that time St. Francis Xavier fought against those prohibitions. And as a fact, those laws have been changed.''

"Modified," said Father Lavelle.

"I know personally a Jesuit whose father is a rabbi," said Jim.

"With a dispensation. You see that's how the law was changed. It is still there, the one thing the Church would know when it called on the Jesuits to provide its one man was exactly how much Jewish blood he had. Taint. Free of taint."

"An unfortunate term in an unfortunate time."

"And you are here, aren't you, Jesuit?"

"Do you think I was brought in because your findings are invalid because your mother was Jewish, Father? Is that what you think?"

"It doesn't matter now, does it?"

"Is that what you think?" asked Jim.

"It would not be the most impossible event, even if it is certainly one of the more minor ones."

"Is that what you think?"

"You heard a yes."

"You think that?" said Jim, his voice rising on purpose.

"Yes. Yes. I think so. Yes."

And then Jim's voice dropped very low, almost a whisper.

"You're missing an important fact, the most important fact," said Jim. "Why you could not be the one."

"Yes?" said Father Lavelle.

"You believed the body was His."

"I do."

"But you see, that means your investigation ended when you left the cave. And that is where the Church's has to begin."

Father Folan had made his point. But it was really setting up something else. All the framework for pulling out Father Lavelle's personality had gone into this next question.

"When you entered that cave, I see from what little information I have, you believed in the Resurrection. When you left you did not. What was it, ten minutes, a half hour? And it was totally changed."

"I saw Him. I read the plaque. I saw the stone. I saw the Golban data. It's Him, Father, and unrisen."

"Pierre, I am not an archaeologist, but I do know the Romans crucified thousands. In one rebellion in Galilee alone three thousand men were crucified in an afternoon. They used to give those things out like parking tickets. Why that body? Why so quickly did you accept that it was Him?"

"There is the time, the data, the plaque. The body was crucified. It was found in a rich man's tomb, which is odd in itself, because usually only the lowest were crucified. But Jesus, in the Gospels, was placed in a rich man's tomb, and so was this."

"And in the Gospels the sign above Jesus' head was in Latin and Greek, too."

"No, just according to St. John, and that is considered the least accurate Gospel. It was written to convince not to report. Or are you one of those who believe those paintings with the silly sign above the crucified head reading INRI, using Roman abbreviations for Jesus of Nazareth, King of the Jews?"

"Why did you accept Dr. Golban's data?"

"You mean I should have investigated her tainted blood?"

"I asked a question," said Jim.

"She is an archaeologist, why should she lie?"

"I didn't say that, Father. Please, I know you are in great pain, and I feel for you. I do. Let me carry this now. This is mine. The Holy Father has given it to me."

There was no answer but the beaten lifeless stillness in the man whom Jim wanted to cradle in his arms and tell that everything would be all right. He wanted to tell him all the stories Jim knew he would not respond to but should, about the darkness before light, and the death before the Resurrection, that sign that the sin of the world had been conquered, the victorious Christ, who could be victorious over this man's hell.

Father Lavelle's dossier had said he had often gone into the wilderness alone for days at a time, and so Jim began with that question, how long had it been since he had gone to the Judean wilderness?

"A month. I would go there, and return, and return from the nothingness. You see, there the question is clearest. Are we all an interruption of nothingness, or do we come from something and go to something? Have you been to the wilderness? You can walk there from Jerusalem."

"And who asked you to observe the body? Dr. Golban?"

"No. No. A representative of the Ministry of Religion, Christian Affairs. Mendel Hirsch."

"And how did he hear about it?"

"I presume from Dr. Golban. She discovered it."

"I see. Why did she dig there? What caused her to dig in that spot on Haneviim Street?"

"It was an assigned dig. You see, when people want to build and they uncover something of archaeological value, by law the area must be excavated properly before they can continue."

"What had been discovered, the cave?"

"I don't know. Sharon just said it was an assigned dig."

"Are you friends?" asked Jim.

"We knew each other," said Father Lavelle.

"Do all archaeologists in that area know each other?"

"We all know of each other."

"But you knew her."

"Yes."

"How well?"

"I once lectured at a class of hers."

"And she knew you were a priest?"

"I don't know. I didn't go around in vestments. Or even a collar. I lived at the House of Isaiah, on Agron Street, near the American Consulate. Do you know about the House of Isaiah?"

"It's a Dominican residence. You all work in Israel," said Jim, leaving out Cardinal Pesci's comments that the residents of that house had to be assumed to be pro-Zionist. Pesci had stressed that.

"Do you know who suggested that you be chosen to examine the dig?"

"No."

"And you don't know why you were chosen?"

"It is possible they knew me as a Christian and an archaeologist."

"There are others who fill the same bill, Father. I'm trying to determine why you were chosen, why the Catholic Church. Certainly there are Protestants who are archaeologists. It appears that the Catholic Church was chosen."

"It is Him in that cave tomb. Why are you looking for all sorts of dirt under fingernails and time of day and who said what and who did what because of what and intended what? It's Him."

"That someone like you, Father, believes that, is exactly why the Church wants to know who said what to whom and why. We want to know every speck of dust in that cave. Because we don't want to lose you, Father, we don't want to lose one soul because of this thing, and if we've lost you . . ."

Jim's voice cracked. On one hand, he was the professional working toward building his facts, on the other, he was feeling for this man's despair. "We don't want to lose you, Father."

"Are you through, Father Folan?"

"I can come back tomorrow."

"I want to finish today."

"I've got a lot of questions."

"Whatever you want, but let us get through this thing today."

Jim did not want to continue. Father Lavelle needed rest and relief. But most of all Father Folan felt he needed Him, the One he no longer believed in.

"You know, there are lots of possibilities yet to be explored, including some scientific dating that I have yet to fully understand. But have you ever thought that that cave came from one period and the body another? You don't know yet. You don't know, we might not have some proof, putting the body twenty years after Pontius Pilate was back in Rome. You don't know. It is you, Father Lavelle, who has made the leap of faith by declaring it is Him."

"Ah, the Jesuit mind," said Father Lavelle, impregnable to compassion, imprisoned in his grief.

Father Lavelle did not look at Jim or even nod but stared at the crucifix on the wall with the lettering both of them knew was unlikely ever to have hung over the head of Joshua, son of Joseph, later to be called in Greek, Jesus the Christ . . . the man who came from Galilee one spring for a Passover in Jerusalem and an appointment with eternity.

The rumpled sheets of the bed had dark lines where Father Lavelle's shoes had made marks. Jim paused at the door and returned.

He reached under a light blanket covering the feet, and untied the shoes, and put them neatly under the bed, and then removed the socks. He pulled the blankets back up over Father Lavelle's feet. How fragile the feet had seemed, thought Jim. They had blue veins and tiny bones and yet they had carried that poor man such a long, long way.

The physical evidence about Christ was as Jim had suspected. None. Pesci's office had set up a meeting for him with an elderly Belgian priest, teaching at a seminary near Rome. Why this man was chosen, Jim was not sure at first. But he confirmed what Jim had expected to hear.

"What we know of Christ Himself we know through the Gospels. Nowhere in the Gospels is there any description of Him," said the elderly priest.

Pesci had given Jim an office for such meetings. It made Jim uncomfortable just to sit in it, because this was the sort of ornate presence that required a cassock. It was European royalty, not American Jesuit.

"Do you think that the writers of the Gospels refused to describe Him because of the Jewish tradition of not describing God?"

"That is an interesting theory," said the old priest. "But I would say that there was nothing extraordinary in his appearance. For we have an example of Muslim tradition against graven images, which is also from the same root as the Jews. And they speak of specific features of their Mahdi, the one who is to come. So then, it might be allowed."

"In which case, the Gospels might not have described Jesus because He was so ordinary for his time."

"More than likely. How much do you know about the Shroud of Turin?"

"I know that the Church has never come to a position on the

shroud. I believe a study was done outside the Church that showed it was not forgery. But what else, I do not know.''

''Well, it shows the negative imprint of a crucified man. Many believe it is the shroud that covered our Lord.''

''The shroud is just too dubious. I need firmer stuff. That isn't something solid enough. It is physical, but unproven whom it covered.''

''I know by how quickly I was summoned that what you are doing is important,'' said the old priest. ''I can say no more but to look at the evidence on the shroud.''

''The Church hasn't done work on the shroud, has it?'' said Jim.

''Cardinal Pesci can get you whatever has been made available to the Church,'' said the old priest.

''I should look for something through Pesci on the shroud?''

The old man nodded.

At the afternoon reserved for Jim, Cardinal Pesci allowed as how he had heard rumors of a report done on the shroud. He would be able to get that report for Jim through His Holiness, if it existed. He reminded Jim that, in deference to His Holiness, he too was making efforts to adhere to papal secrecy. Jim's name was not in his appointment calendar. This afternoon Pesci would be officially listed as ill.

''I have one outstanding question that you might answer for me, Your Eminence. Why did Israel choose us? Why the Catholic Church?'' asked Jim.

''Ah,'' said Pesci, beaming. ''The main question? Why? Why should the government of Israel, whom we don't recognize, invite us to be the one to share this secret? Why?''

''I don't know, why?''

''Maybe you will help us find out why?'' Cardinal Pesci lit a long cigarette. The cigarette paper was colored green. There was wine, which he offered to pour for Jim himself. Jim refused. Cardinal Pesci began an explanation of the Church and the Middle East which lasted the afternoon, the intricacies of Arab interaction, Western interaction, Church interaction. But one thing was clear from all of it, the great events never seemed to end, not even the Crusades, which Cardinal Pesci said he believed still lingered in the back of the Arab mind.

"The resentment is abated now because they have Israel to focus on, but let their hate turn to us and you will see how vulnerable our Arab communities are, how vulnerable our interests are."

"Is that why the Vatican never recognized Israel?"

"We do not recognize Israel because its borders have never been settled with Jordan."

"That means the Church does not have to recognize Israel until the Arabs do. Or just about that," said Jim.

Pesci smiled.

"Well, quite obviously there are dealings between the Vatican and Israel, Your Eminence," said Jim. "We have holy places there, many that I know of."

"You only offend an Arab by what you do publicly for his enemy," said Pesci, nodding with an even broader smile. "The enemy is always more important to the Arab than the friend."

"So it is only the public relations with Israel that are a danger. Obviously we have private ones, because frankly, Your Eminence, you seem to have everything in order and working rather well."

Pesci nodded. "Understanding all this, we must now ask ourselves, how have the Jews survived? By their cunning. And now we have a Jewish state afloat in a sea of hate, sending us a Zionist who has discovered the body of Christ. Come, come. You don't have to be a secretary of state to be just a little bit suspicious."

"I don't think Father Lavelle is part of any plot. He is severely depressed."

"What does it take to look depressed, American? A long face?" Pesci smiled.

"Medically I think the man would have to be considered depressed."

"And I would want to make sure I trusted the doctor who came to that conclusion," said Cardinal Pesci.

Jim moved the conversation onward. He had always thought that generalizations about entire people were the product of lazy minds. He could accept the difficulties of the Vatican in the Middle East but he could not accept that all Arabs hated or that all Jews were cunning. It seemed, however, more common to Europeans to describe entire people in simple sentences.

As to the survival of the Jews, Jim had always thought it was part of God's plan, and later learned that indeed it had to do with the Second Coming. Pesci apparently overlooked the theology of the matter.

"Specifically, do we have any evidence at this point of Israeli subterfuge? What do we have?" asked Jim.

Suddenly there was a rapid knocking on the large main entrance door. The door opened silently on perfect hand-oiled hinges.

Cardinal Pesci looked up, startled, his flesh quivering under his loose chin.

A middle-aged monsignor, with fluttering hands and weeping eyes, glided quickly across the carpeted floor, sputtering rapid Italian. Jim's Latin enabled him to pick up a few words about death. He recognized Lavelle's name.

Cardinal Pesci listened, nodding. Then he turned to Jim.

"Father Lavelle has created a serious problem. He has committed suicide in his room."

Jim's breath stopped. He started to speak. Nothing came out. He got up from his seat, still holding his notebook.

"I must go to him," he said.

When Jim got to the room, a nun was gesticulating wildly, and the priest who had been sitting outside was weeping with his head in his hands. The door to the room was closed.

Jim opened it. Two bare blue-veined feet hung in midair. Those delicate toes were dark from settled blood never to be pumped back up to the heart. Father Lavelle was hanging by the bed sheet from a light fixture in the middle of the room. A chair stood upright to the left of the feet, just above the ankles.

The tan had darkened bluish on the face, and the tongue stuck out slightly at the mouth, while the eyes stared stupidly, so placidly stupid, up at the ceiling. Father Lavelle had let himself strangle slowly without moving his legs a kick.

It was not one of those suicides where someone hoped possibly to be saved from himself.

Jim Folan touched the feet. They were already cold.

He shut the door behind him, and he was alone with the body.

"How could you do it? How could you do it? We've just begun, Pierre. We've just begun. We've just begun. He's God, Pierre . . . He's God . . .''

Jim stood up on the chair, and hugged the small man to him with one hand while he untied him with the other. He lowered Father Lavelle to the floor, trying not to let him fall, but stepping off the chair, he fell himself. People ran in and he ordered them out.

He wanted oils for the last rites.

"Oils. Unguent. Unction. Oil Unctus," said Jim, and they all looked confused. "Extremo Uncti," he said. And they understood. He shut the door behind them. They were not to be in this room.

Jim knelt by the body and prayed that no more suffer like Father Lavelle from this thing that had been found in Jerusalem. He prayed that Father Lavelle somehow be accepted ultimately into heaven despite what appeared to be the final mortal sin of suicide.

He prayed, and when he looked down at the man who had been hanging like so much baggage, this human life who had made himself just weight by his own hand, this purposeful waste of such a tender soul, Jim Folan said, "Ah, shit." And he cried.

And then the oils came with worried priests, whom Jim dismissed. He put his thumb in the small jar and rubbed the oils between Father Lavelle's eyebrows, and there, kneeling on the floor beside him, gave him the last rites of the Church, under the possibility that when it was too late to move his legs Father Lavelle had at the last moment regretted the taking of his life.

"In the name of God, the Almighty Father Who created you," said Father Folan, "in the name of Jesus Christ, Son of the Living God, Who suffered for you, in the name of the Holy Spirit, Who was poured out upon you, go forth, faithful Christian. May you live in peace this day, may your home be with God in Zion, with Mary the Virgin Mother of God, with Joseph, and with all the angels and saints.

"My brother in faith, I entrust you to God, Who created you. May you return to the One Who formed you from the dust of this earth. May Mary, the angels, and all the saints come to meet you as you go forth from this life. May Christ, Who was crucified for you, bring you freedom and peace. May Christ, the Son of God, Who died for you, take you into His kingdom. May Christ, the Good Shepherd, give you a place within His flock. May He forgive your sins and keep you among His people. May you see your Redeemer face to face, and enjoy the sight of God forever. Amen.''

Father Folan did not need to look at the little book the Italian priests had brought him. He knew the words quite well in English. He had said them for his mother, and for a cousin. This was his purpose in life. He was a priest.

But for Father Lavelle, he whispered one more thought into the dead ears:

"May you see now and for all eternity that He is risen.''

Cardinal Pesci did not hear of the prayers. He heard only that the American went right into the room, and when he left he had cleared out all the notes and had opened every book in case some piece of notepaper had been kept in one of them. Then the American asked everyone who had had any contact with the priest what they knew about him.

But what impressed His Eminence most was that this American, with the innocent Irish face, had so casually informed the Secretary of State that he would use Lavelle's room in the Dominican residence in Jerusalem, since now it would be vacant.

His cover story would be simply that he was continuing one project of Father Pierre Lavelle. Perhaps, thought His Eminence, the Pope had seen this ruthlessness, and had only told his Secretary of State a pretty little story about the man's strong faith as being the main requirement. Perhaps the Pope was smarter than everyone thought.

No one told Cardinal Pesci that James Folan had wept.

6

Going Up to Jerusalem

Jim Folan arrived in the land of Israel to defend the faith with his Georgetown overnight bag, a ream of white paper, and an old green portable typewriter he had borrowed from a Swiss nun.

His shirt and chinos, so fine for Boston, clung to him in the noon heat of the eastern Mediterranean like heavy blankets of punishment. Even his socks were wet.

He was the first to customs because he had nothing, and because all he brought was in that overnight bag. It aroused questions, as he realized and should have known it would. Right here, almost forty Puerto Rican pilgrims had been gunned down years before by terrorists. Just because they were walking by.

As Pesci had pointed out, this was a land under siege, and everyone appeared so normal he had forgotten about it. "I am here to see Dr. Golban. She will vouch for me," said Jim, and refused to answer any other questions.

He would take all the time he needed. He would make sure nothing was left unexamined, no matter how seemingly irrelevant. He had the resources of the Church at his call, Pesci had assured him, and Jim knew something else, coming from a technological nation, something His Eminence did not quite understand.

There was no greater time in all history to prove the exact nature of the bones than now. Ninety percent of all the scientists who had ever lived were alive now.

In some way, even though man couldn't see it with the naked eye, almost everything left some molecular trace. These technicians would be used in such a way that they would not know what they were working on. But they would not be brought in right away. And they might not even have to be brought in at all if major discrepancies about the validity of the whole were found.

That Jim Folan could do himself, very carefully. This, of course, would be fine with His Eminence, who had hinted that he did not want to rush.

"If it had stayed another two millennia where it was, it would not have been tragedy for us, if you understand."

But Jim was not going to slow things down. In this world things got delayed enough without planning. And he suspected, with his experience as an administrator, that if he purposely tried to slow things down, then somehow everything would work faster.

The requested secrecy of His Holiness, however, was guaranteed to consume enough time. He did not take his notes with him but separated them into fifteen different packets, none of which contained enough information to let anyone know the nature of the suspicion of what had been discovered in Jerusalem. The name "Jesus," of course, was never used.

The packets would be courier-delivered in diplomatic pouches to the apostolic delegate on Rue Shmuel Ben Adaya on the Mount of Olives over the course of two weeks. Officially, he was not a delegate to Israel but to the people of the area. Through that office Jim would keep in contact with Pesci, and submit major findings.

Jim still felt overwhelmed by what he had been entrusted to do, but reviewing things he planned made him feel better. He could not forget those poor blue-veined feet hanging in the middle of that room in the Vatican, however, and he reminded himself that, while it appeared the poor man had hanged himself as a bitter testament to what he had found, he still did not know enough about the man to be sure that that was the reason.

That was only the reason he discussed when he was alive. And what was, and what a man said was, could not be accepted as the same thing. The greatest investigative tool a person could have was knowing exactly what he did not know. And he did not know why Father Lavelle had taken his own life. Yet.

Jim looked at his watch. The woman at customs looked at him.

"Would you page her again?" said Jim. Very quietly a young man in a khaki police uniform took up a position behind the customs counter. Jim knew the young man had been posted on him.

He stood by the customs counter watching the people of Israel claim their baggage, wondering if they knew what a miracle this whole thing was, how it had been foretold they would return to this land on wings. How superstitious and improbable that Biblical prophecy must have sounded in a time when the only travel was by foot or animal.

He saw a dark old woman with two large shopping bags waddling through customs with two children behind. She wore a bright yellow print dress, wide as a tent, and a print cloth head cover, and smiled a gold-toothed smile, and from what country she came or her parents came or their parents came he could not imagine. Jim assumed it was somewhere east of Israel, or south. Or perhaps they had been the Jews who never left, or the Spanish Jews who had come to Safad in the fifteenth century. He had read of that holy place where they had studied.

He saw people he would have bet were Irish, and German and Slav and African. One woman was so black he was sure she could not be Jewish, but there she was, speaking Hebrew.

The tribe had scattered, and brought back with them the blood of those nations they had journeyed through. Perhaps they had stayed a few centuries, perhaps they even thought it was home, but here they were.

Jim Folan remembered a debate once in his Chevrus High School on the color of Jesus, and he would love to have offered the Jews of Israel now as proof. Although he hadn't really needed them at the time.

There had been a lot of talk about the color of Jesus, and some students had heard some blacks saying Jesus was black. One student had said no one knew what color Jesus was exactly, but he thought he probably looked like the Goldbergs down the block, who were white and blond, so baby Jesus could well have been blond.

Another student said people of the Middle East were dark and he saw a picture of Arabs and they were dark, some darker than others, but dark.

"The only thing Jesus was not was black," said Father Braun, who taught the class.

A few of the boys clapped. Father Braun noted who they were but said nothing.

"That's racist. That's a racist remark, I think," said one of the better scholars in the back row.

"No," said Father Braun, "that was not a racist remark. The applause just now was racist, because they were happy He was not black. I am not happy that He was not black. I am just saying that we have evidence He was not black."

"What evidence?" demanded the student. He was the best in the class, and everyone was sure he was going to become a Jesuit. Chevrus High was run by Jesuits and was known for producing Jesuits.

"The Bible. The Old Testament," said Father Braun.

"Prove it," said the student.

And Father Braun, who liked to be challenged, and encouraged students to challenge him, read from the Old Testament about the Queen of Sheba, who was "black but beautiful."

And he put the book down and said:

"If the Jews were black, they certainly wouldn't mention that Sheba was black. Such as if we were talking about you, we wouldn't say a white kid came to class. We never would say that if we were white. But if we did, you could be pretty sure we weren't white. Do you see?"

"Well, that doesn't make Him white," said the student.

"No, it doesn't, but in the Song of Solomon there are references to beauty as white, 'neck like ivory towers,' and 'white face under black locks.' And since the people were white, we can assume He was white."

"I heard Jews have colored blood," said another student.

And then Father Braun had been noticing Jim looking out the window at the spring buds that always took so long in Portland, Maine.

"Jimmy Folan, what do you think?"

"Well, sir, Father Braun, I think this is the dumbest discussion I ever heard, sir. Father Braun, sir."

"Oh, really. And why is that?" said Father Braun with a menacing smile. Jim heard some snickers behind him.

"Because we are talking about Jesus. And what He is is so much more important than what color He might have been, and that makes the whole discussion dumb. It's like, like talking about the greatest ruby, sapphire, or something that ever was, and here people are going around talking about the color of the shopping bag it comes in. I mean, that's stupid and, yes, I think so. It's stupid."

"Do you know it is a sin to call someone stupid, specifically prohibited in the Bible?" said Father Braun.

"I was referring to the topic of the conversation. And I think you know I was, sir."

"I do now," said Father Braun. "You have just given us all the best student answers to any question this year, and I just wanted to make sure it was as good as I thought it was. There are moments in teaching that I feel make a life worthwhile. You, Jimmy Folan, have given me one of them."

Jim had felt tears come uncontrollably to his eyes and he was embarrassed. He didn't know where to look. Later, when Father Braun had asked him whether he ever considered becoming a Jesuit, Jim had said he hadn't. He had always thought Jesuits were for smart people, really smart. Bookworm kind of people.

"Think about it, Jimmy. You have a mind, and that is something special God gives. What are you going to do with it?"

And that started him thinking of the Jesuits. Later, in Vietnam, when nothing seemed to make sense, Jesus did. And so did the Jesuits. More and more they made sense for Jimmy Folan's mind.

Now, looking at all the colors of the people of the world who were Jews, James Folan would like to have had Father Braun's class here to solve the argument, or perhaps even begin another one.

One exceptionally beautiful young woman was making her way toward the customs desk, as though about to lodge a complaint. He guessed she might have been from some Arab country. Her complexion was more golden than brown, her hair richly black, and her eyes soft, doe-like, a warm, rich brown.

Her face was elegant, with soft hints of high cheekbones, and precisely full lips, without makeup. She wore a khaki blouse, and shorts exposing legs so sleek, Jim Folan removed his eyes, reminding himself he was a priest.

The woman spoke Hebrew to the older customs woman, somehow able to ferociously inhale a cigarette without missing a beat of conversation. Her raven locks were pulled back tight into a beret, but wispy light strands had escaped and were floating around her ears like silken jewelry spun by the breeze.

She looked at him. Jim turned his head.

"You," she said.

Jim looked back. He felt he had just been addressed by a policeman.

"You," she said again in English.

"Yes," said Jim.

"You are Dr. James Folan," she said with a soft Middle Eastern accent that seemed to caress the consonants and float the vowels.

"Yes. Folan. James Folan," said Jim.

"I am Dr. Golban. I am glad to meet you. You have no more bags than that?"

"No," said Jim.

"You don't plan to stay long. You're leaving tonight, what?"

"No, I just sort of hurriedly came. I'll stay as long as I have to."

"I see. So the choice of you is some sort of rush or accident?"

"No. Not at all," said Jim. "Do we have to talk out here?"

"No. Anywhere you want."

"On the way to Jerusalem," said Jim. She extricated him from customs, and guided him past some dark taxi drivers with large amounts of gold jewelry around their necks. She spoke sharply to them, and Jim gauged from his incredibly sparse and rusty Hebrew that insults had been exchanged.

Dr. Golban took him to an old yellow Volkswagen beetle, with dents and bumps and a blue front fender.

The seat covers were new green plastic material and the engine made a pitiful plea for junking.

Nevertheless, from that coughing, whining, screaming engine, Dr. Sharon Golban got the beetle up to what Jim estimated was almost sixty miles an hour very quickly, and kept that pace out of the airport, onto the highway to Jerusalem.

"Excuse me, please, would you watch where you are going?" said Jim. His bag was on his lap, and his hands were sweating. They had just gone by another car with only inches to spare and the bug was still accelerating.

"I am watching," she said, turning to look at him directly as they missed a Mercedes-Benz bus by what must have been no more than a layer of paint.

"All right, now?" she said when they were on flat openstretch highway between green irrigated fields bordered by golden brown hills.

"Yes. I feel safer."

"Well, I'll slow down more if you want."

"Just look at the road."

"I am looking at the road now. Where did you do your work?"

"Georgetown University."

"Good school."

"Thank you," said Jim.

"I must admit I was apprehensive over whom the Vatican would send, especially when I did not see any of your work anywhere. But Georgetown is an excellent school. Whom did you work with?"

"Well, I don't think anyone you've heard of. I'm not an archaeologist. Look at the road, please."

"What is this? I am driving. Do you wish to drive?"

"Just look at the road."

"I am looking at the road," said Dr. Golban, staring Jim directly in the eye for what must have been a full minute. It had to be a full minute, or at least it felt like it. She turned back to the road in time to avoid a full head-on collision with a military jeep passing a truck.

"So you are not an archaeologist at all?" she said.

"Right," said Jim.

"You are a priest?"

"Yes."

"You don't dress like a priest."

"How do you know what a priest dresses like?"

"Nowadays I don't know. I used to know. But with Dr. La-velle and you now, I do not know."

"You were friendly?" asked Jim.

"Pierre Lavelle is a good archaeologist, and he examined the dig briefly, and then left."

"How briefly?"

"Very. He looked at my notes and the photographs and went to the site, and then left. I must say, I felt sorry for him. He was disturbed by it. I never knew he was a priest. He was such a good archaeologist. He is a good man. I take it you are just a priest, nothing else."

"I am the one who is sent," said Jim.

"And I am under instructions from our Ministry of Educa-tion to assist you in anything you want, and my new department head is Mendel Hirsch, Director of Christian Relations for Je-rusalem. You've heard of Mendel Hirsch?"

"Yes, I have," said Jim.

"You should get along well."

"Why is that?"

"Director Hirsch is not an archaeologist also. I must tell you, I am not going to lie to conform to either of your wishes. I will tell you that."

"Have I asked you to lie?"

"Not yet."

"You expect me to?"

"I expect you to be like the people who throw stones. Yes, somehow people who think they speak for God think they are above normal human constraints. They throw stones if you drive on Saturday. They try to stab you, yes, with knives, if you disturb a graveyard. You people don't even think you speak for God after a while. You think you are God. All right, there you have it. Right there. That is it. That's what I feel about you," said Sharon. Her face flushed, her jaw set, her dark eyes low-ered with hostility.

"Excuse me, Dr. Golban, but if I am correct, I think you are describing the actions of a certain sect of Jews in Jerusalem, not the Catholic Church."

"Same thing. You're all alike. They stone people to death. What did you do, burn them?"

"I haven't burned anyone. And I think you are referring to isolated events of five hundred years ago."

"What about Khomeini? He's not yesterday. How many has he killed?"

"Khomeini is a Shi'ite Muslim leading Iranian Shi'ite Muslims."

"Same thing."

"By definition he is not," said Jim. He reminded himself she was serious.

"All of you who claim everyone should act according to the way you hear it from God feed from the same trough. Maybe you don't burn people or stone them or cut off their hands or heads or whatever, but you do it in subtler ways. You do it to the truth, as though it is some kind of danger to you."

"I happen to believe that the truth leads to God."

"And that which doesn't you'll destroy, right?"

"Dr. Golban, I have not asked you to lie. Nor do I see myself asking you to lie. Nor do I think you would, should I ask you. I would appreciate your judging me on what I do and not the lowest standards of every extreme deviant action by any sect anywhere at any time."

"I just want to let you know what I think."

"Well, you certainly have," said Jim. He wondered if it was something he said. But she was just too hard too quickly for him to have been the cause of this. He was catching the severe resentment of this woman for things he obviously had nothing to do with.

Jim thought of being diplomatic and saying nothing because he did not need a major argument within the first hour he set foot here. But also he felt he should let her know what he thought of her actions. After all, perhaps she did not know how hard she appeared.

"You know, to me, you sound prejudiced," said Jim.

"No. That means judging beforehand. I have had ample experience with rabbis, thank you. And I have seen otherwise intelligent human beings devote lifetimes to haggling over subordinate clauses of codified superstition. That to me is murder of a mind, too. I have yet to see any evidence that any of you are any different."

"You said Father Lavelle was a fine archaeologist."

"He was an archaeologist when he entered the cave. When he left it, poor man, he was a broken child. The murder of a mind."

"How do you know?" said Jim.

"He was crying."

"You saw him cry?"

"I saw tears on the hewn steps when he left. I mean, there it is. Presented with archaeological evidence, he broke down and cried, not because of his poor archaeological training, not in the least. The man was a graduate of the Sorbonne and had worked with Yadin and Shilo and McAlister, so of course he was solid."

"Who?"

"You don't know Yadin, Shilo, and McAlister? Next you'll tell me you haven't heard of Kathleen Kenyon."

"No, I haven't," said Jim.

"Among many important accomplishments she devised the way we all excavate a large city. Before her they just used to dig down, removing era after era. She developed a way to dig down in a grid sort of thing, leaving stratification so you could see the levels. You see?"

"I see."

"You were not joking when you said you had not heard of Kathleen Kenyon?"

"No, I wasn't joking."

"I didn't think so," said Dr. Golban. Now she not only was avoiding glancing at his face, she was looking out the opposite window in despair, her hands rising from the wheel of the wildly chugging Volkswagen. Jim reached for the wheel and collided with her hands.

"What are you doing?" she said. "Are you trying to get us killed?"

"I thought someone should be steering."

"I was."

"Your hands were off the wheel."

"For a moment."

"Please look at the road."

"This is ridiculous. Do you know I was ordered to give up lecturing this semester just to assist you?"

"Please watch the road. If this will relieve your worry, I am going to bring in an archaeologist whom I will choose later. I am going to bring in a geologist, and all the other technical people the twentieth century can offer. At the end of this investigation, we will know every possible fact man can know. You can be assured of that.''

''That is not my concern. I care that I have to work with you. I care that I was asked to lie, and have to live with a lie.''

''Just what was this lie?'' said Jim, careful not to show how much he was really alerted by this.

''To the volunteers. Mendel wanted me to swear to some hokum story about why the dig had to be closed suddenly. The minute politics comes in, lies begin.''

''In what way?''

''The fact that Israel doesn't want to be held responsible for this find, as though we are attacking allies or something. I mean, it is there. And why do we have to go about this like some criminals?''

''You mean secret?''

''Yes. Why?''

''It is a favor your government is doing for the Vatican.''

''Why, have you stolen something? Have you done something criminal?'' said Dr. Golban, looking directly at Jim, waiting for an answer as a large tractor trailer hummed up the road toward them.

''Please look at the road.''

''I am,'' she said, staring directly at his eyes, and just as angrily finally turning back to the road in time to miss the truck. Jim decided to keep quiet while Dr. Golban was driving, so as to reach Jerusalem alive.

He cradled the overnight bag in his lap and just watched the autumn fields go by, fields which, according to a brief survey he had read, produced three crops a year.

As they climbed the hills to Jerusalem, Jim remembered the oft-used phrase of the Bible, ''going up to Jerusalem.'' It was both a spiritual and a physical description.

Jim noticed how green the land became with the intensity of trees the closer they came to Jerusalem.

The little yellow Volkswagen spit furiously and the car rattled and passed another truck.

Dr. Golban lit another cigarette. She was surly and silent.

Jim ventured what he hoped was a question not sufficiently emotional to get her to take her eyes off the road. He was still not sure why she was so angry. That amount of anger seemed entirely inappropriate.

"Was this a Roman road once?" he asked.

"No. This one will take valleys. The Romans like their roads under the crest of hills to move legion columns free of ambush. You can see their roads over there," she said, nodding to the left in the far distance.

It struck Jim that all the time he had studied Roman history and the history of its empire he had been studying about a place over there somewhere. Just talking to Sharon, he knew now everything he had ever read about the Roman Empire, and the life of Jesus, was not a "there" anymore, it was here. All around him, in the terraces of olive trees under the new forests planted by the Israelis, in the stones that talked to people like Dr. Golban. It was here that He was crucified, just up the road, and here that He was buried, and here that He rose again on the third day.

Right here, at a point in time, the offering up of God unto His Father was the sacrifice for the salvation of all mankind. From that point onward, all people had access to heaven through His blood. And somehow not only did Jim feel it was all here, but he sensed somehow that it was also now.

And then Jerusalem came into view, a warm brown-gold city on two hilltops in the distance, under the smiling sun of God. He could see the frustration in Dr. Golban's face soften, and a joy reflected by this city on a hill. The face became warm and delicate and fine, looking at the city.

"Dr. Golban, forgive me if I am wrong, but I sense a distinct hostility toward me on your part."

"You are correct."

"May I ask why?"

"Because you have come here to disrupt a perfectly scientific archaeological dig. It is hard enough to scientifically estimate what has happened by the fragile fragments left us without someone with a preconceived set of suppositions taking charge."

"Isn't this your dig?"

"If it were, would I be bothered by your religious beliefs, by your lack of credentials? But if you are supervising this particular dig, then it certainly does bother me. Yes.''

"I had thought that this was your excavation, and I was just observing.''

"No," said Sharon sharply, as they turned down a gentle slope into the city itself, losing its overview by the rise of close gold-brown buildings, all of the same warm yellow stone. The air was somehow wine-cool, and Jim felt a sense of joy with the very stones of the city itself.

Most of the buildings were two stories high, and each had that warm brown facing. Everywhere there was greenery, trees and shrubs, and neatly laid-out streets.

There were a few more people in dark Orthodox Jewish suits. Except for the presence of Arab kaffiyehs, the people could have been from any American or European city, he thought.

Then he saw a donkey make it up a road, with an Arab on him carrying two large bundles. Then he saw several donkeys, and large stalls of produce that seemed to swim in flies. Down the street was a wall with parapets and a large ancient gate.

"That's the Old City," said Dr. Golban, nodding toward the street. She parked the car. "Suleiman put up that wall.''

"Suleiman, the Magnificent," said Jim.

"Yes.''

"He drove out the Crusaders.''

"No. No. Sal Ah Din defeated the Crusaders up north.''

"Saladin," said Jim, confirming who he thought it was by giving it the English pronunciation he had learned.

Sharon got out of the car. She didn't lock it. Jim got out also. He waited for her to lead him somewhere. There was a storage building from which crates of food were loaded, an empty lot across the street, and an empty lot to which Sharon was pointing.

In the lot were stakes with bright yellow ropes surrounding a hole approximately forty feet by forty feet.

"Is that it?" said Jim.

"This is Haneviim Street.''

"Is everything secured? Can people get in or out freely?''

"Absolutely not. The stone has been moved back over the tomb. You would need several people, and I mean several, or a crane to move it, and we have an Arab watchman at night, and nobody is going to move it during the day.''

"So everything in there is secure?"

"Yes. And we have dropped a few plywood eight-by-eights over the stone.''

"To protect against what?"

"Anyone thinking it might be a tomb."

"Why is that?"

"We are near Mea Shearim. There is an ultra-Orthodox sect that believes God has given it the right to stone people, lie, stab people, and generally do any harm for the sake of not disturbing the dead,'' said Sharon. "Well, let us go look at the dig.'' She started walking toward the roping around the hole.

"No, I don't want to look at it,'' said Jim. He shook his head and did not move.

"Wonderful,'' said Sharon. "Would you mind telling me why?''

"There are other things I have to do first,'' said Jim.

"Wonderful,'' said the beautiful Israeli archaeologist. And she was laughing in despair.

The laughter was a bit infectious.

"I can see what you're thinking,'' said Jim, smiling. "But I do have my reasons. I really do.''

"That's what I said,'' said Dr. Golban. "And no fact will ever change them.''

7

The Holy Sepulcher?

Father Folan discovered the purpose of the Israeli moves too soon, and too suddenly, and with too much finality. By the time he knew of it, the Israelis had gotten what they wanted.

The reason His Eminence Almeto Cardinal Pesci hadn't thought of it was that it was quite simply too obvious.

Dr. Golban had driven Jim to Director Hirsch's office off Ben Yehuda Street. Director Hirsch, a middle-aged Israeli, was affably correct and courteous. Dr. Golban smoked sullenly. Apparently there was tension between the two.

Director Hirsch made many references to the Vatican hierarchy, correctly referring to each title in that intricate structure. When he talked of Jerusalem, he overflowed with ecclesiastical titles of the many Christian sects: "His Excellency, His Beatitude, the Archimandrite, the Patriarch, the Right Reverend, the Very Reverend, the Reverend Custos, and Venerable Brother."

As he mentioned each, he nodded to pictures of them on his wall.

One could see the multitude of different Christian faiths on Director Hirsch's wall. They also demanded an answer to a very big question Jim had been asked by His Eminence Almeto Cardinal Pesci, himself, back in Rome.

Through Pesci's office, Jim knew Hirsch's job was not new with Israel. Because of the multitude of Christian sects, and because of the many claims to holy places, whoever ruled Jerusalem had to provide a mediating service. This had been done by Turks and British and Jordanians before. In fact, when the British took Jerusalem in 1917 these experts at empire immediately announced, "Status quo."

And that meant that the centuries of intricate relationships to time and place at holy sites would stay the same because it was beyond the skill of man to rearrange them without religious warfare.

Jim let Director Hirsch serve him coffee and cakes. Dr. Golban just took coffee.

"How did you get assigned to this project?" said Jim to Director Hirsch. They all spoke English. Jim noticed Dr. Golban perk up. Maybe this would be news to her also.

"You want to know why I am involved in this?" said Director Hirsch.

"Yes," said Jim.

"Well, when we realized what we had, someone had to coordinate things, and it fell on me with my knowledge of Christian hierarchies."

"All right. Now I know why you. Why us? Why the Roman Catholic Church? Why not the Greek Orthodox, the Russian Orthodox, the Church of England? The International Council of Churches? Why the Roman Catholic Church?"

"I could say that because your founding head, the first Pope, was a Galilee lad," said Director Hirsch with a warm smile.

Jim smiled back. Sharon lit another cigarette and exhaled.

"But we know you know that St. Matthew left for Cairo just about the same time St. Peter left for Rome," said Jim. "So you might just as well have chosen the Copts. And the Greek Orthodox have claims in your eyes equal to us. Just as old. So how did we get this honor?"

"Because you are the most formidable Christian sect."

"Why did you want formidable?"

"You've got to ask yourself what we wanted from the body, Father Folan."

"That's what I am doing."

"Think of our history, yours and mine. All right. We have been looking at each other for two millennia," said Hirsch.

Jim noticed the voice drop an octave. It became leaden and strong. Each word must have been felt many times. It was like a giant wall without enough space between the blocks to insert a sheet of paper. There was no room here in what he said for any leeway.

"In the Diaspora, in your Europe, there have been some hard times. Not the least of which, Father Folan, were done with religious overtones. Easter for you is a happy holiday. I remember pogroms as how it was celebrated. Easter and the Good Friday of the crucifixion. You know who was blamed?"

"You are also aware of the Jewish schema whereby Vatican II absolved the Jews for the crucifixion of Jesus. That the death of Our Lord was for all mankind, for the guilt of all mankind."

"Yes, I know, but I am talking of memories that go deeper. Do you know what our first reaction was? Our first reaction was, 'Oh, no, not this!' We didn't want to be blamed for this. We thought Christians would be saying, 'Look at what the Jews are doing.' "

"Why didn't you bury it?"

"That was not undiscussed."

"You considered it?"

"Yes."

"But you didn't do it?"

"No."

"Why not?"

"Because even if it is buried, it is still there."

"Why not destroy it?"

"Can you believe that if we destroyed it, and ultimately word got out that we destroyed it, it would be considered an act of aggression against Christianity?"

"That's farfetched."

"For computers, Father Folan. Not for people," said Director Hirsch.

"Father Folan, we explored a multitude of possibilities should we proceed with this dig either as a normal archaeological dig or a special one. In either case, word would have gotten out about the nature of the body. Here in Israel, when we plan, we go through scenarios. Best case, worst case, most probable, least probable, et cetera."

"I am aware of that planning tool," said Jim.

"In this matter there was not one good thing that could come to us from being associated with this find. The negatives were inexhaustible. The best possible thing that could have happened, if we had let this proceed and become public, would have been a massive controversy and only modest blame on Israel limited to the ever-present anti-Semite. That, my good Father Folan, was the best case."

"And so you decided as a first step to call us in as part of the solution to your problems."

"Oh, no, Father Folan," said Director Hirsch, beaming. "You are not part of the solution. You, Father Folan, *are* the solution. It is your dig. We are here only to assist. No Jew, no Israeli will have any authority over this dig."

Jim Folan glanced at Dr. Golban. She put her cigarette out in her coffee cup, and announced:

"Please, excuse me from this, thank you."

Then she left the room.

Director Hirsch apologized for her being a scientist and not a woman of the world.

"I can see her point," said Jim. "I can see it very well."

"Of course, Father. We do too. Now what shall we do with your dig?"

Sharon Golban got a phone call two days later at her apartment that Jim Folan, do not call him Father, call him Jim, would like to see her the following day to interview her and discuss the dig.

"All right, come on over. I'm at Beit Vagan. Do you know how to get here yet?"

"Is that your apartment?"

"Yes."

"Do you live alone?"

"Yes. No one will overhear."

"Let's meet somewhere else. Perhaps more open," said Jim.

"It's open enough. I'll open a window. I have my books and notes here."

"I'd prefer somewhere else, if you wouldn't mind."

"I do mind. It's a nice apartment. Messy a little, but I'll clean it up."

"Do me this favor. Please."

"No. What's wrong with my apartment? You haven't even seen it."

"It's not your apartment. I shouldn't be alone with you in an apartment."

"Why?"

"For me it is an occasion of sin."

"Why? What have I done?"

"Nothing, Sharon. I am a priest. For me to be alone with a woman in her apartment would be an occasion of sin."

"That's incredible. That's insulting. That assumes I am going to jump on your penis the minute no one is looking."

"Dr. Golban, where can we meet?"

"Do you want me to wear a chador, Ayatollah Folan?"

"I will meet you at Mendel's office."

That night Sharon bought a bag of new autumn apples, and with an extra packet of cigarettes and a glass of wine settled down with her old textbooks in preparation for the meeting the next day with the Vatican's man.

She could see her dominant student interest scrawled over the first chapter of St. Matthew, the beginning of the Gospels.

"Test Sunday on the Synoptics!!!!"

And somehow, as it always did, it all came back, how the professor had stressed that the Pentateuch, called the Torah, was what the Christians called part of the Old Testament, indicating, of course, that there was another one.

And somehow, as it always did, it all came back, how good the Synoptic Gospels were as reference in large areas of Second Temple period history.

She noticed her old notes about the political struggles of the time, and how the Gospels helped place many factions so accurately.

She focused on that Passover when the Nazarene had come to Jerusalem, and why the Romans were there, and what Caiaphas, the high priest, wanted, and even the interests of the Pharisees and Herod himself. Things started to make sense in relation to the dig.

She made more notes. "Review attitude of apostles toward crucifixion shortly before and after believing they witnessed resurrection . . . Negative attitude toward tomb as toward cross . . . How many centuries before cross could be acceptable as Christian symbol? Unique nature of early Christian movement.''

And she thought briefly about the clay wall, how well it blended in with the cave. She made notes. She could not do a scenario of probability until she went back and saw exactly how well the wall blended, and performed other tests. One did not jump to neat answers or one found oneself neatly stupid.

Holy men needed neat answers to the universe. Archaeologists had to deal with minute disputable facts. That was the glory of truth. It was so rich.

Sharon lit another cigarette and wrote down ''Holy Sepulcher.'' That, too, had to be reexamined.

There was a Church of the Holy Sepulcher that, until now, archaeology had shown to be the place of the probable tomb of Christ. But why?

Weren't the Jews driven out of Jerusalem during the destruction of the Second Temple? And that would mean Christians too at that time, because then they were considered another Jewish sect.

And if they were all out of Jerusalem, who would be left to say a certain tomb was the tomb of Christ, the Holy Sepulcher? And the less certain the accepted site of the Holy Sepulcher, the greater possibility another one was, perhaps one on Haneviim Street.

Sharon went to a wall in her bedroom–living room–study combination and got the history book she wanted. She was right. There was a period during Roman administration that Christians were not in the city either.

These things were facts to be explored further, by either herself or that priest, if ever he got around to it. The old excitement was back even if she had to work with that man.

She took another apple, and went back to her Gospels.

Sharon liked the Gospels for another reason. She liked the common sense of the man Joshua, called Jesus by the Greeks, and the Christ, which meant in Greek the anointed one, or Messiah.

''It wasn't what went into a man's mouth that made him holy, it was what came out of it.'' Beautiful. So much for the *kashruth*, the dietary laws.

''Let the dead bury the dead.'' He could have been talking to the Orthodox sects, who would kill people today for disturbing a Jewish cemetery. The fuss they made over proper burial. And they would stone him today if he told them that.

She could see Jesus coming to an archaeological dig and telling the crazy Orthodox sects they should worry about the living and not the dead. And she could see them accusing him of being blasphemous, first, if he spoke Hebrew at all, because some thought that was only for holy uses, and then throwing stones at him or even using knives if he told them their first duty was not to the bones in the earth, bones of people dead not for days but for centuries.

The use of the Old Testament prophecies was interesting because the Christians took all the prophecies about the suffering to mean it would happen to a man, the Messiah. The Talmud taught that the prophets had talked of the people of Israel in the Torah. Man and people, two interpretations.

She read until three in the morning because she had no class the next day, or for the duration of the dig. And each time she came to one passage she felt as moved as the night she had reviewed the Gospels, cramming for a test:

"My God, my God, why have you forsaken me?"

It was so incredibly human, she wanted to cry. She had felt that despair herself. It was just what she would want to cry out at times of extreme loneliness, if she could cry out, if she hadn't felt so utterly abandoned and useless to the world when her Dubi had left her that day, that dismal rainy winter day, without even a note, just his clothes and personal possessions gone from the closets and two thousand Israeli pounds she had been saving. Not even a good-bye. Not even a nasty note. Not even the least bit of an argument.

It was not the money loss that remotely bothered her but the fact that he did not care that she needed it. He didn't care. He didn't care at all.

A year and a half later he had phoned with the most ridiculous story of gangsters being after him, and he had to take the money to run and live. And, to save her life, he had not left a forwarding address, because she might be in danger if they knew.

"Dubi," she had said on this transatlantic call, "that is so much nonsense."

"I swear."

"That's unbelievable."

"I need money to come home. I'm tired of America. I miss you, Sharon."

"Then come home."

"I can't without money."

She wanted to send him the money. Even remembering how she felt talking to him on the phone, her body ached for the want of him. There never was a lover like him. Never. None of the men touched what he could do for her. And she had thought, to hell with it, I'll send him the money and at least I'll have the man I want. I'll have him here.

So he was a liar. She had never loved him for his intellect anyhow.

She sent him the money and didn't hear from him for another six months when he came up with another transatlantic call, collect, and an equally urgent plea for more money.

"Come here first, then maybe we'll talk about money. I know if I send it it will be gone."

"All right, then how about money for a divorce? You can't get married again unless you have me for a divorce. That must be worth something."

"Maybe."

"Will I get it?"

She had hung up so he would not hear her cry. He phoned a year later, with another fancy story, but wanting only $100 American to settle a divorce in Israel. She agreed. But he had to be here. And they'd talk. She was sure the talk would take place in the bedroom.

And all right, she wasn't proud of it, but dammit, she wanted him. It wasn't her fault he had made in her an appetite for him that never left, and never quite got satiated with another man.

He didn't come but he did call for more money again, and this time she just didn't send it at all.

Helpless was the awful word for it, and while Jesus, this prophet or God, or Son of God depending on the Christian belief, was made helpless in more noble circumstances, nevertheless Sharon Golban could feel what he felt there in those last moments. Humiliated. And she had done this to herself. She knew who Dubi was, and if she thought about it she probably knew who he was the day she married him.

But even thinking about him now, she wanted him. And that was the most humiliating part of it all. Still wanting him.

If she were correct, those of Jim's faith, Roman Catholicism, believed Christ was God, not just the Son of God, but God Himself with the Father and the Holy Spirit.

And that brought up a question. If Jesus were God, how could the Catholic Church explain why He had felt despair, how could He think the Father had forsaken Him?

Also, there was a proven miraculous prophecy. Any historian could check it out. Matthew wrote before the fall of the Second Temple, one of the gigantic structures of the ancient world, that Christ had said his words would outlast it.

Now if Christ had known that, why didn't he know in that moment of despair that he would be resurrected?

Was that despair on the cross an act of a man who expected resurrection?

She would have to ask the priest these questions. If she were going to be assigned to his dig, then she would learn something, too.

But Sharon did not get a chance, and in the end that next day, she would not even care about that.

She met Jim at Director Hirsch's little office. She had her notes, and her big question, in a small handbag.

Mendel Hirsch was there, Jim Folan was there, and an ashtray was there, near where she sat.

Jim Folan asked the first question:

"On the first day of the dig, what did the ground look like?"

"It was a partially excavated empty lot."

"And what did you wear?"

"What?" said Sharon.

"What did you wear?"

"I don't know. Clothes. I wore clothes. Why are you asking this?"

"Please bear with me. I have my own questions, which might seem unreasonable to you, but they are reasonable to me. What did you wear? Do you remember specifically?"

"No."

"All right, what was everyone else wearing? Who was there and what were they wearing?"

Sharon looked to Director Hirsch. She asked him in Hebrew: "What is this going on?"

"I understand a little bit of Hebrew," said Jim in English. "I understand this is difficult for you but please bear with me."

"All right," said Sharon, "they wore clothes too." The interview went on for hours like that. Hirsch left. It was a pack-and-a-half-of-cigarettes interview.

She put aside completely any thought of asking Father Folan about Jesus' despair on the cross, the theological explanation.

Finally he took out a special notebook, in which there was no discernible writing. It seemed like a combination of abbreviations. It was code, of sorts.

"What are your reasons that make you think the bones are those of Jesus Christ?" he asked.

"I never said they were. Not exactly."

"What?" His head jerked up. He had very open blue eyes. In other circumstances the man could be quite attractive. There was something very strong and honest about him. But of course he was a priest and therefore so professionally warped in his thinking that he would be worse than Dubi Halafi. Dubi was an outright ignoramus. This man had to go through years of training to get that way, and it must have been years before she noticed how apparently disconnected questions on trivia always came together in some intelligent form of cross-reference. He was not stupid. She was sure he was asking similar questions of others. He would have made a wonderful policeman.

"I said I never declared openly that it was the body of Jesus Christ. I said, formally, that what was discovered conformed at that point to the Gospels."

"You mean there is more to be done?"

"Absolutely," said Sharon. "But first let me explain that I jumped to that conclusion in my own mind, which was highly unprofessional of me."

"Tell me about it."

"I was so excited about finding the disk with the writing that I started to do broad analysis on the spot, that is, figuring out what it meant. And I just raced along mentally and then it hit me. Who was the Jewish king crucified? There was no Jewish king crucified. It was a mock sign. The man was Jesus.''

''So you think it is Jesus?''

''I think there are tests to be done, scenarios to be explored.''

''What tests?''

''Hallelujah, hallelujah, a question I am most fit to answer,'' she said.

He smiled. He did have a reasonable sense of himself, she thought.

She started to explain the difficulties of carbon dating the bones. The substance most amenable to that dating was collagen, and that was found in the connecting tissue and skin, which apparently had all gone in time. They were the very elements that made radiocarbon possible.

But the disk itself could provide perhaps the best dating, since it was kiln-fired, and that lent itself to the new process of thermoluminescent dating, incredibly accurate if one had the time and money to find a matching piece of kiln-fired pottery for which a singular date was known.

''You see, what you are looking for is the amount of light emitted by a crystalline material above the normal incandescence, which in itself can give you a variable time, but when you match with . . .''

''So the disk can be used for dating?'' asked Jim.

''I thought you wanted to know the process.''

''Later. Right now I am just looking for the broad outlines.''

''Fine,'' said Sharon, slumping back into the very hard and uncomfortable chair. She looked at her watch. She had been here for hours. '

''Now, what would you say is the main archaeological source book for this dig?''

''You want me to answer that?''

''Yes.''

''Matthew, Mark, and Luke.''

''Yes,'' said Jim, smiling. ''I've heard of the Gospels.''

''Not the way I have. May I go now?'' said Sharon.

''Yes, and thank you.''

At the door she remembered something. The bones were now exposed to fresh air since the clay bricks had been broken through. The bones should be coated with polyvinyl to protect them. This would not only stop deterioration but would keep the bones in place if the coat was thick enough. She owed it to the dig to mention it. The bones, after all, were almost two thousand years old, and very fragile.

"Jim, I think there is something you should do right now."

"Thank you, Sharon, I have my own schedule."

"Well, all right," she said. And left the office wanting to cry.

8

The Proof of Christ

Autumn heat stole moisture from the body in that part of the world. Jim Folan had been warned to drink more than he thought he needed, and rest at midday.

At noon, however, Jim set out for the apostolic delegate's on the Mount of Olives, just beyond the Old City walls. It was a walk of several miles from the House of Isaiah on Agron Street.

His body did not want to move, and his legs dragged, and Jim Folan felt good about the strain. He had reasoned that if he pushed himself now in the heat, and suffered now, he would be able to function better in Jerusalem after the hard conditioning period.

Everything for him had required struggle before he succeeded. This would be no different, no matter how immense. He was like a little child again, he realized, making a deal with God—"If I suffer, therefore You have got to help me."

But there was something else to pushing himself in the noon heat. This he could do. He could make his legs move. He could force himself to keep going. That was the one thing he could control.

As he reached Mamila Street, at the northwest corner of Suleiman's walls, he could see brown and white bare walls beyond the distant Mount of Olives. That was the wilderness. When the Bible said Jesus went to the wilderness, it meant just that. There was no abbreviation of time there for a reader to imagine a long trip on a donkey. You walked out into the wilderness like a hike to the suburbs.

A man could fast out there for forty days because the wilderness was not a forest, which was a common misconception, but rather incredibly desolate desert hills. The word Zion itself meant "wall against the desert."

Did Father Lavelle used to go out there by himself? Jim wondered.

His evening examination had uncovered lately that he really resented Father Lavelle for not disproving the find immediately, for not being the Church that Jim Folan's mother had told him would always protect him. He felt Lavelle had failed not only himself but also his Church and ultimately Jim. And while Jim Folan knew better intellectually, did not believe this, it was something he had to acknowledge he felt to be at peace with himself and his God.

It also allowed him to more fully feel the compassion poor Father Lavelle so deserved. And that was good.

Jim tramped along in his pain, remembering boot training as a Marine. Well, he was a soldier of Christ, and soldiers had to know how to endure pain. At the end of the Old City walls he reached the Kidron Valley, the other side of which was the Mount of Olives. It was hot and his mouth was dry. He could see to his left a large black stone church, which looked dark with time. A sign along the road explained it was the church that marked the spot from which Mary was traditionally believed to have been assumed into heaven. On the right was a magnificent church with a grand mural, surrounded by a large garden of very old, gnarled olive trees.

Jim glanced at his little hand-sized map. That was the street he had to walk up to reach the delegate's residence. The map also explained what the olive trees meant. The church and the trees were the Garden of Gethsemane, now looked after by Franciscans.

He could have rested by the walls of the garden, but he chose to push on up the hill. Gethsemane meant "olive press" in Hebrew, and Jim could hear in his imagination the stone press grinding olive and pit, Geth-Sem-Manee, Geth-Sem-Manee, round and round, stone against stone, crushing pit and meat, round and round Geth-Sem-Manee.

There was the cave to his right where Jesus and the apostles stayed before entering Jerusalem on that Passover which would become Easter forever after. Jim pushed on, the sweat now profuse upon his brow, his shirt wet at the arms and back, his breathing a rasping pain, his throat and mouth dry.

When he reached the cool stone-roof vaults of the apostolic delegate's residence, people were running around to get him cool drinks, and Jim realized what a fool he had been. They wouldn't let him move from his chair, and the apostolic delegate himself, a Canadian monsignor, brought him a water-soaked towel and a shirt of his own.

The whole walk in the noon heat had been a grandiloquent, self-centered exhibition for his own relief because he couldn't take the emotional pressure. Not the least of which came from that hostile Israeli archaeologist who had every right to be angry with him, and whom he didn't want to be angry with him. Some examens didn't need preparatory prayer—they hit you in the face. The truth was either hidden or flagrant. Somehow it was never reasonably observant.

"Thank you, thank you. I'm all right. I did a foolish thing. I'm not used to the weather, and I walked several miles in the noon heat," said Jim.

"Why did you do that?" asked the monsignor.

"Sometimes, I am not too bright," said Jim, getting a grapefruit and carbonated water drink that was more quenching than anything he had ever tasted.

Bougainvilleas flourished along the yellow limestone walls, kept immaculate by Arab gardeners.

He drank several grapefruit and soda drinks, and realized the delegate himself was not the man he wanted. The monsignor, of course, would do everything in his power to assist, as per his Lord Cardinal Pesci's instructions, and, of course, exert maximum discretion in all matters relating to Father Folan, officially an American citizen traveling on an American passport.

What the monsignor had to offer, however, was his assistant, a British priest named Father Walter Winstead, who handled all communications, courier and coded telex, and the delegate's funds. Father Winstead had one problem, the monsignor warned Jim:

"He has a curiosity that tends to get the better of him."

"Thank you for telling me, Monsignor," said Jim.

Father Winstead's office was a bright, window-lit room with immaculate red tiles on the floor and a counter separating Father Winstead from the world. Behind him was a room with dark machines and a sign in English, French, and Arabic saying that no one should enter.

Father Winstead was a pale man with thin, bony fingers and very dark eyes that gave Jim the impression the man would love nothing more to do with this American Jesuit visitor than to file him, probably under "American Jesuit Visitor."

He wore a black cassock, and was very young. He had $500 he had been ordered to release from Cardinal Pesci's office to Jim, at Jim's request early this morning by phone to Father Winstead's office.

"I am the one you spoke to. I am Father Winstead. You must be Pesci's nephew. I've never seen funds authorized so quickly."

The $500 was more than Jim had held in his hands since he had been a Marine. His own Jesuit allowance was less than $20 a week for personal expenses in one of the more costly American cities.

"It's all here," said Jim. "Thank you."

"It certainly is. We couldn't get that much so quickly if it were for the Second Coming. Money is so tight nowadays. The Church is in a financial bind today that it hasn't been in since before the Second World War. It's awful. I see you have an open-ended authorization from the Secretary of State for funds."

"I think I had been told that, yes," said Jim.

"Of course if something is important, that important, then it is worth it," said Father Winstead.

He nodded to the room with the dark machines. "That's the code room," said Father Winstead. "We can send your messages directly to His Eminence in code if you wish."

"Thank you," said Jim. "I'll remember that."

"Although, frankly, anybody who cared probably could break our code with a pencil and a half hour's experience," said the priest. "I don't know where Pesci thinks we're operating, as though we are surrounded only by Jewish peddlers and Arab goatherds. This is a major event around here. These people are tops. When the Egyptians and the Israelis fought in the Sinai, it was the second largest tank battle in all history. The Israelis have more tanks than NATO. Did you know that?''

''No,'' said Jim.

''And the Arabs have more tanks than the Israelis,'' said Father Winstead. ''You know the monsignor said to me the other day after a delayed transmission, he said, 'Who do you think might be listening in on us?' ''

Jim waited politely for Father Winstead to answer himself.

''I told the good monsignor, 'Whoever wants to. Whoever wants to.' And they wouldn't have to delay our transmissions either. They could get them in milliseconds. So he said, 'Why not change the code?' And do you know what I answered?''

''No,'' said Jim.

''I said, 'Why bother? There is nothing I am going to come up with that they are not going to have broken immediately. I'd spend five days on a new code, and they'd spend five minutes breaking it. Not to mention the Russians.' ''

''The Russians. Where do the Russians come in?''

''You have to assume the Russians, you just do.''

''So you don't know for sure. It is an assumption.''

Father Winstead chuckled. ''As sure as anyone can be, we are sure.''

''I guess you picked up something,'' said Jim.

''If that would help you in your purpose, I would tell you,'' said Father Winstead. ''However, I don't have the least idea what you're about.''

''Right,'' said Jim.

''I am not at liberty to let you know how we know, but I can tell you you are looking at the whole Vatican communications complex for the most crucial area of the Middle East.''

Jim smiled.

''Someone else known to be very good at these things let us know.''

''The Israelis?''

''Officially, we have no official contact with the Israeli government. However, we are very, very busy with many Israeli citizens who happen to hold government posts.''

''I would think that you would get more equipment,'' said Jim.

"More equipment? I wouldn't have time to use it. Between 4:30 and 5 P.M. I transmit, taking on the best in the entire world. Do you know where we have the most sophisticated code equipment, Father?"

Jim shook his head.

"Between the Vatican and Castel Gandolfo in that crucial war-strained area of central Italy connecting His Holiness' winter residence with his summer one. Do you know why I am sure we are God's Church? Do you know why?"

Jim smiled. He sensed what was coming.

"Because," said Father Winstead, "there is no other reason for our survival. None."

"Is this Russian thing recent? Stepped up or what?"

"You haven't shown me your laundry, Father," said Winstead.

"I can't trade. I'm sorry. But your information could help this thing I am on. Although I don't see how for sure. It's something that would be good for me and the Church to know."

Father Winstead shrugged, and Jim guessed that, like most good gossips, he enjoyed the giving as much as the receiving.

"Well, the Russians are always around, in a way, but about two weeks ago we were informed there was some increased form of Russian monitor on us. For what reason, I don't know."

"Are you sure it is Russian, not Arab?"

"These people who told us know the difference."

"I see," said Jim. "Do you know why?"

"They didn't say."

"The Israelis?"

"Who else?" said Father Winstead. He disappeared into another room and had Jim sign for two briefcases with the seal of the Secretary of State on them. Jim signed, but before he left the delegate's residence he broke Pesci's seal on both briefcases to make sure they were not empty. It was a mistake because inside one of the briefcases was still another case, and this one had a seal that sent more electric curiosity through Father Winstead than it seemed his dark eyes could handle.

"The papal seal," said Father Winstead. "Are you here for the Pope?"

"C'mon, Father," said Jim, closing both briefcases.

"You are, aren't you?" said Father Winstead.

"Thank you for the money," said Jim Folan, and took a ride from the delegate's chauffeur back to Isaiah House and the room once occupied by Father Lavelle. As Jim had suspected, the papal seal covered a report on the Shroud of Turin. The Church had looked into it. And had decided to keep it quiet. The old Belgian priest was right.

Father Lavelle's room overlooked a courtyard of eucalyptus and almond trees, and gravel walks between beds of flowers. To the right was the American Embassy for the old Israeli side of Jerusalem. To the left was an order of Arab nuns, devoted especially to the Rosary.

Most of Father Lavelle's books were in French. Jim interspersed his own notes into Father Lavelle's books. It was either this or rent giant safes and attract attention.

The Dominican brothers at Isaiah House welcomed a priest to say Mass for them, and did not ask too many questions, except about Father Lavelle himself. On that Jim used a mental reservation, saying he saw him in Rome and that he was still there.

Father Folan did not like these mental reservations. They were supposed to be in lieu of lies, but he had always felt that, if you meant to misinform, even using the truth was a lie. It was the Vatican Secretary of State's province, however, to announce the suicide, not Jim's.

The chapel in Isaiah House contained no statuary, just a giant missal in the center, where a crucifix ordinarily was. It reminded Jim of how the first Christians must have prayed, but he understood that this lack of statuary was in deference to both Muslim and Jew, who would feel uncomfortable in the normal Catholic Church. Statues and icons and incense came from the countries Christianity settled in, letting the local people use their own forms of prayer. In fact, the Latin used for so many centuries in the Mass was actually Vulgate Latin, or the Latin of the streets, used originally so that the common people could understand it. There was a story about a Catholic priest who, when ordered to use the common Latin of the streets in Rome, would wash his mouth out after every Mass.

In his first Mass in Jerusalem, Jim had prayed for Father La-

velle. His second, for his mission. And his third he offered up
for himself.

A later message from Cardinal Pesci said any positive word
would be appreciated, and that had to mean disproof. It also
meant that the Pope himself wanted speed because Pesci had already come out for as much delay as Jim wanted.

In a way, this relieved Father Folan of a decision. Reasonable speed, he had discovered right away, required the help of
Mendel Hirsch to cut through the Israeli bureaucracy. Hirsch
had what was called "Vitamin P," or "Protecksia." It gave
certain clerks and administrators that special impetus to do their
jobs the way they were supposed to. Helpfulness seemed to be
random. In one department he might have people running all
over themselves to help him. In another, he could have been
stricken with a heart attack and no one would have called an
ambulance until he was sure it was his place in line.

The cure for all of this, to make service uniformly good, was
Mendel Hirsch, who loved running interference for the representative of His Lord Eminence, Almeto Cardinal Pesci. Jim
would have preferred to keep the Israeli government out as
much as he could.

He had already planned to recruit his own pathologist, geologist, technicians for the tests, and, most of all, his own archaeologist. As much as possible, they would know as little as
possible.

But in this phase of the investigation, Hirsch was a necessity.
He forced the woman in the Department of Antiquities to get
the exact slip prohibiting Nasir Hamid from building his basement until it was archaeologically excavated.

And then he made her get immediately the slips that came before and the slip that came after, something she had argued
about but succumbed to. Jim never could have gotten that by
himself.

Jim had seen some rough red gum marks on top of the author-
izing slip, which meant it had come from a pad. Therefore, the
one before should have left a writing imprint on Nasir Hamid's
prohibition, and his on the one after.

Jim held each up to the light. They matched.

If there were some kind of fraud, it was in just this sort of

thing that it would show up, because then the slip would probably have been very carefully prepared in some office.

"It is a routine assigned dig," said the woman angrily. But
this was not quite so. Jim knew that any Israeli official being
asked about this had to report who asked. Mendel had told him
this was done as a precaution for His Eminence Cardinal Pesci.

"Who wrote out this slip?"

"I did. I do them all," said the woman. She was not happy
being pressured by Mendel.

"What did you eat that day?"

"Did I spill something?"

"No," said Jim.

"As a matter of fact, it was a morning, and I had a tomato
salad," said the woman. There were more questions about the
weather and what people wore that day. Jim got just the right
mix of accuracy and confusion and contradictions that smelled
of truth.

"Okay," said Jim to the woman. "Now we've got this piece
of mosaic, floor you say. And you said it was before 430 C.E.
because it had a cross on it, and after that date Emperor
Theodosius, Byzantine, said the cross is too holy to walk on.
Right?"

The woman nodded.

"Well, I'm wondering why the laborer brought the tile to Tabinian in the first place."

"For money. There is a market in antiquities."

"And Tabinian would in turn sell something like that?"

"No. He is not supposed to."

"But something like that can be sold?"

Jim watched the woman.

"Sometimes, but he is under obligation to report anything
like that. And he lived up to his obligation."

"I see," said Jim. "And where is the piece of mosaic floor
now?"

In a small town near Jerusalem, Jim saw the warehouse where
the piece and the entire floor were supposed to be stored. The
warehouse had a corrugated tin roof and was roughly seventy
yards long. Jim tried out his Hebrew and stumbled through a

conversation. The watchman, with the keys and a note pad, found the Golban dig listed in the pad.

He opened the warehouse door and pointed to the first mosaic floor on the left. The warehouse was stacked to the ceiling with layers of earth, tile, fabric, and more earth, tile, and fabric, like a giant layered Viennese pastry of floors.

"Lucky that our floor is right here," said Jim in Hebrew.

"Yes. Yes. Take the floor. You have the permission. Yes. Yes. Your papers are in order," answered the man. He wore old gray pants and cracked shoes. He hadn't shaved for a couple of days.

"This is the floor?" asked Jim.

"Right here. This one," said the man.

"I want to see it."

"Take it."

"I just want to see it."

"It's yours."

"I wish to observe, to oversee it. Yes?"

"You can take it."

"I don't want to."

"You have the papers. Take it."

With elaborate pantomime, Jim showed himself examining an imaginary floor.

"Yes. Come. Of course," said the man and motioned to the floor he had been pointing to. Jim climbed on top of the stack. It was the lowest stack in the warehouse. The others stretched to the ceiling. He walked along the gauze, which had apparently been shellacked to hold all the squares together in the same order in which they had been removed from the dig. Every square was virtually even.

In no way could a tractor digging a foundation have made any of these squares. They were all the produce of saws. Nowhere was there a jagged piece with a portion of a cross on it to match the story of the laborer and the antiquities dealer.

"This is the floor from the Golban dig?"

"Yes," said the man.

"Thank you," said Jim. "May I see its papers?"

"What?"

"Papers. How do you know it's the Golban dig?"

"No. No. Take the floor."

"I want the one from the Golban dig!"

"Oh no. Back there. Too much labor. No. Take this one. It is a good floor."

"I want the other. I want to see the other."

"No."

"Mendel Hirsch is a friend of mine. Mendel Hirsch."

"So? It means nothing."

Jim asked to use the telephone in the man's shack near the warehouse, and phoned Mendel Hirsch to explain what he wanted. In five minutes there was a phone call back, and the man answered. He said a few words, and then led Jim back into the warehouse, a third of the way down, and pointed to a layer three quarters of the way up.

"I think it's that," he said.

By nightfall both Jim and the man had the stacked floors above it laboriously moved. It wasn't the Golban floor. Two days later, sweaty with dust in his mouth from centuries-old floors that had been dug up in Israel, Jim found the Byzantine floor that had started the whole thing. It had strips of plastic glued to it with the date of the excavation and Dr. Golban's name. Its corners also matched the written description on the watchman's pad, and, most significant of all, it had a jagged piece unlike the smooth squares, and on that piece was a portion of a cross, the cross which Emperor Theodosius decreed in the year 430 was too holy to walk on.

It was less than ten by fifteen feet, and had obviously covered a small room. There was a peacock in beautiful pink and brown, surrounded by a sea of grape-purple tile. It had many crosses.

It was the floor that had started it all.

"Good. Thank you," said Jim.

"Is that it?" said the man.

"Yes."

"You don't speak good Hebrew," said the man, still puzzled.

"Thank you. Thank you," said Jim, smiling to show him gratitude for the help with the floor.

"No. You speak bad Hebrew. Not good," said the man.

"Yes, thank you," said Jim.

* * *

In three weeks Jim managed to get most of the small, corroborating interviews. There were some conflicting stories on small details but this was usually because someone didn't remember accurately. There were enough minute strokes of such subtle shading that Jim had to conclude that, unless something major leaped up and screamed phony, he was not dealing with fraud. He still had three major interviews to do in Jerusalem, and therefore when Mendel Hirsch asked him how long it would be until he saw the site, he had to say he didn't know.

"Sharon has been calling me quite often, saying there are things that have to be done, and that you are not doing them," said Mendel. He had come to his office this holiday especially to facilitate more of Jim's requests. It was Rosh Hashanah, the Jewish New Year, five thousand and some years since the creation of the world according to ancient Jews, and this reminded Jim that when Christ came down from Galilee the Jews were already dating into the three thousands, more than an entire millennium than Western men were dating now.

And even then the Egyptians were considered ancient history. Man had been around this part of the world recording and building a long, long time.

"I have my own methods, but assure her I will get to it. Do you think I should call?" asked Jim.

"It might help and it might not. She was raised in a rather narrow academic atmosphere, and, as you can see, professors are not prone to compromise. Then again, who is, yes?"

"Well, I can see her point," said Jim, extending his own charity to its limits.

"About how long will your work here take?" asked Mendel.

"As long as it takes, whatever it takes. I will do this thing."

"Will you need Sharon further?"

"Yes."

Mendel sighed. "She is not an easy woman, you know."

"She's rather beautiful on the outside," said Jim.

"If you like that kind. You're not supposed to notice, I thought. But men are men. If we were all saints, Father," said Mendel with a resigned smile, "I don't think we would need countries. But need them we do. Have you seen Yad Vashem?"

"That's your memorial to your holocaust?"

"Yes. I go there once a year, and each year it gets harder.

Sometimes I wish I would never go. Sometimes. But wishing does not make things so, and every year I go.''

"Do you think I should see it to get a better idea of who you are?" said Jim. There was a sadness in the man, which now he showed. Jim felt it was there always, even under the joyous solicitude. It was constant. Perhaps on the side, not center stage, but constant.

"The big mistake I think people make is that Yad Vashem is to show the Gentiles. You know, everyone who visits here who is important is taken there, but I guess it looks like we run it down for everyone else. But I tell you, Father Folan, what you get out of it is your business. That is there for me. I will never let myself forget. Never.''

There was silence for a moment, and then, almost in a whisper, with all the illusion of softness, Hirsch repeated the word again.

"Never," he said.

"Ken," came the beautiful singing voice over the telephone. It meant "yes" in Hebrew.

"It's Jim Folan. Hello," said Jim. He had planned to use his young and wobbly Hebrew, but when he heard her voice, he wanted to be sure he spoke well. So he used English.

"Hello, Jim. How are you doing?"

"I am doing fine. In a few days, hopefully, we will go down to the dig.''

"Well, good. Fine. At last. You have been researching?"

"Yes. Yes."

"Good, then you are getting some background in archaeology and we can talk better.''

"I am sort of saving that part," said Jim.

"You haven't?"

"No," said Jim.

He heard contemptuous laughter at the other end of the phone.

"I will be getting back to you soon," he said.

Nasir Hamid insisted Jim partake of sweet coffee and candies before they began their talk in Mr. Hamid's home.

There were low couches slightly higher than pillows, and the floor was stone, as were the walls, the ceilings arching to high points under smooth, perfect plaster.

The room needed no air conditioning, even though this was noon and the winter rains had yet to come to chill Jerusalem. It smelled of roses and there was quiet, although Jim knew outside there was traffic.

"I guess your family has been here forever, Mr. Hamid. I am told you were one of the old Jerusalem families."

"Oh no. Not forever," said Hamid, with a slight acknowledging smile. He wore eyeglasses, and had a somewhat fair complexion, but his eyes were pit black.

"They came with Sal Ah Din."

"Saladin," said Jim. "That was almost seven hundred years ago."

"Yes."

"And how do you feel about your new government? The Israelis?"

Jim didn't know if he would answer the question.

"They are the government," said Mr. Hamid.

"Which means?"

"Which means I deal with them."

"Do you like them?"

"I don't understand the question."

"Do you like them as the government?"

"I am talking to you, Mr. Folan."

"I don't understand."

"If I wish to get my basement built, I will speak to you. You have been sent by the government. So I do not understand why you ask these questions."

"I see you think I am from the government."

"Yes."

"Well, I am not. I am not the government. The Israelis are cooperating with me, but I am not the government."

"Then you have nothing to do with my basement?"

"I didn't say that."

"What, may I ask, do you have to do with my basement?"

"I am working with the government on that dig, and when I am finished, then I believe you will be able to build your basement."

"I am sure you can understand, Mr. Folan, how I would look upon you as the government."

"I do. But I cannot punish you."

"I am already being punished. I am paying taxes on land I cannot use. That is a punishment."

"I guess it is," said Jim, and was quiet to let Mr. Hamid know that he, himself, had nothing more to say on the subject. Eventually, Jim did point out that when he was done, and he did not know when this would be, but he was sure it would be less than a year, and it might even be as little as two months, Mr. Hamid, he was sure, would be able to build his basement.

Mr. Hamid answered every question, but nothing more than the question. He offered nothing. Jim kept him the better part of the afternoon. And still Mr. Hamid's courteousness did not wither. He answered all the little questions about the dig, and then some big ones, such as that particular piece of land being in the family's hands for a century and a half, and that it had once been a food-selling stall and had never had a big building on it.

Moreover, that part of Haneviim Street had been right at the Mandelbaum Gate, the dividing line between Jordan and Israel from 1948 until 1967, when the city was reunified.

Even now Jim could see the remnants of Jordanian sniper fire in pock holes on stone buildings near there, undoubtedly having come from the parapets controlled by the Arab legion. No one was going to plant anything three stories down at that spot for those nineteen years unless they tunneled in from miles away. And that would be checked out by his geologist.

All the details of the problems of building a basement to a store, and specifically why Mr. Hamid felt Haneviim Street would be a good location for an appliance store, fit into what sounded accurate, especially in the little details. Never once did Mr. Hamid question the silliness of Jim's questions, such as what Dr. Golban wore the day before the dig was closed, what Mr. Hamid saw at the bottom of the dig, who called out first, how long they were down there, and why Mr. Hamid thought the dig was closed.

"From what I hear, the Religious Party of the Jews had some influence in closing it. Why, I do not know for sure."

Jim nodded. He was hearing Hirsch's cover story for the closing of the dig, and the dismissal of the students.

"What do you think of Dr. Golban?"

"She is a fine, worthy person, despite her education."

"What do you mean?"

"An educated woman is like a sharp chair. Not exactly comfortable."

"So she was abrasive?" said Jim.

"Not in the least. I would consider her one of the finer people I have been blessed with meeting. Educated and yet thoughtful."

"That's quite generous of you."

"I am not exaggerating."

"Surely you can't mean that?"

"I absolutely do, sir."

"You have to say it because she is an Israeli official for you. Correct?"

"No. I do not have to."

"Well, you haven't attacked any other Israeli official."

"That is not praise."

"What do you think of me?"

"Please, sir, this is my house. I do not insult people in my house."

"I would consider it a gift for your assessment of me and what you think I am doing."

"As to what you are doing, you are incredibly clever. You have asked so many questions about so many things I do not even suspect what you are after. As for yourself, I am sorry to say, you are very much like Director Hirsch, who has spoken to me."

"And that is?"

"Both of you, I am sorry to say, are so fixed on something that is of ultimate concern to you that you do not even think of me as so much dust under your feet. I am like a cat. Only if he makes noise will he be noticed. Either you will chase me off, or you will give me milk. But only when I in some way disturb you or, more important, what you are doing."

"Mr. Hamid, you are right and I am sorry."

Nasir Hamid accepted this with a precise and almost minute nod. He invited Jim to stay for the evening meal. Jim declined.

* * *

Mark Prangle from Lansing, Michigan, was the last student volunteer on the dig left from the summer, but he was the most important one.

He had discovered the round stone covering the tomb first, and he had done something to make sure the stone had not been moved the first night.

Jim met him on the steps of the Christian Youth Hostel, about three blocks from Haneviim Street. Jim talked as one American to another, and Mark, in his blue jeans and Israeli sandals, took it at that.

Mark was a pleasant and intelligent young man whom Jim would happily have recommended for acceptance to Boston College. He had enthusiasm, and enough courage to be positive, which would be refreshing for a freshman dean to see nowadays.

Unfortunately, Mark never stopped asking questions. And invariably it was about Sharon as they walked the streets and talked in the coolness of the late afternoon. Mark had stayed in Jerusalem just to take Sharon's course, and now that she wasn't giving it he had decided to go home.

"Is Sharon all right?"

"She's fine," said Jim.

"But she's not lecturing this year," said Mark.

"She's working with me."

"What are you doing?"

"I am trying to get technical things squared away. As you know, she has run into a religious problem with the dig."

"I heard about the Religious Party. Terrible, but it's their land. It's the only land that we know for sure anyone owns," said Mark.

"How is that?" said Jim.

"The Bible. The Bible gives the land of Israel to the Jews and anyone who believes in the Bible accepts that deed. Do you believe in the Bible?"

"I do," said Jim.

"Are you a Christian?"

"I am."

"Then you too believe it's their land."

"Yes," said Jim. "But how much and where? The borders

of Jewish land here historically have been all over the place. And borders have to be compromised. Because, frankly, there are complications.''

''Nothing's complicated if you believe in Jesus Christ,'' said Mark.

''I think you're confusing our position with God's. To us it's complicated.''

''Not if Jesus tells you what is right.''

''I agree.''

''And He does in the Bible.''

''But you've got to interpret it correctly. You can get incorrect things from the Bible too. It does require the grace of God to get out of the Bible what's in there. Without His grace, the Bible is just another book.''

''Are you a Catholic?''

''Yes,'' said Jim. Mark offered him a can of Coke and some dates from the spring of Ein Geddi, supposedly, according to Mark, the best dates in the Holy Land. ''Jesus,'' said Mark, ''might have spent some time at the spring of Ein Geddi. He's all over here. I can feel him. Can you feel him?''

''I try to,'' said Jim, steering the conversation toward the mechanism Mark had used on the first night and how the covering stone had been discovered.

It was at bedrock, everyone thought, the limits of man, when Mark had noticed chisel strokes on a piece of rock, and then he had called Sharon. She verified that it was indeed worked stone, not bedrock.

''What was she doing on top of the dig?''

''Smoking and talking to the Arab who owns the property. She smokes too much. She is so beautiful and she smokes all the time. I told her what it's doing to her lungs, that it would take ten years off her life. And she said those were the ten years she didn't want anyway.'' Mark smiled. Jim could see a fortune in braces having gone to make those teeth. Why he assumed Mark was not born with good natural teeth, he did not know. He just had the feeling that the big-boned young man with the remnants of acne on his face, and sandy brown hair, had to have had incredibly expensive orthodontic work.

''So then she came down and then what?''

Step by step, Jim got the details of that day.

"She wouldn't even smoke in the dig. That's how careful she was when other archaeologists would smoke anything and anytime. But she did smoke the second day, after we found the body."

"Why do you think that was?"

"There are some people who are so beautiful inside that they are riven by any thought of suffering. I think seeing the skeleton reminded her of suffering in her life."

"She is an archaeologist, Mark. That would be like a dentist being upset by a tooth."

"Well, she certainly was flustered."

Jim nodded. This verified Sharon's reaction.

"What do you know about the body?"

"Well, we got a picture of it but I didn't see it developed."

"Do you know the cause of death, any marks or anything?"

"Not that I know of. Maria, she's gone back to Holland, got the picture with the Zensa Bronica."

Jim nodded. He remembered those pictures the first night, of the skeleton and the disk lying on those vertebrae. Apparently Dr. Golban had not mentioned to the volunteer crew what she had seen in later notes, that what appeared as a dark smudge on the black and white film was actually orange, the remnant color of a crucifying spike.

"She said there was writing on the disk and that really got us excited, you know. Really! To find something with writing on it is an archaeological triumph, you know. It tells you so much."

"And then she read the disk to you, right?"

"No, she just stood there and then she led all of us out of the tomb, and she was sick or something because she looked pale, and she was upset and lit the cigarette right in front of the stone itself, and so we all figured she was upset by something. It reminded her of something horrible."

"And that was the second day. But the first day, you just dug to the stone?"

"Right, and I put a match down, sort of just to make sure, you know, that no one would come in and steal something or leave something. Like my own seal."

"And everyone saw you do it?"

"Right."

"So if someone wanted to enter the tomb that night and leave something or take out something they could have taken away your match and then put it right back."

"No," said Mark.

They had been walking along the Old City walls, past the Jaffa Gate, south and downhill toward a valley. Palm trees and shrubs and neat, tender grass made the walls seem like great lengths of gardens. Across the valley they could see blue and white villages on distant slopes. According to the signs, Bethlehem was the next right turn.

Mark took a little box of matches out of his pocket and pointed to the six sides, a stick of wood that had been machine-tooled in the millions, a hundred probably costing less than a penny to cut. Mark dug a thumbnail into the white wood.

"This is what I did. And I remember facing it into the stone but I didn't tell anyone."

"You mentioned that you put the match there, why not the mark? Didn't you trust the rest of the crew?"

"I was embarrassed. After Sharon had said the stone had been there a couple of thousand years, and it could last another night, I didn't want to mention the nail mark."

"Why not?"

"Because I got that from Sky King on television, when I was a kid. It was a trick he used to foil bank robbers. I felt kind of stupid, you know."

They passed the open gate, and Mark nodded into the city. "That's the accepted place of the Last Supper, although they're not sure."

They continued to walk around the walls of the Old City, and Jim could now see how difficult an attack by ancients would have been through the southern part.

And they came again to the eastern part of the city, and Mark pointed across the Valley of the Kidron to the Mount of Olives, for they had passed, he had said, the Valley of Gehenna.

"There. Up there. That's where He will come again," said Mark. And Mark quoted the Bible, and pointed across the valley, which was a graveyard on the far side of a deep valley, which ran through the southern half of Israel, he said, to the Dead Sea.

"Read the Bible, His words are in there. Don't pray to statues," said Mark sincerely. "He's coming back over there. Read His book."

"I know you mean well, Mark, but the book is only part of the faith."

"It's the only part. It's the one thing you know isn't going to lie to you. Now I don't mean to be insulting. You've got to know a Pope can lie to you."

Some Arab boys came up to them wanting to sell bits of antiquities found along side roads or traded, Jim imagined, like American kids would trade baseball cards back home.

Behind them was the Temple Mount, the Temple having been destroyed nineteen centuries before, as Jesus had predicted. Jim, even now looking back up the hill upon which that great Temple had been and where now the Muslims' mosques sat, felt the hugeness of it.

And larger still was the death of one man.

"Coin from Herod. Coin from Herod. Coin from Herod," insisted one urchin.

Jim shook his head. Mark ignored the boys too. But they would not leave.

"Byzantine. Do you want Byzantine?"

"He's coming there. And He has only one book. That's the only thing we know. The only thing."

"May I ask you a question?" said Jim.

"Sure."

"Why do you believe that book?"

"Because it's God's book."

"Who told you?"

"God. I know."

"That's what you feel now, but why do you believe the Bible is the word of God? Who told you?"

"Well, first, my father."

"And who told him?"

"Well, I guess his father or his mother or a preacher, and it made sense."

"But who told them? Why did they believe it?" said Jim.

"Crusader coin. Beautiful Crusader coin. Perfect condition. Make an offer," said one boy, shoving a large black disk in front of Jim's face.

"Preachers before them."

"And before them?"

"More preachers."

"And before them? Why? Why do you believe the Bible? I'll tell you why," said Jim. "Because the Church said that was the book of God. The Church said, as part of tradition, that these books are true, and the word of God. That's why you believe."

A hot wind blew up out of the Valley of Gehenna and Jim could see that the young man was thinking.

"No," said Mark finally. "That's not why I believe in the book or Jesus. Not because somebody says this man said this at this time. And you can prove that here or this there, or any of that stuff. None of it. You know how I know . . ."

Jim turned to the Arab boys and shook his head forcefully. They understood that.

"How?" asked Jim.

"In my heart," said Mark. "And that's the only way you can know. In your heart."

"There is more," said Jim.

"And if you need more," said the young American, "I feel sorry for you." He lowered his eyes when he said that.

Suddenly the wind shifted out of the valley, and it was no longer hot with the day's baking of the sun, but was cool to the point of discomforting chill. The breath of autumn was coming now from the wilderness.

Tabinian, the antiquities dealer, was difficult to pin down on a time, so Jim had to phone Sharon and tell her he was ready.

"Do you really want to see it? Really?" asked Sharon.

Jim was phoning from Isaiah House.

"Yes. I do."

"I thought you were avoiding it?"

"I'm ready to see it. Ten tomorrow?"

"All right. Good. I'll phone Mendel," said Sharon.

"What for?"

"You want to roll back the stone, don't you? You can't do it alone."

"You mean it is a big stone?" asked Jim, remembering how Mark, Matthew, and Luke made reference to how big the stone was, showing that just a few Roman guards could not have moved it, the great stone that the priests felt would protect them all from the removal of the body.

"Not big so much as heavy."

"That could be a great stone in Aramaic?" said Jim.

"Absolutely. Same word. Is something bothering you? I get the feeling you are delaying. If you want to delay some more, go right ahead. I can't stop you."

"No. Let's do it. We have to do it, and it is right on schedule. Right on schedule," said Jim.

But that night in his examen he realized he had felt protected in a way by having to study the surrounding facts first. He had hoped for a while to find just the sort of evidence that might cast some severe questions as to how the body got there. There were none, and now it didn't look as though there were going to be any.

9

Atonement

Jerusalem was quiet as judgment day. Hardly a car moved, and the traffic lights blinked to empty streets. The shops were closed and Jim could hear his footsteps as he walked up the normally busy Jaffa Road and to the northwest corner of the Old City.

This was not Saturday. It was Tuesday. He remembered his first shock at how quiet Jerusalem became on a Saturday, until he remembered that was the Jewish sabbath, Shabbat, and he was advised if he wanted to do anything or buy anything, he would be best off in Tel Aviv.

But this morning was quieter than even Shabbat. It was eerily quiet and reminded Jim how he used to feel when the streets were sometimes empty back in South Portland. God had come and gone, taking his own with him and leaving Jimmy Folan behind. So quiet on this chill autumn morning in Jerusalem.

Down the street, near Damascus Gate, he saw Arabs busy as usual. The Arab produce stores on Haneviim Street were open as on every day except their holy day, Friday.

Sharon was standing on the street blowing into a paper cup of steaming coffee. Soldiers lounged around a three-quarter-ton truck just behind her. She had been talking to the soldiers.

"What are they here for?"

"To roll back the stone," said Sharon. Her delicate brown eyes were still soft with sleep.

"Soldiers will attract attention," said Jim.

"They're all over Israel. What's bothering you?"

"I don't want soldiers. We have an arrangement on some sort of discretion and soldiers violate that discretion."

"All right, we'll do it tomorrow. We'll do it next week. But don't hold me up for another semester."

"Why can't we get someone else?" said Jim. The soldiers watched them. He did not know if they spoke English but they would certainly know the edge of hostility.

"Because it's Yom Kippur."

"Oh. I'm sorry," said Jim. "This is your holiest day, I know. I didn't mean to open the tomb on your Day of Atonement."

"What are you afraid of?"

"I am not afraid, I am just showing respect."

"You've been here almost four weeks and you haven't looked at the dig you came to investigate. I've got to assume you're delaying."

"I'm not," said Jim.

"Then let's go," said Sharon.

"I do not wish to take your soldiers away from their most sacred holiday."

"It's not your religion. What do you care?"

"I care," said Jim.

"Listen, if they really wanted to observe Yom Kippur they probably could have traded off with someone. And if they couldn't, I'm sure they got something from a rabbi saying it was all right. Religious laws are like the weather. They only affect people who can't afford air conditioning or stoves. You've got Vitamin P from Rabbi Mendel Hirsch."

"I didn't know he was a rabbi."

"He's not. But anyone who can bargain in the Knesset is already a Talmudic scholar. There is no religious law so strong here as a few deciding votes. But what am I telling you for? It's got to work the same way with your church."

"Ask the soldiers which ones wish to observe their holiday."

"Their commander has sent them here, Jim. Now, are you afraid of what you're going to see?"

"No," said Jim, and he heard his voice crack. There was no reason for it to crack, he thought. He was not afraid of what he would see. What bothered him was that he had planned to have by this time at least some evidence to indicate if not fraud at least some discrepancies. He was here after four weeks of research with absolutely nothing, shorn of even a possibility that the bones had not been there two thousand years, just as they were found.

"I am not afraid," said Jim. And then he noticed how carefully Sharon was watching his eyes. "I am a bit apprehensive. This is very important. I am not, mind you, afraid of who that was, if you understand."

"I think I do," said Dr. Golban, and for the first time Jim felt a softness in her voice. "I've read your books. I think I can understand."

"Thank you," said Jim.

"But you don't have to worry, Jim. No matter what you are going to find, you already have your mind made up."

"But what if I am honest . . . ruthlessly honest with what we find?"

"Then you're in trouble," she said with laughter, which for the first time was not unkind. She had a beautiful smile, with beautiful long even teeth that somehow Jim felt never had to be wired into that evenness but were natural. Everything about her could be naturally beautiful if she weren't scarred by her prickly hostility to any modern religion.

He was sure she didn't feel the same way about some discovered altar to Baal or Astarte. As long as it was dead, she could live with man's faith.

She nodded the soldiers to the hole and they hauled out two lengths of ladder from the truck.

This morning, despite the chill, she wore a maroon sweater over shorts. Her legs were sleek and beautiful. Her hair was brought back tight in a bun and she wore lipstick, leaving it faintly imprinted on the cigarette. Her dark eyes were sleepy and warm.

Jim's toes had become cold as he stood there in his new sandals. They were part of his one great indulgence, $60 American for his entire new wardrobe, which would enable him to have to get his clothes all washed at once in only every eight days. Isaiah House was not the Vatican with an army of nuns to serve the priests.

"Look," she said, putting a hand on his arm, "you don't know archaeology, but when you get into it, and I think you will, because you're not quite as ignorant as you appear, not in the least . . . when you get into it, you will find that even archaeologists disagree on many things. Even big things like where David's tower was. We had several sites. Even Kathleen Kenyon herself was not always right. In the end archaeology is analysis, which is a fancy word for guesswork. I have no doubt that, given any guesswork, you will have everything just where you want it theologically."

She released his arm and gave him a pat, puffing on her cigarette as she started toward the hole. Jim stumbled trying to keep up with her across the rock-shrewn lot.

At the edge of the dig Sharon put a hand on his stomach to keep him from going farther. It looked deeper than just three meters.

The soldiers were waiting four ladder lengths and two thousand years down at bedrock beside a piece of plywood apparently covering what was supposed to be the great stone. Sharon nodded. One soldier removed the plywood.

Four soldiers got into position, bracing themselves, and with a unified grunt the stone screamed upon stone as it rolled with a lurch, and a little opening, very dark, appeared in the golden brown of limestone.

At first glance the stone had looked small, too small to be the great stone the Gospels referred to as that which covered His tomb. But the weight of it, the difficulty the soldiers had in moving it, the heavy scream of stone against stone removed that bit of Gospel disproof. The tomb was open.

"They have been told," Sharon said softly, "only that we wish to protect this body from religious extremists. I don't know if you are aware of the troubles we have with the religious zealots."

"I've read about some incidents. I've seen it on TV."

"You've seen the police chasing them. You have not seen them throwing stones and using knives, or lying. Having your television cover an archaeological dispute is like excavating the Suez Canal with a cocaine spoon. It was horrible."

"How do you know what we see in the States?"

"I've heard."

"From rabbis?" said Jim with a smile.

"From people I trust."

"Not rabbis?"

"Not rabbis, of course. Scientists."

"Where do you get evidence that scientists are somehow more trustworthy than holy men?" said Jim.

Some of the soldiers were casting glances into the hole. Jim could see what he thought were carved steps down there.

"When you people give as much knowledge, as much light, instead of flames to the world, as archaeologists, I will give you that respect," said Sharon.

"Have you heard of the Biblical Institute?"

"Of course," said Sharon. "It is here in Jerusalem."

"And what do you think of the work done there?" said Jim.

"Solid work. Class A," said Sharon. "Some solid archaeologists come from there."

"And how can you explain that the Biblical Institute is run and staffed by Jesuits, a Roman Catholic order of priests?"

"I know they are supposed to be Jesuits, one of your orders. I knew that. But they don't believe like you do. That's probably why you are here instead of them. Jesuits don't believe like you."

"Oh, really. How do you know?" said Jim.

"I've read academic papers. You know what a man thinks from his papers. I never saw holiness out of the Biblical Institute."

"Dr. Golban, I know they do believe, quite devoutly, and do their work as they say in their motto, 'For the Greater Glory of God.' "

"No. No. That's what they say, so their religious order can support them in their important work. We all do some of it. They can't be blamed."

"Well, I know you are wrong, Dr. Golban, because I am a Jesuit."

Sharon took a step back and looked at the priest again.

"You're a Jesuit?"

"Yes, and I say the Mass, and being a priest is the most important thing in my life."

He could see she was thinking about something.

"Perhaps the uneducated ones believe," she said.

"Have you ever heard of invincible ignorance?" said Jim. Soldiers were looking up now as his and Sharon's voices rose this Yom Kippur morning at the dig.

"What a wonderful phrase. It describes you people so well. You can't be reasoned with."

"It was created by the Church to describe people who no matter what evidence is placed before them will not open their minds."

"That's what I said. You."

"No," said Jim. "You."

"Ignorance is not a function of the scientific mind," said Sharon.

"You win," said Jim.

"Why do you make it a question of winning?"

"Because I give up."

"So do I," said Sharon. "I think you ought to go down now and get a feel for the place. You know, we've got a couple of thousand years to climb."

Jim swallowed and went first, facing the earth as he climbed down, with Sharon explaining briefly the layers of civilization.

When they got to bedrock and she announced they were at the Second Temple period, Jim noted that for Rome this area had been the northern access route to the grain of Egypt, which was as necessary for Rome as oil was now for America.

"Good analogy," said Sharon. "This has been a passageway and a dividing line between East and West intermittently since before Alexander, this eastern edge of the Mediterranean. It all comes together here."

"And went out from here," said Jim, and suddenly he had an insight into the Bible. One of the great mysteries was why the Jews were the chosen people, and a mystery to them especially.

Because, unlike the popular myth that the Jews felt they were chosen because they were in some way superior, the Torah said their God had chosen them specifically, not because they were either bigger or better than anyone else, but despite the fact that they weren't. They were chosen only by God's will and for His purposes.

What if God had chosen them to put them at this crossroads of civilization? Weren't the Jews ordered here? How many passages in their Torah told them to be here? It could well be in the plan of God that they were sent to this crossroads to give birth to the Word, to Jesus, and thence go forth to the world.

If anyone wanted a word to go out to the world in the Second Temple period, here was the spot.

"Well?" said Sharon, showing a flashlight into the tomb, down hewn steps of the hewn cave.

"Okay," said Jim, and lowered himself to get down through the small hole.

"It must have taken a lot of work to carve this out, you know?" said Jim. He heard his voice resonate inside the tomb. A rich man could have afforded that, he thought. Jesus was hastily buried in a rich man's tomb, hewn out of rock—Matthew 27, Mark 15, Luke 23.

"It doesn't smell like it did the first day," she said. "Which is bad."

"Why is that?"

"Because the bones are terribly fragile and they should be protected from deteriorating once they touch the fresh air."

"How would you do that?"

"Polyvinyl. Very carefully coat them with polyvinyl."

"Who would do that?"

"I would. You do it yourself."

"Would that destroy evidence, being under a coat of something?"

"No. No. It would preserve it. It's a very thin coat. Everything shows."

"All right, but where is the body?"

Sharon pointed the light against the back wall where Jim saw a hole.

"That's the clay brick wall," said Jim. "You know, you don't notice it. You don't, not right off, unless you're looking at it."

"We can expand that hole I made just a bit and then coat, by hand."

"All right. Good. The disk is still in there?"

"Oh yes. Nothing has been touched since the day I left it."

"I think we should get Mendel to put in a metal door instead of that stone. We'll be coming here a bit."

"Good idea," said Sharon.

"One with a key," said Jim. His mouth was dry.

"Yes. They can build a frame into the hewn stone."

"Good," said Jim.

"Well," said Sharon, pointing the light to the hole.

"Okay," said Jim. "You know I will be bringing in experts."

"I do."

"And another archaeologist."

"I understand."

"I guess I should take a look," said Jim.

"Yes," said Sharon.

"Who will handle the light?" said Jim.

"Just look. I maneuver the light and explain to you what you are looking at."

"What if my head blocks the light?"

"Then you'll move it," said Sharon.

"Right," said Jim. "Well, here we go. Just walk up?"

"Just walk up," said Sharon.

"Okay," said Jim and walked up to the hole in the clay brick wall, bricks so uneven in formation that they acted like a camouflage in the dark cave.

"Well, look in," said Sharon.

"Yes," said Jim, and the bright harsh light broke the blackness of the little niche behind the wall and there it was. Just a pile of bones, not even connected, so very small.

He saw the orange mark on the legs beneath where the plaque lay, over a vertebra. Sharon was shining the light there.

"See the orange mark? That's oxidized iron. I think they used a smaller spike than usual because even though iron rusts it will tend to last as long as bones in these circumstances."

"I see."

"There might be a piece of wood underneath the tibia or vertebrae which then we could use to carbon-date."

"You can't carbon-date the bone itself, you said?" asked Jim. He felt somehow reassured making such a technical comment.

"No, no. Bone doesn't carbon-date, but often they would bury the cross with the victim."

"Without removing him."

"Yes."

"But he obviously was removed?"

"Apparently, but a piece of the cross might have come with him with the rough spike. You see, spikes were not necessarily smooth in those days. No machine manufacture."

"I know," said Jim. He remembered his brief perusal on the unannounced Vatican report on the Shroud of Turin. Within that was a whole medical and historical study on Roman cruci-fixions on where spikes had to go, and all the gruesome varia-tions.

His eyes moved to the hands and something seemed missing. Something seemed missing from the feet, too. The little fingers and toes. The pinkies were gone.

"The small bones are gone. Were they cut off?"

"Very observant," said Sharon. "No, for some reason, and we are not all that sure why, the small digits just never survive great lengths of time. We don't find the dust they leave or any-thing. They just go."

Jim's back ached and his feet were sore and he realized he had been standing rigid all the while.

"Do bones shrink?"

"No," said Sharon, "but that looks smaller because there is no skin or hair, just the bottom of the heel bones to the skull. You lose maybe three or four inches sometimes. He actually would have been five feet five in your measurements."

"The tallest would be five feet five?"

"Yes."

"No way he could have been taller?"

"No."

"Okay, let's go."

"What?" said Sharon.

"Let's go. Let's close it up. I've got to go somewhere."

"That's it?"

"For now."

"Just leave? You've hardly examined it. I haven't explained the disk."

"Later," said Jim, and nodded toward the doorway.

"I don't know," mumbled Sharon, stepping hesitantly to-ward the light down the hewn-stone steps. "I don't know. Even for a priest, this is strange. There is no way someone from your École Biblique could be brought in instead of you?"

"No. Come. Let's go."

"I don't know," said Sharon. "I just do not know. Occasions of sin, let's see the body. Let's leave the body. I don't know."

The soldiers rolled back the stone on Sharon's orders, and were happy to leave. Jim was the last one out of the dig and promised Sharon he would phone her as soon as possible.

"You won't forget the polyvinyl?" she said.

"Oh no. No," said Jim, and he practically bounced all the way back to Isaiah House. It was an act of will to force himself not to run there with screaming joy. He had it. He thought he had it.

When his door was shut, and when the blinds on the single window that showed to the courtyard had been drawn, Jim Folan pulled out the Vatican report on the Shroud of Turin and, forcing himself to be thorough and methodical, reviewed the secret report to His Holiness Pope John XXIII. It was 212 pages, with a short conclusion, in Latin, which said:

"There is no evidence available at this time to prove that this shroud, referred to as the Shroud of Turin, did not cover the body of Jesus, the Christ. More pointedly, it is in complete conformity with the Gospels, science, and history. It is the opinion of this papal commission that the shroud, known as the Shroud of Turin, did in all probability cover the body of Jesus, the Christ."

By logic the shroud was at least as valid as anything in the Haneviim Street dig. And if that was the case, already he might have the one significant contradiction that would cast solid doubt on any claim that those bones had to be Him. Jim wanted to race but he knew he had to force himself to be methodical.

He read page by page, making sure he understood it all.

How this shroud had come to the West was still a mystery. That had been unverified. One story had it being brought back from the Fourth Crusade in 1203. Some, earlier.

The shroud, 4.3 meters by 1.1 meter, of herringbone-weave linen, had the markings on it as though it covered the body of a crucified man. It showed scourge marks on the back of the man, and blood marks indicating a crown of thorns, and blood where the ribs had been.

The scourging, the thorn marks, the wound on the side, the historical acceptance as the shroud referred to in the Gospels led many to believe it indeed had been the shroud that covered Jesus, the one in which the crucified body had been wrapped when laid in the tomb.

The Church never took a position on the relic during a time when relics of all manner of authenticity flooded Europe. But in 1950 an American pharmacologist established that shreds of cloth attached to tape taken from the shroud showed signs of iron oxide, an element of red pigment. He declared it was a clever painting.

And that brought up questions about why the bloodstains appeared so red after two thousand supposed years. They should have been brown.

Jim remembered just a bit of the controversy, and that vaguely some scientists had proven that indeed the red color was blood. And that was that. The shroud went back out of sight from the public after having appeared only twice in the twentieth century.

The Church still had taken no public position on the shroud, and Jim had thought the Church had just chosen to ignore questions of its validity.

Now he was seeing in detail what really happened.

At least twenty scientists, none of them informed of the project on which they worked, had done extensive research in their fields. It struck Jim as funny that he had thought he was bringing something new to the Church in his manner of investigation. But apparently this supervisor of the investigation had been chosen, just like Jim, for his organizational skills.

He knew this because each report began "While I am not an expert in this field," and then went on to attribute what each scientist said.

The reports on the shroud were in many languages but had been translated into an old universal language, Latin, which Jim could read.

What had been done on the shroud was something only the twentieth century could have provided. Radiocarbon dating, microchemical analysis, fluorescence, radiography, infrared radiometry, optical microscopy, ultraviolet fluorescent photography, infrared spectroscopy, and mass spectroscopy.

Of all of them, Jim had recognized only the last, because someone once had said there was a machine over at MIT, across the river in Cambridge, that could measure flavor and air.

On pages eighty through ninety-five were graphs and other findings, proving without any qualification that the red stains on the shroud were indeed blood. Jim did not understand the graphs, but they seemed laborious beyond human endurance.

Different laboratories were used for different analyses. The linen had been carbon-dated by a lab in England, fixed at 50 B.C.E., plus or minus 100 years, which would put it within the historically correct time of Jesus' crucifixion, 30 to 40 C.E.

The body had apparently been rubbed with olive oil. Minute particles were found throughout the shroud. Olive oil was the staple of the Mediterranean. Particles of spices were picked up, common to preparing the Jewish dead, myrrh and aloe. The weave was common to the finer linen of Palestine at the time, herringbone. There was an entire paper on linen manufacture in Judaea, and Jim forced himself to read it all.

There were five examples of blood older than a half century which remained red, including the blood on an American President's sleeve, that of Abraham Lincoln.

There were other samples going back twelve hundred years that stayed as red as the shroud.

There was also that investigation of what was known of common crucifixion practices, and this would augment Jim's work.

The common form of crucifixion was either tying or nailing a person to a cross, then breaking his bones to increase the trauma, bringing about slow death. Scourging, too, was common. What was uncommon was the crowning with thorns, and the wound on the right side.

"A death by blade was considered a punishment of a much higher level and would defeat the purpose of crucifixion, which was humiliation."

The Gospels, therefore, had described an unusual form of crucifixion. And the shroud conformed to its unusual specifics.

In the opinion of the investigator, a priest who would go as nameless as Jim would, this shroud indeed, in matter of physical evidence, had covered the body of Jesus.

And the height of the man was five feet ten inches.

That was five inches taller than the find of Dr. Golban, and bones didn't shrink. She said so herself.

If the shroud was valid in accordance to the Gospels, then the smaller bones were not. And if this find should not prove a flaw, still there would always be the shroud itself, covering a five-foot-ten-inch frame, establishing enough doubt so the find could never be declared the unrisen Christ.

There was enough room now guaranteed for the Faith to live in. The gates of hell had been once again shut.

He had never doubted Jesus had risen, but he had feared he might prove inadequate to proving the bones were not His. He wished the man in whose room he had discovered this was alive for him to explain it.

Nevertheless, Jim felt all the energy of the universe now course happily through his body. He hid the Vatican report quite carefully among Father Lavelle's books and then almost danced all the way to the apostolic delegate's residence.

Father Winstead glanced at the message the American priest asked to be coded and sent, and then back to the priest. Father Folan was sweating.

"Where have you been running from?"

"Haneviim Street," said Jim. He had actually been running in one way or another, with feet or mind, since Haneviim Street. And he felt great.

"That's quite a run," said Father Winstead.

"Sometimes you feel like running."

Father Winstead repeated the message in a low voice: "Blessed are those who have seen. Major countervailing evidence discovered."

He looked up to Father Folan's eyes, questioning.

"Are you sure you don't want to clarify that?" said Father Winstead.

"No," said Jim.

When the American had gone, Father Winstead went into his code room, translated the message into code, and then punched it into the keyboard of a teletype. Before the afternoon was out, the Secretary of State's office was back with congratulations and a request for specifics. If ever there was a cross to bear for Father Winstead, it was not knowing what was going on with that American priest with such easy access to funds and power.

After dinner, he went back to the code room to type out the

evening's messages that were to be left in the wastebasket, which the nuns would pick up and throw away with the regular trash, and which the Arab gardener would sift through and take to his superiors. This little trick was suggested by the Israelis. One could not stop the scrutiny of other powers, but one could keep them more occupied with chaff than with the wheat of what was going on. The Israelis, of course, wanted something for this suggestion, namely the inclusion of certain specifics in one of the messages, and this of course was declined.

There might be something that would link the Church to one of the Israeli secret operations, and even though the Mossad was supposed to know better, it was Father Winstead's duty to observe discretion for them.

Once, a visiting bishop had asked Father Winstead if he thought the Israelis had penetrated the delegate's office.

Father Winstead couldn't control a laugh.

"Of course. They watch us, Cardinal Pesci must have people watching them, everyone else watches us watching each other. This is the Middle East," Father Winstead had said.

This evening, as every evening, Father Winstead created a message specifically for the trash, specifically to be discovered by the gardener and sold to whomever the Israelis knew the gardener was selling it to.

As in every misleading message of this sort, Father Winstead used some fact of reality that had happened during the day. This day he used Cardinal Pesci's name, which was always good because it implied information about Vatican foreign policy. And then he combined it with something totally random. The name of a street he had heard mentioned that day. Haneviim Street.

10

Look Again

It was a happy Mass. It was a happy morning. Even the elusive antiquities dealer Zareh Tabinian finally returned Jim's phone calls.

Because of his good friend Mendel Hirsch, Zareh Tabinian would give up a morning for Mr. Folan.

Jim postponed observing the coating of the bones to get the interview.

Mr. Tabinian lived in the Old City in a clean, white-walled apartment with immaculately washed linoleum on the floors, the walls white as bond paper, sun bleaching in from a window overlooking a courtyard of yellow-brown limestone blocks.

A large photograph of King Hussein of Jordan hung over the kitchen table. It was the sort of photograph a movie star or politician might have visible. King Hussein was smiling, showing three quarters of a face and wearing an Arab kaffiyeh. It had everything but an autograph, "To my good friend, Zareh."

"King Hussein?" asked Jim.

"The absolute most perfect ruler in the world," said Mr. Tabinian. Mr. Tabinian had a presence as though he was always posing for a statue. He had a large, imposing nose, dark eyebrows, and a very small, dark mouth. He wore one of the few ties Jim had seen in the city.

"Yet, you say Mendel Hirsch is a good friend of yours."

"Of course. I respect the Israelis. But King Hussein is the perfect ruler."

"So your loyalties are with the Arabs?"

"King Hussein," said Tabinian.

"You have done business with him?"

"I still do. The most perfect ruler in the world."

"Substantial business?" said Jim.

"Any business with a king is substantial," said Tabinian.

"Very good," said Jim, and then asked Tabinian to describe the piece of mosaic floor Jim had already seen in the warehouse. It was a form of cross-reference.

"It was a perfect example of Byzantine mosaic before A.D. 430. I paid for it from my own pocket because I knew I had a greater duty to this city. Where, I asked myself, had it come from, this beautiful mosaic? And when I found out, I knew it was a new find. In no way did I wish to harm Mr. Hamid. Do you know him?"

"I met him," said Jim.

"A wonderful, gracious man. Perhaps the most perfect businessman in all the city. I would sooner burn my own shop. You know where my shop is?"

"Off Via Dolorosa, two blocks from the Church of the Holy Sepulcher."

"Yes, I deal in only the best antiquities. Only the best. I wish I could say that for all of the dealers. I am certified, you know, by the Israeli Tourist Ministry."

"You have your grapes, so to speak?"

"Yes. In any case, I wished no harm to Mr. Hamid, and yet, to my horror, this find I had turned in, on whose property I had no idea was Mr. Hamid's, this property turned out to be his. Well, what could I do? I ask you, what could I do?"

Jim shrugged.

"Done was done, and if Mr. Hamid would give me just the slightest chance to explain and make amends, I would crawl on my knees to his residence and say, 'Friend, tell me what you will of me.' " Mr. Tabinian's hands went up with such a glorious statement.

"And you want me to tell that to Mr. Hamid if I see him again?"

"If you wish. Here. A gift. Please take this," said Tabinian. He brought forth from his suit pocket a small silver coin in a plastic case. Jim saw a figure of a god with a spear seated on a diadem. The god had a wreath of laurel. On the other side was a profile. And Jim could read the name "Augustus."

"Augustus Caesar. This is the time of Christ, two thousand years ago."

"Yes. It could well have been in the hands of Jesus Himself. Paid to a taxman. Perhaps Matthew, the publican. You are familiar with Matthew? One of Jesus' very disciples was himself, I am sorry to say, a tax collector. Perhaps he was saved especially, yes?"

"Where was it found?"

"Much of the Roman material we get is from Galilee."

"Jesus was raised there."

"Yes, I know."

"I couldn't take it. How much will you let me pay you?"

"Two hundred dollars American is what I paid."

Two hundred dollars was more than Jim had paid for anything since he had become a Jesuit. But this was a special day in a special place, and he felt he was now not failing his Lord. And since he had the money, and he would repay it to the Church, he bought the coin.

"All right," said Jim, taking out his large roll of Israeli shekels.

"It is a beautiful coin. Do you know we have holy oil lamps from Jesus' time?"

"I'm sorry. I don't have any more money," said Jim.

Tabinian gave him another gift, a small dark coin, which Jim returned. Jim asked more corroborative questions, and felt at the end that, although Mr. Tabinian tended to dramatize extensively, he did indeed verify the last corroborator on the lack of fraud concerning the discovery of the body.

Jim could prepare that part of the report for the courier, making seven different pouches that could be understood only when assembled in Pesci's office.

That took two days. He spent one more day watching Mendel's workers install an iron door to replace the stone at the dig. Jim took both keys, and Mendel was happy that he had them.

Four days later he met Sharon for lunch in a little coffee shop on Ben Yehuda. Her hair was loose over a thick khaki shirt, and the weather was now cold enough for blue jeans. This was the day she would polyvinyl the bones.

Jim had abandoned his sandals for army boots. He ordered ice cream but it tasted too chemical. Most Israeli ice cream tasted of chemicals, and Jim didn't know why, since they had good dairy herds and access to sugar.

Sharon had cigarettes, coffee, and a salad.

"What happened at the dig?" she asked. "What did you see?"

"I went to check out something. I'll explain it at the dig. I don't want to talk about it here," said Jim, nodding at the crowds.

"Fine. But now we are going to be there alone inside, right?"

"Yes," said Jim.

"How do you know I won't attack you as an occasion of sin? Nobody will be there to protect you."

"The dig would not be an occasion of sin because I would not normally be tempted in that sort of a place."

"Oh, it applies to you too. I thought of it just as an insult to me."

"The Church, in its backwardness and mindless superstition, Sharon, has declared that it takes two."

"It's reasonable, you know. If you accept the first premise," said Sharon. "And that is that God cares about that and has given instructions."

"I do," said Jim.

She thought that was funny. Jim noticed she touched him a lot, but not in a sexual way. It was part of her communicating, he told himself. Israelis did that.

On the way to Haneviim Street, he started to explain that she shouldn't hold his arm as they walked, but instead of rebuffing her, he showed her the coin he had bought from Tabinian.

"Where did you get it?" said Sharon, releasing him to glance at the little clear plastic envelope containing the silver coin.

"Is it genuine?" asked Jim.

"Where did you get it?"

"What does that have to do with whether it's real?"

"You bought it, so where you bought it had to do with whether it is genuine, because some people are reliable for certain things and others aren't."

"How do you know I bought it? Well, I did. Zareh Tabinian. Do you know of him?"

"Yes. He will not deal in fakes. It is genuine."

"What do you think of it?"

Sharon turned it over. "Very pretty. But may I ask, is there any special reason why you got this thing? You liked its looks?"

"Augustus, Caesar Augustus, was emperor of Rome at the time Joseph and Mary came to Bethlehem. He ordered a census of his empire, and that was what they were doing on their way here, when they stopped down the road and couldn't find an inn."

Sharon held the coin up in front of Jim's face. "Did Tabinian sell you this as an artifact of the Holy Land?"

"He said he couldn't guarantee that Jesus or Mary or Joseph ever held it."

"I can. They didn't. This came here on either Alitalia or El Al. Maybe TWA. Come," she said, tugging on his arm to make him move faster.

"Wait, it was sort of a gift."

"He knew you," said Sharon.

"Tabinian is highly reputable. You said so yourself. He gave up his own profit to turn in that mosaic floor, you know. He has been authorized as a legitimate dealer by the Israeli Tourist Board."

"Yes. Yes. His grapes. And he may lose them because they suspect he sold an ostracon. That has writing on it, if you don't know. He is trying to make up to Antiquities, that's why he turned in that piece of floor."

"I think he exaggerates, but I got the impression—"

"You didn't get any impression. He got the impression about you and he was right. Come," she said, and she pulled him along after her, refusing to listen to any explanations about how honest the transaction had been.

"I know Tabinian. I respect Tabinian. You don't know enough to respect Tabinian. You don't know enough for anything," she said.

At Damascus Gate she turned into the Old City, and after leading Jim through warrens of dark, covered streets with packed stalls and syrupy smells combined with the faint odor of

Old City sewage, she took him to Tabinian's shop just off Via Dolorosa.

She charged into the shop holding the coin aloft like a standard. She was barely at the counter when Tabinian, himself, hastily rammed his hand into his pocket and pushed $200 in American money at Jim.

"It was a gift," said Tabinian.

"Sharon. He's right. I insisted on paying."

"Do you think he didn't know you?"

"Sharon, I made the offer. I paid for it."

"Take it," she said, grabbing the money in her fist and pushing it into his hands.

"Sharon, I think you're out of place . . ."

"You're out of place. I live here. Tabinian knows that."

"It was a gift before and a gift now. Yes, please," said Tabinian. He was turning red.

"He knows you're going to be gone but I am still going to be here."

"Then I will return the coin."

"No. No. It is a gift."

"Sharon, I feel awful," said Jim.

"Do you want a gift?" said Sharon, pushing the coin into Jim's face. "This is not a gift." She put the coin into Tabinian's hand. And then pointed to his head. "This is a gift. In there is the gift. That's the treasure. Sometime he will show you his private collection, the one he uses to sell special dealers around the world, and then you see a gift, and it is this man's understanding of antiquities. He could have been a professor."

"I like my Mercedes," said Tabinian.

"A good mind," said Sharon. "A monkey can drive a Mercedes. What a waste."

"A rich monkey, Dr. Golban," said Tabinian, smiling with courtliness.

Tabinian insisted they let him serve coffee. Jim felt too embarrassed to say no. Sharon said they were busy but if Tabinian would show his special items they would love to stay.

Jim was impressed with Tabinian's knowledge of the Roman Flavians. He had several artifacts from that peiod, almost all of which were imported. Sharon noted that Tabinian not only imported but was known to do a bit of exporting also. She smiled wickedly when she said that.

Tabinian shrugged, with an acknowledging smile. When they talked about the dating of an object, Jim discovered that much dating of archaeological areas was guesswork, unless of course one had something that could be carbon-dated, or better yet something that could lend itself to thermoluminescence, like kiln-fired pottery. On that subject Tabinian deferred to Dr. Golban, whom he called an expert.

He showed her a small silver coin with a "G" on it, for which he would be asking $500.

"Governor Glaucus, he followed Pilatus," said Tabinian.

"I know," said Jim. "This is like a Pilatus coin I've seen."

"Pilatus, five times more valuable, religious interest," said Tabinian. "So little is left with Pilatus' name."

"I found it," said Sharon, "on one of my digs."

"Ah well, then it is not for sale."

"That means some archaeologists do sell things?" said Jim.

"Never," said Tabinian, with that little, knowing smile.

"I imagine there have to be some archaeologists who live on a very small income who might have sold something not too crucial just to survive in their work," said Sharon.

"As opposed to, let's say, a rabbi, Sharon, who would just be greedy?"

"Well, I don't know rabbis that well."

"Would you stone me if I said something against your great Kathleen Kenyon?"

"She is dead. I don't care. It would just show who you are."

"You're angry," said Jim.

"Please. I have other things," said Tabinian. "Who needs arguments?"

"I am not arguing," said Sharon, refusing even to look at Jim. "Some people have idiot spots in their heads and it comes out from time to time."

"I am just pointing out that you have invested your profession with a certain sanctity, Sharon. And I am willing to bet that some archaeologists have sold some very important and very expensive properties in this shop."

"Never," said Tabinian.

"Not you, of course, Mr. Tabinian," said Jim. "I am sorry I mentioned this shop."

"If it is not me, then yes. They have. Dr. Golban happens to be one of the most honest. Most are, but some . . . some," said Tabinian, and there was a very broad smile on his face. And he locked the doors of his shop, and took them to the rear out of sight of the street, and unbuttoned his shirt. He reached a hand under his left armpit and winced as he pulled. Coming out of his shirt was a wide white adhesive tape with black hairs still on it.

A small, clear, hard plastic envelope protected by gauze was stuck securely in the middle of the tape. Tabinian removed it ever so carefully. Inside was a slick gold coin, so bright it looked as though it had been minted that morning.

Tabinian very carefully handed it to Jim.

"Moabite," he said. "Before the Nabataeans."

"The Nabataeans," Sharon explained to Jim, "were very, very powerful once. There is a whole abandoned city in Jordan they once ruled. Cut entirely out of stone, and highly defensible. Totally abandoned, called Petra."

"What happened to it?" said Jim.

"They sinned and were destroyed," said Sharon.

Tabinian smiled.

"What happened?" said Jim.

"What usually happens. Think. The Romans changed the trade route on them, and the city had no purpose anymore. And poof! Everyone left because you couldn't make a shekel in Petra anymore. It's the way things really happen."

"They could also have sinned," said Jim, "and as His punishment God changed the trade route."

On that Tabinian smiled, for Jim had a good point. Even Sharon said she couldn't disprove that.

But on the subject of passing civilizations, Tabinian became sad. He, himself, was an Armenian, and his grandfather had come to this city, Jerusalem, after the Turkish massacres of Armenians, and there was no Armenian nation, although here was an Armenian, citizen of Israel, citizen of Jordan.

"A Jerusalemite," said Sharon, putting a hand on Tabinian's.

"We were the first Christian nation," said Tabinian.

"I know," said Jim.

"And we have suffered. Where were the Christian nations when we were massacred? Where? Where was anyone?"

Jim was silent.

"Fourteen thousand dollars," said Tabinian with no joy on his face as he put the gold coin back into its pouch. He taped it back under his arm and buttoned his shirt. "You see, I am a rich man here in Jerusalem."

He smiled. But there were tears rimming his eyelids. He was a proud man, Jim realized, and the smile was very brave.

"Thank you," said Sharon softly, and they left the shop and walked back along the Via Dolorosa amid Old City noises of vendors, donkey hoofs, and artisans. Sharon and Jim were silent until they reached the Damascus Gate, where the street had been widened.

"You know," said Sharon, "he would never leave Jerusalem. Armenians have been here for sixteen centuries." And then she smiled, and her tough shell appeared again. But Jim had seen her tender side.

Immediately she explained, while they were at the Damascus Gate, why all the medieval gates shown in movies were wrong.

"The movies show giant doors opening to courtyards of the city, and men charging in, right?"

"Right," said Jim, remembering how he had seen doors bashed down.

"Wrong," said Sharon. "That would be considered a breach in the wall. They never had gates open directly into a city. They always had another wall behind, forcing an invader to turn one way or the other. The one thing they weren't going to do was to let anyone charge right in."

"I see," said Jim, looking up ahead at the dark wall where now vendors sold batteries and radios and candy. They had to turn left and then right again to get out of the Damascus Gate.

"It would force any invader," said Jim, "to lose the power of his charge, and bunch up as they turned."

"Exactly," said Sharon.

"I feel sad for Tabinian," said Jim.

"Yes, well so much for proper medieval gates," said Sharon.

* * *

To polyvinyl the bones, Sharon needed only brushes and a jar of whitish liquid that she had been carrying in a small backpack.

Jim left the new metal door slightly open for better breathing, he said. Actually, he felt the door might somehow not open right, and lock them in for a while. It looked like such an intrusion on the place, even though Sharon said that was just the way ancients would do things—add whatever they had to whatever they found.

Very delicately and very carefully, Sharon applied the whitish liquid to the brown bones. Jim had to stand close to hold the powerlight. He felt a warm flush come up on his face, and then go back down to his body. Sharon's words became like gentle caresses, even though she was talking about bones and dating.

"Excuse me, could you hold the powerlight?" asked Jim, handing it to Sharon.

"Sure, what's wrong?"

"A crick in the back," said Jim. It was a lie. Why did he lie? Why didn't he just say flat-out he was liking it too much? That he had vows he intended to keep and he didn't want to go any further. Why?

"Okay," said Sharon. "It would be even easier." She put the light pack right into the niche itself, so that it illuminated the hole from the other side, casting an odd light on her. Jim could see she was almost hypnotized by her own work.

After a while she wiped her forehead, and said she was tired and needed a rest.

"If you want to smoke, go ahead," said Jim. "The door is open."

"No, no," she said. "You know the jaw hasn't fallen off."

"Which means what?"

"Which means I have been touching the bones, which must create some vibrations no matter how careful I am and the jaw has not fallen off."

"You mean you think there must be some fragment of connecting tissue there?"

"Exactly. Somehow a small fragment has survived there to hold the jaws. The jaws are not connected to the skull by bones, I am sure you are aware."

"What does that mean, exactly?"

"Well, you know you can't carbon-date the bones themselves because the substance you use is a protein called collagen, and in bones you just never isolate enough."

"But you can in connective tissue?" said Jim.

"Exactly," said Sharon.

"So now we can get a carbon dating," said Jim.

"Right," said Sharon. "Now you tell me what nice thing you saw in here last time that has made you such a different person."

"You could tell I felt good?"

"A different man, a condemned man entered this tomb, and a reborn one, excuse the expression, left it."

"Have you heard of the Shroud of Turin?"

"Yes," said Sharon. "I know someone who thought he had done some work on it about ten years ago or so, but he never got a proper answer from the people he worked for."

"Well, for certain reasons, I think the Shroud of Turin is every bit as valid as physical evidence of Christ as this find, and if that is so, then this can never be conclusively proven . . . what some people might think."

"Oh, yes. Yes. Yes. The shroud. It did have that wound on the side, didn't it? What was the dating on it? Did they ever do the dating?"

"You mentioned the wound on the side?" said Jim.

"Absolutely. Odd form of crucifixion. I could see if crowds were getting unruly, and they had to finish someone off fast, but the pilum in the side does not make sense. It would be like sentencing someone to solitary confinement, and sending along twenty obnoxious people to talk him to death. It just defeats the purpose."

"I read that too."

"The normal way of bringing about a faster death was to break the bones," said Sharon. "Which was slow. And, of course, Pilatus asked why Jesus died so quickly, which he would do if some Roman soldier had killed him with a lance."

"And the shroud shows a crown of thorns," said Jim. "Just like the Gospels."

"Not all that unusual. There is a game the Roman soldiers used to play with a victim sometimes, where they did make him an honorary king for a game, but of course not king of a specific people. But in Jesus' case it would have been a natural. And I think they did that because part of the game was playing for the royal robes. I can show you the square where it might have happened. It's inside one of your churches.''

"But the combination of both spear and the thorns is most unusual.''

"Agreed.''

"The shroud had both, of course. You can't tell if that one died by a spear,'' said Jim, nodding to the hole in the wall.

"A pathologist can,'' said Sharon. "Nowadays.''

"You think a spear would leave a mark on a rib?''

"It would have to. That's how those wounds kill, the blade or point bounces off the ribs, and then into the heart. Ribs are like guides to the heart for those familiar with killing.''

Jim shivered a bit to hear her talk so casually about brutal death.

"Therefore, if the shroud is valid as a covering for Jesus, it at least establishes what we have here cannot be proven without a great doubt to be Him. Because the shroud covers a man five inches taller than the bones could have been.''

"To hell with it,'' said Sharon. She lit a cigarette and smoked inside the cave.

"You see, I was really worried when I read back in Rome that no shroud was found with the body. But when I found bones don't shrink and the shroud could not have covered those bones, I knew I had my countervailing evidence. In fact, conclusive evidence. That poor fellow is not Christ.''

Sharon inhaled on the cigarette.

"Is something wrong?'' asked Jim.

"Everything is fine, Father . . . congratulations.''

"What's wrong?''

"I am not going to get in a discussion with you. Get your archaeologist. Do whatever you want. If you think Tabinian's waste of a good mind bothered me, you ought to see what I think of what you're doing.''

"What's wrong?''

"You came here for something and you found it. Let's not pretend this is a dig. *Pax vobiscum. Sursum corda.* Whatever.''

"What is wrong?''

"You have jumped to a religious conclusion and your evidence has a flaw, and if you knew where your argument fell to pieces I might have a depressed priest on my hands. Good. Go with God, Father Folan."

"You may disagree with me, but I would appreciate your treating me at least like an adult. Let's have it. I am here for the truth, whether you believe it or not."

"The Shroud of Turin could never have covered Jesus if you read the Gospels properly."

"How can you say that?"

"Because I read them not as a believer but a scientist. As a believer you are being carried along so quickly you don't notice some things."

"What?"

"I really don't want to discuss this. You will get what you want, anyhow. So let it be this."

"I want to know, Dr. Golban," said Jim.

"All right. I'll make a deal with you. Tomorrow may be the last good day till spring for the beaches at Tel Aviv. You go with me there, and read your Gospels while I swim, and I will explain to you afterward how the Gospels disprove the shroud."

"You couldn't tell me now?"

"Maybe you will see it yourself if you read it like a scientist, like that detective you can be when you are defending your faith. All right. You're a lot smarter than you let people know, Jim Folan."

"You couldn't just tell me?" said Jim, but he knew the teacher in Dr. Golban would not let a mind like his go free without a workout.

The next morning they bought pomegranates, dates, almonds, and the bitter oranges from the new citrus crop, and sesame loaves and Carmel wine, and they set out for the coast.

Jim asked that Sharon drive a little bit more carefully. When Sharon turned from the wheel to assure him how safe she was, Jim gave up asking and said a few silent prayers for their safety. When one of them became vocal by an unconscious slip, Sharon accused him of ridiculing her.

"My driving is not that bad," she said.

"You are really serious," said Jim, truly shocked.

"There are worse," said Sharon.

"A degree of bad is not a qualification for good."

"I said 'not that bad.' I wasn't talking about slow poke, let everybody run you off the road, 'Oh, here come the police' kind of good. I said 'not that bad.' And I meant it."

"You just missed a truck," said Jim.

"Right. Missed it," said Sharon, angrily vindicated, and Jim decided to just close his eyes on close calls, until Sharon accused him of trying to make her feel guilty. Which she didn't. But she would slow down because he was a guest of the State of Israel. Big deal. There, did that make him happy?

"Yes," said Jim, and they drove down from the hills through the land of Benjamin, into the coastal plain, past the ancient port of Yafo, until they reached the new city of Tel Aviv, where they needed a parking sticker for the beach.

Jim sat on the blanket reading a paperback of the New Testament in Hebrew, which was ironic.

Even by the time of the apostles, Hebrew was already a language reserved for Jewish holy works, and only the rebirth of Hebrew as a common language for Israel could have brought about the edition he had now.

Jim looked up at the water. He saw Sharon dive into the little breakers of the blue Mediterranean, and imagined Roman galleys making their way slowly up the coast, and sailors seeing someone as beautiful as Sharon on the shore, her golden body so sleek and perfect, a tribute to Hellenistic worship of the body.

Of course, if she were an ancient Hebrew, she would not be bathing like that. The attitude toward the body, as being something definitely not to be worshiped, was Hebrew to the marrow. And now part of Christianity.

She was wearing too little, just a string bra and napkin-size panties. But she had the body for it, a glorious body for it.

Jim felt lucky that he had never had to wrestle seriously with a woman problem as some priests did. And of course some failed. It was a modern scandal, specifically about the Jesuits.

But like most scandals, this was exaggerated because no one ever gossiped about the great numbers of Jesuits who kept their vows of chastity.

Jim stopped himself from this line of thought. He said a prayer of gratitude that he did not have that problem and watched the beautiful body of Sharon Golban play in the Mediterranean, dive into the little breakers, swim out and then back, and then stand up and let the water roll off, shaking out her luxurious black hair. Some men would come up to her, and she would nod back to Jim, who would wave and then pretend to read.

There was nothing new he was going to find in the Gospels that would disprove the shroud. If he didn't know it by now, he wasn't going to know it in an afternoon.

Sharon would tell him her proof, and he would see what she was working at, and find the flaw in it, and go on. It had to be impossible that the Church could conduct an investigation and miss an obvious fact.

He read snatches of Hebrew in the print he had come to believe at one time was the only Hebrew writing. But the marks on the disk were like handwriting compared to this print, and that is what had confused him.

As he read, the story of Jesus dragged him in, reminding him of his mother reading him the stories in English, and how he had imagined Jesus speaking in English, and Baby Jesus playing with toys just as he had. It was an old friend he met that afternoon, in a different language, in a faraway place from his mother's kitchen. But He was an old friend, as pure in Hebrew as in his mother's voice.

Suddenly, Jim felt cold water splash on him. Sharon was standing over him, shaking her hair out and drying herself. She was close. He could see the flesh of her breast firm before the line of the bra. There was nothing that was held up, and this woman, he was sure, could have modeled the suit, if she chose to.

"Am I spraying you?" she said.

"Oh. No. Stay there. You don't have to go."

"Have you found it?"

"No. But I think I know why you wanted me to go to the beach with you. You could say I am your date, and then nobody would bother you."

"Very good. This is a pickup beach, and I happen to love it and I also don't like to be bothered sometimes by men, so, yes, you are here. I remember reading an article that an American newspaperwoman had written about how aggressive Israeli men are on the beach. It was so funny because it had to be this beach. When you come here, it is like one of your bars in America.''

''Not all bars are pickup bars.''

''Really? But there are bars that are?''

''Yes,'' said Jim.

''What are they like?''

''I don't know what they're like today. When I was a student, I would go to those sorts of places.''

''You must have been very good. You're attractive and have a nice way.''

''No,'' said Jim, laughing. ''I wasn't very good.''

Sharon opened the wine, pouring for Jim first, and then tore off a piece of sesame bread for him, and gave him little bunches of grapes and almonds on a plastic wrapper.

''Is that why you became a priest, because you weren't good with women?''

''No,'' said Jim.

''I didn't think so,'' said Sharon.

''Why?''

''I just didn't think so.''

''No. I had been thinking of it since high school, and I had thought I would like to, but I didn't think I could do it.''

''You mean, give up sex?''

''Everything.''

''Are there priests who can have sex?''

''Some of our Eastern rites can marry. But not in our Latin rites.''

''Do you have sex?''

''That's personal.''

''You don't want to answer it?''

''Uh. I don't have sex. No, it doesn't bother me to answer it.''

''Are you a virgin?''

''No.''

''Did you like sex when you had it?''

''Yes,'' said Jim.

''And you gave it up?''

"Yes," said Jim.

"How?"

"With the help of Jesus. I don't expect to do it alone. He gave me the grace so that I would not be tempted beyond what I could handle."

"Sort of a self-hypnosis?" asked Sharon, biting into a piece of bread but never taking her eyes off Jim. She was locked in like a bird hovering over something, aware of any movement, even while she chewed.

"Unless, of course, Jesus Christ is God, and therefore capable of giving that help that I need to bring me closer to Him."

"All right," said Sharon, rather pleasantly. "Yes, that's possible."

"I thought you didn't believe in God."

"Where did you get that idea?"

"My God, you're a personal anticlerical pogrom."

"Ah," said Sharon. "God and men who claim they represent Him are two different things. Spit out the pits."

"What?"

"You're chewing the grape pits."

"I didn't find what you wanted me to find in the Gospels. I see nothing that remotely disproves the shroud as the covering of Jesus."

"Pits are not good for you."

"Never mind the seeds."

"All right," said Sharon, putting her forefinger on the text in Jim's hand. "Where in there does it mention Jesus Christ was tall?"

"What does that have to do with the shroud?"

"The shroud in your measurements is five foot ten. Yes?"

"Right," said Jim. "That's not tall."

"For Boston, Massachusetts, twentieth century, no. For Waco, Texas, no. For London, no. For Jerusalem today, no. For the Second Temple period, during Herod's time, yes! And nowhere in the Gospels, the Synoptic Gospels, from eyewitness accounts, nowhere does it say He was tall."

"Synoptics don't describe Him."

"Is it possible they would not mention He was tall, that He stood out in a crowd, that He towered over the people who followed Him, that one could see Him at a distance, because He was the tall one?''

Jim thought about that. There was no mention of Christ being tall. Where had he gotten the idea Christ was five feet ten? And then he realized where the tradition came from. He realized it with horror. It had come from the shroud itself.

''Jim,'' said Sharon, ''Goliath, the giant Goliath of the Philistines was six feet tall, maybe six feet one inch tall, in your measurements.'' Jim put down the text and looked out to the Mediterranean, and the painfully blue sky.

''Five feet ten was huge, Jim. They couldn't have not mentioned it. And Jesus was just not big enough for that shroud.''

''Yes,'' said Jim.

Sharon offered him wine, and he refused it. On the way off the beach, Jim kicked up sand.

''I'm sorry,'' said Sharon.

''Truth is truth,'' said Jim. ''The investigation is not over.''

''Absolutely,'' said Sharon. It was getting cold suddenly as the wind shifted coming in off the sea. Sharon said he should have a jacket.

11

Lavelle Again

"Regret previous report on countervailing evidence incorrect. Due to hasty judgment. Reports will follow."

The message was hard to send. The report was even harder. He had not only to explain his jump to a conclusion but then why that conclusion was wrong, and that meant why the report on the shroud was wrong.

He had to explain why so many had missed such an obvious fact. Perhaps because they had to see something that was not there. Or more likely because they had never grown up without the Gospels, because they too learned them as children and could never approach the works like historical documents no matter how much they thought they could.

What was even more brutal was Jim's examen, and there was no escaping this airing of conscience. He had lost a battle for his Church because of a flaw within him. He had been afraid because he feared failure, that he would fail the Church.

When he got down to it, it was pride. He jumped at the first good evidence to make himself look better, to make the Holy Father feel better, as though Father Jim Folan were playing benevolent God.

He had misled his Church and his Pope.

It was good that he was ashamed. What he owed his Church and his God was the best use of his mind. He did not have a right to be afraid. This was God's World, and His City, and His Church, and His Truth.

What God wanted to be known and when, He would decide. Jim was just his soldier.

He apologized for his sins. He asked for help, and the man who returned to the dig the next day was not the one who had left it days before for an appointment with truth on a Tel Aviv beach.

"What happened?" said Sharon. She noticed it immediately. "Is something different?"

"You," she said. She had been chatting with the watchman, who now had a chair and a little shack to sit in because of intermittent rains. As soon as Jim had started across the lot she had run over to tell him she missed him. She wore heavier lipstick this morning, with strong dark eyeshadow. On a face less majestic, it would have looked severe. But on Sharon it had a deep sense of quiet and beauty, a fluid grace that only the best sculptors seemed to capture.

"You think I am different?" said Jim.

"Absolutely, night and day. Who is this man?"

"Who do you think it is?" said Jim, smiling.

She grabbed an arm naturally as they walked. "Well, the first man was burdened, then the next man was elated and that was after the false hope, and then, on the drive back to Jerusalem in silence, there was a man in despair with even greater burdens."

"And who is this?" said Jim.

"This is Jim Folan, I think. Who was always there."

"And who is that?"

"A very nice person, I think. A man in the finest sense. Yes, you're quite a man, I think."

"I thought you didn't like clerics."

"I like the man, Jim."

"The man is a priest, Sharon."

"I try not to think about that," said Sharon.

Jim laughed. He shouldn't like that. He knew he shouldn't like that. But he loved it. She was wearing shorts this day because it was one of those intermittent warm days heading toward winter. Back home in New England it would be called Indian summer.

Jim descended the ladder first and refused to talk as he climbed down, because then he might look up at her legs,

which were so close, and so beautiful, and so incredibly
tantalizing. But more important, he had never looked up at panties in high school and he certainly wasn't going to do it now as
a Jesuit in Jerusalem on a mission for his Pope.

At the bottom, he told her.

"You know, I got everything straightened out through
prayer. I want you to know that, Sharon. I don't know how
much you know about the Church, but pride is a sin. And I,
through pride, had felt I didn't want to be the one to fail."

"I thought so," said Sharon. "I thought you felt that. But I
held back mentioning it. I didn't think my judgment on that
would be proper."

"I didn't think you held anything back, Sharon."

"Fuck you. Is that how you say it? Fuck you."

"I never say it," said Jim.

"I bet you didn't let anyone copy from your paper, either."

"They never wanted to. I wasn't smart enough. Were you a
copier?"

"I never had to," said Sharon.

"Did you let people?"

Sharon laughed. "That was cheating. I never did. I was the
little stinker who didn't let other people copy. And I always
heard from others what a horrible sort of person that was. I was
a bit ashamed of it. It was the best insult I could think of. It certainly bothered me. I assumed it would bother you."

"No. I was not the smartest. I was not the strongest or the
largest, but I was chosen. Because I was chosen."

"You should be a rabbi."

"You recognize the passage?"

"Of course. Our religion is our history. You were chosen
like God chose the Jews."

"I wish I hadn't been."

"I guess we should wish the same thing if you read history."

Jim noticed that there were puddles forming at the south end
of the dig facing Damascus Gate, the water now free to follow
the slope of the bedrock. He mentioned that they should get it
pumped out, and opened the metal door.

They had left the flashlights in there. And when Jim touched
the metal, it felt moist and cool. He wondered how long the

bones could endure the dampness even with the polyvinyl coating.

"That's just one of your problems," said Sharon. "The main one is, how are you going to go about this whole thing?"

"You can understand why we don't want knowledge of this to get out yet. Not because we are trying to hide something, but because, before the full truth is known, there can be quite a danger of speculation, to say nothing of the interference from outside. Could you imagine conducting a dig with television reporters around?"

"I can see your point."

"The problem is, any Christian coming in here is going to know what we have and I can't let one more person know about this."

"Simple," said Sharon.

"I can't imagine a Christian finding a crucified body in a tomb like this and not jumping to an immediate conclusion."

"It doesn't have to be here. You can have your pathologist examine the body in a lab. Many of them aren't done on site, either. The disk can be examined in another lab. You can have one person examine the disk for age and another for the authenticity of the Aramaic. You mentioned you wanted a geologist. Have him look at an empty tomb. But one thing you've got to do, and this is a must in any archaeological dig—for God's sake, don't rush," said Sharon. She had both his arms in her hands, now. "Above all, don't rush."

"I know already."

"I hope you choose the right lab and the right people."

"You know I am going to have to get another archaeologist."

"I know."

"How am I going to keep the archaeologist from knowing?"

"You can't," said Sharon. "Your archaeologist is the one who puts all the facts together."

"The archaeologist will know as much as me," said Jim.

"Absolutely."

"And he'll know where and why everything proves anything."

"He'll have to," said Sharon.

"I don't want anyone else knowing," said Jim. "It's not that

I am afraid of what this is, it is that I am afraid, perhaps, that the evidence won't show who it isn't. Can you believe that?''

"It would be an effort," said Sharon. "I saw your despondency when a piece of cloth was shown not to be what you thought it was. What is going to happen to you if by some chance evidence starts mounting that this is . . . is . . .''

"Is Jesus?" said Jim. He could say the word. Mendel had thoughtfully assured him voices inside the tomb could not be discerned up above.

"Yes," said Sharon.

"I hadn't planned on that."

"What if?"

"You yourself said that in archaeology there is always leeway for different opinions. But let me ask you, what do you think your rabbis would do if I came up with proof that Judaism was flat wrong?"

"Stone you to death."

"You're kidding."

"Maybe they would use knives."

"You're not serious."

"Tomorrow night, if I were to drive through Mea Shearim, I would be stoned. So don't tell me I am not serious. Already, respected archaeologists have been physically attacked by those animals. So yes, I am very serious.''

"But other rabbis would try to prove me wrong. I know rabbis, and I know some very rational rabbis. And they would attempt to disprove my evidence. I do not believe they would destroy the evidence, or me. We don't burn or stone anymore.''

"All right," said Sharon. "But I tell you I was bothered by what I saw in you, coming back from the beach, I was bothered."

"It's all right now," said Jim.

"Are you sure?"

"Yes," said Jim.

"Are you aware that I had a vested interest in that body being Jesus Christ?" said Sharon. Her voice was sharp.

"No, I wasn't."

"Well, you would have found it out. That's how minor archaeologists become major ones. By a famous dig. And that means they get more money for more famous digs, and so on.

But coming back in the car from Jerusalem, I didn't mind not having this dig as my own anymore. Not after seeing you.''

"I'm all right," said Jim, "and thank you for telling me about your vested interest.''

"You would have found out.''

"But you told me.''

"Yes. I did that. I did," said Sharon. She was trying to look at some place where Jim wasn't and she didn't know where to look.

"I'm all right, Sharon. Now don't make me have to worry about you, all right?''

"Fuck you," said Sharon. And turned away.

Jim took a light and went to the niche. The bones were shaded white now, and the jaw was still in place. The covering of polyvinyl was so light that the dark iron showed right through. It was almost transparent. Jim noticed how good the teeth were. He thought briefly that, if he could find a filling, he could pack up and go home. Fillings were recent. Although, the Egyptians had been great doctors, and they might have had some ways to handle cavities, which the Romans might have picked up.

He did know the Egyptians were doing brain surgery back then, so why not fillings? Don't jump to conclusions, he told himself. His eyes kept going back to that rusted iron. To think that people purposely hung a human being on a cross so that he would die more horribly, to create pain, to create humiliation, to create helplessness.

And to think it was done to thousands. And to think how his Lord had allowed Himself to be killed like that, where the most powerful object in the world became a spike that held your legs. Jim said a prayer for the poor fellow who had died like Jesus.

Sharon had regained her composure and was coming back up with more suggestions.

"We can cut the clay wall into sections, although some of it will crumble. Also, there might be something mixed in the clay. Sometimes it happens. We might find a dating object. You know if you found a coin from Governor Glaucus in the clay, that wall could not have been there at the time of Christ's crucifixion.''

"Yes," said Jim. "The wall.''

The clay bricks that had been formed by hand were irregular in line, a technique used thousands of years later in World War II to camouflage ships.

It had dried so that, with the irregular lines, it seemed to blend into the back of the cave so well that several of Sharon's volunteers hadn't noticed it.

Even with the hole she had punched into it, Jim had not been aware of the wall when first entering. He had to be shown.

Now according to the Gospels, Peter saw an empty tomb. Mary Magdalene saw an empty tomb.

And Jim Folan, two thousand years later, saw an empty tomb.

"You know," said Jim, "this looks at first glance like an empty tomb with that wall there."

"Today, but what about two thousand years ago?" said Sharon. He was onto something. But she held back. She had some questions herself. "Do we know whether wet clay back then would be so similar in color?"

"But in the Gospels, when did people see the tomb? They didn't see it right away."

"Good point. If we are going by the Gospels as a guide for possibilities as to what this might be, then we know it was not the time of winter rains, when it would take quite a while to dry."

"It was springtime. Easter," said Jim.

"Friday, he is crucified, and put in the sepulcher, and, let's say, right away this clay wall is put up. Okay?" said Sharon.

"Theorizing," said Jim.

"Scenario. Okay, the next day is Shabbat, so nobody comes here, especially not Mary Magdalene, who is a Jew. According to the Gospels, she skipped Saturday for that reason, and came here the third day, and saw that the tomb was empty."

"That's three days," said Jim. "The Gospels spell out those three days. Good Friday to Easter Sunday, springtime."

"It could be dry by then," said Sharon. "In springtime, three days would make it dry as now, I think."

"As dry as Easter Sunday when—Shhh," said Jim.

"What?" said Sharon.

"Shhh," said Jim.

He heard movement on the ladders outside. Someone was

coming down. Jim went to the steps to look out. He saw a brown leather shoe covered with dust descend to the bottom. The man wore greenish pants, like the guard up on top.

When he bent down to the hole, blood filling his face, Jim saw that he was the guard.

He spoke Hebrew, and Jim caught that he wanted to look around. Jim asked if he spoke English and the guard apologized that he didn't.

"Sharon, stand in front of the small hole in the clay wall," said Jim in English, and then in Hebrew told the man to see for himself. The man looked puzzled, straining his eyes.

"It is empty," he said in Hebrew.

"Yes. Yes," answered Jim in the same language.

"I heard there were bodies here," said the man.

"Rumor. Rumor," said Sharon.

"Then, why was I hired to make sure no one comes down?"

"We can't have our own interests without you knowing?" said Sharon.

"Sure," said the man.

"Come on in," said Jim.

"My back hurts," said the man.

"Well, look in closer," said Jim.

"Do I have to?" said the man.

"You're down here," said Sharon.

"I'm looking," said the man, lowering himself to his knees to peer deep into the cave. Sharon shone the hard light from one of the flashlights on the wall behind her.

"Empty," said the man. "It's empty."

"You sure?" said Sharon.

"Sure," said the man. "I heard there were bodies."

"Well, now you can tell everyone there aren't," said Sharon.

"So what are you doing here, you two lovers?"

"You must know from our voices," said Jim.

"It just comes out mumbled up there," said the man.

"We're making sure that a rock foundation is solid," said Jim, who had just verified that his voice didn't carry.

"It's solid," said the man, knocking the entrance to the cave, and with a grunt lifted himself up from the painful kneeling position. They watched his feet walk away.

"Well," said Jim. "You certainly would think it is empty from the outside. It would look that way."

"Did you check it at eye level?" said Sharon when the man's footsteps sounded high in the dig.

"Mary Magdalene had to see this at eye level, because there is a slight slope down. We can excavate farther south, toward the Old City walls, for you to get a better look."

"That's all right," said Jim, who went out into the base of the dig, and lay down in the little puddles formed by the dips and crannies of the bedrock limestone, and looked into the cave on his belly. Even with the flashlight, which of course Mary Magdalene would not have had, the clay looked like the back of the cave.

"Jim, you're getting wet," said Sharon.

Even from the outside the wall appeared to blend into the back of the cave. Wet clay or dry clay, two thousand years or three days, inside or out, the tomb looked empty.

Back at Isaiah House, inside the gardens, an Israeli was talking to one of the Dominican brothers. Jim could tell some Israelis now, just as he could tell some Arabs, by looks. But mostly one discerned by the clothes. And an open white shirt without a tie, under a sports jacket, was as much a sign of an Israeli as a kaffiyeh was of an Arab.

He understood they were talking about Father Lavelle. He heard the brother, a lecturer on Hebrew literature at Hebrew University, explain that "that man saw Father Lavelle in Rome."

Jim stopped. His Hebrew was better than it had been but still like new legs. His Hebrew was for the reading of the Pentateuch, not for some medical discussion, which this became immediately. The man preferred German. Did Jim speak German? No, said Jim, shaking his head, so they settled on the second language of Israel, English.

The man was a doctor. He was a psychiatrist. He had been treating Father Lavelle, and he was worried about him.

Who was Jim? the psychiatrist wanted to know. His name was Dr. Baumgarten. He had white hair, and stood somewhat stiffly, hands resting one on the other, the top one liberally sprinkled with age spots.

Jim, explained Brother Maurice, was from the Vatican, doing studies in Israel, and had met Father Lavelle in Rome, and was here to continue some of Father Lavelle's work.

Jim wanted to know more about Father Lavelle, but he did not want to reveal the suicide. He did not want questions because that might bring up what had provoked it.

How was Father Lavelle the last time Jim saw him?

"When I met him," said Jim, "he was or—'seemed' is the word—seemed depressed."

"Of course," said Dr. Baumgarten. "Exactly. He is a chronic depressive. That is why I am worried. Do you know what is chronic depressive?"

"Medically, I do not."

"A chronic depressive runs a risk constantly of suicide."

"You mean a major traumatic experience can bring about suicide?" said Jim.

"No. Anything can bring about suicide. A chronic depressive is a suicide that is going to happen unless something is done."

"From what I knew of him, he had never attempted suicide. That is what I was told," said Jim.

"Yes, of course," said Dr. Baumgarten with a sad laugh. "That is the problem with male chronic depressives. The female will make a few attempts before success. The man, unfortunately, will succeed the first time. When they do it, they just do it. Their suicides are not a cry for help, their lives are."

"So, what you are really saying is that they cannot judge reality with accuracy? Sort of interpreting everything at its worst?"

"I wasn't saying that, Brother Folan. You were," said the doctor, assuming Jim was one of the Dominican brothers.

They went into the kitchen of Isaiah House and made eggs and salami and drank wine with it, and talked about the sad life of Father Lavelle, with Jim implying he could help. It was, of course, a lie, even though he never once told an outright lie, but it was the only way he could safely extract from the psychiatrist what he had to know.

Father Lavelle had been under treatment for three years. He was a classic case of a chronic depressive. Outwardly an overachiever, but that was only the deceiving symptom of it.

Chronic depressives need activity and goals. They are like people running up falling ladders. To outsiders they appear to have nothing but energy. Actually they are running for their lives.

In childhood, chronic depressives can be treated by a psychologist or psychiatrist. Usually they are very passive, mistaken as good children, or very angry, mistaken as bad. But by the time they mature, they have to be treated chemically to break the depression.

Analysis alone would not do. Many world leaders are chronic depressives, and many of the sudden deaths when they are out of office are the result of their depressions catching up with them. When they have a cause or a job, they can survive.

Father Lavelle had many causes all his life. He refused chemical treatment, instead going out into the wilderness. He insisted upon God upholding him.

Jim looked to Brother Maurice. Perhaps the psychiatrist did not catch the symbolism, but the two Catholics did. It was in the wilderness that the devil tempted Christ by urging Him to throw Himself off one of the cliffs, trusting to God to save Him, and Christ refused, saying one did not tempt the Lord. Father Lavelle's refusal to accept medical help when it was available, instead of tempting the Lord, was symbolically throwing himself off a cliff.

Jim had a crucial question.

"Was Father Lavelle inclined to make judgments that the worst had happened? In other words, would he automatically jump to the worst possible conclusion without checking out the facts?" asked Jim.

"Brother Folan," said Dr. Baumgarten, still uncorrected as to Jim's title, "Father Lavelle lived the worst possible conclusions and went through life collecting the data to prove them."

They talked late into the evening, and it reminded Jim of Newbury Street back in Boston, where one could have truly illuminating talk, relaxed among educated men. It was one of the little joys of being a Jesuit, and, as in Boston, Jim usually just asked questions and absorbed.

He knew this was not just talking without giving. To be listened to and questioned was a gift also, especially to intelligent people.

He found out that the best terrorists were chronic depressives. Classics. When the cause was won, they would have to fight on other fronts for other causes. If not that, they betrayed the cause when it became a reality.

Jim mentioned he heard that terrorists were really very rational people. Psychiatrists said that.

"Probably a psychiatrist who was a chronic depressive, and shared the same demons as the terrorists he was asked to interrogate. Chronic depressives make good psychiatrists, also," said Dr. Baumgarten, smiling. "They always have their sick patients to hang on to for dear life. And don't think otherwise."

"And saints," said Brother Maurice. "With their troughs of despair."

"Unless," said Jim, "it comes from God."

"Then, one cannot argue," said Dr. Baumgarten.

Which brought up whether chronic depression could come from God, which brought up whether God was capable of evil, which brought up good and bad, and the limits of the devil.

It was that sort of night. Jim retired, filled in his mind. Before he said good night to Brother Maurice, he got either a warning or a bit of advice.

These Dominicans were a mission to both the Jews and the Christians, believing there is a mystical link between the Church and the Jews. Originally, the early Church believed the Jews were competition, and that was where much of what became theological anti-Semitism in Christian Europe stemmed from. The very existence of Jews was thought to be a refutation of Christianity, since if the Messiah had come, then why did so many of the people he was born among reject him?

But the Church had come to realize that one did not negate the other, and both were here for God's purpose until the end of time.

"You will be surprised, Jim, at what we share, and what we don't share, with the Jews."

"I studied Judaism. I know Talmudic argument a bit, the Halakah, and many of the differences of their sects. You don't think I am one of those Americans who think there are three kinds of Judaism, Reform, Conservative, and Orthodox and that's it, and let's light Hanukkah candles with our friends because that's really their Christmas?''

''I said, you will be surprised,'' said Brother Maurice, ''and you will.''

12

A Friend in Need

Warris Abouf knew his time was at hand. He knew Major Vakunin was under pressure from above. Warris saw it in the way
the major's bearing carried even in the way he sat, transferring
his unpleasantness to his spinal column. Vakunin was more im-
perial this day, more upright. He was shorter in his sentences,
less tolerant of answers. Faster with the ultimatum.

"If you can't find someone, we will say you cannot do it and
that is it. Done," said the major. The fingernails of his right
hand tapped the green-felt desk top.

"Oh no, no, no," said Warris. "As I said in the reports, this
is a more subtle, you see, a more subtle project than it would
appear on the surface."

"In all the universities in Moscow, in all the training camps,
you have not been able to find us our Palestinian fluent in Hebrew and knowledge of Vatican affairs? Where is the subtlety?
You take a Palestinian. You take a Catholic and you take one
that knows how to speak Hebrew. I know, myself, of five, and
I am not our expert, Comrade Abouf."

"And I know them. Speaking to one I imagined was an Israeli, I could barely make out his Hebrew. I had to give him a
Hebrew lesson. Two others were not real Christians, and by
that I mean, while they were loyal to us, to the true socialism,
they did not even know what an apostolic delegate was. Is that
what I could call knowledgeable of Vatican affairs? And then

the others who were knowledgeable were, I am sorry to say, people we could not trust.''

"You dismissed them that easily.''

"I would have to stand by my estimate.''

Warris knew that if the major managed to get Warris to change his estimate, then the major was covered, having relied on a subordinate who could be blamed for failure.

Even if the major felt the men were all right, he would not recommend them without having Warris' approval, because then the major would be responsible. What he wanted from Warris was his own security on the one hand, and the easing of pressure from above on the other.

Warris knew the bullying that would come. Ordinarily he would negotiate some compromise. Part of everything Warris had in his life was knowing what his commanders wanted, would tolerate, would push for, would not push for. And he knew this major had to have Warris' approval on a candidate for the special assignment within Israel.

And so the threats came, and the warnings came. The major disclosed that he had defended Warris. He had said in a pinch that his man always came up with what was needed.

Now what could he say? What could he say?

And it was this moment that Warris had prepared for. He showed a sense of panic. He inhaled deeply, as though a flush had overcome him. His hands wrung together. And he stood up abruptly, his body stiff, at attention.

"Sir,'' he blurted out, "I must now do the only thing possible. I must recommend the only candidate possible. One who fits every qualification.''

"Now we are doing business,'' said the major.

"I recommend Warris Abouf, sir. Comrade.'' And Warris threw the major a salute he had learned in one of the camps that had given him the brief mandatory military training. It was a rather inelegant salute, with more fervor than form.

"No,'' yelled the major. "Absolutely not.''

And Warris neatly returned all the major's reasoning about Warris' poor performance combined with the organization's need for a candidate, which Warris had discovered, to his dismay, could be filled only by himself. And he was volunteering as a last resort. Warris felt confident he would now be going home.

Unfortunately, one of the problems about logically backing someone into a corner was having all the logic dismissed by the reality of who was running things, and why they were being run that way. Truth could be so brutal at times like this.

"I'm not letting you go," said the major. "You're too comfortable to work with. I worked with others. Frankly, Warris, you are the decent Arab. I don't even think of you as an Arab at all. You understand me and I understand you. The others are like working with zhids. Now, come now. Be a good fellow and get us someone we can all live with."

"Yes, Major," said Warris.

"Let me be of more help, Warris. And this is confidential. A knowledge of Hebrew can be made up for with a knowledge of Jerusalem," said the major.

"All of Jerusalem?" said Warris weakly. Already, Moscow was cold to the marrow, and all the pink-faced Russian joy, with their winters, always made it more miserable. There was nothing to live here for. His wife, Tomarah, was a woman he slept with. His son was now ridiculing him, with his mother's help. To watch this daily was a worse scourge than the cold.

But Warris was realistic enough to know that his pain and despair were better than being shot or starving to death. For himself, he was a reasonable man. But such was his despair that he made a mistake of concentration, and had to ask that the major repeat himself. He had missed some rarely given technical information.

"I am sorry, please repeat," said Warris.

He had even been prepared with reasons why it would be no risk if he were captured. He never knew who was accepted and who wasn't. All he knew about were the students he interviewed, and there were hundreds. And, of course, that was meaningless information. Any reasonable man had to see that. But there was reason and there was reason, Warris knew bitterly.

And when you were a major in the KGB dealing with an Arab, all the reason was on your side. You let the Arab play with only as much reason as you felt comfortable with, and

when you were uncomfortable, you took it all back. Warris
smiled and nodded.

"We believe whatever is happening between the Vatican and
Israel has to do with some building, some negotiation on Haneviim Street. We have penetrated the Vatican. And we know."

"Street of the prophets," said Warris.

"You know it?" said the major.

"No," said Warris. "Haneviim means 'prophets.' That's
the Hebrew word. 'Prophets.' A prophet is one who speaks for
God. It is what the word means. 'Speaker of God.' "

"Look, you are not a bad fellow, Abouf. Come, we will eat
in the commissary downstairs, I know you like that. Come.
They have shashlik. See, I am letting you know about you,
Abouf."

"Yes, the commissary," said Warris. He always remembered the first meal he had there. He saw meat left over on
plates, and that was when he decided these were the people he
wanted to work for.

But it was not like nowadays, with everything offered to almost everyone. Warris had to work for it. He had to earn his
place here. He had earned his place through his cunning.

One of the African students had been beaten to death in an
important neighborhood. Students at Patrice Lumumba Friendship University said that he was killed because he was trying to
date the daughter of an important official. They said he was
killed because he was black, and there were angry stirrings
when the body was officially lost. Students said gasoline was
poured over his genitals and set afire.

Before anyone could organize a protest, Warris himself organized one, apologizing for the behavior of any particular student, because, as his signs said, "We are not all animals.
Russia, the only friend of the Third World."

It did not totally diffuse the anger among the students, and it
made Warris enemies. But the enemies he made were not nearly
as important as the friends. The enemies did not have extra
meat to leave over on their plates.

Warris went down to the commissary with the major. This
meal, too, would change his life.

A thick-faced woman with big arms brought steaming plat-
ters of shashlik for the major. She was fat. Her blouse was

unbuttoned at the top and as she leaned forward over the table Warris caught the major's eyes. The major's eyes did not look at the shashlik. They did not look at Warris. They did not even look at the waitress herself, but fixed on one spot, that fleshy cleavage pushed up almost to her collarbone.

"Exquisite shashlik," said Warris.

"Yes," said the major, staring at the breasts.

"A number four wine would be good," said Warris.

"Yes," said the major.

And the major noticed that the shashlik had done wonders for the Arab's disposition, because he became that chatty, almost mindless bubbler, happy to serve. He had a little request, too, one that everyone who worked for 2 Dzerszhinsky Square had to get clearance for. It was a camera. He wanted to photograph the family he loved.

Would the major supply personal camera and film, since Warris was not allowed to buy them because of his position?

"Yes, yes," said the major. "You are a good man. Good people deserve to be treated well."

A week later the camera was ready, with one roll of film. Marking on the cartridge in official glaring blue said only the KGB could develop this roll. It was a criminal offense for anyone else to develop it, not that anyone could really photograph anything sensitive, anyway.

Arkady was the first he photographed, in front of the little cartoon bear on the ice-cream stands. Arkady did not want to pose for Warris' "stupid pictures," as he called them, but Warris promised him a trip through Dewtsky Mir (Children's World) and a toy of his choice.

Tomarah was a bit harder to photograph, and Warris discovered that she was the source of Arkady's calling the pictures stupid.

"Why now pictures? Why pictures of me? What is the purpose of a stupid picture?"

"Smile. Laugh," said Warris, trying to align the camera.

"These are stupid pictures. Why do you want me to laugh?" she said. He had gotten her to sit in front of the window, at first explaining that south light made a woman look more glamorous.

"You should laugh because your laughter enhances a blonde's voluptuousness. You are an exciting woman."

"Liar," she said.

"You are saying to me you are not beautiful, precious?"

"You are a liar. That's what I am saying. Liar."

"Get closer to the window. You will look so beautiful with the light coming in."

"I will not laugh."

"You are so beautiful."

"But not laughing. Laughing is not attractive. My eyes squint like Tartars' when I laugh."

"No. Not laughing. Whatever made me say laughing," said Warris, touching her shoulder gently, and stroking.

There had been a time when just thinking of her could make him burn. And even while he understood that she had married him to get a resident's permit for Moscow, he had accepted that just to get into her snow-white flesh.

The sex had been good for many, many months, but in the second year, a year after Arkady was born, it had settled into something that was just there. The fire was gone, replaced by a sort of mutual comfort, in a home where a truce reigned.

But in the last six weeks, since Arkady had told him what the rouge on his cheeks represented, there had been only two incidents of sex, and each a grinding performance of duty lest Tomarah suspect something.

Somehow, she sensed that sex with her had become a labor, and not only did this fail to decrease her appetite, it enlarged it. It aroused her that, like some weary worker, he would have to start up her body like a cold machine. There was the touch on the breast, the kiss on the clitoris, and then if Tomarah said ready, he would mount.

Sometimes she would say, "No. No," and mention more of this or more of that.

This day as he stroked her cheek, she wanted the sex right away.

"After the pictures, dear," said Warris.

"The pictures later."

"But with pictures, I can get excited."

"Liar," she said. "Don't lie."

"I only have to see your breasts," said Warris.

Her large breasts were well hidden in two layers, the first a thick white bra and the second a flowery print blouse, just as opaque.

"You are not a breast person. You like my, you know what," she giggled, patting her very round backside.

"You don't see what men notice."

"They notice nothing. What do they notice?"

"How full you are. Men love the fullness."

"I am a woman," she said, with a telltale grin. "Average maybe. Better. A little."

"Better than better," said Warris.

"You don't fondle me that way."

"Just seeing them is excitement."

"No," she giggled. And not calling him a liar meant she was open for more of the same.

"Oh yes, they are magnificent. Here. Let me open this button," said Warris, reaching forward.

"Not unless you mean business."

"Of course I mean business," said Warris. He opened one button, and kissed his forefinger and placed it upon the white, rising pillow of flesh jutting above the sharp bra line.

"That's too much," laughed Tomarah, closing the blouse again, but not fastening the button.

Warris focused, adjusted the lens for daylight afternoon winter, and snapped the picture.

"Is that all I get?" said Warris.

"Not for the camera."

"I want your picture."

"Why? You have me."

"Not always."

"Well, you should not have me like that always," she said and there was the very big grin.

"One more button."

"Never."

"Let me."

"This is silly."

"Let me."

"Not here," she said, and Warris followed her, trying to read the instructions for indoors. All he saw was that he should keep the camera very steady because indoors there was less light and therefore longer exposure was needed.

On the bedspread, Tomarah opened the other button, then stuck out her chest.

Warris snapped the picture.

"You don't need the shirt."

"Oh, never. Never. Put away the camera."

"I want to see."

"Nooh," cooed Tomarah.

"Yeeees," cooed Warris.

"Put away the camera," said Tomarah.

"No."

"Put it away or I'll break it."

Warris rested it on a wooden bureau.

Tomarah unbuttoned the rest of her blouse and flung it off. Two mounds bumped up through her thick white bra. Her nipples were hard. She was excited.

Warris grabbed the camera.

Tomarah screamed like a little girl being tickled. Warris snapped. It was not a good picture, he knew, but she didn't know that.

"You're awful," she said. "You cheat. You're unfair."

"Stay still."

"No."

"I already have the picture."

Tomarah, with a girl's grin on a woman's lust, pushed forward her bosom, bulging into the straining bra.

Warris was very steady, snapping two pictures perfectly.

"Take it off," he said.

"You wouldn't dare shoot me like that," said Tomarah.

"Go ahead," cooed Warris.

"Here. Nothing," said Tomarah, reaching behind herself and unsnapping her bra, hurling it across the room, her white breasts rising to the hard pink nipples thrusting in front of her like regimental glories.

Warris' hand trembled slightly. He photographed at three different exposures to be sure.

"You love your breasts, touch your breasts. Play with them."

Tomarah raised one eyebrow and, like a matador in a proud

display, in full control of her bull, put her two fingers to the tips of the nipples, and played with them, watching Warris' face.

When Warris did perform the required sex, she needed no more stimulation. She was as moist as a wet marsh, and came to a screaming orgasm almost upon entry.

Several days later, she wanted to play "slut and cameraman" again, as she called it.

"I have no more film," he said.

"Liar," she said.

"Really," said Warris.

"Of course," said Tomarah. "There was never any film to begin with. Right?"

"Right," Warris would say. "Unfortunately, I have returned the camera to where I got it as loan."

"We can pretend you have a camera, no?"

"It's not the same thing," Warris would say.

"Liar," she would say.

The pictures did not come back for a long time, and when they did the corners of the nude shots were dark from finger marks.

Warris had to confess to Major Vakunin one day that indeed his wife had been a great disappointment to him. He suspected she would sleep with some officer. They always turned her on.

"What evidence do you have for that?" said the major.

Warris lowered his head. He let his eyes fall downward. "She was the one who wanted me to take pictures of her. She wanted them to give to someone."

"Who?"

"No one, yet. The poor woman had it in her head she can seduce some man by handing provocative pictures of herself to someone. I told her no decent man would consent to that."

"Of course not," said the major. "I saw the pictures. But I thought they were your own personal business. And does she have them now?"

"No. I have them. And I am going to burn them."

"If you want, I will do it for you," said the major.

"No. No," said Warris. "It is my trouble. You are too kind. I tell you this, however, I am going to stay near her whenever I can, because I know that if I should be away for any length of time, that woman is ripe. Like a plum. Like a pear. Like a well-rounded, juicy peach.''

"You poor man," said Vakunin. "Do not torture yourself anymore. Let me destroy the pictures for you."

And Warris did, handing them over in a little packet.

"You are not just my commander, sir," said Warris. "You are my friend."

13

"Why Have You Forsaken Me?"

Winter was upon Jerusalem, and the rains were cold. Jim bought himself a warm coat for $75 American. He missed Thanksgiving, and football, the other Jesuits and Boston College, Boston, and the officiousness of Father Wingren. He also missed phoning an aunt once a week in Portland, and performing the personal sacraments for the family, such as baptism, weddings, and funerals.

An uncle had died, and he was not there. His little cousin, Mary Elizabeth Coffey, was going to marry a boy from Georgia, and he would not be there.

Pots of chemicals to absorb moisture out of the air were placed in the cave until the plastic cases were ready. These would be opaque, airtight, and crushproof. One would conform to the bones, and the other to the disk. They would have to withstand a truck falling on them, at least. Jim had told the manufacturer the cost did not matter.

He had rented a secure laboratory just outside of Rehovot for the bones. Sharon had supervised the construction of the temperature and humidity controls. Jim had taken care of the more mundane dangers, such as breaking and entering, with locks and alarms.

The clay wall covering the niche had been sprayed so it would not crumble, and then cut with diamond-edged saws into squares. Each square was photographed, and then removed to

Hebrew University, where Sharon was given a laboratory. Jim had a key to the lab.

Making sure every square matched every picture, they reconstructed the clay, which conformed to the arch of the niche. Jim felt when the entire clay covering was removed that the bones of the little man looked somehow naked, and that it was wrong to look at him, so helpless with that disk lying over his spine.

It was as though the clay wall over the niche had been his one blanket of respect and now he was an object again. Several times Jim had prayed for him, asking that, if he were not in heaven already, he be accepted through the blood of Him who had died the same way.

Jim offered up his own loneliness for him.

Rumors kept coming back that he was working on some bodies. These were usually from people in the halls of Hebrew University. There he met Brother Maurice, the Dominican from Isaiah House, strolling with some students, chatting in Hebrew, and he could see how Sharon would not know Father Lavelle was a priest. One couldn't tell, if one didn't know, that Brother Maurice wasn't just another teacher of Hebrew literature.

He was also a citizen of Israel.

Both Jim and Sharon disassembled the wall again on a long metal table, and then hammer blow by hammer blow shattered it, looking for objects in the clay. They found none. They even shattered the little bits, until they had a pile of powder. If they wanted, they could have added water to it and made clay again. They poured it into a plastic bag and labeled it "Niche covering." A small portion was sent to a laboratory even though Sharon said it was clay common to the entire eastern part of the Mediterranean.

"There is a point where thoroughness becomes foolishness," she said, with his right arm firmly in her hand. She had him backed against the main table in their private lab at the university. "No one is more thorough than me. I know what clay is. But I think you'll answer that you don't mind being a fool for Christ, right?"

"I can't be too thorough. Please step back."

"What?" said Sharon.

Jim felt the closeness of her body, her hips against his, her braless breasts pressing against his chest.

She always seemed to have her hands on him when they talked.

"We're touching," said Jim.

"Yes," said Sharon. She seemed puzzled.

"Well, it's uncomfortable," said Jim.

"Why?" said Sharon. "We're just talking."

"But it's sort of, well, sensual."

"I was just talking."

"Could you do it without touching?"

"No. I feel uncomfortable just saying the words, when I know someone. Do you understand?"

"Could you try?"

"Sure," said Sharon.

"Well, are you going to try?"

"Yes, but not now. We're talking," she said.

"If I stay in this position, it is a sin for me, because it arouses desire. I am going to have to move," said Jim.

"Move," said Sharon, stepping back. "I was just talking. You sound like some rabbi calculating sin by where you stand or don't stand. What's the purpose of Christ if nothing changes? He was supposed to bring change, right? So where is the change?"

"You've been reading Christian books."

"I am on a dig. I have a responsibility as long as it lasts. Answer the question. Why has nothing changed?"

"Because, as He said, He came to fulfill the law, not change it."

"You always have an answer," said Sharon.

"Does that bother you?"

"It bothers me that you have a good mind and are wasting it. But it is your mind, isn't it? If you want to believe you are different from the others, then believe." Sharon sighed and looked at her watch. "It is getting on Shabbat Eve and I must go."

"I thought you didn't believe in religious forms," said Jim. "Yet every Friday you leave early."

"The rabbis wouldn't call me a good woman, but I observe Shabbat. I have a family, my brother, whom I share Shabbat with. It's his family and mine. I love them. Paula, his wife, is from America."

"Are you going to ask if I know her?" said Jim.

"No. No. Did you think I would?"

"No," said Jim. "May I walk with you?"

"Certainly," said Sharon.

He wanted to walk with her because he had come to like her companionship, and felt that somehow on Fridays he was always cheated by her leaving early. He wanted the rest of his workday with her.

Outside it was raining, and Sharon wore a yellow rain slicker with a broad yellow hat. She looked like a tall mushroom. She grabbed Jim's arm as he hunched down into his jacket. She knew he could not go to her apartment, but wanted company, so she walked with him in the rain. He found a fast-food store and got a pita stuffed with falafel and tomatoes and onions, and ate it as the rain soaked it, threatening to break the bread.

They walked up to the Dome of the Book, where the Dead Sea Scrolls were now housed, and Jim commented on how the scrolls had helped shed light on early Christianity.

"I have a question about that, Jim. I have puzzled over it, and I had intended to ask you during your first interrogation. I find it the most emotionally appealing part of the Gospels, and yet the most illogical. I don't understand how you can explain it."

"I think I know what you are thinking of," said Jim. He was smiling. The sandwich was bursting, and he had to let it go into a trash can or wear it over his jacket.

Hebrew University was beneath them now in the valley made by one of the many hills of Jerusalem. Across the valley, he knew, was Sharon's apartment, which he would not let himself enter.

"If you know, Jim, then tell me."

"Just before He dies on the cross, Jesus exclaims, 'My God, my God, why have you forsaken me?' "

"Yes, that's it. Why? If he were God, if he could prophesy, if he said, as the Gospels claim, that he would rise again, that he would outlast the Temple building itself, how could he suffer such despair, such hopelessness?"

"Because," said Jim, "He is not Socrates."

"Explain."

"No. You think. You read the life of Socrates, and then you tell me what you think."

"That's not fair," said Sharon.

"You did it to me with the Gospels."

"I'm not strong on the Hellenes. You can tell me, I'm not a child."

"Read the life of Socrates and you tell me," said Jim.

"Let's see, Socrates was a Greek philosopher, and a good man, who was also executed."

"Read the life of Socrates," said Jim.

"I don't like it when you play games."

"You played games with me."

"I also had to have someone to go to the beach. It is not the same thing."

"Right, yours was a form of blackmail. Mine is a form of education. Maybe you will know something of Christianity that is hard to understand."

"All right," said Sharon, with a bite of threat in her voice. "If you are going to educate me, then I will educate you."

"It sounds ominous," said Jim.

"I have mentioned that you should know politically what everyone in the Gospels was doing, where they were coming from, as you say."

"Yes," said Jim. It struck a chord. "You mentioned that when I noticed how the tomb looked empty with the niche covering in place."

"Yes. That is part of it. You have a good memory. You know Pilate was washing his hands from other things than guilt, which he may not have felt at all."

"I would appreciate very much your suppositions. As damaging as you apparently think they are, I would want nothing less than your suppositions."

"Actually, they're not that damaging. They're just suppositions, things we usually put together at the end. I was just trying to force you to answer your riddle."

"We'll both be educated," said Jim.

"Damascus Gate, 10 A.M., Monday morning. You'll see the whole Second Temple period, everyone, Herod, Pilate, Caiaphas. We'll go to the courtyard where Christ was sentenced and

Pilate was politically trapped. We'll see the Second Temple itself, and we'll go right to the end of the Via Dolorosa.''

"To the Church of the Holy Sepulcher," said Jim.

"Yes," said Sharon, and she gave him a little good-bye hug sealed with a kiss on the lips.

"Don't forget," Jim yelled after her. "Why was Socrates different from Jesus? There'll be questions."

He watched her go, and he went back to Isaiah House alone, in the rain, tasting her lipstick on his lips. At first he tried wiping it off, but when it was gone he realized it hadn't lasted long enough.

"Socrates went to his death calmly, rationally accepting," said Sharon, meeting Jim at the Damascus Gate. It was a sunny, wintry day and blessedly dry, so a light sweater was all he needed.

"Good morning," said Jim. He had brought the coffee and Arab bread.

"Is that right, is that right about the death? Was that the point?"

"Yes. Do you want bread?"

"No. Just the coffee. I never have bread until I've had enough cigarettes."

"When is that?"

"When my throat hurts. Is what I am saying right about Jesus?"

"You have it exactly. Socrates was a philosopher and a good man who went to his death accepting death as a natural progression of life. Christ first prayed in the Garden of Gethsemane to be spared what He knew would come, and then, on the cross, despaired of having been abandoned."

"All right, but how does that all fit?" said Sharon. "How can you say to me that Christ despaired because he was not Socrates, tell me that?"

"First of all, which has the elements more of fairy tale, the life of Socrates or the life of Jesus?"

"Well, when you get to the Resurrection I would have to say . . ."

"No. No. The life. The life itself, as a man."

"Oh. Socrates is more of a cartoon character and less believable. He is too perfect. Christ curses fig trees, and most of all Christ fears death. Which I am asking, how can Christ fear death if he knows he will be resurrected? If he is God?''

She saw him smile as she took the coffee. She did not enter the gate. She was not interested in walking. She wanted to know, and there was something here that moved Jim Folan deeply, that was something strong in his life.

''When God was man in the life of Christ, He shared that life. Now some will say manhood is standing up to someone or being brave, but that I believe is a virtue, and not a natural thing necessarily. What is most man about man? And by that, I am sure you know, I mean people. What is it that makes us different from statues, from giraffes?''

''Yes. Go on. The winter is not long enough to explore that one,'' said Sharon. She was not joking.

''Manhood, real manhood, the thing of manhood is knowing you do not control the really great events of your life.''

''Define 'great.' ''

''Whether you are born or die,'' said Jim, ''you have no control over that. When you are born, you will die. And man knows that, and pushes that out of his mind when he can. At the time, just before His death, in that helpless despair, Christ was most a man, significantly the time of His greatest manhood, just before His eternity, and the glory of Resurrection. That helpless despair was our humanity.''

''Ah,'' said Sharon. ''But Christians aren't supposed to despair. They are supposed to hope. Christ, therefore, was not a good Christian.''

''Christ was not a Christian. He was a Jew,'' said Jim. ''And what we have, that He did not have at that moment, was Him. We have His Resurrection,'' said Jim. ''His Resurrection is our hope.''

''His philosophy, I think, as far as people go,'' she said, ''is probably the best in the world. Christ certainly understood people. He really understood people.'' Sharon looked around the stone walkway into Damascus Gate. People were coming in now, as the Old City hummed into its day of commerce and prayer. She looked up to her left at the beginning of Haneviim Street. She couldn't see the street from there because of a rise of new limestone steps. Jim wasn't talking. She looked back to him, and then he caught her eye.

"His Resurrection is our hope," said Jim. "He was not the perfect nice guy, and no one of us should believe in Him because of His philosophy or niceness. Nice guys don't curse fig trees. But God, wanting to demonstrate that we should bear fruit, cursed fig trees. God, wanting to show us we should do good, curses fig trees. Nice guys remember they owe a cock to Asclepius," said Jim, referring to the last recorded comment of Socrates, who, facing his death, showed such calm acceptance that he could care enough to settle a small personal debt.

"God cries out, tasting manhood in the fullest, 'My God, my God, why have You forsaken me?' "

"Yes, but He did provide a way of life for people. A good way of life, of understanding and forgiveness and an awful lot of common sense," said Sharon. "Yes, common sense." She felt her lips tremble. She felt trapped in the very day itself, trapped by this man who knew what he was doing.

"You are avoiding what I am trying to say, Sharon. He was not another philosopher. He was not another good guy. Sharon, I believe He is God. Millions of others do, and billions have gone to their deaths believing He is God. Do you follow me?"

"I don't want to," said Sharon, turning her back, looking for a place to be away from him.

"You understand now."

"I don't want to understand."

"They have lived their lives believing He is God, and everything about God that is God. They have died for this belief. This central belief."

"Leave me alone, Jim," she shouted. "What are you doing to me?"

"There are countless numbers who cannot get through the day without believing in Him, Sharon. You take away His Resurrection and you kill the God of Christ. The Romans only did the body," said Jim.

"Jim. Jim," said Sharon, her face twisted in tears. "Leave me alone. I'm off this dig. I'm off. I don't want it. I'm out. Good-bye."

He saw her throw the coffee cup on the street as vendors looked up and Arab women with their fruits to sell stared quizzically at the yelling. She ran into the compressed crowd, trying to get through the corner of the Damascus Gate, but he caught her.

"You understand now what it means, what you found?"

"I didn't find anything. I don't know anything. Leave me alone. I'm just an archaeologist, you fucking holy man. You bastard. You knew what you were doing. I'm just an archaeologist. Give me a stone, damn you. Take your God." Sharon was sobbing. She would not look at Jim, she would not look at anyone.

Jim took her in his arms and moved her out of the traffic until the crying stopped. He patted her back like a baby's and she did not resist. Finally he whispered in her ear.

"I do," she sobbed. And then she pushed away, and by now everyone was watching, so he pulled her away farther into the Old City. She nodded him up to a street that seemed relatively empty but for some nuns leading Arab children in blue smocks down a stone street, with two high walls on either side. There they stopped.

"Jim, all my life I didn't want to do anything that could hurt someone. Can you believe me?"

Jim nodded.

"And in this profession, unlike law, or medicine, or the military, people's lives wouldn't depend on me. I was free. I could do anything, deal with anything, because I knew it had all happened before. I could come to understandings of peoples and places without one jot hurting one soul, or even affecting one soul. I was free. It was pure research. And now, I don't want to find out what may be down there under Haneviim Street."

"And now you understand."

"I am now not the right person for this dig."

"On the contrary, Sharon, now you are."

"Oh, no. Don't you say that. Don't you say that, Jim Folan. I know you are my friend. Don't do this to me, don't you dare," said Sharon.

"Think about it, Sharon. What are my interests? Where am I coming from? You are going to do that, with Pilate, and Herod, and the rest, today. What about me, now, the Vatican's man? My problem is to keep this secret as much as possible. Who is the most dangerous link in this whole process? The archaeologist. He must know all the pieces. I didn't know whom I could bring in. I didn't know whom I dared bring in. Until today. I don't have to bring in anyone now.''

"Of course you do."

"Oh no. I have a top archaeologist, one who apparently is reliable at keeping secrets, and now I know one who does not want to prove who the find is.''

"An archaeologist should not have emotions, either way, toward a find.''

"Right, but this isn't Archaeology 307, or some other course. I'll take those emotions in the Church's favor, thank you.''

"But what about you? What happens if we prove . . . Well, you know how you were just over a piece of cloth.''

"You're not worried about me, Sharon. You're worried about your watching me. You're worried about your not being able to disprove who that body is. I see now we don't, I see now we may just not have all that room to prove whatever we wish.''

"I can't lie on a conclusion. I just couldn't do it. 'Can't 'is the word, not 'won't.' ''

"And the Church doesn't want a lie. The Church will go with the girl who wouldn't let other students copy.''

"I did worry about you the other day.''

"But not now?''

"Now you can die on the spot with my blessings, Jim Folan, bastard.''

"I am sorry, Sharon.''

"And if I refuse?''

"It will always be the Golban dig, and they will come after you with questions. Now, do you trust other archaeologists to be more thorough than you in finding evidence so that we know for sure what the bones are not? Could you name someone who has as much vested interest in proving a certain point, in sparing nothing to prove that point?''

"You.''

"With your abilities and credentials, Sharon.''

"It should not have been 'seek and ye shall find,' you know. It should be 'avoid and ye shall get.' ''

"Can you believe that, if I had a choice, I would spare you?''

"I don't care. You didn't." She shook her head angrily. Her eyes were red from the tears.

"Well, it is all real now to you, for the first time," said Jim. "So let's get on with your historical tour of the Gospels, where it all happened."

"We can do it at the end of the dig, if we have to," said Sharon. She lit a cigarette, and started back toward Damascus Gate.

Jim noticed a street sign. They were on the Via Dolorosa. He grabbed her elbow.

"C'mon. Let's do it. We're on the street already."

"They are just suppositions," said Sharon.

14

The Gospel According to Golban

Jim had known of the trial of Jesus since childhood. There wasn't a time he could remember that he didn't know it, how Jesus was unjustly condemned and then Pilate, with a heavy heart and much guilt, ordered the just man crucified.

"Pilate may have felt guilty, but he had to wash his hands for other reasons, and he had to do it publicly," said Sharon.

Using the same Gospels Jim had been brought up on, Sharon showed with eerie strategic insight why Pilate had to do what he did that Passover two thousand years ago.

They were on a stone street surrounded by either high walls or buildings. Sharon pointed south, saying just over the walls and a few more buildings was the Temple Mount, where the Second Temple had been. Therefore, the area they were standing on had to be Antonia Fortress, where Christ was condemned.

"Okay, why a Roman fortress here?"

"High ground," said Jim.

"Yes, but specifically in relationship to the Second Temple, because that was where trouble among the Jews would occur if it were going to occur. And the worst time for trouble was Passover. Even today, you can feel the city heat up at that time. Loads of pilgrims congesting in high religious fever. Okay, what were the Romans doing here at all?"

"Palestine was a crucial roadway," said Jim.

"Excellent," said Sharon. "It was the northern route to

Egypt, and Egypt at that time was the grain basket of the Roman world."

"And Rome, no longer self-sufficient in grain, depended on Egypt for grain. It was crucial because the whole city could go if the mobs didn't get their grain dole," said Jim.

"Excellent," said Sharon. "And what Rome wanted from this northern route was for nobody else to have access to it, specifically the Parthians or any Eastern kingdom."

"Like the Persian Gulf today," said Jim. "Rome didn't want any rebellion getting out of hand, because then the rebels might invite in one of the Eastern kingdoms. I taught a bit of Roman history."

"Pilate had another ongoing interest, as did every Roman procurator here."

Jim thought a moment. "They were known to try to make a personal profit, but this was not a rich land."

"Right," said Sharon. "Each procurator wanted to be on the side of whoever was in power, and also on the side of whoever might replace him. They wanted to be on all sides."

"Yes. That would be logical for someone controlling the northern route to Egypt."

"All right, we've got Pilate. Now imagine, in comes this man, at this most dangerous time of religious passion, charged with a religious crime that the Sanhedrin want the Roman authority to punish him for. Now, who are the Sanhedrin, Jim?"

"The Sanhedrin were the religious judges of the Temple. And the one thing I would imagine Pilate would not have wanted was to get into a Jewish religious quarrel."

"Exactly," said Sharon. "But now we come to why Christ was sent here in the first place from the judges of the Temple, the Sanhedrin."

"Because He refused to deny He was the Son of God, and God Himself, which was a religious sin."

"No," said Sharon. "Those were the grounds, but not the reason. Can you imagine if I were to go to your Vatican, and announce your Pope was an impostor and that I was really Pope, what would happen?"

"I don't know," said Jim.

"Think. You know."

"I imagine you would be given a sedative and referred for some sort of therapy."

"Right. But imagine thousands of Italians were following me and I had believers all over the world. A little different scenario, eh? With a mob at my back, storming St. Peter's Square."

"You think Christ had a large following then?" said Jim. "Are you sure?"

"What about the multitudes in Galilee? If we can believe the Gospels, which seem highly accurate, He was doing good deeds up and down the land. He was known. People awaited His coming. This is a man popular among the people. No one wants to be responsible for executing a popular man."

"But they certainly want Him out of the way if He has followers," said Jim. "So they pass the buck to Pilate, who also doesn't want to be the one responsible for His death. Rome has no vested interest in taking sides in a religious quarrel."

"Exactly," said Sharon. "Pilate gives Him all the opportunity to get out of it. He doesn't want to be the one to crucify Him. But Christ won't defend Himself. So, Pilate tries to throw it on the backs of the people in the street."

"And the people want Barabbas freed, not Christ," said Jim.

"Or, at least the voices in the mob, and there is evidence many different power centers might have planted them there, to force the Romans to do what they wanted done. Not that the Romans didn't want it done."

"They just didn't want to be the ones to do it," said Jim.

"Exactly," said Sharon. "So, what does Pilate do after the mob cuts off his last escape from being the one to crucify Jesus?"

"He publicly washes his hands and declares Jesus innocent," said Jim.

"He may have felt guilty, too," said Sharon.

"I don't think so," said Jim. "You know, politically, Jesus was crucified not because the Jews were against Him but because so many of them were for Him."

"Exactly. Now let's go into the church. There's something you should see."

* * *

The stone inside the church was one flight down and was part of an ancient Roman street.

"This isn't as deep as Haneviim Street, is it?"

"No," said Sharon. "The depths vary because Jerusalem is made up of hills, and hills mean valleys, and valleys get filled up faster with human debris."

She pointed to one stone in the pavement that had been covered with a clear thick plastic, bolted into the old floor by modern brass screws.

"Here, see, look," said Sharon.

Jim noticed a circle intersected with lines.

"This is the game of Kings, you see. Do you remember when I told you the crown of thorns was not that unusual, because the Romans had this execution game called Kings? Here is the board. And this is where they probably played dice for His robes. Here," said Sharon.

"I just realized I am standing on the Second Station of the Cross. The original one," said Jim. And then he explained that, when Christians in Europe could not make the pilgrimage to Jerusalem to follow in the footsteps of Christ, they made what were called the Stations of the Cross, modeling them on the original Stations of the Cross in Jerusalem. They were the physical places of Christ's suffering.

"Catholic churches have little models of each station around the church, where people stop and pray, reminding themselves of the places here, what happened to Christ at each place. He got the cross here."

"Probably," said Sharon. A guide was coming with his group of pilgrims and Jim saw several women in black enter the room where this street paving was and kneel down, kissing the floor.

"Does it bother you to be here? I can talk outside," said Sharon.

"No. This is all right," said Jim. "It's good. I've got to start thinking like this."

They followed the Via Dolorosa only a short way before it turned sharply south. North, to the right, less than a thousand yards, was the dig on Haneviim Street. A man could carry a cross on his back to there, thought Jim.

"What are you thinking, Jim?" said Sharon.

"I am thinking that Jesus could have reached what is now Haneviim Street. Damascus Gate is right up here to the right, it's closer than the Church of the Holy Sepulcher, isn't it?"

"Yes, but don't jump to conclusions."

"I'm not jumping, I'm just saying," said Jim.

"This is all nebulous conjecture."

"You weren't too nebulous about Pilate."

She took his hand and guided him left, along the Via Dolorosa. It was not known for certain Christ took this way, but the Crusaders had connected the point of Antonia Fortress with the site of the Holy Sepulcher, and declared a winding way between the two as Christ's Street of Sorrows.

In this age, the streets were shop-crowded, smelling of sweets, and sewage, and animal blood.

Arab butchers had the shorn heads of lambs, the dark eyes open in such innocence, stacked on trays, with the blood running down to the tilted ends.

Shops hawked olive-wood crosses and Stars of David. Confectioners showcased large trays of creamy sweets, with the attendant swarms of flies. Arab men sat in front of their shops sipping small cups of sweet coffee.

Arab women, wearing black shrouds decorated with colorful flowers, knelt on the sidewalks selling baskets of fruit, which Sharon warned Jim against because of amoeba poisoning.

Sharon suddenly turned off Via Dolorosa and led him through a narrow side street, where soldiers examined her purse and all the bags of everyone passing through. Jim had gotten used to this now, and hardly noticed when soldiers checked parcels for bombs at public places.

Occasionally a terrorist bomb would go off somewhere and someone would be killed, but it had become somewhat like auto accidents. And Jim thought people could really get used to anything.

The small checkpoint opened to a broad immaculate expanse of limestone descending down to the Wailing Wall on the left and an archaeological dig on the right. Above them were two domes, one gold and one silver. Jim followed the groups of people descending toward the Wailing Wall, then felt Sharon's hand pulling him back.

"Wait," she said. "Up here you can see it all. The whole area is the Temple Mount, and this is where we get to Herod, and Caiaphas, who is the high priest, and the Sadducees and Pharisees."

"I used to get them confused as a kid. Especially when you throw in the Sanhedrin."

"There is one thing they all had in common," said Sharon.

"What's that?" said Jim.

"The ordinary Jew didn't like them."

"Then Jesus becomes more dangerous."

Sharon made an arch with her hands signifying a great expanse in front of them.

"Now, today, on top, it is all Islamic. The gold dome on the left is the Dome of the Rock, where Muhammad was said to have risen up to heaven on his horse, leaving a footprint in a rock there."

"I've seen pictures of the gold dome. It's quite large. And the silver dome on the right?"

"That is Al Aksa Mosque. Those two mosques could easily have fit into what the Second Temple was. It had the finest woods and imported marbles and basalt. We have found some of the columns through excavations. It was glorious. And it was Herod the Great's gift to the Jews and to the priests."

"But he was on bad terms with his subjects, wasn't he?" said Jim.

"Absolutely. That's why this great builder, one of the truly great builders of the ancient world, gave them the Temple. But the Sadducees, who were in charge of it, didn't trust him and were always plotting against him."

"The Sadducees were the priests of the Temple," said Jim.

"Hereditary priests from the line of the Maccabees," said Sharon. "Caiaphas was the high priest, and that is something special to the Jews, so special that the post hasn't existed since the fall of that Second Temple."

"The Orthodox believe the Temple cannot be rebuilt until the Messiah comes, and therefore, without a temple, they cannot have that high priest, correct?"

"Father, you are absolutely correct," said Sharon. She smiled in slight surprise.

"I studied a bit of Judaism," said Jim.

"Grade A, Jesuit," said Sharon. "So, now look at what we have. A Herodian dynasty the subjects hate, priests committed to the purity of the most sacred site really being swingers in their own way; rabbis who are supposed to bring Judaism to the people being involved in legalism; a Roman procurator who only wants to be on all sides and keep the peace, and into this all . . ."

"Into this all at the most heated time of Passover," said Jim, "comes Jesus of Nazareth."

"Who is said to raise the dead, heal the sick, feed the hungry, and claiming to be 'King of the Jews.' "

Sharon threw up her hands as though she had completed her scenario proving why Jesus had so many political enemies. She headed down toward the giant retaining wall that had marked off the area of the Second Temple, the left of which is now revered by the Jews as their Wailing Wall.

But this time, Jim did not follow.

"You didn't finish," he said.

"I did. I did," said Sharon. "That's just who everyone was. You have it."

"I have more. I have the clay wall in the tomb. That's what you were working on."

"I am a senior lecturer at Hebrew University, and I will tell you when I have something worked out and when I don't."

"But you did, Sharon. You showed me how everyone wanted Jesus out of the way, and why no one wanted to be the one to do it. But Pilate, in the Gospels, was also warned of claims that the body might rise. That's why the stone was there, and the soldiers were there."

"I am the archaeologist, and I don't want you going any further until we complete more technical work."

"But all of a sudden, Roman soldiers, the most disciplined possibly in all history, fall asleep. And the stone, the great stone, is rolled aside," said Jim.

"The Bible is full of miracles," said Sharon. "I don't like to smoke here, and I need a cigarette, so let's see the big dig now, near the old Second Temple steps."

"Sharon, all those who feared Jesus in life feared what would happen to the body. They even had to get the body out of politics. So, what did they do to hide it best? They hid it in a niche of a cave behind a wall the color of the cave.''

"It wasn't their cave, it was Joseph of Arimathea's, a friend of Jesus," said Sharon.

"It was their friend Pilate's soldiers, and their stone."

"Ah, but you see how it backfired on them? Would they do something that backfired?" said Sharon.

"I am at a loss as to what political harm ever came to either Pilate, Herod Antipas, Caiaphas, the Sadducees or their judges, the Sanhedrin, or the Pharisees from the crucifixion and believed Resurrection of Jesus Christ.''

"You don't believe that," said Sharon.

"No," said Jim. "You do." And on that he followed Sharon down to the dig.

Heading toward the Wailing Wall was a group of young Hasidic boys in dark coats and hats, a few of them carrying guitars. Sharon said it was a new movement among the Hasidim to sing what she described as "almost rock songs" to God.

The boys went to the left of the path that led up to the Islamic holy places, while Jim and Sharon went to the right.

Previously, the path had been part of a hill, which ended at the exposed retaining wall, for centuries the holiest spot in Judaism. "Only because they didn't know the rest of the wall was under the ground. But the left side is now the holy spot, and the right, a dig showing the beauty of Herodian stones."

"You didn't terrify me with your scenario, Sharon. I am still here."

"Maybe you scared me after you told me it is all on my head."

"No, Sharon. It's been on mine. It is mine."

Jim saw tourist groups enter with a guide. One guide with a Canadian group pointed out in English that that was Dr. Sharon Golban of Hebrew University, an archaeologist who had given a lecture once to a group of guides.

Jim could see Sharon was a bit embarrassed. He also noticed his own arm was around her waist. He took it away.

The steps Christ had walked on were south of the retaining wall partially reconstructed for tourists. Sharon explained to Jim that the City of David went on down into the Kidron Valley, and there were raging debates among archaeologists as to where certain levels were.

The entrances to the Second Temple had been stoned over centuries before, but Sharon pointed to their outlines.

"Christ drove the money changers out through those portals, didn't He?" asked Jim.

"Yes, and do you know what they were doing there?"

"Blaspheming, I guess."

"Only partly. They were also stopping blasphemy."

"I don't understand," said Jim.

"All right, a clue. We had a diaspora, even then. My family was in Persia, and we made a pilgrimage to the Temple for Passover. So did the Jews from Alexandria, Athens, and Rome. What did they bring with them as a donation to the Temple?"

"Sacrifices?"

"Come on, Jim, you are so smart. They couldn't bring jars of fruit and cattle those distances. What travels well?"

"Money."

"Right. Now, why was the Pilatus coin we found with just the 'P' on it real, and that coin with Emperor Augustus you bought strange to this area? Why didn't Pilatus mint coins with Augustus on them?"

And then Jim suddenly remembered the Dominican chapel with only the book in it and no statuary to offend Muslim and Jewish sensibilities.

"The coins had graven images on them. The coins of Athens, Persia, and Rome had to be exchanged for ones without images on them," said Jim.

"The money changers were there to exchange currencies."

Sharon led him back along to the dig to the excavated extension of the western retaining wall.

Jim already knew what the colors of stones meant. Those blackened above on the retaining wall on the south side of the Muslim path in the middle were those exposed to the air for centuries. But the richer, golden stones were those unearthed by an archaeological dig. He was amazed at the great size and perfection of the Herodian stones, giant multiton blocks between which not a knife blade could fit.

Jim looked at the stone with the face sheared off. He tried

imagining a fire so hot that it could do that to the very stone. It must have been an awesome horror, he thought. The people must have thought it was the end of the world.

And then, strangely, the stones began to sing. Voices came from them. The voices were all around him. They sang in Hebrew. And he heard the guitar beat, and the joy, the rousing joy of the Hebrew song. He knew the words.

"Purify my soul, O Lord, that I may do Thy will."

But it was so joyous, like a cheerleading section at a football game, and it was coming from the Temple Mount.

Jim looked to Sharon, stunned. The top was Muslim.

"Acoustics. The stones carry the sound. Herod put the stones dead set against bedrock. Vibrations carry. They aren't muffled by earth. On the other side of the path is the Wailing Wall. The religious boys we saw are singing."

Jim looked up at the dark layer of earth, cinders from burning, earth from waste, and the stones seemed to sing with the joy of the young Hasidic boys.

The greatest army in the world had destroyed in a single holocaust the greatest temple in the land, driving out the Jews from the city.

And yet, from the ashes came the living voices of the Jews, singing the praises of the Lord. Christ had outlived the Temple, as He predicted. And the Jews had outlived the Roman legions, as no one could have predicted.

When God chose, no man could put asunder.

Jim understood now the mystical union Brother Maurice had talked about. The Jews, like the Church, would be here till the last, labored tick of time, and Jesus returned with the first morning of forever.

Jim looked at Sharon pressed against the wall. The critic of all holy men had her face against the stones. She was kissing them and crying.

And when she noticed Jim was looking at her, she said:

"The sun collects heat on the stone. You can feel it if you put your face there."

And he understood now why she had been so willing to give up her dig. She loved her country, even if she didn't love the politicians.

* * *

At the other end of the Via Dolorosa was the Church of the
Holy Sepulcher, which by tradition enclosed both Golgotha,
where Christ was crucified, and the tomb from which He rose,
the Holy Sepulcher.

It was a large, dark old church that seemed to ramble on in
many directions. Where Golgotha was supposed to be, a Greek
Orthodox priest was offering candles for sale. They had the left
side of the altar. The Franciscans had the right. The Armenians
had incensing rights.

The Copts had the back of the tomb, where they sold crosses,
and someone else had the glittery marble front.

Upstairs were the Abyssinians and Copts, one of which had
locked the other out of their praying quarters. There had been
fights here with brooms over who swept where, indicating terri-
torial rights, and many Easters ago there had been a riot and
fistfights over the holy flames.

Jim knew the whole sorry tale. But while it bothered him,
Sharon seemed oblivious. She went into rapturous detail about
the positioning of old stones proving this spot was more likely the Holy Sepulcher than another tomb found later, even
though the other tomb looked much more like what a Second
Temple tomb should look like. It was limestone, and the one in
the Church of the Holy Sepulcher was imported marble.

"But you see the original tomb and hill of Golgotha were cut
down by the mad Caliph of Cairo, Hakim. That desecration of
Christian sites helped bring on the Crusades. Whereupon the
Crusaders did some desecrating of their own when they arrived,
which helped bring on the Arab response. And so on, et
cetera."

Jim remembered what Pesci had said about the Crusades not
really ending here. Nothing seemed to end here.

And yet people lived here. They got along here and they did
business here, despite the furious divisions.

Jim tried to explain why it bothered him that there was such
contention about rights to spaces.

"What is valuable here is not who has which right to which
space in time, because we're really dealing with eternity. It is
not the rocks, but the soul," said Jim.

"Look, we all have some special thing we like to believe

makes us more prone to good than others. But why should Christians be any better than anyone else?''

"We should be better than we are," said Jim.

"So should everyone else," said Sharon.

"That bothers me and I don't know why."

"Because I am not going to argue with you," she said, and took his hand and led him from the Church of the Holy Sepulcher.

Out in the courtyard, she explained that it was the Roman Emperor Hadrian who really provided the best evidence for supporting this as the spot of the Holy Sepulcher. He built pagan temples on all Jewish and Christian holy spots, and what he covered up was a limestone cave and a little hill.

"How did he know which was the spot?" asked Jim.

"Good question, Jim. We don't know. We can only surmise. Maybe Christians told him, but would they tell him the right spot? After all, he was an enemy."

"Weren't the Jews driven out of Jerusalem a generation after Jesus' death?"

"Very shrewd, Jim. Let's get out of here."

"You've done more work."

"This guess is just a guess and let's not go into it," said Sharon.

"Let's have it," said Jim.

"You know it is just supposition."

"I do."

"All right, I don't think the tomb of Jesus was revered at the beginning. I think it was avoided, like the cross itself."

"It doesn't bother me that there would be no reliable witness to tell Emperor Hadrian that this was the real place of the Holy Sepulcher. This is just stone here. You are onto something more."

"Remember, Christ was not really a martyr in the traditional sense. He was the movement. His apostles had given up everything to follow him. They were totally invested in Him."

"Which means?"

"Which means they had to be incredibly distraught, and in that state a Mary Magdalene could see the back of an empty tomb, and then imagine a risen Christ, and then go on to the apostles in that awful state they were in and tell them, 'He is risen.' And then they too would see Him.''

"And that is a scenario," said Jim, controlling all his feelings, putting on his best of faces.

"I mean, Peter had given up his fishing, and Matthew his tax collecting, and . . ."

"I know," said Jim. "Thank you."

"I'm sorry."

"No. Thank you," said Jim. "Is there anything else?"

"It was just one of many, many possible scenarios," said Sharon.

Jim smiled at her. She was doing her job. She offered many other possible scenarios that afternoon, but they all seemed somewhat desperate, and they were all delivered while intently watching Jim's eyes for reactions.

The rains came again and they were cold. The winter rains of Jerusalem had a special bitterness all their own.

15

Righteous Gentile

Jim knelt and raised his hands before the body on the stone.

He held a thin-edged palette that he was supposed to push forward along the base of the niche very gently, while Sharon, with a board padded with gauze and cotton underneath, ever so carefully tried to keep the bones in place. What they were hoping for was that the polyvinyl coating would hold everything in place, with the help of the light pressure from the cotton and the gauze. If he heard any breaking, Jim was to stop and they would pack each bone separately.

Sharon was on one side, and had to lean over. Jim could feel her breast press against his forehead as he moved the palette forward. It was distracting. She was wearing only an old shirt and slacks. She had taken off her old army jacket and dumped it by the chemical pots, which had become laborious by now to empty. They were filling up with moisture too rapidly, and it was good that the cases were now ready for the movement of the bones and disk.

Already, the disk was in its small case. It would go to a safe in Hebrew University. The body had a moisture-controlled lab waiting for it just south of the city. Sharon had come up with an even better idea for the lab. Why not rent another in the Galilee, where so many crucifixions occurred, and thereby the pathologist would assume that body was unearthed there?

Jerusalem and Christ were just too synonymous, especially since Jim had said he was leaning toward an American or European pathologist, because at this point in civilization Europe and America provided the best doctors. And that meant Christian-oriented.

The palette inched along the stone. It went under the bones just at stone level. Jim thought he heard something.

"Go ahead. Go ahead, it's alright," said Sharon.

Jim pushed farther, steady, his body moving the thin palette, waiting to hear a break from the fragile bones, waiting to hear even a turning.

"Careful, careful. That's it. Go ahead. Go ahead. Slow."

Sharon guided him. In all, it took fifteen minutes to ever so slowly get the palette between the stone and the bones.

"I don't know how you did it," said Sharon, straightening. "My back is killing me."

"I'm use to being on my knees," said Jim. "Remembering who I am."

"Yes," said Sharon. "Well, you see you have good training for something, then."

They taped the board to the palette, so that they had a sandwich of their protected material, and then, with Jim on one end and Sharon on the other, they moved the bones to an open, black plastic case with sides as thick as auto tires.

If downed at sea, it would float. A knife could not puncture it and it could withstand an auto accident.

"Did you notice the jaw still didn't move at all?" said Sharon. "You think we definitely have carbon-dating material then?"

"I think we do," said Sharon. "We might even get some of the cross."

She photographed the empty niche, and then carefully, with a magnifying glass and a camel's hair brush, whisked whatever she could find into a case.

"There's no wood there," said Sharon.

"Oh," said Jim, not thinking about the wood, but thinking about how her hair this day fell over her shoulders.

"Well, not finding wood won't matter if we can get material holding that jaw in place," said Sharon.

The disk was already in its case by the door, a shiny metal traveling case that Sharon had suggested when the plastic cases were taking too long to manufacture. Because the disk was so hard, the extra precaution would not be needed as much. Packing it with cotton would do.

"Well, I guess we can leave," said Sharon.

"I guess we can," said Jim. He had entered this tomb more than three months before, not even knowing about loci and coins of the Second Temple period, and the politics of the place. He could now often tell one stone from another, the Herodian being large with a border like a picture frame, and the Maccabees preferring to dress the faces of their stones with pick marks, like iron rain upon the face.

He could use Hebrew easily, and he had learned that if he had turned away from a fact his Church would have to face it on harder terms later. It would now be science that would carefully examine things the human eye could not perceive. Nowadays, they could even tell what the bones had done for a living.

In the history of man, never had the knowing powers of science been so abundant. The more Jim had discussed with Sharon what was available, the more he was sure that disproving evidence was going to be available.

Sharon lowered herself to walk up the steps, putting the metal case before her. The light was dreary from the winter day. Jim followed, pushing his black case in front of him lengthwise, and thus the body left the tomb after centuries.

Something banged the metal case, loud and hard, knocking it from Sharon's hand. There was a big dent in it. Another crash came, shattering splinters of rock like shrapnel, making a big white mark of impact at the bedrock outside the tomb door.

Sharon reached for her case. Jim suddenly felt a sharp pain in his upper back. Something hit him there. Something hit the case again. Rocks. People were throwing rocks from above. They were being stoned.

He stumbled out to Sharon, and got her back into the cave, covering her body with his. She wanted to get her case, but he wouldn't let her. The rocks could kill them, coming down three stories like that, especially if they were being thrown with force.

One bounced harmlessly off the black case, and he pulled that back into the tomb. They were pinned down there by an artillery of rocks.

He saw the lower ladder jiggle at its base. Someone was descending. He reached for the metal case. A rock cracked close, sending hard limestone fragments into his palm, wounding it.

Yelling came from above. It sounded like Yiddish.

"What are you doing? What are you doing?" he yelled in Hebrew.

But there was no answer in a language he understood.

"What are they yelling?" asked Jim.

"I don't know."

"That's Yiddish, right?"

"I think so. I don't know."

"Great, a Jew who doesn't speak Yiddish."

"What do I need Yiddish for? My parents spoke Farsi. Persian's my first language. Hebrew is my next, and third is Arabic . . ."

"Shh. We don't have time."

A black shoe encased in black tight wrappings appeared, followed by billowing black pants. It had to be the ultra-Orthodox. When the man was at dig level Jim lunged for the case. He felt a blow as the man fell on him. Then another man had his arm, and another had another arm. They were attacking the dig in force. Sharon was out of the cave, screaming. The case was wrenched from beneath Jim, like a log powered by a Roman sling. Jim heard Sharon yelling. Something was ripping. Jim got an arm free. Then another arm. Then his leg was free. They were running. Sharon was ripping her own blouse. The ultra-Orthodox were fleeing her bare breasts.

"Animals," she yelled at them in Hebrew. "Superstitious animals."

Jim got to the last ultra-Orthodox with a good punch in his back. But the case was already on top of the first level with the first one.

It was a useless, futile punch of helplessness. Another rock came down, and Jim got Sharon back into the cave, while under the cover of the rocks, the black-coated men made their escape. Jim took off his own shirt to cover Sharon, who was crying in uncontrollable anger. He had come to Jerusalem on a holy mission for his Pope and now he was punching rabbis.

"Animals. Animals. Animals," she sobbed.

"They must have heard those rumors about bodies being here," said Jim.

"They're from Mea Shearim, where the animals live."

"We've got to get the disk back," said Jim. And then he felt the cuts on his forehead and the pain in his back and noticed how fragments of limestone were still imbedded in his palm.

Sharon tended to him, and he felt her tears on his palm, and the salt stung, but it was warm and good, and his own shirt opened, and he noticed how perfectly formed her shadowed breasts were, how the nipples darkened at the end, where gold became dark brown. And he thought he should tell her to close the shirt he had given her, but he did not want her to stop tending his palm, so he said nothing, and even as he looked at her exposed breast, he told himself he could easily avert his eyes if he had to.

Mendel Hirsch was reviewing the month-long Christmas schedule. At shortly after noon on the twenty-fourth, His Beatitude, the Latin Patriarch, accompanied by clergy, was to leave the Latin Patriarchate in Jerusalem for the square opposite the Citadel in the Jaffa Gate, where they were to collect their cars for the procession to Bethlehem. Fifteen minutes later the Armenians were scheduled to ring the bells of their churches. By 1:15 P.M. His Beatitude had to be through the small ceremony at Rachel's tomb on the way to Bethlehem, and be at Manger Square no later, absolutely no later, than 2:15 P.M.

At 12:45, simultaneously with the Armenian bells, the Greek Orthodox in Bethlehem were to place their icons in the grotto of the Nativity and ring their bells.

If anything went wrong with the first processions on the day before Christmas, disaster would be reaped at the midnight Pontifical High Mass and could foul up everything right through Epiphany. The meaning of Christmas was quite clear to Mendel Hirsch, as it had been to Jordanian, Briton, and Turk before him. Timing. And it was this timing that had to be so well coordinated, because if it weren't, the Greek Orthodox dragoman might be banging head on into His Beatitude, the Latin Patriarch, to say nothing of the Copts and the Syrian Church. And this disaster would go on right through late January.

Suddenly his phone was ringing. The municipal police,

which had been told to keep a casual eye on the dig at Haneviim Street, had some bad news.

An ultra-Orthodox sect had set upon the archaeologist in the dig, apparently causing minor harm, from eyewitness accounts, and the archaeologists had gone looking for the group in Mea Shearim itself.

What should the police do? They were not allowed to do anything in relationship to the dig without clearing it with Mendel's office first.

"You have done everything, now stay out. Thank you," said Mendel, and immediately looked up a number without an explanation beside it in a little pad in the top drawer of his desk.

"There has been some trouble at the dig," said Mendel. "We need the help we discussed . . . No. I do not know exactly what happened, but there has been some physical violence to Pesci's man."

Within fifteen minutes two carloads of very dark young men had pulled into the courtyard outside Mendel's office. They were from the Mossad, and, as planned, they were Yemeni.

It was important that an Ashkenazi, who would be familiar with Christianity, not be used. They had to be Sephardi but, as Mendel had specifically requested, not Moroccans. Moroccans, he felt, were animals. Prone to violence, lazy, irresponsible, and generally untrustworthy.

Yemeni, on the other hand, were intelligent, honest, and reluctant to go for their guns, and, most important, very effective.

Mendel and the Mossad men got to Mea Shearim within four minutes, and quickly found Father Folan and Sharon Golban wandering around the quarter trying to question passersby, looking for their attackers.

Father Folan had a cut on his forehead. His hand was bandaged. He moved his left arm with pain, occasionally rubbing the back of his right thigh.

Mendel sent two Yemeni Mossad to get Father Folan and Sharon into the car.

Jim was startled to see a black man touch him on the arm in the middle of Mea Shearim. Only when they addressed him in Hebrew did he realize these young men in winter jackets and dungarees were Israelis. He was also carrying a concealed weapon under the jacket. Jim saw a bit of the shoulder holster.

Then Jim saw the car.

"It's Mendel," he said.

"We'll get those animals now," said Sharon.

Mendel wanted to know what had happened, and Sharon poured out a story of barbarism. Jim interrupted.

"They took the disk. We were removing the disk and the body from the tomb, and they attacked us with rocks from above. They got the disk. We have to get it back."

"Animals," said Sharon.

"We know the group. They are the troublemakers who follow the Reb Nechtal," said Mendel. "We know where they live around here."

"We can get the disk, do you think?" said Jim.

"And throw them in jail," said Sharon.

"If they attacked you, yes. I guess," said Mendel.

"No," said Jim. "I don't want a trial."

"If I may intrude," said the Mossad man from the front seat, in Hebrew, "I think we ought to establish what we want before we enter the home of the Reb Nechtal."

"I want the disk," said Jim. "We've got to have it back."

"The disk," said Mendel.

"And we do not want a court trial or anything else that would entail publicity, I take it."

"Correct," said Mendel.

"Then, I would suggest we not let them know that. We should make this appear like a police raid on them."

"Isn't it?" said Sharon.

"Not if we are as vulnerable as they are, and they have something we want," said the Yemeni officer.

"What is it, then?" said Sharon.

"It's a negotiation," said Jim somberly.

"Do you think you can reason with animals?" asked Sharon. Jim was struck by the neatness of this quarter. The buildings were very plain, with little, hidden courtyards, and before one entered the quarter one saw many signs admonishing modest dress.

The Reb Nechtal's home was on Avraham Mislonim Street. The Yemeni officer knocked on the door, announcing himself as a policeman. But there was no answer. A crowd of ultra-Orthodox men in black hats and black pantaloons began massing at both ends of the street.

"Mendel, I think you should talk," said Jim. "They are not going to talk in Hebrew, and that officer doesn't know Yiddish."

"Right," said Mendel.

"Not talk in Hebrew, where the hell do they think they are? Some Polish ghetto?" said Sharon. Mendel glanced at Sharon with a fast frown.

"Not you," said Sharon to Mendel.

The Yemeni officer had extra kepahs in his jacket, little cookie-sized head coverings, to be clipped on to the back of a man's head so that, according to the Talmud, the head would be covered before God. A handkerchief was procured for Sharon.

A woman opened the door. She was elderly, and wore an ornamental kerchief.

A dark-haired man in his mid-thirties, with a ferocious-looking beard, stood behind her. He and Mendel spoke in Yiddish.

Jim tried to make out what was being said, but couldn't. The street was filling up, both sides massing with men and boys in dark coats and dark hats.

The Yemeni officer very casually, and smiling pleasantly, went back to the car, and just as casually had the driver move a microphone over beneath the window, where he radioed his contact in the Jerusalem police.

At that moment three special units of the Jerusalem municipal police positioned themselves just outside Mea Shearim, and waited.

Jim looked around. Indeed, this probably was like a Polish ghetto, which was right. The Jews, like the Christians, had gone out to the four corners of the world and, like the Christians, had returned as many peoples with many different customs. A Polish ghetto was as valid a religious trapping as Latin for the Mass. Everything seemed to come home to Jerusalem.

Mendel returned. He had been speaking to Zalman, the Reb Nechtal's assistant. He and Jim could enter, but the unclean woman could not.

"That shit," said Sharon.

"He says you exposed yourself or something. In any case, he will not allow you in the Reb Nechtal's house."

"I think Sharon should be with us. She is the ranking archaeologist," said Jim.

"What do animals care about archaeologists? They operate on smell, not credentials."

"Ask Zalman who has authority here for his group," said Jim.

"It's the Reb Nechtal," said Mendel. "They follow him in everything in their lives, they look to him."

"Is he called an authority unto himself?" asked Jim.

"You mean Fascist," said Sharon.

"No. No," said Jim. "Every rabbi has to quote the Talmud as his authority. These men are so respected that it is assumed they have the Talmud within them."

"They can make up whatever they want, then?" said Sharon.

"No. No. It's exactly the opposite," said Jim. "They have studied the Talmud so impeccably that no one would assume they would make up anything. But, if there is something new, which is unlikely, they are so respected that they are considered equal to those rabbis quoted in the Talmud."

"So I should ask Zalman if the Reb Nechtal is one of those," said Mendel.

"And say we ask an audience with him, that we have a dispute and that we would like to resolve it. Don't get into whose law we are going to resolve it through, just stress 'resolve.' A dispute to be resolved, resolution."

"What makes you think that will work?" said Mendel. "I ask because we have some clout. We can cut off their garbage collection, and we've done that, and generally squeeze them. They do respond to that at times."

"They must know that. And it will help the reasoning process," said Jim.

"Reasoning is not what they do," said Sharon. "They wouldn't be that way if they had any reasoning at all."

"It's all reasoning," said Jim.

He watched Mendel approach Zalman, who looked at Jim suspiciously. With an abrupt movement, Zalman beckoned Jim and Mendel to enter. Jim and Mendel followed Zalman through a small courtyard, and into a large room that looked like a library, with a balcony all around. There were books on shelves all the way up to the balcony, where even now young men and old were coming to stand and look down.

In a corner, behind a large wooden desk, was the object of this reverence and attention, a white-bearded old man in a skullcap, with parchment flesh, and light-blue eyes. He did not look up, nor did he move, but seemed to contemplate his frail hands. Zalman took an honored place to his right.

Neither Mendel nor Jim was to address the Reb Nechtal, it was understood. There were chairs brought by young students for Jim and Mendel.

It was too late now to review his Talmudic logic, but even if he had had months it might not help. So complex and deep was the study of Jewish law that the Gospels themselves considered it worthy of mention that Jesus, before manhood, had discussed law with the elders. For Jews of the time, it was considered virtually a miracle, definitely a sign.

Word came back from Zalman that the Reb Nechtal indeed was one of those who was an authority unto himself. No matter, thought Jim, even an ordinary rabbi would have to be more learned than Jim in this matter. It required a lifetime.

The Talmud was both laws and commentaries on the laws growing since Moses came down from Mount Sinai with the Ten Commandments.

Books were only the written portions of the Talmud. Jim remembered his teacher saying many contended the Talmud had no beginning or end. No end because as man studied the Talmud it grew with the men themselves. No beginning because every written book of the Talmud referred to a previous book including the first.

The Reb Nechtal undoubtedly would use the stricter Palestinian Talmud codified in the five decades at the end of the fourth century instead of the later Babylonian.

"Mendel," said Jim, "thank the Reb Nechtal for letting us appear before him to resolve the dispute," said Jim.

Mendel repeated in Yiddish to Zalman what Jim had said. Zalman answered:

"He says he would be happy to decide, according to the law, what should be done," said Mendel to Jim.

"No. Thank him for accepting us into his house and hearing us in his house, in which he has authority," said Jim, and Mendel did that, and Zalman answered that the law had authority over all of them.

"Nothing greater than the law of God was there"—this, to Jim in English, from Mendel, with Jim sure that Mendel had added the word "God," because Zalman would never say it, but use an abbreviation, the name being too holy to pronounce.

"Ask the Reb Nechtal that Sharon be admitted because she is a scientist," said Jim, and then added that he thought the nature of what they were doing was going to come up, and that Sharon should be there when it did.

To this there was a loud protest. Jim heard a buzzing up on the balcony.

"He says she is unclean because she bared her breasts before men, many men, in a wanton display, and this is not something to bring before the Reb Nechtal."

"Say that she did that to save a life, not as a sexual enticement," said Jim, and Mendel translated that into Yiddish, and returned to Jim with this:

"The law is the law. It was sexual, because that was why they did not stay."

And Jim answered that that was their interpretation, but it would not necessarily apply to a woman saving a man's life. "You must be subjective in the interpretation. Not absolute."

Mendel repeated this. Jim could see a smile crack across the face of Zalman, black beard revealing white teeth. And laughing, he asked, according to Mendel, who is this man who instructs us in the Talmud? Where did he study? Who was his rabbi?

"I think we'd better stick with threatening their garbage. It works better in the summer than the fall, but they're not certain what is down here on Haneviim Street," said Mendel.

"Tell them that I am a Gentile, and that I studied at a Gentile school in America," said Jim.

"Are you sure you want me to say that?" said Mendel.

"Yes," said Jim, and as soon as the Yiddish came out of Mendel's mouth there was laughter from the balcony. Even Zalman was laughing. The only one not laughing at Jim was the

Reb Nechtal himself. His clear blue eyes now focused on Jim, indicating nothing.

When the laughter abated, Zalman asked, through Mendel, what they taught of the Talmud at this Gentile school? Do they teach you can eat ham, or that you can blaspheme? What do Gentiles teach about Jews?

And Jim remembered his first lecture from the teacher he later met on the plane to Rome, the man whose personal life forbade him to be here on this mission.

"Tell him they teach that the reason why someone does something is important. That the Talmud is not an absolute instrument, but a subjective one that needs man."

"I think you'd better rethink that," said Mendel.

"Say it," said Jim.

Mendel glanced nervously up to the balconies.

"The Talmud is what they live for. I don't think you understand what it means. Which is understandable, if you understand? You see . . ." said Mendel. He pressed his hands against the pants legs. He was wiping off perspiration.

"Say it," said Jim.

"You mean you're counting on the fact that we are in the Reb's house and they won't kill us," said Mendel. "People die by accident, you know. Things get out of hand, you know."

"They don't speak English, I don't speak Yiddish, they won't speak Hebrew, Mendel, say it."

"And what do I tell His Eminence if something happens to you?"

"You're assuming it's going to be me who's hurt, not you."

Mendel appreciated that. He smiled. Zalman was making more jokes, to continued laughter.

"What is he saying?"

"He is saying we are trying to figure out whether ham is supposed to be eaten before or after prayers," said Mendel. "Give me again what you want."

"That the Talmud is subjective, not absolute. That is what they teach. The Talmud needs man as much as man needs the Talmud."

"You didn't say that before. That's more," said Mendel.

"I'm saying it."

Mendel began. Zalman was still bubbling with his newfound

humor. Mendel spoke slowly. The mirth left the pale face of Zalman, the brows narrowed and the eyes became dark.

Up on the balcony the little buzzing sounds of side conversations stopped. The room became deathly quiet.

And when Mendel had finished, the room could hear him swallow. Then Zalman began, the voice rising to a shrill pitch, the face becoming red, the finger pointing at Mendel and Jim. One of the men on the balcony banged something and then there were many bangings, and the room shook, and Jim saw one young man climb over the balcony in a frenzy.

Mendel tried desperately to keep up with the translating, but Jim knew what was being said. Blasphemy in the house of the Reb Nechtal, blasphemy against the Talmud, blasphemy against the one whose name dared not be mentioned. Blasphemy with the whore of Haneviim Street, whom Jim wanted to bring in here.

And then an old hand reached out to the wildly waving arm of Zalman. And when Zalman, in his own frenzy, did not see that hand, another man banged him harshly. For it was the hand of the Reb Nechtal.

The Reb Nechtal spoke. It was one word.

"What did he say?" asked Jim. "What did he say?"

Mendel wasn't translating. Finally, Mendel turned to Jim:

"He says you're right. You're absolutely correct."

And then the Reb Nechtal spoke again. And Mendel translated:

"He says Zalman is wrong."

How Zalman was wrong and the Gentile was right would be spoken of in Mea Shearim long after that day. It would be remembered how well the Gentile knew the Talmud, even though he sometimes did not know specifically which rabbi supported which interpretation. It would be repeated often in the quarter of Mea Shearim how the Reb Nechtal himself helped the Gentile with quotations even as the good rabbi argued with him.

How that day of argument went would become a lesson in learning for all.

The Gentile contended, and was correct, that the woman exposing her breasts to save someone's life was not a sin, because the purpose was not sexual but merciful. And so the woman was brought in, but she was indeed dressed immodestly, with arms exposed and wearing the pants of men. And everyone knew, even if that act was not a sin, that this was the sort of woman who would do those sins, and end up, it was sure to everyone, a prostitute dead in the gutter.

Because even when her arms were covered, her mouth was not. She was one of those who dug up graves to look at bones, who treated the dead with shame.

The Gentile, on the other hand, understood that it was an impurity to look upon the dead, and that it was a commandment and a good deed, a mitzvah, that Jews should see the Jewish dead were properly treated. He understood that the Reb's followers used as their authority the teachings of the Talmud.

His authorities were other books, which included some of the philosophy of the Talmud. He also came by authority from his spiritual leader. He too was bound by law.

Wisely, the Gentile established exactly what a body was, therefore also establishing what rights it had, and what obligations Jews had toward it.

A body, according to the law, was any portion of a human bone larger than an olive.

Then, the Gentile openly admitted, a body had been found in the cave on Haneviim Street. But he pointed out there was no indication it had been buried properly.

There was no cloth around it, as was custom. Moreover, there was indication the man had died violently, so the man might not be buried at all, but abandoned waiting to be buried. And when he was asked if there were any other bodies around, he said no. But when he said it was older than centuries, one could not assume it had not been properly buried in a cemetery at that time, because the cemetery might have disappeared. Therefore, one could not assume it was not a body in a proper grave, instead of an accident, waiting to be transported to one and buried.

The body had to stay in the grave. It could not be moved.

What, asked the Gentile, if it had already been moved? And the Reb Nechtal answered that the Gentile would know that, and could answer that. And should answer it.

And the Gentile answered, in truth, that it had not been moved from the tomb, and this was accepted, because the Gentile had no obligation to admit there was a body there in the first place. He could have lied as easily as scientists found they could lie.

But he didn't. And he made this promise, that he, himself, wanted to find out the identity of this body, that he might find out if the man was a Gentile and not a Jew, in which case the Reb Nechtal and his followers would be freed from any obligation toward the body.

But Zalman said any investigation was a desecration, and then the Gentile brought up the crucial point!

What happened to all the Jewish bodies in lands of the Gentiles, where sometimes no respect was given the living Jews, let alone dead ones?

Therefore they were not obliged to give a proper burial, Jim said, but only to try to give the bodies a proper burial. And on this the Reb Nechtal smiled, for everyone later would know that the Gentile had surmised what was in the Talmud, when he didn't really know for sure.

And an agreement was made that the body would get a proper burial, and this would fulfill the Reb Nechtal's obligations. But it would be after the Gentile's investigation, which would fulfill his obligations. At all times the body would be treated with respect. But the Reb Nechtal said the body could not be moved around, for it might fall into untrustworthy hands. So, it was agreed that one of the followers of Reb Nechtal would be the one to sit on the chair above the hole and make sure the body never left.

The Gentile agreed, saying he too was bound by what was possible. But the Reb Nechtal insisted that it be the Gentile who was responsible for it all, not the woman who used the sacred language for common talk, or the government official. If the Gentile was the one who was responsible, then they all had done what they could do. And what the Gentile wanted, that the suitcase be returned that day, would be done. And there were apologies for any physical hurts, because that should not have been, said the Reb Nechtal.

And then he proclaimed his reasoning by his Talmudic authority, why the Gentile should be trusted above Jews.

For Jim it was the first word he understood of the Reb Nechtal, and they had been discussing the Talmud for almost three full hours. And he was mentally numb with exhaustion.

These words were in Hebrew because they were holy writ:

"The righteous Gentile is as blessed as the high priest himself."

And Jim knew the Reb Nechtal was talking of the only man in the Hebrew race allowed to utter the name of the holiest of holies, and this only once a year, and this when the Temple was once again standing. A man who could not exist for the Jews again until the Third Temple was built, when the Messiah came.

Outside, Sharon commented on the fact that the body could not be removed from the cave. She said, "Well, he really stuck it to us, didn't he?"

"What are you going to do, Father?" said Mendel.

But Jim was not listening. He did not know it, but the crowds that were now surrounding their slow-moving car leaving the quarter of Mea Shearim had come to see the Gentile who had successfully argued law with the Reb Nechtal himself, the righteous one.

16

Christmas

The problems were enormous, and Jim returned with Sharon to her apartment to discuss them, unless, of course, as Sharon pointed out, it was "still an occasion of sin, or larger than an olive," whichever Jim and his new friend in Mea Shearim would decide.

"Where does the olive come in?"

"You agreed that a bone became a body at the scientifically established size of an olive. Ah, but Reb Folan, are we talking about a ripe olive, a new olive, olive oil, does that constitute olive? And what about the Spanish olive, or is that Gentile olive, and only for special occasions, is it righteous?"

Sharon went into her bathroom to change. She was still wearing Jim's shirt from the afternoon. Jim waited in her bedroom-living room combination, looking at the lights of Jerusalem at night.

In the distance was the Knesset on the left, and up above the valley which housed Hebrew University was the white, ice-cream cone mosaic top of the Dome of the Book, where the Dead Sea Scrolls were housed.

Sharon's bed was unmade, and quite broad with a brown bedspread rumpled at its feet. Books on archaeology crowded the walls, just like in the Reb Nechtal's study.

Jim's hand throbbed. There was a bottle of brandy and a glass that Sharon had set out for him. She had also put some fruit before him, a bowl of strawberries and orange pieces. He was tired.

He was mentally exhausted from the intellectual combat in the Reb Nechtal's home. He didn't want to fight with Sharon. He had a problem, now that the body had to stay within the cave. He needed her to solve it. The case with the disk rested between his feet. He would put it in the safe in their lab at Hebrew University tomorrow.

He poured himself a quarter glass of the pink-red brandy and sipped it. It was good. It warmed him and took the cold out, and made the exhaustion comfortable.

Sharon returned with her hair pulled back, her face freshened, and wearing a pink bathrobe and sandals.

"Why is it, now, that my apartment is not an occasion of sin, in other words, a sin by even being here? Why not now?"

"Because I have overriding problems about the investigation, and I need you for them, and there is probably something I forgot that has to be solved tonight."

"Smaller than an olive, right?"

"Right," said Jim.

Sharon went into her small kitchen and brought back a bottle of antiseptic, cotton swabs, and some gauze. She pulled a chair up to Jim and then carefully began ministering to his palm. He remembered her tears and he remembered what her breasts looked like, and he could see the same outlines in her bathrobe.

"First thing we have to do," said Sharon, "is get a dehumidifier into that cave, and that means an electrical outlet down there. Mendel can get wires run down there. And it would be nice to have them run underground so there isn't that big directional signal to the entire world, screaming for everyone to look at what is going on. Right?"

"Right," said Jim, wincing.

"I'm sorry," said Sharon.

"That's all right, keep going. It feels good," said Jim. Her touch on his palm was sensual as well as healing.

"Okay, now that we stabilize the bones by lowering the humidity, we have to take care of your other requirements. We can put the body under some kind of cover when the geologist comes in to prove there were no other entrances into that cave.

And you can tell him that you are looking for a way out because you want to tunnel, and ask if there is any original tunnel.''

"Won't he know it's a dig?"

"It had been, but now the basement for Mr. Hamid is going in, and you want to expand, and you don't know if there had been tunneling here before, and if there had been, you won't have to cut through bedrock.''

"Better," said Jim. "Now what about the pathologist, who will have to look at that crucified body in a rich man's cave? And why are we making such a fuss over that one body?''

"Can't be a Christian. That's out. Can't be a Westerner, Christian or not. Although you have problems right there, because anyone with the level of scientific expertise we need has got to be Western-educated, and that means Christian-exposed.''

"I've been checking on that. Have you ever heard of William Sproul?''

"Sproul. Dr. William Sproul of the Hotchkiss Institute in Indianapolis, Indiana. He lectures here. He is Methodist. That's a Protestant sect.''

"I know. How do you know he is a Methodist?''

"He's quite religious. He'll come here usually for Easter and Christmas, and that's when the university can grab him for lectures. He is absolutely a perfect choice. From the bones he can tell what a person did for a living, what ethnic group, et cetera, incredible things. He is a perfect choice,'' said Sharon.

"And the one soonest to recognize what I am here to disprove.''

"Correct," said Sharon. The wound was clean, and she wrapped gauze around it, and then taped the gauze to Jim's hand. She peeled an orange for him, and cleaned the wound on his head, which was not severe. As she did so, her thighs rubbed between Jim's thighs.

There was a pleasant tingle to it, and he told himself he should tell her to step back. As she worked on his forehead, her breasts touched his cheek. He really should stop this, he told himself. He really should. It was already going too far.

"So what can we do about it?'' said Jim.

"We are going to have to flat out lie, successfully,'' said Sharon.

"Wonderful, you help the Church, and you learn to lie. I learn archaeology, and I end up punching people in the back."

"Welcome to Jerusalem," said Sharon.

"What is it about this place that intentions spit in your face?"

"Do you want a bandage for your head?"

"Sure," said Jim. He felt his body was tingly warm. Sharon went into the kitchen to get a smaller bandage for the forehead, and Jim was going to tell her not to stand so close when she came back. Of course, perhaps it meant nothing, and he certainly didn't want to insult her, what with all she was doing for the Church and everything.

She didn't have to do all this for the Church. Not at all. So when she came back, and took the same position, with the breasts touching his cheek again, and her smooth thighs inside his, and his face becoming hot, he knew he should say something. He was only lying to himself about the Church service being so important that he could be here. He had to tell her. He had to tell her now this had gone too far.

"What do you do when you find other bodies?" he asked. "I mean, this whole area is highly intensive with graves, you know. What do you do? What does anyone do when they find bodies, like when digging a road or something? Is there always a religious dispute because the body is assumed to be Jewish?"

"We find a lot of Crusader bodies," said Sharon.

Jim smelled her body, which was without perfume but a stronger perfume, of clean womanliness.

"Uh huh. You do. You do find them. Bodies?"

"Uh huh," she said, and he felt her hands fall down behind his neck, and she was lowering her lips to his, and he wasn't telling himself anything at this point. His right hand was on her perfect breast, fondling the hard nipple, and she was kissing him and he was kissing back, and then his tongue was in her mouth, and he didn't even know where he had learned that.

His shirt was coming off, and she was leading him to the bed.

"I shouldn't," said Jim, and she had his pants off and he had her bathrobe off and he saw her flesh was golden smooth, first to his hand, then his lips and tongue.

He felt between her thighs, wanting her, wondering when to enter, until she pulled his penis toward her and into her.

He felt the delicious wet warmth around his organ, and on the first thrusting movement of her hips, he spent. It had happened again.

He started to pull away but she held him there.

"Hey. Shh. Kiss me. Kiss me," she said.

He kissed her lips, he kissed her nipples, he kissed her neck, and kissed her lips again, and kept doing it while stroking her smooth belly, and then he felt her moving under him, and he was strong again inside, hard inside the walls of her vagina, a man thrusting again, and again, and her eyes narrowed as he drove her to completion, not stopping but triumphing in her, again and again, and her banging his back, and sobbing her relief. And he was still strong, hard as Lebanon cedars, and again he gave her relief.

He remembered reading where women were aroused by playing with the clitoris, and he did that, too, until she said she was already too sensitive there.

They lay together for a while, with Jim kissing her cheeks. After all, he told himself, now was not the time not to do something. It was done and then some.

He was still erect when she pulled from him, and went into the bathroom and came back with a wet cloth. She wiped clean his penis and its head felt raw. Even gentle touches were harsh.

And when it was clean, she lowered her head and he felt her very soft sucking mouth around his organ, and he was going to say stop, but he had already sinned. He had already violated chastity.

And since he had already done it, it certainly wasn't going to change anything now, especially when he wanted release so much and he felt it coming, with a groan, a glorious, explosive groan.

And when he was spent this time, it was, of course, absolutely clear. He had only been lying to himself.

Sharon crawled up his body, kissing him.

"Oh, shit," he said. "Damn."

"It wasn't good?" she asked.

"It was wonderful," said Jim. And then he sighed. "Dammit. It was wonderful. Dammit, I thought I was stronger than that."

"You know what you are unhappy about? You are unhappy

that you are a man. And you are a man, a magnificent man, if I must say so.''

"A man isn't a penis, Sharon.''

"He is not not a penis, either,'' she said.

"But I had put that part away. I had rigorously kept my vows. I had taken that energy and given it to God. Do you understand?''

Sharon nodded. She moved her body into Jim's and he folded his arms around her.

"What are we going to do?'' he said.

"I don't know,'' she said.

"We've got to stop this,'' he said. "That's what we're going to have to do. We're going to have to stop it, and you're going to have to help me . . . I said you're going to have to help me.''

"Jim,'' said Sharon, rolling over to get cigarettes nearby on a night table, "I said I understood. I didn't say I approve. I understand why your Aztecs cut out the hearts of sacrificial victims, also.''

"So, you are not going to help?'' said Jim.

Sharon took a long inhale on her cigarette and went to the table for Jim's brandy. Without clothes her backside was even more lovely, two perfectly rounded pillows, moving with barefoot grace.

She brought him his brandy glass, and as she bent down Jim's hand rose to feel her right breast. He just wanted to do it so much. She kissed him.

"Shit,'' said Jim. "You know I should leave! I should get up and leave.''

"Where are you going to put the disk? We're closer here to Hebrew University.''

"Right. I'll put it there tomorrow. I hope you can see now the results of an occasion of sin.''

"I do,'' said Sharon. "I think I wanted you since the first moment at the airport.''

"Same here,'' said Jim. "I think it was the same here. But it has to stop. If you care for me, you'll help.''

"Uh huh,'' said Sharon, sitting down on the bed next to him, stroking the hairs of his stomach.

"Going to stop it. Tomorrow. We'll figure out what we will

do and then, dammit, we'll do it. That's it. Over," said Jim.
"Do you know you have a magnificent body."

"Only when it's used, Jim."

"I never used to think lust would be my weakness. I was so
sure that wasn't going to be one of my problems," said Jim,
and he told her how he used to have a problem with premature
ejaculation before he entered the priesthood, how he used to
wonder sometimes whether that wasn't one of the strong motives for his becoming a priest.

He talked of the priesthood, and of New England, and how
there would usually be snow by now in South Portland, Maine,
where he had been a little boy. It was so natural and so good to
talk like this with someone whom he was close to in mind as
well as body. He was thirty-five years old and this was the first
time he had ever enjoyed the comfort of falling asleep with
someone in his arms.

In the morning, even as his eyes opened, he said, "No."
Sharon was sleeping next to him, and he realized fully he had
been lying to himself. He dressed even as he luxuriated in the
smell of her, the joy of her apartment. He was supposed to be
sorry for what he did. But he couldn't feel it. He regretted the
sin of it, but not the act itself.

Actually, as he thought about it, he regretted that the act was
a sin. He was even tinkering with thoughts of changing the
Church law instead of himself. He was shocked to find that his
great ability to lie to himself, the reasoning process that was to
lead him to God, had been marshaled as his felicitous guide to
the bowels of hell.

He had even told himself that since he had been exposed to
Sharon in service to the Church, vital service, it became less of
a sin. He even had himself believing for a while that if he continued an affair with Sharon, and that it helped the Church,
what he did was not a grievous breach of contract with God but
actually a service to Him.

Even on the mildest inquiry, this one did not hold. But there
was his mind working against himself, lying to him, because
his whole body wanted to stay in bed with Sharon that morning.

He went up to the university, and entered the lab and locked
the door, and opened the safe, and opened the case, and exam-

ined the disk, which was perfectly safe, and put the disk in the safe, and locked the safe.

So much for all he could do without Sharon. He phoned her from the lab.

"Where the hell are you? Don't ever leave me like that, Jim. How could you do that?"

"I had to put the disk away."

"Dubi left me like that. Don't ever leave me like that."

"Your husband?"

"Yes."

Adultery, Jim reminded himself. He had commited adultery. Not just fornication, but taken another man's wife.

"Sharon, we've got to stop this."

"Don't say it over a phone, dammit. Say it to me."

"I won't go to your apartment. It is an occasion of sin. I'd be lying to myself if I thought I could go there safely."

"You're at the lab?"

"Yes."

"I'll be there."

"All right. But never again in your apartment," said Jim. And he was firm on that.

They made love on a lab table when she got there. And he didn't even know how it got started. She had walked in, he had started to explain exactly how they might work together without tempting each other, and her clothes were coming off. They were coming off in his hands, and his in hers.

And they were making love again. And this time he vowed that when he ejaculated prematurely he would pull out and leave it an unpleasant sexual experience for Sharon, and, quite naturally, his problem, that last physical defense for his spiritual disaster, failed to function as expected. Sharon orgasmed twice before Jim did, and then hurriedly told him to dress.

"Hurry, hurry," she said. "Do you know where we are? I could lose my job. It would be a disgrace."

"Sharon," said Jim, putting his shirt on inside out, "if we continue like this, every place is an occasion of sin. Our meeting is an occasion of sin. We can't be together."

"So that means another archaeologist to replace me."

"That would be a risk for the Church, wouldn't it?" said Jim.

"Oh, yes. Yes," said Sharon.

"I couldn't do that to the Church," said Jim.

"No," Sharon agreed.

"Too much of a risk," said Jim.

"Too much," said Sharon.

"I will not do that to the Church," said Jim, with the gravity of a papal decree.

By the weekend he was living at her apartment, and Father James Folan, S.J., celebrated Christmas in Jerusalem with a last Mass for the brothers at Isaiah House, and a bottle of Carmel wine for his girl friend.

Father Walter Winstead got a Christmas gift in January. It was not the Church's Christmas, but the Armenian Christmas, and it came from a Mossad representative who suggested that he stop referring to Haneviim Street in his misleading messages left for the Arab gardener.

"You mean they are really picking up on them?" asked Father Winstead. He didn't even bother to disguise the joy in his voice.

"I am just suggesting that you stop. For many people's benefits."

"Is there something going on on Haneviim Street?" asked Father Winstead.

"If I knew, would I tell you?" said the man.

"No. But do you know?"

"If I knew, I wouldn't be delivering messages in this weather to you."

"And what would happen if I continued to use Haneviim Street in the messages from the garbage?"

"I don't know."

"It may be that this whole thing somehow doesn't even have anything to do with us, but rather with you."

"Could be."

"It could be that the mention of Haneviim Street fits in with something I am not even aware of, and will never be aware of."

"Could be," said the man from the Mossad, who wore a little fur hat and a jacket trimmed with fur that was wet now from the January rains.

"Exciting, isn't it?" said Father Winstead.

"No," said the man from the Mossad, who had to go out in the rain again.

On the Orthodox Christmas, January 7, the one celebrated in Moscow, Warris Abouf mutilated himself. He did it with a hammer, and he did it to a toe.

He did it after several attempts. He did it after a long wait looking at the toe, and looking at the hammer, and realizing he could not keep increasing the power of the blow because the last blow already hurt too much, and the toe wasn't even swollen, let alone broken.

As he waited he reminded himself why he was doing this. He told himself that he was doing it for his life, for his self-respect, to at least take the chance of getting back to where he felt he belonged.

All the pressures were working properly on Vakunin. Unfortunately, the major had found a way out. There was still an increasingly urgent need to find an Arab-fluent Hebrew with knowledge of the Vatican. The major had confided that even a Russian had already been lost on that project. This must have been a promotion for the captured agent because there had been some sort of hint before that he was a Jew.

And Warris knew through Tomarah's actions there was another man on her mind. Whether she and the major had already tasted each other, he didn't know. But she walked around the house with little unshared pleasantries inside her, and Warris assumed that she and the major had at least made contact. What Warris had not counted on was Major Vakunin's solution.

Why not, said the major, make another broad sweep of installations, even to the training camps producing the chaff? Who knows what hidden intelligence one might find under the cultural exterior.

And to make sure what he was hearing, Warris this time said:

"Major, I might have made a miscalculation on one of the students at Patrice Lumumba. I should work harder on him. I will stay here diligently."

"No. They're no good," said the major. "You've tried them before. I've accepted that. That's accepted already. So they are out. You must leave Moscow."

"I think we just might be successful this time."

"No," said Vakunin.

From this, Warris knew Vakunin was now willing to risk a possible chance at success. And it could be only because he wanted something even more. He wanted Tomarah. The passion was working.

But if Warris left Moscow, the major would get Tomarah, and that pressure on the major to get Warris out of the country might be lost. Indeed, given a good chance to get to know Tomarah, the major might want Warris close to her permanently.

Warris had to keep things difficult for them to get together, and to do that he had to stay in Moscow, and to do that he needed an excuse, and a perfect excuse was a broken toe.

It would be a break that would ease in pain enough to move on only when Vakunin's plight got so bad that he had to send Warris to that assignment inside Israel.

So, on Christmas Day, while Tomarah and Arkady were out, Warris took the hammer into the bathroom, shut the door, and hit his toe gently to get range with the hammer, and then brought it down harder. But as he brought it down, he decelerated, because he didn't want to hurt himself. It ended up hurting.

So he hit harder and it hurt more. And he hit harder a bit, just a bit, and it hurt more, a lot. What he needed was one single hard dramatic stroke.

And that was the one thing he couldn't get himself to do to that poor toe. And so he thought about what had brought him here, and how logical the solution was. A broken toe would keep Warris in Moscow closer to Tomarah. Warris could not, he would say, approach a fellow Arab if he were wounded, because, he would say, Arabs did not trust wounded people. It was the sort of thing Vakunin would believe of Arabs.

Then, Warris would allow as how the toe might be healing, healing enough for a trip to a sunny climate where he knew it would heal. He knew Vakunin would break. He knew the man.

Perfect plan, perfect part of the body, and all it needed was one decisive hammer stroke.

Warris put down the hammer and went to the parlor, poured himself one big drink of vodka, swallowed it in a single burning gulp, returned to the bathroom, shut the door, picked up the hammer again, and thought about his toe.

It must have been a half hour before he heard the door open, and in that time he had been addressing that rotten toe as the one thing that stood between him and home. He was building up a hate for the toe, but never quite so sufficient that it would quiet the toe's contention that whatever Warris did to that toe, Warris was doing to himself.

"Hurt me, and I'll hurt you," said the toe in Warris' thoughts. That confident little arrogant toe. That traitorous toe.

If an eye offends thee, Warris told himself, pluck it out. But that was Biblical, and he wasn't going to pluck out an eye, either.

There was nothing an eye could do to him that would make him do that. Warris was a prisoner in his body.

And then he heard real voices. His son, Arkady, was talking to his mother, Tomarah. And Arkady, the Arkady Warris had kissed on the belly and made gurgle as a baby, that Arkady said to his mother:

"Is the zhid home?"

The toe went with one stroke. It was easy. When Warris left the bathroom limping, there were tears in his eyes. And it was not because of the toe, which he informed Tomarah and Arkady he had just broken. Arkady laughed.

And Warris wept.

In the third floor of the Vatican, His Holiness was hearing from his Secretary of State how the high number of Slavic priests in attendance at Christmas service might have given an inaccurate picture of the truly Catholic nature of the Church.

Not that His Eminence Almeto Cardinal Pesci was one who thought Catholic meant Italian. But it was true that Italians tended to blend into the scenery, so to speak, and were accepted as administrators of the Church, almost like the weather. Italians, unlike Slavs, just did not stand out. It was a fact of the Church. Had been for centuries, probably almost since the Church came to Rome with Peter.

His Holiness wanted to know about the American priest. And when he said it like that, there was only one priest he could mean when speaking to the Secretary of State.

"He is progressing, Your Holiness."

"Is he close to his findings?"

"I don't know. As you remember, he did make some calculations concerning the Shroud of Turin."

"And what did you think?"

"I didn't give it all that much thought, Your Holiness. We are so busy now with the number of Slavic priests, just from an international standpoint . . ."

"Did you think he made a good case?"

"I didn't give it that much thought, Your Holiness."

"Even if it were proved true, the shroud would be just a relic, a lost, precious relic, but a relic. Did you read the Gospels in the light of his report on the height of Jesus, and the height of people at that time?"

"Read the Gospels again? I don't have time, Your Holiness."

"I reread them. They are truly water to a thirsty spirit. I find nourishment and rest every time I return to them."

"If you find them relaxing, then, certainly, Your Holiness. I have always felt that the Pope himself is the one to get the least rest. Pius XII liked walks, they said."

"The priest had clung to the shroud to disprove the find, and then the shroud itself was torn away from him," said the Pope. He felt sadness for the American priest. He had prayed for him several times.

"I am sure the Jesuit will work it out, Your Holiness," said His Eminence Almeto Cardinal Pesci, moving on to important matters of state, and then ending the morning session repeating what he had heard from a French cardinal about the lack of French clerics in the Vatican hierarchy, and how the Church was opening itself up to just those sorts of comments from everywhere as long as it kept replacing Italians with any other nationality. And he assured His Holiness he was not singling out Slavs. It was just that they were noticed.

Mendel Hirsch had to report to superiors, not for them to hear how well Christmas went, but on what was happening on Haneviim Street.

"Do they know yet?" he was asked.

"Not that I know of. I've just installed wiring down to the dig, heating, and a humidity control and lights. There will be a long stay. We had the trouble with that Reb Nechtal sect."

"The Jesuit, it is being said, had an impressive knowledge of the Talmud. The Jesuits are something, eh? The Reb Nechtal group will now trust only him, and not you, Mendel," said the superior.

"Well, you know, when they are not speaking Yiddish they speak Russian," said Mendel Hirsch, carefully reminding his superior that there was a feeling among many Polish and Lithuanian and Galician Jews that Russian Jews were a bit insensitive to other people's feelings, a sort of lack of *Yiddishkeit*, which translated into "nice Jewishness." The essence of the statement was that the Reb Nechtal had chosen the Gentile over Mendel because of a Russian sort of harshness. That Mendel's superior had a Russian background was not what Mendel, of course, was meaning. But it might explain why Mendel was not chosen to be the trustee of the agreement between the Reb Nechtal's group and those who ran the dig.

"It also might be, dear Mendel, that you used to eat ham sandwiches in front of the Wailing Wall."

"That was in a time when we felt we had to get the religious element out of Zionism. It was a statement that we were a political movement, you see. Not bound by ancient laws."

"Well, some people remember, Mendel. Maybe the Reb Nechtal remembered."

"And maybe somebody reminded him."

"Do you think we want Pesci's man in there, instead of our man? Be reasonable."

"You know, it was at a time when we thought that if we could get the religious aspect out of the thing we might face less anti-Semitism."

"That was 1939," said the superior, showing how wrong the strategy had been, because that was the year Hitler began his war and the destruction of Jews. And with that statement, they got back down to business, with nothing else having to be said. It was all unobstructed work thereafter.

The department head of archaeology at Hebrew University dreaded the moment he faced. With Dr. Sharon Golban, he always had perfect proof that his department did not discriminate against either Sephardi or women.

Dr. Golban had been a fanatic for archaeological procedure,

and a fanatic about student work. She had been known to dismiss an entire class because they were unprepared. She would fail an entire class, too. Everyone knew that, and knew what a hard marker she was. Yet, it was impossible to get her to be more lenient or understanding. It was as though she was out to prove she would out-Ashkenazi an Ashkenazi, or out-European anyone.

She had not been pleasant when told she was given the leave for the autumn semester, even though she had agreed to it.

"What else was I going to do? You stuffed it down my throat, and with it already stuffed, you then say, would you care to eat, and how sorry you are. Well, thank you for nothing."

That was what she had said for the fall semester. She had also added she was willing to give up only one semester. But there was going to be a fight of fights if there was even a hint of her having to give up another semester. Even a hint.

Now the department head had the responsibility of telling her she was on indefinite leave from the university.

She came in to his office happy, dancing in on the knock. There was something different about her this day. She still avoided lipstick, and her hair was still severe, but there was a softness about her today, an easy laughter, a willingness to enjoy the moment. The department head smiled nervously.

"What a lovely, lovely necklace," he said.

"Yes. I thought I would wear it today. It was a bribe, you know. Actually not. I joke. It was a gift of appreciation from an Arab businessman who was glad that I kept him informed. I got it on the last dig. Do you really like it?" she said, lifting up the necklace Mr. Hamid had given her so graciously, and which before was too flamboyant for her, but now was just right.

"Beautiful. Exquisite. I am afraid I have bad news for you. You are on indefinite leave."

"I thought that was what you were going to tell me," said Sharon. "You know, for the first time I understand what Mr. Hamid saw in this necklace. The man saw me in the necklace. You know. It is amazing what people will know. People can even see what you will be or could be."

"Absolutely," said the department head. "You know, of

course, we will welcome you back after your leave, and you will have your rightful seniority, and everything."

"Yes. I know."

"So you are aware you are on indefinite leave?"

"Absolutely," said Dr. Sharon Golban. "The rest will be good. I will come back refreshed."

In a New York City bar, a Moroccan Jew from Israel realized the horrible truth of America. It had taken him a long while to finally acknowledge this, but in the grimy slush of Fifth Avenue, where so much money was, with the ice water totally permeating his socks, Dubi Halafi had to accept he was not going to become a millionaire.

He was not going to make it on his dark good looks. He was not going to make it on his large penis. And he was not going to be able to successfully steal it without being caught.

America was not easy.

American Jews were not going to welcome him as a partner in their businesses.

American Jews were Americans. They might talk for Israel. They might send money for Israel. But when an Israeli like Dubi Halafi should possibly be a little bit short of funds, and possibly mistakenly fail to ring every little penny in a cash register, they would fire him like some nigger, a word he had learned his first week in this new country, a word he suspected some might use for him when his back was turned, although he was not as dark as a Black.

Blacks were friendly to him because of his dark skin, but they were Americans, too. They talked of Third World, but they were on the hustle, too. The worst thing was that he and they were competing in the same market. And they had a better chance because there were laws that protected them.

But there was no law that protected Dubi Halafi in his new country. And he could not return to Israel, because he had left telling everyone he was not going to hang around for spare change but going to America to make big money, where a real lover could be a millionaire and drive Cadillacs and Rolls-Royces. What was he getting there in Israel—the leftovers from some professor whose family looked down on him?

A man who left to become a millionaire could not return

home owing for the wet suit on his back. Everyone would say, "Dubi, millionaire, buy me supper." That's what they would say, and they would hate him for not doing so. Sure, he could cut up anyone who talked to him like that, but how many could a man fight? There were limits.

But that cold day, Dubi smelled golden hope. He was bartending when another Moroccan Jew told him he had heard from someone who had just arrived from Jerusalem about Dubi's wife back in Israel.

"I don't care about her," said Dubi, and used a Moroccan slang word for a skinflint. He was remembering how he had covered himself and offered his own body for the mere cost of getting him to Jerusalem. Less than cost. Just a helpful few dollars. That he didn't intend to use the airfare, Sharon couldn't know. She was Talmud stupid in a way, and that meant someone who just studied and didn't know the real world.

He had written her off as worthless.

"She is living with someone now," said the man, who had heard this from a friend, and immediately Dubi saw Sharon crazy in some kind of love, and himself selling her that divorce, which was just one of many possibilities that would force her to open her pocketbook.

"With a Gentile, too," said the man.

"The whore," said Dubi righteously. He was working up the proper feeling for the best kind of settlement. His money was back in Israel.

17

And Ye Shall Plant Trees

He had betrayed his God, his Pope, his order, his vows, and even his dead mother.

"What have I done to your mother?" asked Sharon.

Jim was in a pair of undershorts, drinking awful coffee and reading notes in Sharon's apartment, preparing to remove the jaw from the skull this day at the dig.

"You haven't done anything. I'm sorry."

"That doesn't make me feel better," said Sharon.

"I've broken every vow in my life by living with you. I don't know of anyone I haven't betrayed by living with you."

"Me. What about me?"

"I am betraying you by telling you this. It's not your burden."

"You mean I get you only for the laughs?" said Sharon.

He stood up and hugged her. She felt so good in his arms. He felt so good holding her, the very act of the giving of his body warmth felt holy and good. That's what it felt like. What it was, was mortal sin.

"We were poor, Sharon. I know there is the impression in the rest of the world that all Americans are rich. We weren't. And my father had this drinking problem and when I got out of the Marines, I could have supported my mother."

"You were a good son," said Sharon.

He felt her lips say this on his bare shoulder.

"Well, yeah. I tried to be. I really did. And I wanted to be. Not just for approval or anything. I chose to do it."

"Good for you," said Sharon.

"Thank you," said Jim. "Well, my mother, who never had an easy life, chose to do without to share in my priesthood. She gave a son to God, do you see?"

"Human sacrifice," said Sharon.

"No," said Jim, pushing her shoulders away so he could look at her. "Sacrifice of certain daily things, but not the life, you see? Because if you love something, you give up something for it, because you love the other thing more. You see? Like you thought Tabinian should give up his money for scholarship because of his good mind, you see?"

"That's Tabinian. He has his problems. But I want to do what I am doing, why not you?"

"Did you want to take second place to a holy man on this dig?"

"No."

"Why did you?"

"Our streets might seem peaceful to you, but we are surrounded."

"But you gave up the dig because you loved your country more."

"I don't think survival is really a choice, Jim. It is not an option one chooses or does not choose. So I did it, yes."

"Well, I chose," said Jim. "And then, I chose again." And he hugged her, and kissed her neck and smelled her hair in the morning, and it all felt so good, how could it be wrong? Which was what a seventeen-year-old kid should think, not a thirty-five-year-old Jesuit selected from all the soldiers of Christ to defend the faith.

Good for you, Jim, he told himself, not without bitterness. And then he forced himself to a working compromise. His first mission was for the Church, therefore his own feelings had to be secondary. If guilt got in the way, he had to ignore it, or betray his mission further.

Perhaps he might be lucky. Daily routine often wore on passion. He had seen it in so many relationships, especially those that seemed the most furiously wonderful. Like his.

Perhaps his passion for Sharon was that way, precisely because it was new. The whole thing was new to him. Perhaps time, God's great healing tool, might cure him of it. He might just drift away from Sharon in time. It had happened to others, why not him?

But as he dressed he remembered he was no longer doing his examen, and he had to give up saying the Mass, because not only was he in a state of mortal sin but he did not have an immediate intention of amending that state.

On the other hand, he had seen Sharon change before his eyes, hear her say she had never been so happy, hear her comment that he was the first man who seemed to have everything.

In the car, going to the dig, with rain pelting the Volkswagen top, and the streets running so heavy with water that Jim saw how ancients could store in winter cisterns a supply of water for a year, he asked her what she meant by his having everything.

"You're such a fine person, and there's, well, the sex, too. It's so good."

"You mean you never enjoyed it so much?" said Jim.

"It is special with you, Jim," she said, and she smiled so softly, and so nicely, he became excited, just sitting there watching her in the cramped bug.

"It wasn't good with Dubi?" said Jim. She had told him about how he had hurt her so much in so many ways.

"With Dubi it was great, but it was the only thing, you know."

He fought with himself not to ask the next question.

"Was he, uh, better than me?" asked Jim.

"That's pride, Jim. I'm counting sins," said Sharon.

"No, it's not pride. If some man gave you more pleasure, I want to know."

"Dubi was Dubi, Jim. I feel like a full woman, now, Jim. You love me. Me. Dubi was a warm, active dildo."

"He was better," said Jim.

"You don't understand what a woman feels."

"He was better. Say it. I will not mind. I am curious. He was better. Say it. Say it."

"I won't."

"But you mean it," said Jim.

"No. I mean what I mean. And I say what I mean. You want me to mean something else."

"I don't know what the hell I mean," yelled Jim.

"Well, neither do I," yelled back Sharon.

"Is that so?" said Jim.

"No," yelled Sharon. "I know exactly what I mean. I love you."

"Okay," said Jim. "You know we have no long-range future."

Sharon pulled the car over. Never before had Jim seen her stop for anything. This time she parked, and turned to stare at him directly.

"What do you want from me, Jim?"

"I don't know. I don't want to lose you and I want you to go away."

"Good. I'll do just that."

"What?"

"None of your business. Why are you doing this?"

"I'm sorry," said Jim. "I really am."

"The one thing I have feared all my life was loving someone and being left by that person. You know?"

"So you fall in love, first with a lout and then a Jesuit," said Jim, and he was crying.

And she was crying. But she thought about what he said, and then she was laughing. And he laughed. They laughed with tears on their cheeks, hugging each other, taking this precious moment in Jerusalem.

At the dig one of Reb Nechtal's men sat in a wooden shed, doing his mitzvah for the dead, and that meant being there to see that the bones were not moved unless, of course, they could be proved to be Gentile. He nodded to Jim and Sharon as they arrived, and Jim returned the nod.

A wooden stairway anchored into the walls now replaced the ladders. Electricity had been run five feet under the surface of the lot and then dropped through a drilled hole down to bedrock, where it came out under a shield of plastic that stretched to the metal door. All the improvements had been done in one night under the guise of street repairs.

Jim had suspected this was the work of the Mossad, and asked forgiveness of Sharon if she thought this was paranoid.

"Sounds like the Mossad or Army to me. I can't imagine the

Jerusalem municipal authority running a line in one night, and having it work, no less. That's a year of paper work, let alone the *histadrut*, which will demand that one man dig, the other hold the shovel, another drive the truck with earth, and everyone get overtime and vacations. This is Israel, not South Portland, Maine, where everything gets done well."

"Not everything gets done well in America," said Jim, smiling.

They entered the cave, which was warm and dry. Jim had put the body on a case with an opaque plastic shield over it, much like a gigantic dust cover for a photograph.

Sharon knew that he insisted there be no levity inside the cave itself, in accordance with his promise to the Reb Nechtal that the body would be respected at all times. And this included a prayer before the body was touched and that the prayer was to Jesus, not incongruous with the promise to the rabbi, since it was how Jim showed respect.

The bones were still on the palette Jim had carefully edged under them. He moved his hands with stately precision to the head, reminding himself how he moved saying Mass, turning his whole body to turn the hands. He could not help glancing at the orange marks on the tibia. He pressed the jaw, ever so gently. It was supposed to come off. He looked to Sharon.

"I can't do it," he said.

"That's all right," she said. She stepped in front of the manmade platform on which the palette rested, and asked for a small pick. Ever so gently she worked it into the jaw. Jim turned away. He heard scraping, and he stared at the side of the cave. He knew the jaw was off now, and he knew she was collecting whatever hardened connecting tissue had once held the jaw shut.

"That's it," she said, and Jim saw the jaw was off, with just a shade scraped from the skull beneath where the openings for the ear were.

She showed him a dark rocklike substance, with small dusty fragments around it.

"That's it, huh?" said Jim.

"Uh huh," said Sharon. "That's plus or minus eighty years in dating."

They put the cover back, closed the dig, and went up to the surface.

Sharon had given Jim a list of three places nearby that could do carbon 14 dating. She also said he could send it overseas if he would feel better. He had chosen the Weizmann Institute of Science at Rehovot.

Sharon was the first person who ever explained carbon dating to him clearly.

"To take the mystery out, carbon 14 dating really measures how long an organism has been dead. And it does it by measuring the amount of carbon 14 released. Now, how does that work, and why does it work?" said Sharon, and she answered her question.

"Plants, which are the basis of the food chain, absorb carbon 14 through carbon dioxide. We eat plants. We get it. We die. We stop collecting it, and start giving it back to the atmosphere in carbon dioxide gas as we decompose. And we can tell from the rate of emission, and from what is left, how long this has been going on. Okay?"

"Sounds simple," said Jim.

"In theory. In practice measurements are not that easy because of competing radiation even from the measuring machines. I think of it as an art in a way."

The Weizmann Institute at Rehovot was a modern, technological campus. Sharon personally knew the woman who would do the carbon 14 dating. She spoke pleasantly with her, reminding her it was a rush. Jim felt uncomfortable near this middle-aged technician. On her right arm was a tattooed number. She had survived a Nazi concentration camp.

Jim realized he was looking at the arm just as he was reminding himself not to look at the arm.

While waiting for the report from the Weizmann Institute, Sharon and Jim prepared the disk, which they had retrieved from Reb Nechtal.

At first they had planned to tape over half the disk and photograph that for one expert to examine, and then do it to the other half for another expert, and then have someone else examine just two indentations in the disk to ascertain that indeed this was done by hand a long time ago, and not by some modern tool.

But with their two heads together they came up with a solution, so fiendishly clever they even joked about going into a life of crime. The solution could have come from Solomon.

They cut the disk in half with a diamond saw and locked away the half that said *"Melek,"* because any scholar seeing that half would become overwhelmed with curiosity to find out which king it referred to. The portion with *"Yehudayai"* was hand delivered to a Semitic scholar in the Biblical Institute for his analysis. Any aberration, or scholarly clue, would be just as present in the left side as the other.

Jim had Sharon deliver the disk half lest the Jesuit at the Biblical Institute was one of the ones who had been called to Rome. He might recognize Jim, and attach Vatican importance to that half.

The man's name was Jeremiah Murphy O'Connor, S.J., D.S.S.

"Another Irishman," said Jim when Sharon returned to the lab at Hebrew University.

"Really. I thought he was English," said Sharon.

"He might be a British citizen, but he is of Irish descent."

"Jeremiah Murphy O'Connor is not an English name?"

"Of course not."

"Doesn't sound English?" said Sharon. "Jeremiah Murphy O'Connor, Winston Randolph Churchill."

"Not in the least."

"Maybe they sound alike because Ireland and England are so close?" said Sharon.

"They don't sound remotely alike."

"I guess you can tell the difference," said Sharon.

Driving to Weizmann Institute to pick up the report, Jim asked what would they do if they found the carbon dating gave them more than an eighty-year difference from the crucifixion, 30 to 40 C.E.

"Your dating of the disk becomes less crucial then, and, of course, you would get the greatest gift of your life."

"Do you think that will happen?" said Jim.

"No," said Sharon.

"I don't either," said Jim. "That Pilatus coin is good circumstantial dating."

"Yes, but don't forget those coins were still in use during the reign of Governor Glaucus."

"Which means?"

"Which means that the date of the find could be twenty years after our known limits of the crucifixion, and both the coin and the carbon dating couldn't tell it."

"But the kiln-fired disk dating could, right?" said Jim.

"Only if we use the matching method. If we measure just the thermoluminescent glow of the disk, we get no better range than the carbon 14 dating, seventy or eighty years either way. But if we can get a kiln-fired piece that we know the absolute date of, we can match the glow curves and the two pieces and get within ten years, plus or minus."

"Then, I would say we would have to get a piece we knew for sure was fired between 30 and 40 c.e. But how do we do it?"

"You find a piece with writing on it that says, 'Dear Pontius, here are some more oils for washing, because I hear you are washing your hands a lot lately.' "

"Is that hard?"

"Not easy. But if you have the time and the money and the influence, it is something I would like us to do."

"I would like not to have to," said Jim.

Sharon went into the building where the carbon 14 dating was being done while Jim waited in the car. She came back, with a sigh.

"We have to. It came in at 50 c.e. It's within the range of the crucifixion, easily."

That night, Jim did not want to be left alone. He wanted Sharon to be with him.

"It's Friday night. I've got to go to Paula's. I do it every Friday night."

"Don't leave me alone," said Jim.

"But I've got to go. It's my family."

"Take me," said Jim.

"Someone I'm living with, to Shabbat Eve?" she said, horrified.

"Well, you know, it's not exactly not a sin for me either," said Jim.

"But Shabbat Eve?"

"Yes. Your sister-in-law doesn't have to know we're sleeping together."

"Paula will know. She'll know."

"Sharon, you are an archaeologist, a senior lecturer at Hebrew University, and I am a Jesuit. I think we can possibly fool someone who to your own admission had only one year of college and then dropped out to marry your brother Avrahim. All right?"

"You do make sense," said Sharon.

So that evening Sharon put on her very modest Shabbat Eve dress, and Jim put on his cleanest chinos and newest shirt, and the two colleagues who only worked together went to Paula's house to share a harmless Shabbat Eve dinner.

Paula answered the door in a print dress over her ample frame. She carried a wooden spoon, still dripping.

"Hi, I'm Jim Folan. I'm working with Sharon. I'm glad to meet you, Mrs. Golban. Sharon has told me so much about you," said Jim, in his smoothest voice of honest authority.

"She's a married woman," said Paula, pointing the wooden spoon at Jim's eyes.

"He knows that, Paula. Please."

"He should remember it."

"I don't know what you're talking about," said Sharon.

"Yes, you do," said Paula. "But it's Shabbat Eve, so come on in."

Dr. Avrahim Golban welcomed Jim profusely. He had Sharon's dark-features and regal bearing. The son, Rani, was courteous. He wore a kepah on his head but the father did not. Mari ran to Sharon, and hugged her and kissed her. She was a pretty little girl, with very blue eyes in her Persian face.

She announced to the family that Jim was beautiful, and that if Sharon didn't want him, she did. She thought that was funny. So did the father. Paula said the dinner was ready.

Dr. Golban said Shabbos prayers, as Paula seemed to monitor every word he said, that it be correct. Then she served dinner.

Dr. Golban wanted to know what kind of food Jim thought he was eating.

"I would assume kosher. I can't imagine Mrs. Golban serving anything that was not strictly kosher,'' said Jim. He smiled broadly at Paula. Paula served him vegetables.

''But what group would you say the food comes from? Kurdish? German? What?''

''Well, considering it's stuffed cabbage and potato pancakes, it seems typically Jewish to me.''

''Jewish, it is plastic. Plastic,'' said Dr. Golban, and then he went on at length to describe food that he liked. The children thought that was funny.

Dr. Golban described Persian cooking, with its subtle use of lemon flavoring, how the meat would be chopped into inch-square cubes, and how the sauce and the rice and the meat would all blend into a unity.

He talked of Arab cooking, which, while not the food he grew up with, still had taste.

''I have a friend who, when I go into his house, I sit down and they bring before me many dishes. And a big plate of rice with almonds and raisins, and I dig my hands in like this,'' said Dr. Golban, with grinning gusto, and he thrust his hands forward into an imaginary pile of rice with almonds and raisins and sauce.

He clenched his fist. ''The rice sticks into a ball. And you eat that.''

The Arab was his friend whose wife was once a patient. Arabs would bring the whole family to the hospital. Dr. Golban had cured the man's wife and had forgotten about it, until he had a stone porch built and the builder wouldn't charge him. It was, of course, the same man, Haj Suleiman Labib, who would not charge. Dr. Golban had been to his house as a guest, and he had had Haj Suleiman Labib here as a guest.

''And he liked the food,'' said Paula.

''He was a guest, he had to,'' said Dr. Golban.

''The food is plastic,'' said Mari.

''You, eat,'' said Paula. ''And if you don't, if you don't have a good Shabbat, you know what?''

''Daddy said it.''

''You don't say it.''

There was another threat for violation of Jewish law that night, this time to Rani, who had been lackadaisical all week in the ritual cleansing of his hands on rising, and if Paula saw that, who knew what God was seeing? Again the awesome punishment of "You know what."

The ritual cleansing on waking reminded Jim how Jews thought sleep was a ritual impurity, and for the most astounding reason. During sleep, man lacked free will. The idea of free will placed humans in the cosmos in a way so different from many other religions and philosophies.

One could look at both Judaism and Christianity and say, here, here is the common root. For what that said—which was so incredibly different from all that went before and so much that came after—was that man was not an animal, a piece of machinery, part of a state, a cog in a historical process. Free will meant he could choose to love God or not. It said to Jim, every time he confronted it in its different forms, that man is not here for a season, but for eternity.

Jim looked over to Sharon and saw Paula watching. He wanted to be on Sharon's side of the table, touching her, being close to her. Did he have a choice here? Where was his free will?

He had one. He was just too weak. He could leave Sharon, which would have been like tearing out his belly with a hot iron. No. He could do that easier because once your belly was out, you couldn't put it back in. At this point he could not leave her and stay away. He could not. So where was his free will?

"Do you think Sharon is beautiful?" said Mari to Jim.

Paula, the director of proper feelings at the table, something even God never claimed, answered Mari for Jim:

"He feels Sharon is married. He feels that if Sharon wants to get a divorce, she should find her husband. And he respects her because she is not some kind of loose woman who worries about the size of her anatomy. No woman who ever worried about sizes ever got a good husband. That's how you get bad husbands."

"Is that how you feel?" asked Mari, holding her fork over her plate. She was so adorable, trusting that her question would be answered honestly. Her eyes were so blue and her dark skin so smooth with innocence. Jim did not really know what to answer. He didn't want to lie. He also did not wish to face Paula's wrath.

"Your mother has made very good points about living. I certainly would say they are good points," said Jim.

"But how do you feel? Do you feel the way she says you feel?"

"Well, your mother is talking about incontrovertible law."

"Do you think Sharon is beautiful?"

"Define beauty," said Jim.

"Something that is pleasing to you," said Mari, dangerously cutting off Jim's retreat. That was not what he wanted her to say, because he had intended to get into a discussion of what beauty was, and the little innocent girl just about ended it.

"Then, an apple becomes beautiful," said Jim.

"Yes. Is she beautiful?"

"Your aunt is certainly prettier than an apple, Mari," said the Jesuit.

"Real beauty is inside," said Paula. "Beauty is not apples. You eat apples," said Paula, as though the term was impossible with human relationships, and in her mind, thought Jim, probably was.

"Is she beautiful inside?"

"I think that is your aunt's great beauty," said Jim. "She is a fine, decent, moral woman."

"I think so too," said Mari.

Sharon hugged her and kissed her cheeks. "I love you," she said to Mari, and then also kissed Rani, who winced.

"I'm sorry, you have a bruise on your cheek."

"Where?" said Paula.

"It's nothing," said Rani. "Nobody ever saw it."

"How did you get it?"

"I was hit," admitted Rani.

"And were you hitting too?"

Rani lowered his eyes.

And thus on Shabbat Eve, in the city of Jerusalem, did Paula pronounce the punishment for disobeying a parent, which was a violation of Jewish law, as ancient as the First Temple stones.

And this was the punishment she had been threatening all evening:

"No 'Little House on the Prairie.'"

Later, when the children were asleep, Paula said she disliked

taking that American television show away from them, because
it always had a morality so difficult to find these days.

Jim said nothing, but smiled in weak agreement.

Outside, as they walked to their car, coming close only when
they were out of sight of Paula, Sharon said:

"She liked you."

"That's liking?"

"She doesn't like the idea of any romance between us."

"I'm glad she didn't ask if I were married."

"She will," said Sharon.

Saturday was spent in bed, talking about themselves, and on
Sunday they went for long walks around the city, because the
sun had come out briefly.

Jim confided that he had had fears about becoming a priest,
that he couldn't make it.

"But you did change your mind?" said Sharon.

"Yes. I did, because the Jesuit I was talking to at the time
said I wasn't expected to make it alone."

"You mean, the help of God?"

He said he couldn't make it through a day himself as priest
without Jesus. And so I said, 'Okay, Jesus. It's your problem,
not mine. I'm counting on you for help.' "

"Ah," said Sharon. "God as a friend."

Jim felt her squeeze his arm, and they walked quietly through
the hills of Jerusalem.

Monday began the search for the matching kiln-fired piece of
pottery. Throughout the week reports kept coming back from
Sharon's colleagues that there was no kiln-fired pottery in any
museum with writing referring to Pontius Pilatus.

"Do you want to go the illegal trade?" said Sharon.

"Not yet," said Jim. "If we have to, we have to. What are
our chances, even if we go illegal?"

"I don't know," said Sharon. "I'm not that familiar with the
illegal market."

"Well, then, that will be a last resort," said Jim.

"Good. I'm glad," said Sharon.

Shabbat came around again, and again they went to Sharon's
brother's house, but Jim went early to play Frisbee with Rani

and Mari in a nearby park. He was showing off his ground skimmer when he saw a park sign.

He was playing Frisbee in the Valley of the Cross, the place from which tradition said the wood for the cross had been taken. Part of it was now a Boy Scout park.

On Shabbat Eve, he heard Dr. Golban describe the beauties and glories of Persia.

"May I ask why you are here, then?"

"Because I am a Jew," said Dr. Golban.

"But you sound so Persian."

"We were there for twenty-five hundred years," said Dr. Golban, and he talked more about Persia and said that, to his surprise, he was using classical Greek remedies that he thought were Persian.

"How did classical Greek medicine get to Persia?" asked Jim.

"You've never heard of Alexander the Great?" said Sharon.

"He married a Persian princess," said Mari.

"He was a great general," said Rani. "But he overextended himself, though."

"I found out they were Greek remedies only when I came here. It was hard, you know, because they did not accept my Persian medical education. For good reason, too."

"There was a choice," said Sharon, "of staying in Persia, Iran, with respect for his medical skills, or coming here with his little sister and learning again. I was brought here at twelve."

"Let me ask again, even though you have answered. Why did you come?"

And Dr. Avrahim Golban rose from the Shabbat table and kissed the forehead of Rani and then Mari.

"When I was a boy, my big fear was that my father would not be able to defend me. My children in Israel do not have that fear," said Dr. Golban. "You have heard many things about Islam. The Muslim neighbors in our village were the most beautiful people in the world. I can cry for missing them now. But I tell you, Mr. Folan, it was as recently as twenty-five years ago that it was not more of a crime than a twenty-gold-piece fine in that Islamic land to kill a Jew. In our village, our Muslim neighbors would defend us."

"We were lucky, because our village was good to all minorities," said Sharon, "Zoroastrians, Christians, Bahai."

"Here, we defend ourselves," said Rani, and he put a hand on Mari's shoulder, next to his father's hand.

"You see," said Avrahim, his voice trembling, "my children will not miss Persia, and that beautiful land and our beautiful neighbors."

Outside, going home, Sharon explained to Jim that in her brother's house there was a conflict within Judaism.

"He's Persian. They have adopted some of the Muslim customs. Paula, of course, is Ashkenazi to a T, to a T."

"So what do they do?"

"They do it the woman's way and the man complains. The candles and types of Friday night prayers over the *chaleh*, bread that is Ashkenazi. As a matter of fact, about a hundred and twenty different kinds of Judaism showed up in the great return, with only a single common belief they all shared."

"What was that?" said Jim.

"That the other one hundred and nineteen were doing it wrong."

By the next Friday night, Jim was calling Dr. Golban by his first name, and Mari absolutely loved Jim and was going to marry him, and Sharon couldn't because she was a married woman. Paula thought Jim was too thin and not eating enough, and Rani wanted to know what Jim did for a living.

"I teach at Boston College in Boston," said Jim.

"They have a good nursing school," said Paula.

"They have many good departments."

"I've heard that the only good one is nursing."

"Well, that's a misconception," said Jim, who did not need to go to the homeland of Christ to hear that Boston College had only one good department, and one that he had nothing to do with, to boot.

The national holiday of Tubashvat was close, and Jim offered to plant a tree in their backyard, which they accepted. This was an important thing with Israelis. But when he returned to Sharon's apartment with the apricot tree he had bought, to show her what they would take to her family, he found someone blocking his way.

A younger man with dark curls and much jewelry tinkling on his exposed, hairy chest waited at the doorway to Sharon's apartment.

Jim excused himself, and opened the door with the key.

"Who are you?" said the younger man in Hebrew.

"I live here," answered Jim in Hebrew. "Who are you?"

"I am the rightful husband of the woman you are living with."

"Oh," said Jim.

"Oh," repeated the younger man with indignation.

"You must be Dubi Halafi."

"I am."

"Well, Sharon will be home later, why don't you come back then?"

"I am here now. I am her husband. I belong here. By law." He made a grand gesture with his fingers, his voice resonating on the word "law," as though it was just something he had discovered.

"Come back later, please," said Jim. It was not begging. He was firm.

Suddenly, an ugly knife was at his throat.

"No Israeli court would convict a husband trying to get into his own home. Heh?"

Jim did not move. He did not want to give in to the man, and he was so angry he almost didn't care what happened. He thought of bashing the tree into Dubi Halafi, maybe even killing him in the fight. After all, the man did draw a knife, and Sharon said he had a minor criminal record, a thing she found out only after they were married.

He might be able to kill that man right now, and get away with it. After all, who knew what Mendel Hirsch's influence could accomplish? And this man would be gone forever.

In a flash, Jim thought of Biblical precedent. David and Bathsheba. Right. But that was an example of a sin.

And what he was doing here was thinking of endangering his mission for Christianity, for his own lust.

"All right, come on in," said Jim. He opened the door and Dubi angled his way in front of Jim so the door could not be shut on him. He strode around the apartment, commenting on how well his wife had done while he was struggling.

Jim could see that Dubi dressed to exploit his sex appeal—from the tight white pants to the jeweled chest.

He could see how Sharon would think of Dubi as sexy. She had never called Jim sexy. She would run up behind him and hug him and say how happy she was, but she would never call him sexy, not so that he would believe it.

When Sharon arrived, Jim hurried to the door to let her know what she was walking into. It was simultaneous with her discovery.

"Dubi," she said, and Jim saw her face instinctively light with joy. He felt a sword pierce his own heart, and he said a quick silent prayer he regretted, even as he said it, for its blasphemy:

"Jesus. Please don't let her go with him!"

"I am back, and I see you are living well," said Dubi.

"One does live better when one's pocketbook isn't rifled," said Sharon.

"When I returned, I thought I might be able to arrange a divorce for you. But now that I see what you are living with, I see you need a real man. Need a real man, Sharon." Dubi smiled with the content of a leopard.

"Dubi," said Sharon, putting down some packages on the table in the kitchen, and returning to the living room–bedroom so that her words would be heard and understood. "This is a man," she said, putting her arms on Jim's shoulder. "You are an organ."

Dubi blanched. But he recovered quickly.

"A man without a penis is not a man."

"This man has everything a man should have. He is a whole man. Just go, please."

"You're a whore, living with a Gentile, and I'm not leaving. You've offended my honor."

"Excuse me, Dubi. Sit there, Jim," said Sharon, and she went to the telephone.

"You can call the police. You are my wife, and you are living with another man. Guess who they will throw out?"

Sharon dialed.

She got Mendel Hirsch. She explained that their mutual guest was having difficulties in her apartment and faced some danger. Then she hung up.

Dubi waited, confident. He even sprawled out on the bed, laughing.

Sharon stood by Jim.

Within ten minutes a car pulled up outside.

"Now we will see," said Dubi.

Sharon opened the door. Three dark Yemenis in suits entered. They were the escorts in Mea Shearim. Sharon pointed to the bed.

"I am the husband. I belong here. That man must go."

"Please, sir," said one of the Yemenis softly. "This is her apartment. Please leave."

"I am the husband."

"It's her apartment."

"Where's your identification?" said Dubi.

"You don't want to go to jail, and we don't want trouble. Why don't we go outside and talk?" said the Yemeni softly. Jim wondered what the man could really do against that knife of Dubi's. The Yemeni had such delicate black features. He was not a big man, either.

"Are you some muscle that whore has hired?"

"Let's talk about it outside, please."

Dubi flashed his knife. "We talk here," he said, and then interposed an American word: "Nigger."

Instinctively, Jim thought the Yemenis would react strongly, but then he remembered it was not a word they had lived with. The Yemenis might not even know what it meant.

Later, Jim would understand why the Yemeni could be so polite and calm with a knife pointed at him. But at that moment Jim, like Dubi, took it as a sign of weakness.

"Make me," said Dubi contemptuously.

The Yemeni asked once more, and Dubi moved on him. The knife went onto the floor, and Dubi's knife arm was instantly behind him in the Yemeni's grip, and Dubi was doubled over perfectly, with his head on the floor, while one Yemeni stepped in front of Jim and Sharon so they wouldn't see what was coming. They heard a single blow, and Dubi was blissfully at peace with the universe. One Yemeni picked up the knife and they lifted the sleeping Dubi to his feet and had him out the door, wishing Jim and Sharon, as they left, a most happy Tubashvat.

Later that evening Mendel called to say that Dubi Halafi was on an El Al flight to America, where a job was waiting for him.

"He had a sudden desire to return," said Mendel.

The apricot tree went into the ground behind the house of Dr. Golban with the singing and clapping of hands. Jim had dug a very deep hole, much deeper than one would have assumed was needed. But Sharon said that was necessary, so the tree could root.

And even as he packed the earth back around the tree, he realized he had told himself the greatest lie he could have invented. He had been counting on time to enable him to leave Sharon, for the days to wear at the love.

But like a good tree, it had taken deep root. Out of Paula's sight, he squeezed Sharon's hand, as everyone sang the blessings of the earth.

18

Ash Wednesday

Jim and Sharon pulled a heavy tarpaulin over the opaque plastic cover concealing the body.

"Okay. Now push against it. Go ahead. Fall," said Sharon.

Jim pushed, as though accidentally coming into the cover, with the horizontal thrust of his left hand. The cover groaned but didn't move. Not an inch.

"He can't accidentally see the body now. You've got to lift off the tarpaulin," said Sharon.

"Why does that work?" asked Jim. "Equalized pressure?"

"I don't know," said Sharon. "But it works, doesn't it?"

"Good," said Jim. He gave a little nod to the tarpaulin cover.

"Why did you do that?" asked Sharon.

"Do what?"

"Bow."

"I was just agreeing that the tarpaulin was a good idea."

"You did that before the cover was on. You do that all the time."

"No, I don't. But I do respect the body. I have a promise to the Reb Nechtal to honor this body."

Sharon said nothing. But the bow did not look like honoring a body. It looked like reverence.

"We've got to hide the dehumidifier," said Jim.

The dehumidifier in the niche was too heavy to move up the

ladder to Haneviim Street, so they put that under a flap of the tarpaulin.

The thermostat control could be taken out completely, and was unscrewed from its wall casings, and its bulky wires rolled up, so that they both just fit into the long, plastic bag they had once intended to remove the body in.

"Maybe the cover won't hold now?" asked Jim.

"Do you want to try it again?"

"Too late now," he said.

They turned on strong, battery-powered lanterns, and then unscrewed the light from above and hid the wires, also under the tarpaulin.

"Looks like a dig again, kind of," said Jim.

"That's what we're going to say it has become. An archaeological workshop, which we are closing. I'm in charge, remember," said Sharon.

"Fine. Do you think this is going to work?"

"No. But I don't think he is going to matter anyhow. I don't even see why we need a geologist in the first place. You can see no one planted the body through another tunnel. Secret tunnel. Secret body. Things don't work like that."

"Is everything all right? I don't want the moisture to get in here too long," said Jim.

"The clay," said Sharon. Jim shone the lantern on the pack she was carrying. Inside was a plastic bag of the same light, red-brown clay so common to this area. She took a handful and smeared it into the ceiling where casings for the light fixture had been set, covering them, and then into the holes in the wall where the thermostat had been set.

"Okay, ready," said Jim, as he bent down and climbed up the steps, and through the low opening.

It was sunlight outside. The stone was hidden by a large plank of leaning plywood, and the pump to keep the water from building up the base lay under another tarpaulin.

"Hut, hut," said the Reb Nechtal's man, pointing at the black bag Jim carried.

"Wires, thermostat," said Jim. "Heat. Hot. Humidity. Tools."

The man would not let him walk to the street. Jim had to open it. When the man saw the wires, he looked at Jim, smiled and nodded.

"He wanted to make sure it wasn't a body," said Sharon.

"He doesn't check the little bags," said Jim.

"That's foolish," said Sharon. "You could take the damn thing out in olive jars if you broke it up right."

"Don't talk like that," said Jim.

They put the bag in the back seat of Sharon's car. They waited half an hour, and then the geologist, who wanted everything explained to him, arrived. He drove up in a jeep and wore an army jacket.

Jim went along as Sharon lied her head off. They were on an archaeological dig, and they found some valuable things, and they were lucky to find a very cheap watchman. They had a door down there that locked because of the valuable things, and now they were closing it up, and they wanted to help the owner of the property, if they could, by finding out if there were any fissures in the rock, any possible ancient tunneling, so the excavation wouldn't take that long.

The geologist was suspicious as soon as he looked down into the dig.

"How deep is the basement going to be?"

"Three stories, at least," said Sharon.

"Right," said Jim.

"Hmmmmm," said the geologist suspiciously.

At the bottom he cast a baleful glance at the metal door with the lock set into a frame, covering a hole into the cave.

"How long have you been working down here?"

"Awhile. We're closing up," said Sharon.

"Giving it back to the owner," said Jim.

Inside the cave, he looked at the tarpaulin. Then at the walls.

"When did you uncover this?" he said.

"Some time ago."

"Then how come it feels so dry?"

"I don't know," said Sharon.

"Does it feel dry?" said Jim.

The geologist took the lantern from Sharon, and made one sweep around the cave horizontally, and then one vertically, and handed the lantern back to Sharon.

"I don't know what this shit is, Dr. Golban, but you didn't

need me. This is limestone. There is no crack anywhere. There has been no tunneling. You know that.''

He walked up the little tomb steps, and through the door without pausing.

''Well,'' said Jim. ''That's a valid report. I'll just put his name down on it. No tunneling, no fissures.''

''Right,'' said Sharon.

''You're getting good at lying,'' said Jim.

''Jim, that bothers me. I am not lying about the facts, I am lying to people to protect your interests.''

''I know that, Sharon. I was joking because it did seem like an uncomfortable position, in a way.''

''No. You don't understand. I would never falsify anything to make something appear different for history.''

''I know,'' said Jim.

''No. I am a liar. I am a liar. You are a liar and we are going to be found out by Dr. Sproul. If the geologist knew something was wrong, Dr. Sproul is going to find out everything. Everything. That's it, Jim. Everything.''

''No, the geologist didn't know what we had. He was just suspicious of us. I can live with that,'' said Jim.

''He wasn't Dr. Sproul.''

''We fooled the Jesuit at the Biblical Institute. We have his report in detail about how valid the writing on the disk half was. He even thought it probably referred to some Roman captives because of the rebellions that went on here. That's why the label 'Jews, *Yehudayai*.' He had no idea what the disk was.''

''He is not Dr. Sproul,'' said Sharon. ''I've been to his lectures. The man is eerie, he is so logical.''

''Yes,'' said Jim, ''but even he is not going to suspect, if he believes that we have dated this body at 500 B.C. And he has the word of Dr. Sharon Golban of Hebrew University.''

''Yes,'' said Sharon. ''And everyone knows she would never lie.''

They picked up Dr. William Sproul at Ben Gurion Airport and drove back through the late winter fields of Samaria, not yet producing the flowers of olive, pomegranate, and date.

''I am glad to be here in Israel early. Usually, I arrive no earlier than Easter and stay for part of your digging season, or come after digging season and stay for Christmas," said Dr. Sproul.

"That's good," said Jim, not knowing why he said it was good.

"I will do my Lent here in the Holy Land," said Dr. Sproul. "Are you familiar with the exact meaning of Lent, Dr. Folan?" He turned to the back seat, where Jim sat.

"Yes, I am," said Jim, who had been introduced as an archaeologist.

"It's a meaningful period for a Christian. It prepares you for Easter. The problem with Easter in the States is that it has become rabbits and Easter eggs and pretty clothes on Easter Sunday."

"Uh huh," said Jim.

"Now I have got nothing against those things, but the children lose the real meaning. Easter is God's hand on man. It is the Resurrection of our Lord, and the promise of your resurrection. Easter is a lot holier than Christmas. You have Palm Sunday, when Jesus came to Jerusalem, Good Friday, when he suffered his crucifixion to share our death, and then you have that great day, Easter. It is the most important day. It is the Christian holy day."

"Yes," said Jim.

"Now, you take Christmas. What is that? We don't even know when Christ was born. The Catholic Church picks a date out of a hat, and Christendom goes celebrating it for two thousand years."

"It wasn't exactly out of a hat. The Church did it to coincide with a pagan sun festival of gift giving, which it superseded."

"The blazes you say. You go into a department store and you show me Christ, will you? You've got Christmas trees from the German pagan rite, Santa Claus, some other Nordic tribalism, and the gifts. You ask any American child what Christmas is and he will give you an answer that will fit in with pagan Rome. Gifts and good cheer. Well, dammit, that's not Christian. I'm sorry. Every time I get to the Holy Land, I touch down talking. I'm not like this ordinarily."

"Dr. Sproul is usually quite subdued," said Sharon.

"You can't get angry about a fact, but you can get angry at what we have done to Christianity."

"Excuse me, Dr. Sproul, but you don't have a lien on theological bastardization. You are entering a city where the revolt against Greek ways was led by the Maccabees, whose descendants ended up following Greek ways. The Pharisees started out to bring Judaism to the people, whereupon they got bogged down in externals," said Sharon. "You are just part of a tradition. That's all."

"You're not especially Orthodox, if I remember," said Dr. Sproul.

He turned around to the back seat to see why Dr. Folan was laughing.

"I am not. No. He didn't have to laugh," said Sharon.

"You know each other well, I take it," said Dr. Sproul.

"We've been working together," said Jim.

"Now, you've got this rather special body you wish me to examine, and it is at least 500 years B.C.E. Correct?" said Dr. Sproul, and his voice suddenly became quite soft, almost like clouds in the blue winter sky.

"How do you know it is special?" asked Jim.

"You didn't have to offer to pay my way. You could have asked me when I was coming back again, instead of when could I."

"It is special," said Sharon. "We have carbon dating of bones that absolutely puts the body 500 B.C.E. plus or minus eighty, of course."

"Who did the carbon dating?"

"Weizmann Institute."

"That's good. You'll let me see the report."

"Sure," said Sharon, and Jim knew they were now going to have to get a phony one made up.

"I ask for that only because you would be surprised how many slip-ups you encounter with technical things."

"Sure," said Jim.

"Right," said Sharon.

He went on about dating of bodies, and how the bones themselves encapsulated what a person did in life. Such as a particular spine fracture, which helped him identify what started out as a half skull in Skokie, Illinois. The fracture was common to athletes, and it was discovered ultimately that the body belonged to a sixteen-year-old ballerina who had been missing from a nearby town.

Bones would enlarge, depending on the kind of jobs a person did. Calcium deposits would build up in different places. The size of people differed with their diet, and Jim, as an American, would have to know that the second generation of immigrants was always taller than their parents because of the diet.

One could trace the Little Ice Age in Europe from the thickness of the pelvis.

"I guess that's why they say you know what a person is thinking, from the bones," said Jim.

"You know a lot, but you never know a person. A person has to be alive for that," said Dr. Sproul seriously.

"This body is special because it was crucified. We think it's the first Babylonian crucifixion we have discovered," said Sharon.

"Did the Babylonians crucify?" asked Dr. Sproul.

"The Persians did," said Sharon. "That's who the Romans got it from."

"But did the Babylonians? You must be talking Nebuchadnezzar at that date."

"They could have picked it up," said Sharon. "There is nothing like a bad habit for sure-fire imitation."

Dr. Sproul laughed. He didn't want to go to his hotel room. He wanted to see the body right away.

"Had some trouble with the Hasidim, you say?"

"They're not Hasidim. Hasidim is just one group among the ultra-Orthodox," said Jim.

"But you made a deal with them on the body. Couldn't remove it, you say?"

"Right," said Jim.

"You see, I don't think they believe in real Judaism. Those clothes aren't from the Bible or the Talmud. They're from eighteenth-century eastern Europe," said Dr. Sproul.

Sharon laughed agreement and parked the car.

"The clothes are only a device to let women know the men should not be accosted for lewd things because they are holy men. Like a priest's collar," said Jim.

"And what about their long sideburns, *peot*, Dr. Folan? You know, the Bible doesn't say which locks should not be cut.

Could be the forelock. They just chose the sideburns to let grow."

"Right. Like the Western Church chose December the twenty-fifth. The important thing is that they're doing the work of the Lord, right?" said Jim.

"I can't see doing it that way," said Dr. Sproul.

"That's why you are a Methodist," said Jim, nodding to the Orthodox guard who was stationed at the dig. "And that's why he is Orthodox."

Dr. Sproul laughed.

"The problem is not that he believes in his laws," said Sharon, "but that he is making us live by them."

"Good point," said Dr. Sproul. "I would prefer using a laboratory to examine the body. Laboratory light should be the best of sunlight. Darkness breeds imagination, superstition."

He peered over the edge of the dig.

"Twenty-five hundred years is a long time down, isn't it?" he said.

"Yeah," said Jim.

Dr. Sproul had bought the date and story, so far.

When the metal door was open and Dr. Sproul followed Sharon into the tomb, Jim crossed himself quickly and said a little prayer.

"This is a tomb?" said Dr. Sproul, looking around when the lights were on. "A good-sized tomb. Man was crucified, you say?"

"Yes," said Sharon.

"How do you know?"

"Orange line on his tibia. That's oxidized iron."

"Correct," said Dr. Sproul. "But you found some dating evidence for the First Temple period, 500 B.C.?"

"Right," said Sharon.

"For the Second Temple period, I would say oxidized iron is a right assumption for crucifixion. But frankly, Sharon, I don't know if your find really is crucifixion for 500 B.C. What do you think, Dr. Folan?"

"Me?" said Jim.

"Yes," said Dr. Sproul.

Sharon looked at Dr. Sproul, worried. She had said she

would bail Jim out if he got in over his head. Obviously she felt
he could answer it.

"I think any oxidized iron line means a spike. And on the
tibia, what else is it, except some gigantic accident? Would
they nail a dead body anywhere? I doubt it. Only crucified bodies have it, in my experience."

Dr. Sproul nodded. He filled the bowl of a pipe. Sharon put a
hand on his arm. No smoking.

"He was found there?" asked Dr. Sproul, nodding to the
niche.

"Yes," said Jim.

"No other bodies?"

"No."

"It's an awful lot of tomb for one man, especially a crucified
one. Of course, we don't know how disgraceful crucifixion was
to the Babylonian. They could have done it to the wealthy and
powerful, too. After all, they did take the Jews into captivity."

"My family," said Sharon, "were rescued by Cyrus the
Great."

"The first Diaspora," said Dr. Sproul. "I always liked that
passage about the writing on the wall. That's where it comes
from, you know. When the writing hand told the Babylonian
king his kingdom had been judged and his days were numbered."

Dr. Sproul thought about that, and smiled. "Just sort of setting where everyone was coming from, which you archaeologists do when you study a dig. You know who is where for what
purpose, so you don't go putting your own values on things."

Jim nodded. He remembered how well Sharon had set the
scene that Jesus had walked into, His very admission of the
truth being a death sentence to that life that threatened the sta-
bility of the northern route to the empire's grain basket. In the
end, they did not kill Him for who He was, but for who they
were. Jim had to remember Dr. Sproul was setting his scene for
approximately 500 B.C. This was the Babylonians, not the Romans. He could not make any reference to Roman rule, or the
Sadducees, descendants of the Maccabees who revolted against
Alexander's generals.

Alexander had yet to conquer the Persians, who had yet to
conquer the Babylonians. Rome was a little city on a river. The

Persian empire was about to be great. And the Jews were going into exile for the first time. As the prophets had foretold.

Jim went to one side of the opaque cover, Sharon to the other. They lifted it off, and carried it to the base of the tomb steps.

The bones were exposed again. Only the portion where the jaw had been cracked off was the original brown. The rest had the whitish cast of the polyvinyl.

"Sort of big, wasn't he?"

"Beg your pardon?" said Jim.

"Big. How tall is he?"

"Five-five," said Jim.

"That's tall for the First Temple period."

"Very big?" asked Jim.

"No. It's just that at that time the Roman roads weren't in, and one thing you need for nutrition is roads. A good road network is the first requirement of good agriculture because it encourages farmers to grow food for profit, you see? And, to boot, Romans put up aqueducts up and down this area. So people were generally smaller than before the Romans came."

"How much smaller?"

"Two or three inches. You see, this fellow would be the normal size for the Second Temple period. He'd also be tall if he were found in a suit of knight's armor in Europe. Had a lot of five-footers in medieval Europe, what with the Ice Age and all."

"Uh huh," said Jim.

Dr. Sproul put the unlit pipe in his mouth and hummed to himself. Jim swallowed. The cave smelled somehow musty again, like before the dehumidifier went into action. Jim reminded himself to breathe.

Behind Dr. Sproul's back, Sharon nodded encouragement, and mouthed words that she loved Jim.

Maybe, thought Jim, God had sent her to him as a comfort in God's mission.

And maybe that was another self-deception. He could have relied on Jesus. The Mass and communion were not unknown for comfort. Neither was confession, which he hadn't been to since before Christmas. Adultery, Father Folan reminded himself, was not a spiritual support from God.

"Well, I don't think he was a field slave. Look here at the legs."

Jim got behind Sproul.

"You see, there is no buildup of bone that a field slave or a soldier would have. Marching, or anything like that," said Sproul.

"Perhaps royalty?" said Sharon.

"No, no. Look at the arms. This man worked with his arms, but not his legs. He was a potter. A carpenter, stonemason, some kind of craftsman who required arm strength."

"Uh huh," Jim managed to say.

"Doesn't mean he wasn't a holy man. You see, Jewish holy men at that period all had occupations, too. They did not have that intense ritual priesthood, such as later."

"You're talking about the Sadducees," said Sharon. "Not the Pharisees."

Dammit, thought Jim. Why does she have to bring it back to the beginnings of Christianity?

"Right, St. Paul. St. Paul was a Pharisee who was told to stop persecuting the new Jewish sect that followed Christ as the Messiah. And Christ himself was a carpenter," said Dr. Sproul.

"Oh," said Jim.

"You didn't know that, Dr. Folan?"

"He knew that," said Sharon. "Of course he knew that."

The next day Dr. Sproul was back with his equipment. Jim did not go down to the cave with him. He spent the day in the church at the Garden of Gethsemane, run by the Franciscans. A pilgrim group came in, and Jim heard the Latin Mass said again, reminding him of his childhood as he had grown up with his friend Baby Jesus.

The Latin was supposed to be only the form not the Mass itself. The words were the vehicle. That was what he had been told, and did tell himself when people complained about the Latin Mass being replaced by English.

"It only sounds more holy," he would say tolerantly.

But in his sin, and desperation, the Latin Mass by this pilgrim group, allowed to be said in the old universal language of the Church because this was an international city for the Church, this Mass was water for his blistered spirit.

"Et cum spiritu tuo," Jim answered the priest. And he left church somewhat comforted. Dr. Sproul, according to Sharon, had found a blade mark in the ribs, and established it was going upward into the heart, and also that the edge of the spear was round and not bladed like most other spears.

Sharon had to lie about that, saying the pointed, nonblade spear was common to Babylonians.

"But he was guessing Romans," she said.

"How much was he guessing Romans?" said Jim.

"Not with vigor," said Sharon.

"Hold me," said Jim, and they embraced, and he let his head fall to her shoulder. "Tighter," he said, and then he felt himself wanting her, and this night he knew the love was her gift.

"You didn't enjoy it," he said.

"Yes, I did," she answered. "I enjoyed giving to you."

And as they lay together in the darkness, she told him how much of a woman he made her feel.

"I feel good about that, Sharon. Partly."

"I know," said Sharon.

"I love you."

"I know," said Sharon.

The next day Dr. Sproul, the world-famous pathologist known as the "bone man," was leaving. He did not want to stay for Lent in the Holy Land. He wanted to go home. He had found where the spikes had rubbed between the ulna and radius in the arms, so the arms were not tied, but impaled just beneath the wrists.

Under intense examination of the skull, he had found where the skull had suffered four minor indentations extending from the coronal structure along the frontal, about three inches above the supraorbital notch. Apparently, the skin had been pierced right to the skull with pointed objects, which were not strong enough to dig in deep. Not metallic.

"Thorns," said Jim, reading the report in Sharon's apartment. "A crown of thorns."

The report concluded that the body was that of a thirty- to thirty-five-year-old Mediterranean male.

"What did he say about the carbon dating of the bones? Did he examine the phony report you made up last night?"

"No," said Sharon. "He just kept repeating that I wouldn't lie to him and he had to accept that date." Sharon paused.

Jim lowered the report.

"He asked me who was in charge of this. I told him you," said Sharon.

"Yes?"

"He wished you luck and he said prayers, his deepest prayers, were with you."

"I don't see where he mentions no bones were broken. That's the first thing he should have noticed, you know. That's the normal way to end a crucifixion. It's what made Christ's crucifixion fulfill the Hebrew prophecy that no bone of the Messiah would ever be broken. He missed that," said Jim. "That's strange. That's the strangest part of all."

He looked out the window. He felt numb. He gazed at the white top of the Jewish Dome of the Book, which housed the Qumran scrolls, those scrolls which he had been told in his studies helped establish that the Gospels were accurate in their depiction of what society would be like in the Second Temple period.

He felt Sharon's arm around him. "He didn't want to notice the bones weren't broken. He clung to the dating."

"I don't know what to do. I don't know what I can do," said Jim.

"There is no choice about the matching piece for the disk now."

"You mean we have got to have a date outside 30 to 40 C.E.?"

"In the light of everything, especially Dr. Sproul's report, about a carpenter in his mid-thirties . . . and everything else, you have nothing else."

"You said, at the beginning, that there was always a way to disprove something, always an area for doubt."

"Because usually we get a rock and a shard and a coin. I didn't know Dr. Sproul would be that corroborative."

"And what if the disk, within that fantastically sharp ten-year swing of plus or minus, gives us 30 to 40 C.E.? We would have nothing left then."

"I would say, right now, there isn't an archaeologist in the world who would not testify to the awesome probability that the bones are Him.''

"I thought so. All right. The disk.''

"Let me get that dirt off your forehead,'' said Sharon, licking a finger to wipe away a smudge right in the middle of Jim's head. But he stopped her hand.

"It's not dirt,'' said Jim. "It's ash. It's Ash Wednesday.''

Warris Abouf landed in Beirut on a Syrian plane with a Syrian passport during a lull in the shelling. Debarkation had to be quick because no one could guarantee the shelling wouldn't resume again.

"Who is shelling whom? Which faction?'' asked Warris in Arabic.

"Does it matter?'' answered another passenger, taking up his bags for the rush to the terminal and the sandbags.

"Not to me.'' Warris smiled. He was home. If he were dead on the tarmac, he was still home. There had been courtesy on the aircraft. There had been respect on the aircraft. Russians in the group were no longer the masters. They were just tourists.

Even his toe did not hurt him that much anymore.

It was less than a single day before that he had been called to 2 Dzerszhinsky Square. And when he was not taken directly to Major Vakunin's office, he thought perhaps he was headed toward Lubyanka Prison, which was right behind. At that time he thought perhaps he had miscalculated: perhaps Major Vakunin would send him to jail instead of home, to get at Tomarah, undisturbed by a nearby husband.

But Major Vakunin himself sat in a subordinate seat in a large office. Warris addressed himself instinctively to one man sitting on the side, whom he felt was in charge. It was a mistake. The major told him loudly what a fool he was, and that the man behind the desk was running things, not the fellow on the side.

Now the fellow sitting on the side had thick eyeglasses, and an ill-fitting Russian suit. He did not look impressive, and he was so old one would think he was retired. But Warris knew by the way everyone else stood that he was the power in the room.

"Quiet,'' said the man to Vakunin. "He is smart. He knows. Look, Abouf, we are in a bind, and we need you. You are a smart fellow, and we appreciate your care in your work. But we have to have someone who can be trusted and we have to have him now.''

"Who, sir?" said Warris.

"You're playing a game. I am too old for games, and I am too old for lies."

"The Palestinian, fluent Hebrew, knowledge of the Vatican," said Warris.

"Yes. We need you. It's you. That may be bad news for you, it may be good. Will you go for us?"

"Do I have a choice?" said Warris.

"Everyone always has a choice. It is just not a palatable one," said the old man with the power.

"I am willing to go. I was willing to go before."

"We didn't know that," said the man, and Warris could feel the anguish radiate from Major Vakunin behind him.

"In Jerusalem," said the man, "there is something going on in Haneviim Street. It has some Vatican reference but we do not know what it is. All right, we have lost two agents already, and a third has found nothing. We want to know what is so special that it would involve the Vatican Secretary of State and the Israeli government? What?"

"What are we looking for?" said Warris.

"That is it, we do not know. But it must be important because the Mossad has put a shield around it."

"What if I am caught by that shield?"

"If you are caught and you talk, we will kill you."

"But what if they torture me?"

"What torture? They'll put you in a room and talk to you a lot. If you break, we will kill you. They will not. Remember that."

"But everyone knows they have torture in their prisons. I read it in *Pravda*."

"Warris, I would expect that sort of a statement from Vakunin. Not from a fellow like Warris Abouf, who has survived by his own worth all his life and not by whom he married, and whom he doesn't offend. Vakunin and these others will take care of the details. Good luck, Warris. It always hurts to lose a good man."

"Thank you, comrade, sir," said Warris, struck by the

fact that the first time he ever got real respect was on his leaving.

The details were that he would meet men in the Beirut airport who would take him to Abu Silwan, his contact who would get him into Israel. He was given a Syrian passport, and clothes with Beirut labels, and American dollars. He was not even allowed to keep the picture of his son, Arkady.

And thus ended ten years in a foreign land where he was not wanted, except to be used.

At the Beirut airport he did not have to find his contacts, they found him. They were two young lads with machine guns, army fatigues, British cigarettes, and a new Mercedes that made Warris' old Volga look like a sick cart. In fact, this car was so luxurious it had cigarette lighters in it.

The home of Abu Silwan was outside Beirut, in what the young men called "a safe area." He loved their voices. He loved their hands moving as they talked, and their eyes, which spoke also.

The house they took him to was glorious, with glass all over and deep carpets on the floor, and color television sets all over, and whiskey in crystal glasses, and faucets of gold with sinks of marble.

He heard groans from another room. There was someone in pain there, pitifully weak, crying for mercy. And then there was a soft laughter, and then nothing.

A man of Warris' age came down the hall drying his hands on a towel, which he gave to a bodyguard. There was a red spot on his white jacket. It was blood. He had just washed his hands.

"Well, Warris, you are looking very, very good. What did you do wrong?"

"Sir?" said Warris. The man looked familiar. There was something about the face that was very familiar. "Bashir Hussein. Little Bashir Hussein. From Patrice Lumumba. Yes. I remember you were very, very intelligent."

"I am Abu Silwan now. My revolutionary name."

"Yes, of course. Of course," said Warris. Now he remembered. He had classified Bashir Hussein, now Abu Silwan, as both intelligent and prone to violence. He could not take his eyes off the stain on the suit.

Abu Silwan noticed Warris' eyes. "A traitor. We have so many traitors," he said. "So many."

The voice was like the hiss of a snake, and Warris knew Abu Silwan would kill him as easily as peeling a fig, and with as much thought. Even in that luxurious white suit, Abu Silwan was a menace.

"What did you do wrong to lose that good position, Warris?"

"Nothing," said Warris. "I am the only one who can do this thing they need."

"Come, come. You are not leaving that nice position in Moscow and facing Zionist torture because you have not done something wrong."

"I haven't," said Warris.

"Come, come! I am not a Russian. I am your friend. Your old friend. One needs compassionate brotherhood in these troubled times of traitors. You befriended me in Moscow, I befriend you here."

"Yes, yes," said Warris.

"So, what did you do?" said Abu Silwan, and Warris knew this was a man who had to be satisfied.

"I stole," said Warris.

"They didn't give you enough? The pigs. They think because you are an Arab, you will work for nothing. They are like that, the Russians. Good that you stole. Good."

Abu Silwan embraced Warris, and told him he would not have to steal in the home of Abu Silwan, for they were brothers. Everything in Abu Silwan's house was the property of Warris Abouf.

"Unfortunately, you must leave for Jordan tonight, because everything is arranged, and the Russians, you know how they are, rush, rush."

"Yes," said Warris, even now being guided right back out the door.

"The greatest danger we face and are ever going to face in the Arab cause is traitors," said Abu Silwan, guiding him to another Mercedes, which was forming into an armed convoy for Amman. "They have been our greatest enemies, they are our greatest enemies, and when we win, there will be no scores left unsettled. I am glad you are on the right side. I like you. If it weren't for traitors, the Jews would be hiding behind trees this very day, and the trees would give them up."

"Of course," said Warris to the very same logic that had started his family on their trek more than thirty years before.

"Traitors. Revisionist, defeatist traitors. Struggle till death."

"Absolutely," said Warris.

On the way to Amman, he remembered what his father had told him about their home in the Galilee, how neighbors had said the Syrian armies were coming, and any that did not rise up and fight the Jews would be considered traitors. And they would be killed. But those who did fight would not only have honor, but the homes and property of the Jews as well.

And that was 1948. In 1967 traitors were the ones who stayed behind on the West Bank of the Jordan to live under Israeli rule. In 1970 it was the traitors who did not join the guerrillas in their fight against the reactionary King Hussein, tool of the American imperialists and Zionists.

Warris was old enough to remember that argument, because one side of the family stayed in Jordan and the other, with his father in it, retreated with the guerrillas to find a new place outside of Beirut in a refugee camp, where Warris was lucky enough to be selected for Patrice Lumumba University and Moscow, where he learned about more people he was supposed to call traitors.

He had always thought that, perhaps, if no one was calling anyone else a traitor, he would be this very moment not traveling by car at night in an armed convoy, but safe in his bed in his home in Galilee, with a son who loved him and would inherit the olive trees that he would plant, if they were not there already.

In Amman he did not go immediately to the arranged contact but to a distant cousin, part of those Abouf who stayed in Jordan and moved no farther. All the Abouf, it turned out, were prospering under the reign of King Hussein.

They would not let him stay in a hotel under pain of insult. He was one of them. He would go no farther. He was home.

Warris' first message back to Abu Silwan contained intimations of the unsuitability of the contact. Warris was sorry to say the man might be a traitor, and it would be traitorous to risk such a valuable mission at this time. He would have to stay where he was.

19

Palm Sunday

It was the worst time to see Zareh Tabinian, and yet Tabinian was the best person to help them. Jim and Sharon had no choice anymore, they would have to go into the illegal market.

But this was the worst time to take the time of any antiquities dealer. The holy season was upon them, and with each passing day and with each increase in the number of tourists every piece became more valuable. Antiquities moved closer and closer to the personae of those involved in the Passion. Bountiful Roman oil lamps somehow were associated with the good centurion who recognized Christ as a holy man. Pontius Pilate's wife had strewn enough mirror fragments around the Mediterranean to cover the retaining walls of the Second Temple.

And there was hardly a silver coin that could not have been part of the thirty which paid for the life of Christ to Judas Iscariot, the traitor.

But in this fevered time, Zareh Tabinian put up a sign that said in English, Arabic, and Hebrew that the shop was closed.

"Welcome, friends," he said, and took them to the back room, where he ordered coffee to be brought in from a nearby shop, and served sweet cakes and relaxed as though this were a casual visit.

He sat forward in his chair, but his smile was ever present, and he waited on Sharon's words.

"We are looking for something. We have exhausted museums and all known legal collections," said Sharon.

"I hear you have come into some money," said Tabinian.

"How is that?"

"What I hear is that you have money and you are willing to spend it if you get the right piece."

"Your sources are correct," said Sharon.

"Unfortunately, you want Pilatus. Something with Pilatus' name in writing on a kiln-fired piece. Not stone, not silver, but kiln-fired."

"Yes," said Jim.

The coffee came and Tabinian was quiet until the young serving boy left. Jim noticed the crates in this back room, marked Egyptair, Olympic Airways, Alitalia, and El Al. Briefly, he wondered if the old Roman legions might not have carried things away from here which were now being brought back, so that only by remote accident were pilgrims actually buying the real artifacts of the Holy Land.

There was something different about Tabinian this day from the last time. Now his back was straighter, and he was very careful to stay on the edge of his seat. Sharon apparently did not notice this.

"There is a piece of kiln-fired pottery with Pilatus' name on it," said Tabinian.

"Where?"

"Unfortunately, you will never get it."

"How much did it sell for?" said Jim.

"If I knew, then I might be suspected of being the dealer. But this man gives up nothing, not for money or anything."

"I have resources," said Jim.

"No, no. Trust me to know there are those who will not give up things. You must understand why people buy ancient things. Why should they have to own them in the first place? His ego will not allow selling it."

"So we can forget Pilate," said Jim. "Pilate is out. But you have closed your shop for us."

"What can one do for perfect friends who come to call," he said. "And to be frank, for the last few weeks I have been intrigued by the Golban quest. Why kiln-fired, I asked myself? Is it possible that the whole thing is not some religious connection? That Pilatus' name is only desired because of dating? And then I remembered Dr. Golban being such an authority on dating. Am I correct so far?'' asked Tabinian.

"Yes," said Sharon.

"May I ask why you did not come to me first?" said Tabinian. "Am I not a friend?"

"Yes," said Sharon. "You are."

"But you thought, oh, Tabinian deals in illegal things. I will not deal with Tabinian, right?"

Sharon nodded.

"And so now you come here for your illegal dealings, the honest professor from Hebrew University."

Sharon nodded. Jim could tell she was mortified.

"Good. I just wanted to know that some of us are not all that much better than others. If you used your brain properly, Sharon, you would drive a Mercedes too."

"She is here for me," said Jim. "She is helping me. She would never do this if it weren't for me."

"That's all right, Jim. I'm doing this, so let's get on with it," said Sharon.

"So you want a date, yes?"

"Yes," said Sharon.

"Thirty-two A.D.," said Tabinian.

"Plus or minus what?"

"One year at the most."

"Impossible," said Sharon.

"At least over five thousand dollars," said Tabinian.

"Then it doesn't matter," said Sharon. "What else do you have?"

"Well, something from the Tenth Legion, eight hundred dollars."

"No," said Jim. "The Tenth Legion was here a long time. It was an institution. Some legions were older than my country."

"Good point," said Tabinian.

"What is your piece?" said Jim.

"Caiaphas, the high priest. A tributary jar to the temple."

"The high priest was a lifetime appointment. How can you say plus or minus one 32 C.E.?" said Sharon.

"Ah, the beauty of this Caiaphas piece is that it refers to the earthquake."

"Thirty-two C.E.," said Sharon, excited. "I worked at a dig

in which a floor had been cracked and that was how we knew the date.''

''This kiln-fired piece contained a portion of honeyed fruit, and the writing referred to the fruit as the Jew's temple offering, that it was reduced because of the earthquake. Apparently the donor had problems because of the earthquake. What we have is Caiaphas' name, probably put there by a clerk, accepting a reduced temple donation. It's a big piece,'' said Tabinian. He held out his hand to show the size of the shard. It was the size of an elongated dinner roll.

''Where can we get it?'' said Jim.

''It is out of the country, as so much of the valuable antiquities are.''

''Which country?'' said Jim.

''Please,'' said Tabinian.

''Jim, he has his ways. This is a very difficult and subtle thing. It's all illegal. You can't go rushing in,'' said Sharon. And then to Tabinian, ''How long and how much would it cost us to get a fragment of that shard? You've done a brilliant job in dating for our time period.''

''It will take at least a month. It is in France, you know,'' said Tabinian.

''No. It's not,'' said Jim.

''Jim,'' said Sharon angrily. ''Mr. Tabinian will do things, but will not do other things. I think you have insulted him wrongly.''

''No. I appreciate what Mr. Tabinian has done, by letting us know of the existence of the piece. But there can be only one reason why he needs a month in this era to supposedly find out how much it would cost. We have telephones. This is the twentieth century. Mr. Tabinian hasn't sold it yet. He is using that time to feel out a price.''

Tabinian smiled.

''How much exactly?'' said Jim.

''I don't know, there is someone who already is quite interested.''

''We just want a piece of the piece. He can have the rest after we're done with it,'' said Jim.

''Unfortunately,'' said Tabinian, ''I cannot sell a piece of it. The private collector is a French general, a friend of the

Dessaults', who manufacture the Mirage jets, as you know. Now what does a private collector need with a piece like this? It is not to add to mankind's knowledge, but to show off to friends. Maybe even to know that he alone has it, you see. Taking away a small piece from it robs his feelings of exclusivity.''

"How much?" said Jim.

"I do not wish to make him an enemy."

"How much?"

"Seven thousand dollars."

"I'll get it," said Jim.

"You can get that much money?" asked Tabinian.

"Tomorrow morning."

Tabinian, who had been sitting rather stiffly this day on the front of his seat, asked Dr. Golban to leave the room momentarily. When she was gone, he carefully took off his jacket and pulled his shirt up out of his pants, revealing a giant gauze bandage in the small of his back.

"Take it off," he said. Jim gingerly unpeeled the white surgical tape from Tabinian's hairy back. He emitted little cries of pain as the hair went with the tape. Inside the tape was the shard, the same reddish color as the disk in the safe in their lab at Hebrew University.

Tabinian called for Dr. Golban to come back in, and they spent the rest of the afternoon examining the fragment. The writing was, of course, Aramaic, since it was obviously some Temple clerk's calculation.

They made several attempts to complete sentences, interrupted where the shard of what was left of the jar was broken. The notations were inscribed in a faded black ink, very much like the ostracon Tabinian said people accused him of selling once to a German professor.

"For this, this help, I think I can have that bad mark removed," said Sharon.

"Ah," said Tabinian. "And all my life people have been telling me two wrongs do not make a right. But now it does."

"Is it possible," asked Jim, "that the jar was fired old, kept around for twenty years, and then filled with the temple offering?"

"Oh no," said Sharon. "A Jew would never use an old jar for a temple offering."

"Why is it you seem so willing to understand your religious law as long as someone isn't practicing it?" said Jim. And that was his joke.

"Perhaps," said Zareh Tabinian wisely, "Jewish laws cannot hurt her when they apply to the dead."

Father Winstead had to disobey the monsignor's order for the monsignor's own good. The monsignor had to know the American priest's business.

"Within less than fifteen minutes Cardinal Pesci's office wired in seven thousand dollars to Father Folan."

"Is he still here?" said the monsignor.

"Do you think we could get seven thousand dollars from Cardinal Pesci like that?"

"No."

"Doesn't it make you wonder?"

"No."

"Doesn't it make you wonder that his response was coded, he will know 'yes' or 'no' shortly. The man's been here the entire winter, getting moneys as though he's Pesci's illegitimate son, and now seven thousand dollars, and a 'yes' or a 'no.' Doesn't it intrigue you?"

"That's not intriguing you, Father Winstead, it's punishing you. You're very unhappy."

"You're not bothered?"

"No," said the monsignor pleasantly.

"I don't see how you cannot be."

"Spring is here. Easter week is coming. It is here where He rose. That is why we are here. The redemption of mankind happened here, and it is beyond me, Father Winstead, that when infinite good abounds, you worry about someone else's money."

"Infinite good doesn't pay the light bills," answered Father Winstead.

The monsignor smiled. He knew Father Winstead was a good man and a good assistant, it was just so sadly funny how the man would worry about light bills when this was where God chose to offer the Light Himself.

"I don't know what is so funny," said Father Winstead.

"I was thinking about the Resurrection, and how even great

trials are made trivial by the great promise of a happy ending. The beginning.''

"You would," said Father Winstead, "which is why the Church, in its great wisdom, has me here to pay the light bills.''

"I'll do it," said Jim.

Tabinian's Caiaphas piece was set in a horizontal vise over a table in Sharon's lab. Jim had a surgeon's saw.

He felt Sharon's hand cover his palm. She looked worried. He knew what she was worried about. She was worried about him.

"I'll do it," said Jim.

"I love you," said Sharon. She backed away. The shard was hard, and while the saw was precise, it was slow. He wanted to tell her he loved her. He did love her. But he was too filled with despair this morning to allow himself a moment of peace. And for love one needed some fraction of one's soul to be in peace.

This very morning, before he exchanged money for shard with Tabinian, he had committed the greatest betrayal of his life. Jim Folan had turned on Jesus as no man ever had. It did not happen in bed with Sharon. Nor had he handed Him up to the authorities for thirty pieces of silver, which when analyzed was less of a betrayal, because Judas did not know he was selling out God.

Judas was turning in someone who said he was God.

What Jim had done that morning happened in a flash, and it happened in his head. It was a little wish.

He had thought for just a moment that if Christ did not rise, then he would not be sinning with Sharon, that all that felt so incredibly good, was good. If Christ had not risen, it made Christianity invalid, along with what it said were sins.

He had been willing to trade in that one thought, his momentary innocence, for the hope of the world.

Good for you, Jim Folan, you low bastard, he thought.

And realizing what he had wished, he told his God he was sorry.

But he did not feel forgiven, least of all by himself.

The saw cut the hard kiln-baked sheen on the shard, rock-hard with time and fire, making reddish dust on the paper beneath the vise.

It seemed he would never cut through the shard, but he would just stay forever, moving the saw back and forth, and he also thought if he were to stay over this shard sawing forever, then forever the word would be silenced that He had not risen.

And then, almost as a surprise, the saw was through the shard, and that thumbnail-sized piece was on the paper beneath the shard.

He picked up the camera and stand with which he had photographed the shard before sawing, and placed the stand legs on the marks where they had stood before, so there would be a picture of the shard at the same angle after it was cut, with the thumbnail-sized piece beneath it.

He made a note of the number of the second picture on a bound pad, and then picked up the piece and put it back where it had been on the shard, and made another photograph. He then wrapped the piece and put that in a plastic box labeled B. He wrapped up the shard, and put it in the safe, taking out the disk that had been found on the skeleton, back at the cave.

And he did the same thing for the disk, and it reinforced his despair that the disk felt exactly as hard as the shard. Time and fire.

"We can bring it up to Rehovot tomorrow," said Sharon.

"No. Today. Today. Yes, today. Today."

"I love you," she said, but the words came from a distant place, a place of the world that was not time and fire and the great yes or no of existence. It came from a woman who loved him, whom he had let love him, whom he had encouraged to love him. Whom he, dammit, wanted to love him.

"Thank you," he answered, because he knew she wanted to comfort him. At least he didn't have to hurt her.

But at the Weizmann Institute, he would not let her come with him to the lab.

"This is mine, Sharon. It is all mine. And I am heartily sorry I burdened you with it."

He saw her think how to answer. She was not letting him out of the car. She held his arms in her hands.

For a long while she did not speak.

"I love you, Jim," she said finally. And then she turned away, letting go of him. She was crying.

Jim went to the lab Sharon had described. A young man was waiting for him, all excited about the matching piece.

"It's the matching piece that makes this dating precise, otherwise you just verify the range little better than a carbon date," said the young man.

"Uh huh," said Jim. He knew they measured the glow emitted by crystalline material above the normal incandescence when the clay was heated to five hundred degrees centigrade. He also did not need explained to him that they did not need a multitude of average firings when they had two pieces, because they could just match up the glow curves to see if the pottery was fired during the same period.

Thermoluminescent dating worked, because when a piece of clay was kiln-fired at seven hundred to eleven hundred degrees, the natural thermoluminescent energy was driven out. That was time zero, whereupon it started regaining energy. And TL dating simply measured how much of that energy it had regained, just the opposite of the carbon dating, which measured how much of carbon 14 a substance had lost.

"Okay, what is your dig?" said the young man.

"Call it the Golban dig."

"She's already got two in here that are on file. Her first was Golban."

Jim thought of his own name for a moment, but he didn't want that. He hadn't wanted that for so long and so desperately. He was not going to take this thing to himself in its last breath when he didn't want it on its first.

He thought of Haneviim Street, but he had promised secrecy and that just might compromise it. It had become second nature to him to take precautions of secrecy, so Haneviim Street was out.

And he thought of Messiah or the Hebrew word *Meshiah*, which would of course be the most appropriate, and, at the same time, the worst possible name for anyone who did not want the world to know what he was about.

"Masada," said Jim finally. It was the place of a last stand of Jewish zealots who chose death rather than Roman slavery. A very last stand. Did they, like the Reb Nechtal's group, believe in the resurrection of all men for judgment? Or did they believe that death was the end of man, that it was all over?

Could he ever think of death as the end of everything? And wondering that, Jim in one moment sensed how barren life would be.

"Jesus," he sobbed on the steps going down from the lab, "how am I going to live without you?"

Four days later, with Sharon sharing his pain, and every once-comforting prayer now thrown back in his face by reality, Jim got the call from the Weizmann Institute at Rehovot.

Sharon had the phone and offered it to Jim, and he saw she did not want to bear the final news.

And he didn't want to hear it either. The technician asked through the phone held at arm's length from Sharon, speaking to the room:

"Is anyone there? Anyone there?"

"Some people pray like that," said Jim, rising to the phone, and taking it. "Yes," he said.

He heard the details, and then he thought perhaps he was lying to himself with his ears. The man wasn't making sense.

"Wait. Would you repeat what you said? It's very important," said Jim.

"Seventy C.E."

"What?"

"You've got an absolute maximum leeway, at most twenty years in either direction, and a safe ten. I would put your matching piece right on the button. Seventy A.D."

"What's the earliest it could be?"

"Stretching everything, it could not have been fired before 50 C.E. You should have seen the glow. It was perfect."

"Could you be wrong?"

"There is no way it could be 40 C.E. or 33 C.E.?"

"Only with a miracle. If you know how to rearrange glow, then you can do it."

"God bless you. God bless you. God bless," yelled Jim. And, hanging up the phone, he screamed out to Sharon:

"Hallelujah. He's risen."

Sharon was laughing and crying for Jim. Jim laughed. Jim cried. Sharon jumped. Jim jumped. They tried to hug each other, but they were jumping too much. Finally, Jim grabbed Sharon and squeezed her.

"You're back," said Sharon. "Thank God you're back."

Suddenly the release from the burden came upon him, and he couldn't stop crying. Even in his tears of happiness, he told Sharon he was not the sort of person who cried, and she agreed with him. Although both of them had cried a lot since he came here.

And then there were real tears, when all the held-back sadness came out full, and all he could say was, "Thank you, Jesus. Thank you, Jesus."

It was decided that this time he would not rush into his report back to the Vatican but get the full written report from Weizmann Institute, combine it with everything else, and then return to Rome.

Sharon thought this was wise, and since he was also a human being, they should take at least one weekend together before he returned to Rome. Who knew how long he would be there? And they had not slept together well since Dr. Sproul had done such a stunning analysis on the bones.

"You must see Galilee in the spring."

"I had hoped to do it, but not quite like this," said Jim. "Shacking up with a girl friend before I went to the Pope."

"You did your job, Jim. You did that for your Church."

"I want to marry you, Sharon. I want to get a dispensation from my vows and marry. I don't want to live without you."

"I can't get a dispensation. I can only get a divorce if I can get to Dubi again. We're not as reasonable as the Vatican. We've had a few more years of entrenched nonthinking."

"You're feeling better too." Jim laughed. She grabbed his ears and kissed his lips sharply, a reminder that he was hers.

They made reservations at a kibbutz on the Galilee, and took the north/south road that had been so crucial throughout history. It extended clear from Damascus to Cairo.

On this road, too, you could see one of the problems of the Middle East. From heights, the coastal plain and population centers of Israel were within gunsight. And Arabs were living there. It was the West Bank, their homes were there.

"I don't think there is a physical peace here," said Jim. "I think it's in the mind."

"That's not all that comforting."

"Worse hatreds have been solved."

"Sure," said Sharon. "When better ones take their place."

By car, it was less than a half day to the Galilee, a trip that might have taken Jesus a few days. But it was this road that he took.

The hills were alive with spring flowers, and he could smell the turned earth through the open windows of Sharon's coughing yellow car. Before they reached the kibbutz hotel, Kfar Gzion, Sharon proudly pointed to stacked black stones on the side of the road.

"Migdal," she said. "That means tower."

"Mary Magdalene," said Jim. "Mary from the town of the tower."

"Yes," said Sharon. "We are in the Galilee."

And Jim crossed himself.

"What did you do that for?"

"I just felt like it. I just got chills. Good chills."

"Save them for tonight," said Sharon. "You're so funny."

It was a fine room in the kibbutz hotel, and they couldn't wait to get the door closed and the curtains down. They left a trail of their clothes on the floor to the bed and finally had each other, full with joy and passion and lust.

When they were done, they clothed themselves enough for modesty and pulled open the blinds to look across the dark blue of the Sea of Galilee and the brown mountains of Moab and the Golan Heights, very clear this day. Beyond that was Syria. The road they had taken continued to Syria, but no one, of course, could take it in either direction until there was peace.

"I wonder if people there are as happy as I am now with you. But I don't think so," said Jim. "Nobody is happier than me."

"I am," said Sharon.

"No, you're not," said Jim.

"I'm not sinning," said Sharon.

"Do you want us not to have sex until we're married?" said Jim.

"No," said Sharon, exaggerating the horror.

"Then shut up," said Jim. But his voice was light.

They had dinner late, when it was dark across the Galilee,

and lights twinkled sparsely like distant heavens on the mountains of Moab, named for people who were no more.

The main course was St. Peter's fish, and Jim wondered out loud if Simon the fisherman ever thought as a young man that all the fish in this lake he worked would one day be named after him.

"He certainly wouldn't expect to be a Jesuit," said Sharon. She was smiling her trap smile. Jim recognized an attack on religion was coming. Sharon had put that away during Jim's depression during the bulk of Lent. But now she was back with a vested interest in illuminating all the contradictions of the Roman Catholic Church because he was a priest.

"He wouldn't be a Jesuit because we weren't formed for over another millennia?"

Sharon grinned broadly. "He wouldn't be a Jesuit because he was totally tainted on his mother's and legal father's side."

"Oh, that," said Jim. "How long have you known about that?"

"About a month, but you were so sad, I didn't bring it up."

"Let me explain."

"Jim, don't explain. I love it. I love it. It's beautiful. The Society of Jesus wouldn't let in Jesus. Oh, Jim, that is beautiful."

"Sharon, stop laughing. It was a silly thing."

"I love it. Mary is out. So are the apostles. Pilate is in. Peter is out. You would keep out Judas, and that's okay. But Joseph is out. Not him. Adolf Hitler, Attila the Hun, Genghis Khan, and the Marquis de Sade, yes."

Jim caught her laughter, and was laughing with her even as he tried to explain.

"What happened was, originally the order had many converted Jews, and during a time of great tension, during a time when many Jews converted to save their lives . . ."

"Oh, the dirty Jews." Sharon laughed. "If saving your life isn't anti-Christian."

"Will you stop? It was a silly law which in practice is not done today."

"Did you ever worry that your son might not be able to be a Jesuit?"

"Not when I took my vows, no," said Jim.

"You're mad," said Sharon.

"You're not going to listen."

"I'm not going to believe in what you're mad about."

"Do you want to hear my argument, my thought-out invincible Jesuit argument to which you cannot rationally respond?" asked Jim.

"Yes," said Sharon, enjoying the combat.

Jim stuck out his tongue and made a Bronx cheer in her face. A table of women in black with white bands around their bonnets looked over, shocked. They were nuns.

Jim wanted to crawl under the table. Sharon couldn't stop laughing.

When dinner was done, Sharon was still laughing and they returned to the room reeling and hugging, very much in love at this beautiful time.

That night they agreed to stretch out this time as much as possible by leaving before dawn on the day after Shabbat, and picking up the report on the disk from the Weizmann Institute that morning. It was no more than a two-and-a-half-hour drive if they pressed it. And in that way they would have one more evening in this blessedly beautiful place, where they were beautiful, and, Jim felt, also blessed.

It was two days they had. They swam in the cool Galilee, and sailed on kibbutz boats, and waved to fishermen and water skiers, and even to the mountains of Moab, which was the land of Jordan now.

They laughed a lot. Sometimes they were just quiet together, feeling each other's being. They shared every thought. From toothbrushes to the lily they found growing wild and white, they said how they felt. And more often than not, each one knew.

By the time they got their jug of coffee in the hotel kitchen for their drive to Rehovot, they knew they had shared a special time.

And Sharon thought, If I have nothing else in my life, this has been more than I ever expected. Thank you, God.

"I just thanked God for our time," said Jim.

"Did you?" said Sharon, and held back that he said what she had thought, because then she would have to explain, too, that in thanking God she also sensed this might be more joy than a person was allowed.

It was not logical, but she knew that whatever they had they would never have again. Something as precious as life was going to be over.

It was 9 A.M., and the sun was up over the Weizmann Institute in Rehovot when Sharon parked the bug and accompanied Jim to the lab. She wanted to talk to the technician about the new advances in thermoluminescent dating.

"I always suspected that someday they would go beyond just matching, and be actually able to date, like a chart on the glow curve. I mean, not plus or minus eighty, like carbon dating, but quite precise stuff. Plus or minus ten. And, obviously, they have already done it with your piece."

"That's how they got the 70 C.E.," said Jim.

"Exactly," said Sharon. "And I want to know how they are doing it. I have a reputation for being an authority on technological dating."

"I have time, take all the time you need," said Jim.

But when they met the technician at the lab, he seemed puzzled. He gave them the report on the matching pieces, which was two typewritten pages, accompanied by thick computer printouts. He also gave them a bill. He kept nodding as Sharon talked about the new dating method, that they might even be able to discard the need for a matching piece if they could date by precisely charting the emissions alone.

"We can't do that yet," said the technician.

"Well, then, how did you get 70 C.E. from a matching piece that was 32 C.E.?" said Sharon.

"He didn't say 32 C.E.," said the technician. "I didn't say anything. I didn't give you a date. I wanted a yes or a no," said Jim. "That was all I expected. You gave me more."

"You said Masada. Masada fell in 70 C.E.," said the technician, taking back the report, and checking his writing again. "You said you got the piece from Masada, right?"

"No. I only said Masada. I didn't give you the date."

"Was the date of the matching piece 32 C.E.?"

"Yes," said Jim.

"Then your date is a perfect 32 C.E. We got a perfect glow match."

Sharon drove slowly to Jerusalem with Jim sitting numb beside her, the report on his lap. He was going back to Rome and he had to let them know that.

But the little car could not get up to the apostolic delegate's that morning of the first day of the work week. Israeli soldiers stopped all traffic. A procession was coming down the Mount of Olives, with people singing and carrying palm fronds. It stretched clear up over the hill.

It was Palm Sunday.

20

Ecce Homo

Warris Abouf awoke to the call of the muezzin that prayer was better than sleep. It was not his faith, but it was his language.

He rolled up the mattresslike bed on which he slept and put it in the closet, so the room could be used for other purposes than the mere eight hours in which he slept.

He washed and put on the Western suit so prized in the business world, and then went out for morning coffee and fruit and sweet rolls with his cousins.

It was the day after Palm Sunday, and the beginning of his work week. He was an assistant to his cousin as an accountant, but he was sure he would make a good salesman because, as he said, he knew people better than he knew numbers.

And he knew he was home. There was talk of a good marriage for him, with all his cousins agreeing that even though the Russian marriage did not count at all, only a fool would mention it to the family of the prospective bride.

He was not yet able to tell them of the humiliation from his son, or the Russians. But he did let them know what he did for the Russians.

And this, they told him, was never to be mentioned to anyone.

"This is a good country," said the eldest cousin. "Hussein is a good king, blessed be his name. He is wise. But this is also a difficult time to be a king in this country."

And it was immediately understood that Warris should never

293

mention what he did in Russia. It would only cause difficulties with security forces. That he had been in Russia at all was going to cause a little inquiry, but not much. That could be taken care of. The police were neither unreasonable nor adverse to friendship with a good family. And Warris, said the eldest Abouf, was of a good family.

At this Warris embraced the old man and wept. But that morning he had some worries. He did not know why, but it could be that instinct, honed on a decade in the Communist system, made him feel something was going to come of him very soon. It might be meaningless residual fear, he told himself. Then again, what one learned in Russia was that one was never hurt by protecting oneself from even the wildest suspicions.

So he told the eldest Abouf that morning that he still had fears of Abu Silwan, "a killer, a real killer."

"He is not the only one who can kill," said a younger cousin. But the elder lifted a hand, showing this was not what was wanted. The elder, Hossan Abouf, wanted to know more about this Abu Silwan, where he lived, things he said, little details that Warris might not think important.

The very luxury of the man's house bespoke power in this part of the world. That he was also, in Warris' estimate, a form of executioner meant he was a powerful one. The references about traitors and his being Moscow-connected undoubtedly meant the As Saiqua, which was the Syrian faction in the PLO.

Amman, it was reasoned, would not be the safest place in the world for this Abu Silwan. But it was also agreed that Jordanian forces could do only so much, and probably only after some of the Abouf were dead. Publicly, the Abouf supported all factions aimed at liberating Palestine from the Zionist entity.

Privately, one took courses of reason, and tried to avoid feuds that could last hundreds of years. Which was why politeness and courtesy were a necessity, since a chance remark or some slight to dignity could lead to decimations of whole clans.

Much of the killing in Lebanon was the extension of these sorts of feuds, as they had been during the riots in the thirties against Jewish immigration, which quite naturally had Arabs killing more Arabs than Jews.

The thing the Abouf did not wish to do was create some sort of feud with the powerful Abu Silwan. Even if they should be able to kill Silwan that might be only the beginning and his precious Abouf might pay in blood for decades.

Yet, it was also a fact that this man living in Lebanon could not come dancing down to Amman and say to the Abouf, you send this Abouf here or that Abouf there. No matter what Russia had for plans. This was not Moscow. It was Amman. And even though they were Christians, they were not without power. This was not Iran, this was Amman, and they were Arab.

But it was also decided that any future messages to this Abu Silwan of the As Saiqua should be discussed with the family.

Warris should not act alone anymore, because he was no longer alone.

And on this morning Warris Abouf was filled with the joy of being home, which meant he was no longer alone.

But in the late afternoon, as he was struggling with figures, there was a telephone call, and he recognized the silken voice of Abu Silwan. He was told to look under his desk. There was a package there, by his foot. He was told to open it.

As soon as he saw the clock face and the wires, Warris almost dropped the package.

"Yes, it is a bomb, but you must act quickly to diffuse it. We do not want another martyr. The red wire must be plucked from its base. Do it quickly, or you will die."

Warris' fingers seemed unable even to close on the very small wire, which seemed so well anchored.

"Now, be careful. Do not move it, for now is the most dangerous time. Keep it very still. Very still, for it will explode as you put it down. Now, Warris, let us talk."

"I have nothing against talk. Why did you do this? I am not a traitor."

"I tell that to my people. I say, 'Warris is an Arab.' But they say Christians are not really Arab, I am sorry to say. There are fools like that in the world, don't you think?"

"I am most Arab. I am Palestinian like you, Abu Silwan," said Warris, the bomb right in the middle of his lap, over his sexual organs. He imagined everything of him being blown out, along with the pelvis.

"But, I say anyone who wrongly accuses someone of being a traitor is a traitor himself."

"Yes," said Warris, who already knew where this conversation would end. His messages of delay because of traitors were no longer acceptable. He had to find something else. Warris tried to think, but all he could do was imagine what a bomb in his lap would do.

He said "yes" many times. He said "no" many times, such as when Muhammad Silwan said there were those in the movement who said that now Warris Abouf felt safe because he was with his family, his rich family, rich as Christians, because they were Christian businessmen who hadn't fought the Jews.

But Muhammad did not feel that way about Christians. "Some of our best fighters are Christians. Yes?"

"Yes," said Warris.

"I told them you are ready to move."

"Yes," said Warris.

"I told them let the Abouf live."

"You would kill an entire family?"

"Me? I am your compassionate brother, Warris. I am the one taking the bombs away. But forgive me, I am sorry to say, they must kill all the Abouf, and why?"

"Yes, why?" asked Warris.

"Because the Abouf are a proud family. Why wait to be killed in turn! End it now. I see only deep, abiding peace with the Abouf. But the Abouf must not be intransigent. You must do what you have been sworn to do, and then if the worst should befall you, you would be a hero martyr, and the Abouf would be received among their natural organic allies instead of set against them."

"I see," said Warris.

And then, of course, the purpose of the bomb and the conversation came down to a man he was to meet at dusk near the public gardens.

"Now, remove the blue wire," said Muhammad Silwan.

"Blue? I thought you said red."

"The blue is even more dangerous, Warris, my brother," and then the phone was dead and the operator came on asking if the party calling from Damascus was through, as Warris fumbled the blue wire off the bomb.

Warris did not tell the elder, Hossan Abouf, and he certainly did not tell the younger Abouf, who would want to fight. To tell them would require they defend him for his honor. And he knew a single family could not stand up against the As Saiqua.

If families fought families, such as in the olden days, the Abouf could make alliances and survive. But not now, not against this thing of governments and movements.

If the Abouf stood against the As Saiqua, it would be doomed, and by honor and ties they were bound to defend Warris. And so that day Warris Abouf, whose lifelong occupation had been staying alive, housed, and fed, gave up these very things for what he suddenly found he valued more. His family.

He, himself, could not believe he was doing these things, but the incredible part of this giving up everything was a release beyond imagining. The great momentary fear suddenly disappeared when he went to shake its hand.

Warris wrote a note to the elder, Hossan Abouf, explaining that he took it upon himself to do this thing for the As Saiqua. If he were successful, he would return to the family in Amman. If not, he knew he went with the prayers of the Abouf.

"Better to live a month with my own than to rule a lifetime among strangers," he finished. Hossan, he knew, would understand what he was saving the family from.

Hossan might not even tell the younger ones, for fear of what they might do. Even the imagined anger of his family made Warris' eyes tear. And he gave the note to the wife of a cousin of Hossan, knowing she would not be aware of what was happening, and would take a while to give it to her husband, who would not immediately give it to Hossan.

By then it would be too late for anyone to do anything about it.

The decision was not the hard part. It was accepting that the good life had been one month, and might well be over.

The contact he met at the public gardens made him feel as though he had never left Moscow. There was so much suspicion, so many tricky little cross-questions. Warris guarded every word.

The contact gave him Israeli identity papers and took his Syrian passport. He gave Warris Israeli shekels and a telephone number in Tel Aviv that was to be called at 2 P.M. on weekdays for contact.

He also gave Warris a pointed knife, very much like an ice

pick. He was to use it on the man who sailed him across the Dead Sea.

"I can't kill anyone. I have never killed anyone. I was sent for my mind, not my strength."

"Then be prepared to spend your life in Israeli prisons. He works for Israel, that is why they let him through. He will guide you to a cave, leave you there, telling you you will be safe, but the ones who come for you will be the Israelis."

Warris protested again: "I can't kill."

"It is not a big thing. It is big only because you have never done it. Wasn't it a big thing before you mounted a woman? Yes. It was a big thing, but after a while it is nothing. It is a cup of coffee. The big thing is not the killing. It is staying alive."

Warris was told how to slip the knife between the ribs, and that the reason the knife was like a pick was so that it would not stick in the ribs. Anywhere under the armpit would be fine. But he had to push it all the way. The ribs would guide it. No little scratching, because the traitor had a gun, and he could use it. Warris had to push the blade, really push.

Warris was shocked to find that the traitor who was to be killed was a fifteen-year-old boy. They set the boat off the shore after a Jordanian patrol had left. The boy made light conversation that Warris tried to avoid.

There was no light, this night, to travel by from stars in the heavens. It was murky black, and Warris was told the water they now rode through was so salty it could burn sores and ruin motors.

It was still dark when they touched land in Israel. The boy hid the boat, and then guided Warris inland to a cave. Warris was exhausted by the trek at night.

The boy left him water and some food and told him not to travel until the next night.

"Excuse me," said Warris, and pushed the knife into the boy's back, all the way, and, kneeling down, kept it there, as the boy collapsed.

But the boy did not die right away. He gurgled, and moaned.

"I'm sorry. I'm sorry. Please die. Please die. Please die," said Warris.

But the boy was not dead. Warris climbed out of the cave and waited outside. Perhaps, he thought, he could get help for the boy, and save the boy, and then the boy would be saved, and since he had saved an Israeli spy, he would get time off. And then, having done his duty, he could return to Amman, showing he had been a martyr.

He knew the tales of Zionist torture were political and not operational. He knew he might not even get many years if the boy lived, and he prayed that the boy would live. He didn't want to kill him. Of course he didn't.

And then there was silence from the cave. Warris went back in. The boy was still. Warris felt for a pulse on the wrist. There was none. He gave the head a little tentative touch with his shoe. Nothing. Dead. Gone. Good.

There was a pistol in the boy's hand. Warris took it. He scrambled from the cave over rocks, crossed a stream, and found another cave, where he went in just as the sun rose above the mountains of Moab, bringing light to the world and his crime.

He heard patrols during the day call out in Hebrew, but none found him, and on the next night he made his way to a road, and there he fell in with an Arab man riding on a donkey, and Warris could see he had peasant clothes, and Warris had the clothes of Amman, a city. So he took off his dark, striped jacket, and opened his shirt, and spent time with the man, who had four sons, and two daughters, and worked for a great family in Nablus who owned land near there.

The man told him how he could get a ride into Jerusalem merely by facing the traffic, and soon an Arab would pick him up, and, on rare occasions, an Israeli would stop.

Warris tried this, and soon a businessman in his Mercedes from Deir El Kilt gave him a ride, and asked what a well-dressed person was doing walking through such a barren place with only a few kibbutzim and tourists around.

Warris said he had a friend who had driven him out here but had to return suddenly to Jerusalem.

Fortunately this type of man did not like listening, and instead wanted someone to hear about his success, his friends, his opinions on the world, house building, sewer pipes, God, women, the tough Israelis, armies, Galilee Arabs versus Nablus Arabs, the proper way to purchase grapes, cars, and the absolute all-time perfect motion picture, to which there was none really to compare in the world.

In this way Warris was not asked another question until Jerusalem. On the way he was impressed with the quality and frequency of fine Arab houses, but he did not question too much because that would give him away.

He asked only the price of such fine houses in this occupied land.

"Your soul," said the driver, nodding to a passing Israeli army jeep.

Warris did not pursue this. He had to assume that every Arab he talked to, other than his contact at the number in Tel Aviv, was an Israeli agent. By now the patrols had probably found the boy by smell.

So Warris had killed a man. He didn't have time or space to dwell on it. He was in the land of the enemy, and he was too busy staying alive.

He slipped the gun under a bag on the floor, in case police or patrols should search the car. He saw armored cars and Israeli soldiers. They looked like such young boys. But it was always young boys. Those were the ones who fought the wars. So were the Palestinian soldiers, so very young. They were all young.

He hadn't killed a boy, he had killed a soldier. Did it matter? No, thought Warris, it does not matter. Staying alive matters. Protecting the family matters.

He did not get off at Haneviim Street, but at the eastern end of the walls of the Old City, at Notre Dame de France. He saw holes in the walls, and assumed this had been the dividing line when Jordan held the Old City and the Israelis held just about all the rest.

On Haneviim Street, near the Damascus Gate, according to the maps he had gone over back in Moscow, there were Arab businesses, mainly fruit-loading stalls. He strolled over, pretending to buy fruit, and he found out they were mainly suppliers to vendors. They didn't sell single fruit, but that got the conversation started. And Warris asked where the big building of the Roman Catholic Church was, and they pointed in several directions. He specified Haneviim Street, and they pointed Warris to a convent up the street a good way out of sight.

"I've heard of the convent," said Warris in his native language of Arabic. "Lots of men go in there."

The men who had gathered around him were shocked.

'Oh, no. Never. No men are ever allowed in there. Never. Never."

It was possible, but unlikely, reasoned Warris, that anything of a major diplomatic nature could involve solely women. It was probably not the convent.

"No, I mean the great building the Roman Catholic Church is going to construct," said Warris.

Going to build? They all wanted to know this news, so they too could tell others. There was no building that they knew of. An Arab warehouse was supposed to go up, but that had to be stopped, and, as the visitor could see, next door was only a vast empty lot with a Jew sitting by a hole that, everyone said, would remain forever.

"You could tell I am a visitor?" asked Warris. Oh yes, said everyone. He acted just a little bit strange, and talked with just a bit of a strange accent, but not that strange, everyone assured him.

But it was, Warris knew, enough to single him out. He walked up Haneviim, with its gracious buildings and embassies, until it merged with the shopping district.

And he realized he had expected something to leap out at him, and nothing had. He walked back on the other side of the street, reading signs on buildings. There was nothing that came to light. He remembered his father saying how, when his father was a little boy, he had gone to Jerusalem for Easter, and he had a Jewish friend who lived there. The friend had come from a nearby village, and he was the only one Warris' father had known in the city. So he had stayed there that Easter. Warris' father would talk often about that friend, but not in the refugee camps, for fear of what the others would do.

When he was almost at the produce market, Warris glanced across the street at a new shed. An Orthodox Jew sat in the shed.

A hole that would be there forever? That was what the vendors had said. Warris walked over to ask about this hole from the Jew.

"Shalom," he said. The man did not answer. He asked if the

man were hard of hearing. He asked why the man was not answering him, and the man, obviously reading a Hebrew text,
would answer nothing.

Warris tried Arabic, and the man looked up and smiled,
shrugging his shoulders. So there was one language he
wouldn't, and another he couldn't.

And this was just too ridiculous, after all, finding a Jew in Jerusalem who would not speak Hebrew.

"*Sukin syn,*" Warris cursed in Russian, which meant "son
of a bitch." And the man answered in perfect Russian, asking
what was Warris' problem, and why was he swearing in a holy
spot?

"Because," answered Warris in Russian, "you do not answer me."

"I am answering you here. Look. Don't blaspheme. You are
in a graveyard. There is a body."

"Where? Down there?" asked Warris, pointing to the big
hole.

"Yes. It is not to be disturbed or blasphemed."

"I see," said Warris. "May I look?"

"Look. But don't curse."

"Fine," said Warris, and walked to the edge and looked
down. Ladders stretched down three levels, the lowest being a
good twelve meters down. There was a small metal door set in a
hole carved in rock. To the left, it looked as though someone
had abandoned a great sheet of plywood.

"May I go down and look?"

"If you don't have to be there, you do not play there," said
the Orthodox Jew.

"Why?" said Warris.

"That is holy ground, burial ground."

"Down there, hewn out of rock, way down there?"

"Yes."

"It is such a small opening," said Warris.

"There is only one body."

"One body?" asked Warris.

The man nodded.

"What is under that plywood boarding down there?" asked
Warris.

"I do not know. A Gentile, a good man, wanted it that way."

"How do you know he is a Gentile?"

"That one argued the Talmud with the Reb Nechtal himself. We all know of him where we live."

"I see. Might he have come from the Vatican?"

"The Roman Catholic place?"

"Yes?" said Warris.

"We think so."

"Why?"

"I don't know. But there are those of us who know those things and they think so."

"I see," said Warris Abouf. "Has he been here a long time?"

"What is long?"

"Since autumn."

"If that is a long time, he has been here a long time."

Warris asked if the body were that of a man, but the Orthodox Jew did not know the answer to that. Was there any special commotion about the body when it was discovered? Warris asked, and this, too, the Orthodox Jew did not know.

His group was living up to its obligation and that was why he was there. They were waiting for the Gentile to prove whether the body was that of a Jew or not.

Warris took one more look at the plywood. It was there not to protect stone, which could endure the elements better, but to hide it. Now why would anyone want to hide a stone?

From the Arab produce dealers nearby, Warris got more information. The dig was going along according to schedule when suddenly it stopped, and Nasir Hamid was told that his property could not be used by him for an indefinite time by the Israelis. And if Warris knew what was good for him he would not ask any more questions about that hole because the Israelis were picking up people who did that.

"Thank you," said Warris to his fellow Arab. He didn't have to ask any more questions. The plywood hid the stone because anyone who knew the Gospels knew that a great stone had covered the hewn tomb. And there was only one body the Vatican would care about so much to involve diplomatic channels.

They had found Him.

21

Good Friday

He was the direct successor of Peter, who came from Galilee here to Rome, he was the Bishop of Rome and the Vicar of Christ on earth, and on this Good Friday, he was awakened two hours before dawn by a priest sworn never to reveal he had been so awakened. For at eight in the morning he would return to his apartments, and pretend to be awakened again. Only a few would know the Pope ever had this secret meeting at all.

So, too, for his Lord Cardinal Secretary of State. As a precaution, this meeting was never to have taken place.

The American priest had returned. His investigation was complete. The Lord Cardinal Secretary of State said that he had seen portions of the report, but it was too complex for him.

"Did he give a yes or no, Lord Cardinal?"

"He seemed strange now, Your Holiness," Almeto Cardinal Pesci said.

The answer was in the priest's face, that once brave bright Irish face. This fine mind, this tough soldier of Christ, this rock of faith within the Jesuits, stared dully ahead and did not rise to kiss his sovereign's ring.

His face was pale, his eyes were gaunt, and his mind was hiding somewhere from the pain of the world. He wore a Jesuit cassock.

When the priest saw Pesci kiss the papal ring, he too did so, and His Holiness tried to look into the eyes. But those eyes, too, hid, lest meeting other eyes, contact might be made.

The room was bare, the rug rolled up and taken away. Faint square shadings on the wall were where tapestries had hung. There was a metal table in the middle of the room, surrounded by two high-backed chairs and one small metal one for the priest. It was, as the Lord Cardinal had said, as safe from technological eavesdropping as the Vatican could provide.

"Well, James, what have we?" said His Holiness. They all spoke English.

"As His Eminence knows, I have divided the report into several sections. And the findings of each section were summarized."

"But there was no conclusion."

"I want to give the facts as I found them."

"Please," said His Holiness. And the man's voice was comforting. Jim had not slept this week, nor had he taken the invitation to Mass. He could not even pray anymore without weeping.

He began with his elimination of the possibility of fraud, from the tomb not having another entrance, and other facts which would make the planting of a body impossible, the validity of witnesses, and the ever-important minutiae which matched.

"Whatever was found there was not fraudulent, whatever it was. We knew that early on," said Jim.

"You said so, early on. I was never convinced they could not have put all the evidence there for their own purposes. I am talking of Israel," said Cardinal Pesci. He sat, content in his flesh covered by billowing red cloth.

"When?" said Jim.

"Any time at their convenience," said Cardinal Pesci. "They control all of Jerusalem, you know."

"But it's a place, Your Eminence. Haneviim Street is a real place with real people. Someone would have noticed something. There was no tunneling in from the back, because the limestone showed that could not be. The volunteers would have noticed fresh-packed earth. Two-thousand-year-old dirt is different from yesterday's, you know."

Pesci asked His Holiness if he might smoke, and, being given permission, proceeded to use one small corner of the tabletop because there were no ashtrays in the room.

"Ah, but why did the Israeli archaeologist ask, that, when the rock to the tomb was discovered, they wait a night, eh?"

"They had worked all day and, interestingly enough, we have proof the stone wasn't moved, from an American Baptist, Mark Prangle."

"The proof that no one entered the cave came from an American with pro-Zionist tendencies, correct?" asked His Eminence.

"Yes," said Jim.

"Suppose, that night, the Jews put a body they had been saving into the cave?"

"What about the clay bricks, Your Eminence? They were dry."

"Some clay dries in a night. Do you think Israeli technology is incapable of producing clay that dries in one night? They have one of the most sophisticated arms industries in the world. They have modern science. I cannot believe they could not produce a brick that does not dry in a night."

"And in one night come up with a body that carbon-dates within the time frame, and a disk that dates to within twenty years of the death of our Lord?"

"Perhaps they were waiting for just such an occasion. Perhaps they had planted it before the archaeologist got there," said Cardinal Pesci.

"The Arabs around there knew of no recent digging. The owner of the lot, an Arab, was inconvenienced by this. All the details showed it was a legitimate find."

"Maybe they did it before," said His Eminence.

"When? Before 1967 it was the dividing line between Jordan and Israel, and there was sniper fire going on there. The Jordanians wouldn't let them walk around without shooting at them. Nothing was built there for nineteen years that wasn't a barricade."

"Why not before the founding of Israel?" asked Pesci.

"Dating wasn't that exact then. The technology of this dating is new. They couldn't have been that exact fifty years ago. The only reason we know what we have found with exactitude is because of the new technology. If this body had been found a mere hundred years ago, it would still be anyone's guess as to what it is," said Jim. He did not address the cardinal as His Eminence.

Cardinal Pesci put out the cigarette on the table.

"You used an extraordinary number of Israeli citizens in that technological corroboration, Father Folan," said His Eminence.

"I did."

"Don't you think that was a bit unwise to use so many Jews?"

"You keep coming back to the Jews, as though that is prima facie evidence of some fraud. But as a matter of established fact, the Jews are the least likely to have any vested interest in disproving someone else's religion. They do not seek converts, like Christianity or Islam. They do not care what you believe, and therefore do not have to burn you alive or break bones or pass crazy laws against you. The existence of Christianity or Islam is no theological threat to them. You might as well be the chief priest of Baal or Astarte for all they care," said Jim, adding, "You Eminence." There was anger in his voice. He felt his face flush.

"You seem to know a lot about Judaism," said Cardinal Pesci.

"We have work to do, Lord Cardinal, come, come," said His Holiness. "In what ways, James, does the find conform to our Gospels?"

Jim explained what a rich man's tomb was, how the stone in front was small in height, but a great stone. He explained how someone could have come up to the tomb at that time and thought it empty.

"And what about those who saw Him resurrected?"

"If that is so, then of course he did, Your Holiness," said Jim.

"But you have something else related to that?" said His Holiness.

"I have theories based on the nature of his followers," said Jim, and only at the Pope's request did Jim verbally give Sharon's theory about Christ and his followers, how He was the movement, and how they had invested so much and were now ruined. He was not a martyr to them, He was a failed God until the Resurrection.

"Either seeing that the tomb was empty or hearing that it was, despite that great stone, might lead some severely depressed people to believe they saw Him," said Jim, and then he quickly went on to Dr. Sproul's most convincing evidence that the man was in his thirties and had worked as a carpenter. But most damning was the method of crucifixion, and for this Jim showed a black and white photograph of the right ribs. It was a blowup, and the small, round indentation signified entry by a foreign body.

"While there were thousands of crucifixions all over that land, Christ's crucifixion was unusual. The normal way to speed up death was breaking the bones, not spearing someone. That defeated the whole purpose. To die by a weapon was honorable. Crucifixion was to humiliate someone, strip him completely of everything," said Jim. He was crying. Why was he crying? Why were his lips trembling?

He could see tears rim the eyes of his Pope. The man had sympathy for him. Pesci lit another cigarette. And Jim went on about the crucifixion, and then how the shroud would have conformed to this unusual crucifixion, except for the height, and how Aramaic would have been the most likely language for the disk.

He tried to stop crying but couldn't completely, so he just went along as though the tears were not there. Pesci had arguments about the disk, quoting St. John's description of three languages, Greek, Latin, and Aramaic, as those being used for the sign that said "King of the Jews."

"You don't understand what a disgrace crucifixion was, Your Eminence. Those were high languages for that place, the languages of the rich and the powerful, not for who Jesus' followers were. You know he was crucified because he had followers. And they humiliated him in front of the people who spoke Aramaic. They would not have disgraced those languages like that."

And the heavy tears were there again. The wracking sobs took him, and he had to wait a minute to quiet down to answer a very silly question from Pesci.

"No, Your Eminence, even though many pictures have INRI, Jews wouldn't understand a Latin abbreviation. It would have been only for Roman officers, possibly. And why humiliate him only for Romans?''

"What do you have against Romans?'' asked Cardinal Pesci.

"I beg your pardon, Your Eminence?'' said Jim.

"I hear nothing but anti-Roman sentiment. I think we should note that.''

The Pontiff, ignoring Pesci, pressed on to hear more of the report. Jim explained how some of the dating was new, and the Pope seemed to grasp everything quickly. He even said "Good" a few times when the explanations were especially lucid. Jim had lost all reference for what was good and not good in explanations.

It was Cardinal Pesci who noticed a light crack through a heavy curtain, and then checked a watch and warned His Holiness that soon he would have to be back in bed to be awakened. Above all, this meeting was never to have taken place. Jim accepted the warning.

"Your Holiness,'' said Cardinal Pesci, "I have one last question, which I think is highly relevant.''

"Yes. Yes. Go ahead,'' said His Holiness. His hands were forward on the table, large fingers touching thumbs like that of a blacksmith, thick and wide. But the eyes were incredibly sharp.

"Father Folan,'' said His Eminence, making sure the lines of his imaginary ashtray were neat lest someone think he had a tendency to just put out cigarettes on tables, "you intended originally to get a corroborating archaeologist, and yet you changed your mind. You used the original archaeologist.''

"Yes. I did it for two reasons. I saw that she actively did not wish this find to be . . . to be, to be what originally she thought it might have been. And so that was good. And you have got to realize . . . you've got to realize . . .''

"Go on, James,'' said His Holiness.

". . . you've got to realize that the archaeologist was the one other person who had to know everything. Did we want that?''

"A good point,'' said Pesci. "But do you think the fact that she was your mistress might have had anything to do with her selection?''

Jim Folan couldn't breathe. He couldn't lift his eyes from the stark tabletop. He heard his Pope talking to him.

"What?" said Jim.

"Is that true?"

"She was my mistress. And I love her. I do. I took her in adultery. I did," said Jim, and then he lifted his eyes to that of his spiritual sovereign. "But that was not the reason I chose her. I told you that reason."

"I believe that, Father Folan," said His Holiness. "Now, James, as to why we are here. Do you think they found the unrisen body of your best friend, James?"

"We have the Gospels. It depends on how you interpret them, you know. It's all in interpretation, you know. Your Holiness."

"James. My Jesuit. My soldier. Yes or no."

"I gave my evidence."

"James, what do you believe?"

Jim looked to Cardinal Pesci. He was so content, so safe, and Jim would have traded anything for that safety, that safe place of Cardinal Pesci, instead of being hung out here, in shame. All he could feel was shame. Shame before his Pope. Shame before all that he ever valued or served, only grateful that there were not more here to see him like this.

And Jim opened his mouth to answer, and then covered his eyes in his hands to hide the world in blackness. And even the tears now had deserted him.

What came from his lips was a moan, was a cry, was a wail.

"Father, Father," he said to his Pope, "why did you send me?"

And then the tears came almost like a release. When he was quieted, and Cardinal Pesci was reminding His Holiness of the time element, Jim felt two strong, warm hands on his own.

The Pope waited until Jim looked up.

"When there is nothing else, James, there is Christ. When all is stripped away, you can see Him clearest. There will be a time when science can disprove what it appears to prove, just like there was a time when it couldn't prove these things. So, this now, James, is what I ask of you, good soldier. Rest. We will call on you again."

"I am not a good soldier, Your Holiness," said Jim, grabbing the hand with the papal ring and kissing it.

"Ah, but you are. You have fought the good fight, and you have suffered. We know that. Share it with Jesus, James. Share it with Him. He wants it. It is His. Do not let His good soldier go with these untended wounds, James."

His Holiness told the good Jesuit once more, "He is risen," and then personally took him to the door, as the poor young man told him how much he wanted to believe. He had tried to take the notes with him, but was told that was no longer his responsibility. There were other duties for him very shortly.

When he was gone, the Pontiff turned to his Secretary of State.

"Well, Lord Cardinal, what do you think?"

"I think we send our surreptitious thanks to the Israeli government, and of course return some similar kind of favor."

"As a priest, not as our Secretary of State, what do you think?"

"But I am Secretary of State, Your Holiness."

"What do you think of the body?"

"The Jews won't dare make it public because then we can accuse them of being behind it all."

"Do *you* think that is His body?" asked the Pope, nodding to the pictures, which he would soon ask his Secretary of State to take possession of.

"With apologies, Your Holiness, I am your Secretary of State, not the Pontifical Biblical Institute, or your Archaeological Commission, which you yourself chose not to use."

"You think it is, don't you?" said the Pope.

"I never really wondered that much, Your Holiness."

"Is it that you never cared?" asked the Pope with sudden chilling amazement.

"That is an extreme way to say that my concerns are for the Church, and its real problems."

"What we saw with that priest, that Jesuit with the strong faith, is a problem. That is our main problem. We have lost two priests, the first of whom may have been strong in the faith. I do not know. But the second, the American, it shook my foundations, too, just to look at him. We must have the body. We must have the disk. We must have the secrecy of Israel. There is no question about that.''

"They will ask a price, Your Holiness. Why do you think they chose us?''

"Didn't an early report say they just wanted it off their hands?''

"The Copts could have taken it off their hands. So could the Greek Orthodox, the Abyssinians. Even the Church of England might have taken it off their hands, but we as the Vatican have the only thing they want, recognition as a state. That's why they chose us. They did not offer all the help to our innocent American because they wanted to escape a few more nasty words thrown at them. I know the Jews.''

"I think not,'' said the Pope. "But if recognition is their price, we will pay it.''

"This priest you chose is not that strong in the faith, Your Holiness. After all, adultery . . .''

"Lord Cardinal, not once did you hear from him that his adultery was not a sin. In our opinion, James Folan was the best. And it is the best, the best, the best of our flock, Lord Cardinal, who will suffer most if that discovery in Jerusalem is loosed among them. No. Pay the price.''

"The time has passed when it would be easy, Your Holiness. The Church has many Arab communities. They will become the focus of unbridled hate.''

"We can survive blood and suffering. Pay the price.''

"The Arab world is highly fluid, the only constant thing is hate. And it has Israel for that focus, but the hatred is constantly turning here and turning there. We are too weak to turn it away. I know the Arabs. Even before Israel, that was all they had.''

"Pay the price,'' said the Pope.

"Your Holiness, when we entertained the schema exonerating Jews from special guilt for Christ's crucifixion, we came under immense pressure from Arab governments, and do you know the ones who most fought the passage of this? The Arab Christians. They knew. What will happen to them if we recognize Israel? And what will we say to the world?''

"That it is about time we recognized that the Jews have come home, according to the Testaments, and that it is time the Israelis recognized the Palestinians have a home, also.''

"Arabs don't care what you do for Arabs. They care what you do for their enemies. A bloodbath will ensue, Your Holiness."

"It will pass."

"And what about Jerusalem, Your Holiness? We have properties and interests and claims in that city."

"Let Jerusalem take care of Jerusalem."

"It is diplomatic stupidity of the highest, highest order. What will future generations of the Church say?"

"Yes," said the man responsible for a much larger church than the one that went with Peter from Galilee to Rome, "that there will be future generations of the Church."

Mendel Hirsch was in the busiest time of his year when he was whisked away to the Prime Minister's office.

"Do those idiots know tomorrow is Easter?" he screamed. But the demand came from too high an authority, and when he got to the office, he saw the Prime Minister was there, and the Foreign Minister, and the Chief of Staff, and a man whom he did not know. He found out quite quickly by the man's remarks that he was the head of the Mossad. It was always a secret who held that post.

"Well, Mendel, the Vatican wants the body and accouterments we stumbled on," said the Prime Minister.

"Is that Cardinal Pesci?" asked Mendel.

"Yes."

"I am surprised he didn't contact me," said Mendel, concealing hurt in his voice.

"What do you make of it?"

"I knew they were concluding soon."

"They verified it," said the man from the Mossad.

"How do you know?" said Mendel.

"Through a half-dozen sources, and also consulting the archaeologist, Dr. Golban."

"Is she working for you?"

"No, she was supposed to be working with you, Mendel," said the man from the Mossad.

"Well, they want the proof that there was no Resurrection," said the Prime Minister. "And what do we want?"

"Recognition," said the Minister of Foreign Affairs.

"That is a big thing. A very big thing," said the Prime Minister. "Just how valuable is this body?"

Mendel began on what Resurrection meant, to pre- and post-Chalcedonian Churches, who Christ was to which rite, and finally when he was told to state exactly what it meant to the Catholic Church, he ventured, "Nothing."

And to explain to his startled audience, he gave an example.

"Let's say we discover an absolutely authentic scroll. Absolutely authentic. And it says the writer made up most of the Pentateuch, that he was an Egyptian nobleman who spun this tale to a bunch of slaves to get them to follow him into the desert. And once they are there, he finds they are too unruly, so he goes to a mountaintop, and makes up a fact that the one God told him there are ten things everyone should do, a good set of guidelines for wandering in the desert. You know, to keep peace among these people."

"What are you getting at, Mendel?" asked the Prime Minister.

"Do you think it is going to make any difference to that crazy group in Mea Shearim? Huh? So what? You show that thing there, they'll stone you to death. What I am saying is, I don't think the Vatican should care that much."

"They do," said the man from the Mossad.

"How do you know?" asked Mendel, and everyone looked at him with surprise and just a little bit of contempt. It was an extreme act of naïveté to think that the Mossad would reveal a source to him if it at first had chosen not to do so. Even the Premier would ask only how valid a source was, never who.

"Mendel," said the Prime Minister, "we are going to ask for recognition. Therefore we do not want any casual slip-ups when we have to move the body to the Vatican. Instead of the Mossad assisting you, now you work under orders from the Mossad."

And then the report on James Folan, CIA, S.J., thirty-five, was read, as Mendel was told he could leave. Outside the office one of the guards commented about a bomb killing two in a city marketplace, and to Mendel it was two more added to the six million, plus those killed after and those killed before, which was why he was a Zionist, when he never believed in the God of the Jews.

* * *

The Middle East commander for the KGB got news of the bombing on his way to a highest-level meeting. An aide stuffed the message in his briefcase.

The aide was urgent. But aides were always urgent. They were always urgent and impeccably uniformed, and seemed to have constantly to justify their positions.

The commander wore a common suit made in Russia, and did not feel he had to justify anything of his position. He had seen too much too often to do anything more than his job until he died. And if they took that away from him, they could have it. He had been right on the importance of Haneviim Street, according to the latest reports. And he had been right on the intelligence of the Palestinian, Abouf.

And that, too, did not matter. He had been right so many times before. He couldn't read the note without lifting the thick glasses onto his forehead. Two Jews had been killed by a bomb, a bomb in a small market less than two miles from the Israeli Knesset. The PLO was calling it "a deep penetrating phase, advancing toward the Zionist government itself."

"Nothing," he said, giving it back to the aide for filing. Some Palestinian who probably had harbored a bomb maybe a year or two had finally planted it where Israeli citizens passed, and run back to his house. If he planted enough bombs, he would ultimately be caught. If he stopped, he would cease to be even a minor factor in the Middle East equation.

The commander had developed a nose for the Middle East. He knew that one day you could have an entire government almost in your pocket, and the next day nothing. An ally meant someone you could use at the time. Never was there a place where more words were spoken that meant less. Never was there a place where violence had so little meaning.

He thought the Arabs were the only people he knew who celebrated assassinations and mourned peace treaties. If they weren't bombing Jews, they were bombing themselves.

How many efforts had failed to get the Palestinians to form a unified command structure only to end in some fire fight when one faction disagreed with another?

And two more had died, and many more would die, and it all didn't mean a thing. Years before, he would have said, rather, a hundred thousand deaths to move mankind forward rather than one that did nothing.

But he knew, in his years, that it all meant nothing.

That was the secret of his courage. That was how he faced the highest leadership this day inside the Kremlin, telling them what had been discovered in Jerusalem.

There was laughter and applause in the windowless room with the large felt-covered table. A few of the older ones even started the applause.

"They found the body. They found it. Good-bye, Christianity," said several.

But the man who had seen too much did not join in the celebration or laughter.

"God is dead, and they have the body to prove it," said one who could claim scars from fights with the Czar's Cheka. Everyone was applauding except the man who brought the information.

When the good humor abated, he said:

"We have only established that the Israelis have discovered the nature of the body in this archaeological dig to the satisfaction of the Vatican. The Vatican has, we have discovered on highest authority, asked for the body and accompanying artifacts. Israel has responded with a request for recognition."

"We won't let that one go through," said a general. "We've got them all. Good-bye, Church in Poland. Good-bye. That's it."

"No," said the man who had brought the information. "It will not be the end of the Catholic Church, nor will it be the end of Christianity. Religion is not based on a rational system of proofs. It survives because of needs. If we offer proof that Christ has not risen, those who believe will not believe us. Some will fall away, but Christianity will remain because it fills too much in the human personality."

"What, do we have a Christian here?" he was asked.

"No, a man who has seen too much, comrade." He could have offered communism itself. There were workers dying to get over the Berlin Wall to the West to escape communism, where students were struggling to bring about just that system, supposedly for their benefit. No one in the world could convince them they were not saving the masses, least of all the masses.

The struggle for communism filled their emotional needs, and the real results of communism itself would have little effect on them. It was always the communism yet to be tried that really worked.

He could have mentioned this, and he knew which of the leadership would accuse him of treason and which would understand.

But he was too tired to bother with this fight, and had given it up long ago. He just did his job.

"I don't think exposing evidence of the body, if the Israelis would let us get some, that is if we could overcome them, would do any appreciable good. But there is a minor, if temporary, good that could befall us. If we make sure that the transfer of the body in secret goes through, then the Vatican will recognize Israel, and the Christian position in the Middle East will be significantly weakened for a while."

"Not permanently?"

"Permanence is not a function of the Middle East," he said, suppressing the first thought he had, which was, yes, there was something permanent in the Middle East. The Koran, the New Testament, and the Old Testament. Only the word remained there. And he was sure *Das Kapital*, too, would remain, for it, too, was a hope, and hopes never died no matter how unreal they were. But he was not about to bring any of this up at this table.

Abu Silwan got two messages in the darkest of morning as he manned his revolutionary suicide outpost, with the help of a Japanese Red Army volunteer, who had the tightest vaginal cavity that was ever his glory to enter.

The first message was that he was to bring back his man who had successfully completed his mission and keep him from disclosing whatever he knew.

Abouf could damage something that was going on that Moscow wanted to go on. It was now Silwan's responsibility to return Abouf to Moscow quietly or make sure he was silenced.

Apparently, Abouf had failed to follow orders to leave Israel immediately. Possibly this was caused by confusion with contact. It was now up to Silwan to see that it was done.

The second message was almost too unimportant to be bothered with. If he had to be bothered like that, he could always have his revolutionary suicide outpost in the firing line of Beirut instead of in the strategic hills placed outside the city.

Revolutionary cadres had struck the day before at the power center of Zionist Jerusalem, killing two and escaping unharmed. This meant possible reprisals by air.

"They never bomb here, why did you bother me?" said Abu Silwan to the messenger.

He had to think about important things. Why did Russia want the Vatican and Israel to be successful at something and, most important, who was betraying whom?

Jim Folan returned to Jerusalem on an El Al flight, seated beside a woman asking why he did not eat his meal. He said he wasn't hungry. And she asked him if he had lost a loved one.

He said he had. And she answered that loss was part of life. In another time he could have told her that loss also had meaning. Now, there was no meaning.

Sharon was not there to pick him up, although he looked for the yellow bug, which he could recognize even by its cough. He had phoned the Friday night of his report and said which flight he was making.

He was first to escort the disk on one flight back to Rome, and then escort the body on another flight. In case there was a crash, the Church did not want both being discovered together.

He was not to wear a collar, of course, and both the Israelis and the Vatican Secretary of State believed everything would be safer if the passage looked routine. No great military convoys. They would move safest under the armor of secrecy.

Cardinal Pesci himself briefed Jim. He wanted Jim to know that what he had said in the special meeting was not personal, and he hoped Jim would not take it as personal.

"What?" Jim had said numbly.

"I hope you did not take my position as a personal thing."

"No, no," said Jim. "I wasn't even thinking about that."

"Of course. Let me say that if there is anything this office can do for you, it will do it. Now, we have a minor thing. I sense that Mendel Hirsch, who has been so helpful, might feel somewhat slighted by being left out of recent important negotiations. Please give him this, if you would." It was an autographed picture of Pesci himself.

"Okay," said Jim. And then added, "Your Eminence."

The radio had told one of Cardinal Pesci's assistants that there had been another bomb in Jerusalem, a mother and daughter killed. The aide was worried about that. Jim said those things happened, but caused a lot fewer deaths than auto accidents.

As a matter of fact, the Israelis had lost more people in traffic than in all their wars.

Jim remembered that, as he waited for Sharon's car. And it did not come, so he hired a shiroot, a taxi which took several people, and they left him off at Beit Vagan, Sharon's apartment. The driver warned everyone that certain parts of Jerusalem were closed off this day because it was the Christians' Easter.

With a mercy whose source he did not know, the driver did not explain what Easter meant.

Sharon was not home. Jim waited awhile, and then went up to Hebrew University. It was a normal school day here. But Sharon was not in the lab. So, he walked up to Naveshanan, and the door to Dr. Golban's house was open, and the apartment was crowded and noisy, and Jim did not recognize the language. He pushed his way in and there was Dr. Golban and Rani, sitting on low boxes and their garments were rent. They were sitting shivah. Suddenly seeing Jim, Dr. Golban said, "No more Ashkenazi. Enough Ashkenazi for Paula," and sat down on the floor, giving up the low box. He was sitting shivah. The Jewish ritual for death had changed from the Ashkenazi to the Persian way.

He suddenly felt tugging at his arm. It was Sharon. Her eyes were painfully tear-red.

"There was a bomb left at the store Paula and Mari used to shop at. It went off yesterday. We buried them this morning," said Sharon, and she fell into Jim's arms, crying. It was the first time he held her in that place. Paula was not there to stop them.

22

Forgiveness

It was a Passover of tears. Several times Dr. Golban informed Jim that he was grateful for the Seder, and the duties of the Seder because that eased the pain. One must keep occupied.

The Arab patient who had become a friend, Haj Suleiman Labib, came to the house to show respect, and when the crowd found out he was an Arab, the mood became ugly.

But Avrahim, seeing this, went to Haj Suleiman Labib and asked him to perform the act of rending Avrahim's garment for him. This was a Persian custom, not Ashkenazi. Ashkenazi rend their own garments to show grief. By asking Mr. Labib to do this, Avrahim established him as a friend before all the Persian community gathered there that day.

"We all grieve this day," said Labib. "Only a fool does not grieve when the good die." And everyone agreed it was a brave and caring thing for Mr. Labib to have come at all. For they would have feared if the situation had been reversed.

Sharon had said already there was a woman in the Persian community who would probably marry Avrahim and prepare all the meals the way he liked them, but he would never love her, Sharon was sure, as he loved Paula. The fighting and the arguments were, if Jim could believe it, the way they expressed love. Sharon missed Paula's accusing spatula that tried to direct the moral destiny of the Golbans. But she was so pained by the loss of pretty Mari, her niece, that she could not talk about that at all.

When Rani mentioned he missed Mari complaining that girls didn't have as important a duty in the Seder as the boys, Sharon had to leave the table for a while.

But when the red wine was poured, and the matzoh shown, Jim became numb to his bones.

Sharon explained to Rani and Avrahim that Christ had come to Jerusalem for the Passover, and before he was crucified he had participated in a Seder meal. And he had taken the wine, and said this would be his blood, shed for the forgiveness of sins, and the matzoh would be his body, and that for nearly two thousand years this was the central element of Jim's religion, and that priests of Jim's religion would do these things as commanded, and it was called the Mass, the important ceremony of Jim's religion.

"How could a man forgive sins?" asked Rani, which had been a question asked two thousand years before, and Jim knew he could no longer sit at this table. He apologized and excused himself.

He heard Sharon answer that Jim's religion thought of Jesus as more than just the Messiah but God Himself, which was how he could forgive sins.

"That's the only One Who can forgive sins," said Rani. And Jim heard that as he walked outside in the warm spring day. The tree they had planted in February was budding close to blossom in the small backyard.

Looking down, he saw a square stone with what appeared to be spike marks on it, one of the common stones along the path. He recognized it as a Maccabean stone that had probably been unearthed here.

He could tell a Maccabean dressing from a Herodian dressing on a stone, and knew what balking was, and strata were, and what the Second Temple period was. It was all as familiar to him now as his four years at Georgetown University.

He knew all the things that could not for one instant quench his anguish by a drop. So he walked. Helpless, he walked, thinking he had no direction, he walked, and he found himself headed toward the Old City, with its limestone walls looking as medieval as they really were.

And he came to the street of the prophets, Haneviim Street, and since he was there, he went to see the body. The Orthodox man was there. Mendel had assured Jim that when the body was to be moved, something would be worked out and that he was not to contact the Reb Nechtal anymore because, in the transfer of the body, muscle was going to have to be used. There were going to be no more nice negotiations through the Talmud, according to Mendel.

The iron door over the little hole that Sharon's group had discovered, in what should have been the end of their dig, opened with his key.

Jim turned on the lights in the cave, folded back the tarpaulin, and lifted up the opaque plastic cover, and there he was, bones as dry as when they found him.

He tried to pray but could not. Whenever he had any spiritual obstacle before, and of course none like this, he would ask Jesus for help. And the help was always there.

Now he could very well be putting Jesus into his carrying case of black plastic. He knew the facts said so. It was him.

"Who will forgive my sins?" said Jim to the bones. "Who will take them upon himself and offer them up to God?"

And then he knew. He was alone. For the first time in his life he was alone. Sharon was waiting for him, her care was waiting for him, her rich body was waiting for him, a family was waiting for him, but now even with all those intimate people, Father James Folan was alone.

He started to lift the body, but told himself it would be easier when he was going to move it finally. There was no point in putting it in the case now. Besides, he couldn't. Not now. Not until he had to. Not haul him like some luggage.

And then Jim Folan found himself with his knees on the stone floor that chisels had cut millennia ago, and his hands were in front of his face, and he was looking at the bones there on top of the case, and he clasped his hands.

"I don't care. I love you. I love you. I love you. I'm sorry, Jesus. I'm sorry. I fornicated. I committed adultery, I don't know how many times, with Sharon. I love you. I'm sorry. I'm sorry."

He said these things as he rocked like an Orthodox Jew in prayer, his hands in front of his face, his body leaning forward and then backward, his knees and toes on the rock before the case.

He stayed there awhile with his friend who had died on the

cross, and then he covered him with the opaque plastic, and put back the tarpaulin, turned out the light, and left. On top of the dig, the Orthodox guardian of the body nodded to him. He seemed younger than the ones who had stood duty during the winter. Jim nodded back.

"Good man, good man," said an Arab in Hebrew, grabbing Jim's arm as he reached the sidewalk at the end of the empty lot.

"Yes?" said Jim.

"You are a priest, aren't you?" said the Arab. His Hebrew stumbled with a heavy burden of some accent that seemed to smother the words themselves.

"What makes you think so?" said Jim.

"I know of you, good man, and I know what is in there," said the Arab.

"What do you want?"

"I want to put my life in your hands."

"Why do you want to do that?" asked Jim. The man had a week's unshaven growth on his face, and his once-white shirt was as filthy as his suit jacket. But a filthy formal jacket was not uncommon for an Arab. They wore them like overcoats. What struck Jim was that the jacket matched the pants.

"Because I want to save my people, and you wish to save your church."

"I don't know what you are talking about."

"You have not heard rumors that the Roman Catholic Church will recognize Israel soon?"

"This is a nation of rumors," said Jim, who had overheard some people discussing that fact, and had wondered about it only briefly.

"It is so," said the Arab.

"So. If you know so much about the Roman Catholic Church and that I am a priest, you must know priests are not consulted about such facts. So, why do you come to me?"

"Because you yourself are the only man who can make amends for the great Jewish crime about to be committed against your church and against innocent Christian lives."

"Go fuck yourself," said Jim in English and turned to walk away.

But the man followed him, apologizing, not wishing to offend, but saying he was risking his life just to talk.''

''I have been waiting for two days around here, trying not to be seen by the police. I am on the run. I have been waiting for you, yes, you, the one who has been coming here for months with the woman. You are the American who asked questions. Yes, you do not think you are noticed but you are. We are Arabs around here, but we have eyes. You are the one, and you can save your church. My name is Warris Abouf, and I am an officer in the KGB, despite the dirt on my clothes, and now I have put my life in your hands. Collect it if you will on King Faisal Street in the Old City. Walk from the Lion's Gate toward the Via Dolorosa and back. I will be there. If you wish to collect my life, I will be on King Faisal Street.''

Jim looked at the dark eyes of Warris Abouf. How did the man know so much? Why did he risk so much? Jim's first instinct was to tell Sharon, and then possibly Mendel.

But those were just the people who would have to turn in this man who called himself Warris Abouf. Jim felt uncertain now about what to do.

And then suddenly it was as if the man had read Jim's eyes, because he turned away as though he had seen that one chance of doubt, that one lure that worked.

Warris Abouf scurried into a fruit vendor's house and then out a side entrance, with the man yelling at him. Warris had not had a place to rest his head since he had left the cave by the Dead Sea.

He could hardly believe he was doing this. All his grown-up life he had been so careful and calculating for his safety. Now he was risking possible prison here in Israel or death elsewhere to disobey an order that had told him to run for safety.

The contact by telephone arrangement had even specifically ordered Warris to leave immediately. He was told not even to go near Haneviim Street again. Just go, and disclose to no one what he had previously reported to his contact. And there was even a congratulations along with it.

No order could have been more blessedly received. Immediately Warris had headed toward the Jordan River, north of the Dead Sea.

He knew leaving was much easier than entering. All one had

to do was spot some cover on the Jordanian side, and choose
the most propitious time to run there. That was what he was
told. The Golan, too, was not all that bad if one stayed off the
main roads. It was coming in where the difficulty lay. And so
he would go home, but on the way he discovered something
ugly and threatening.

He had been given a ride most generously by other Arabs,
but even before this car entered the new Israeli Road in the
nearby wilderness, he was asked if he was a Christian. Now, no
other Arab had before asked this question and Warris became
immediately suspicious. He had not spent a life reading subtle
movements on blank Slavic faces to miss this sign from a
brother Arab.

"No," he said. "I believe in Allah and that Muhammad was
his Prophet."

"What do you think of the Zionist Vatican conspiracy?" he
was asked, and said he was hearing about it for the first time.
And the driver explained it in ominously anti-Christian terms,
terms he had not heard since he was a little boy when he had
gotten into a fight with Muslim friends because he said that the
Holy Trinity was not the Father, Son, and Mary, but the Father, Son, and Holy Ghost.

And they had claimed the Koran said otherwise, and they
beat him up for saying the Koran lied.

He had grown up with both stories of Muslim brotherhood
for Christians and of persecution. There had been good times
and bad times. Times of alliance and times of war.

But never before had he heard such harsh terms as he was
hearing now in the car. Never the blood hate, and that ominous
word "traitor."

Perhaps it was only the talk of these few, and perhaps it was,
after all, just talk.

A leftist radio station that morning in Beirut had predicted
openly that the Vatican would join the Zionist imperialist conspiracy.

"What a foolish thing," said Warris. "I do not believe it.
Why would the Christians do such a foolish, foolish thing?"
asked Warris.

"Why did the Maronites join the Israelis? Why did the Christians inflict the Crusades and colonization? The problem with

us is that we are too compassionate, too forgiving.'' And everyone in the car agreed that only a knife could cut the Christian greed for Zionist gold.

Worse still was the talk in the town from which he had chosen to walk to the Jordan. He could tell it was a Christian community because the stores were so big and modern. The talk there was of memories of the riots during the thirties, when many Christian communities had been attacked by roving Muslim bands.

''We will be all right,'' said one merchant. ''But forget those in Syria and Jordan.''

''Jordan,'' said Warris, moving into the group discussing the events in a coffee shop on the main square. ''But what about Hussein?''

''Hussein? Hussein is run by his army and they are Bedouin. They were the ones who kicked out the PLO from Jordan. He just followed. This time they may well join the riots against Christians.''

''It will be bad, then?'' asked Warris.

''I doubt if anyone in Jordan will survive,'' said the man.

''Syria will be as bad,'' said another.

''Not Syria, they have a long, long, good history with the Muslims there,'' said another.

''Which will be all the worse for it. You will see,'' said the man who had predicted disaster for the Christian community in Jordan.

Warris' first thought was to get his family out. But to go where? Where in the Arab world would be safe after this?

There was only one reason why the Vatican would recognize Israel at this time, reasoned Warris, and it was of course that body.

He tried to tell himself there was nothing one man could do in a great disaster, that he was helpless. But he knew he was not. He was just the man who might be able to do something, just the man who might save his family.

And so without even a plan he found himself headed back to Jerusalem, to save his family and their home.

It was the one thing he would risk his life for. But as he traveled, his fine mind began placing people and things, and courses of action began appearing.

The most dangerous man for him was Abu Silwan, but if he could show Abu Silwan that the struggle was being helped by Warris disobeying the order then Silwan, a man most aware of traitorous currents, would be on his side. Silwan, most of all, would understand.

It took no genius to realize that the key to all this was the body, and if there was that Jewish guardian sitting by the hole, then the body was still there.

And if it were still there, it could be removed, and, just possibly, the disaster for his family and his home could be averted.

He did not know how he would remove the body as he worked his way back to Jerusalem, but he thought if he could enlist the help of the Vatican's man, then removing the body might not be impossible.

He had to at least try. He would see this man, look into his eyes, and if this man could be turned, Warris Abouf would do it because he knew people.

If nothing worked . . . Still, Warris had to try, because if nothing worked, there would be no home for him and his family anyway.

All of these things he continued to think about even after he had met the Vatican's man and made his way circuitously to King Faisal Street, making sure to wander through the Arab quarter randomly as a precaution that he was not being followed.

Finally, he entered the rock-paved way of King Faisal Street, and stood under a stone arch, waiting. Warris watched workmen install a large pipe for sewage removal. Several times he thought he saw what had to be Israeli police, but then, down the street, in that heavy, leaden pace, came the priest. It had worked. He was here. And if he was here, the battle was three quarters won.

As he talked, Warris watched the man's eyes. The eyes would tell everything. The eyes said whether the man believed or distrusted. Immediately Warris saw in the blue eyes of the priest that he resented talk of grand conspiracies, so Warris carefully moved away from that.

"I was just talking in broad senses. Of course, people do what they must, no?"

"I don't even know if I should be here," said the priest.

"You are only doing what you can do. That is all we can do. I am not asking you to betray your church. I am asking you to listen. If that is a betrayal, turn me in now. I will wait here."

"No, you won't," said the priest.

The man did not like exaggerations. He did not like fawning and was repelled by it. He liked his truth hard, and he liked specifics.

Warris explained his reasoning. For twenty minutes, under an examination sharper than that of Vakunin, Warris explained that the body itself had to be the price for recognition.

Omitting any words such as extortion, Warris established that the body was the price for recognition. Then he went into detail about the harmful effects to the Christian community if recognition occurred.

"It will not hurt Americans. It never hurts the strong. But it will hurt the weak. I am Arab. I know my kind."

"So, why are you doing this? I thought you worked for the KGB."

"Shhh. Shhh. Please, please. Not out loud again."

"Why are you doing this?"

And Warris explained about his family in Amman, and almost as though in a grand confession, Warris exposed his longing to be home.

He had never known a home except with his family in Amman. He had never known anyone to whom he should show such loyalty. And almost by accident he struck the one chord to play.

"I owe it to them not to fail them. Perhaps I won't succeed because it might be beyond me. But, I must try," said Warris, and seeing the response in the eyes about failing a duty possibly being beyond one's control, Warris worked on that in all its variations until the man said:

"I don't know. I just don't know."

"I do not know either. Maybe we will fail," said Warris. He had him. He knew it.

"Let's just hear what you would suggest. I am not making any sort of commitment. I just want to hear."

And Warris outlined several plans. And to each the man said, "No."

"I'm thirsty," said the man, and they both went to a nearby

store to buy grapefruit juice and soda water. "My name is James Folan."

"And do you have a plan, Father Folan?"

"I do."

"And what is it?"

"I just don't know if I should do it. I just don't know, Warris Abouf."

"Are you afraid it will fail?"

"Maybe."

"But you do agree that the body should be taken out of politics, out of barter, yes?"

Jim swallowed. His mouth was dry. "Yes. Yes. I do." He drank down two bottles of the pale drink, and then said, "O God, help me. Will you ever help me?"

The plan was to meet at the Kibbutz Kfar Gzion on the Sea of Galilee in two days. Midnight. Could Warris get there?

"Yes. Yes. Of course."

"From there, we cross at the Golan, which is nearby."

"You will have the body?"

"And other evidence. Yes, in Syria we go directly to the papal nuncio."

"Absolutely. I am for that too. I am Melchite Catholic. If it is stolen, then, of course, the Israelis cannot trade it for recognition."

"All right then, that is it."

"And if you are not there?" said Warris.

"If I am not there, I am not there. But I will be there. Look for a yellow Volkswagen, very beat up."

"One last warning. Be quite careful of whomever you are close to," said Warris.

"What do you mean?"

"That person will be the Israeli agent," said Warris, and suddenly he saw a fury in those blue eyes that could burn down a city with rage.

"You don't know that. What is that shit?"

"In truth, I would like to tell you I had made a mistake, because you are most angry now, Father Folan. But you must be aware of this. This is how they all operate. They get someone to be close to you to watch you. Not just the Jews."

"You don't know that," said Jim.

"For both our sakes, please think about that," said Warris Abouf, who knew he had just successfully passed his most dangerous moment, knew it in the man's eyes.

"Jim, what's wrong?" said Sharon, getting into bed with him, leaving her clothes on the chair nearby, trying to snuggle up to him for warmth.

"Nothing. Nothing is wrong. I just wanted to know how limitless our expenses are from the Israeli government. You seemed to have done rather well not teaching this year is all I am saying."

"Jim, please don't do this to me. What's wrong?"

"The whole world is wrong."

"I feel we're becoming wrong, Jim. I can't take that now. Not now."

"All right, then let's not talk."

"What's wrong?"

"Do you really think I am a better lover than Dubi, or was that just something you said?"

"Why now?"

"Do you think I believed that?"

"I never said you performed better than Dubi. I said it was better with you. And it is. Because I love you. You feed the whole woman, Jim. Dubi fed this," she said, and she gave a sharp motion of her right hand between her legs.

"Ah . . . ahhh . . . shit," said Jim, in English, finally.

"What?"

"I know you love me."

"Of course, I love you. What's the matter with you, you stupid, crazy lunatic?" yelled Sharon, furious to the point of tears. "You. What's the matter with you? You hurt me."

"I love you."

"Thank you for nothing. I don't need this now. Not now," said Sharon, and she asked him angrily if he wanted some orange juice, and he said he did, and he suggested that maybe they needed a trip back to the Kibbutz Kfar Gzion on the Sea of Galilee.

"We'll never have that time again, Jim," she said, bringing him the orange juice and filling it with some brandy because he liked it that way.

"We'll have another time."

"You never do," she said.

And Jim knew she would go with him.

The key was to move everything at the last minute, and put it in the tiny bug without Sharon knowing it. That, Jim assumed, would be the easy part. The hard part would come later, he thought.

"Oh no, the money man," groaned Father Winstead, running from one phone to another. "Could you come back tomorrow? We are inundated. Some Communist radio has been broadcasting to the Middle East that we're going to recognize Israel and the phones have not stopped."

"And what do you tell people?" asked Jim.

"I tell them that we have yet to receive word of any such occurrence. Which is 'Hell no' in diplomatic language."

"I have to have the money. At least five hundred dollars more. But this money I am going to repay."

"On your vow of poverty?"

"I'll be more poor," said Jim.

"Sounds like less pregnant, Father Folan," said Father Winstead.

The money came just as quickly as before, but this time Jim thanked Father Winstead.

"Pray for me, will you?"

"And you for me, Father," said Father Winstead.

With the five hundred dollars he bought opal earrings to match the necklace Sharon loved so much, the one the Arab owner of the lot had given her. He put a note in it, and then let the jeweler wrap it. He was sure he was being taken, although he tried to bargain. The note said, "Sharon, I will love you forever, Jim." It was in English, because that was his language.

The next morning Jim asked Sharon if he might borrow the car because he had a surprise for her he had to pick up.

"It's big?" she said.

"Not bigger than a Volkswagen trunk," said Jim.

Sharon held her hands roughly four feet apart in width. "Well, it must be an American mink coat for a million dollars."

"You will get your gift at the Sea of Galilee."

"Sounds Biblical," said Sharon.

She smiled, and in that smile Jim could see a little island of joy in her grief. That was how life handled grief, bits of joy and living coming up in brief spaces and getting larger and more common until the grief itself was an island and a memory.

But for Jim, only his expressions changed. What was there in pain was still there, like a sharp rock only occasionally covered by a rise in water, but always there, unmoving, planted.

He drove up to Hebrew University and parked outside. There had been several Palestinian bomb attempts at the university and cars had not been allowed in since because they might be packed with explosives that could cause major damage. The university had learned to live with bombs, and Sharon was learning to live with Paula's and Mari's deaths, so why should Jim's loss be irredeemable?

Was it because the Redeemer was lost?

It seemed like forever now since he had said a Hail Mary. Would he get used to that?

As he entered the lab and opened the safe for the disk, he forced a Hail Mary, and it felt blessedly good.

The case that had brought the disk from the cave was lying under it, but he didn't want to use that one, in case Sharon might accidentally stumble on it. So he got a plastic shopping bag, and stuffed it with papers, and then put in both sides of the disk.

If Tabinian had been representing the Vatican instead of someone as important as the Vatican Secretary of State, Jim suspected that the Church might have gotten the body at what he was sure was the original price, just taking it off the Israelis' hands.

But that was at the beginning, when things were simple, and he was sure now, just as he was that first day meeting Hirsch, that the Israelis would not dare claim the Vatican had stolen the body. Because that would bring them just what they wanted to avoid in the first place.

Maybe the Vatican would recognize Israel, anyhow. He had always thought it should. But it would be done free of using Him as barter.

Outside the university he put the bag in the trunk. There really wasn't much room left, two and a half feet at most.

But he had planned on that. Two and a half feet was the limit of the size of the bag the ultra-Orthodox were letting through. Anything larger might be a skeleton.

Jim drove the yellow bug to a baggage shop, and, with the trunk open, bought an overnight bag to fit.

At the dig the guardian of the body nodded to Jim, his black hat moving precisely as always. Jim nodded back.

It was the first good, warm, warm day of spring, almost summer, and somehow the man wore the same black clothes he seemed to wear in winter. If both of them could speak the same language, he might find out why, someday.

This climb down would be the last time. Already, the weather was claiming this incision into history as its own, with the shades of earth and debris all coming to the same patina.

Inside, the cave was dry and hot, with the dehumidifier still working. Jim removed the tarpaulin, and then the opaque plastic cover. Carefully, he rolled a light layer of cotton onto the bottom of the small bag, and then slid a card under the bones of the body's right hand without the cartilage and ligaments of life, and without the bond of polyvinyl keeping it stuck to the palette, the hand became a light palmful of carpal, metacarpal, and phalanx bones, which felt like so many very light beads. He was faster with the left hand. He laid the arms and legs adjacent on the next layer of cotton, and then the pelvis, which he had to take out again to get it to push up into the rib cage. And finally the head, the skull, and that small orange fragment that had pinned his legs so long ago.

And the zipper would not close on the bag, so he took out all the pieces of what was once a man, and he tried again, starting with the rib cage and skull, and then laying in the hands and feet around it, and again it would not fit. Four ways it would not fit, and where the polyvinyl had not covered, the brown bone was beginning to break off in his hand.

They are just bones, Jim told himself. No matter who it was, they were just bones. The bones were what was left of the man, not the man. And who, after all, had said let the dead bury the dead, if not Him? He would be the most understanding. He would be the most forgiving. Didn't Jim know that?

Jim took one very deep breath and then with both hands pressed down on the bones. They cracked easily, like breadsticks. He groaned. He pressed again and cried out as though someone were breaking his bones, and then it was done. The blue bag would zipper.

He left the cave for good.

The Reb Nechtal's man only smiled when he saw the same small bag that went in. A body was so amazingly small when it was just the bones, like a couple of basketballs. Jim put the bag in the trunk, and it fit. Now it fit nicely. It all fit.

When Jim was a little boy, he had wondered why everybody didn't fit nicely into his place in the world, and now he understood how the thing was done to make everyone fit. You broke people. Because everyone had to fit. When he picked up Sharon he told her about people fitting, even as he told her her gift was in the trunk and their overnight things should go in the back seat.

"Why are you so upset about people fitting into the world, dammit?" said Sharon. ".You're a Jesuit. You're supposed to fit."

"I'm a human being."

"Welcome to the rest of us. You don't have to yell at me."

"Why are you yelling at me?" said Jim.

"Well, why are you yelling at me?" asked Sharon.

"I'm sorry," yelled Jim.

"All right," said Sharon.

"Aren't you sorry?" said Jim.

"All right," said Sharon. "Who drives?"

"Go ahead," said Jim.

"You don't like my driving," said Sharon.

"Wherefore is now different from any other day?" said Jim.

"I'll drive," said Sharon.

And they left Jerusalem and drove north up to Galilee, through land that had once been swamp and which was considered worthless because of the diseases swamps breed, now drained and tilled and loved back to usefulness. Through the beautiful spring-kissed land of Abraham and Isaac they drove, in dull, sullen silence.

They registered at Kfar Gzion, and then, alone in the room, realized how hard being angry was. And also how very silly it was.

"I'll like you if you bought me an expensive gift," said

Sharon, and then they both laughed and touched each other. But this time when Jim wanted the love to be so good, good for Sharon, it seemed as though she were doing the same thing. And it was not as good as always, it did not satiate certain longings which he could not define. He felt somehow incomplete.

"I will give you your gift tomorrow morning."

"Why tomorrow morning?" asked Sharon.

"It's a morning gift. You don't give a morning gift at night."

"No," said Sharon. "You never do."

It took Sharon a long time that night to fall asleep, because she was talking about herself, about how she had first come to Israel and vowed to be a better student than the Ashkenazi, how she had not really loved Persia like her older brother had, and then another aspect of why he left.

"I think he just felt it was time to go. You know, two thousand five hundred years, and it is time to go. We were there before Islam, and in the time of Christ we came to Jerusalem with our coins of graven Persian kings, and when Alexander conquered Darius we mourned for our fallen king. I guess there is a time to go. It does not mean that it is a pleasant time to go, or an easy time to go, but like death, it is time to go because it is time to go."

She said, as she settled into the calm that preceded sleep, "Sometimes I wonder why we Jews don't feel that way, you know. Good-bye, world. But then if we were not Jews, what would we be? You have to be something, yes?"

"I love you," said Jim. "I will love you forever."

And there was contentment in that beautiful dark face as she closed her eyes and went to sleep. Jim stayed with her awhile, and then he put the opal earrings on the night table, and, daring not even to kiss her lest he wake her, went out to the car and waited in the spring night. It was dark. The clouds shared the night with the moon.

"Are you there?" came the voice in that struggle with Hebrew. It was the Arab, Warris.

"I am here."

"Good," said Warris.

Jim had trouble with the bug's engine, and when it finally got going, he saw a figure in a man's shirt running toward the car from the cabins. It was Sharon in his shirt in the night.

"Jim. Jim. Where are you going?"

"I'll be right back."

"You're leaving."

"No."

"What's this?" She pushed the note from the earrings into the car. She noticed Warris. "Who is he?"

"Someone I met, Sharon. I'll be back."

"You're leaving me. Don't, Jim. Jim don't leave me," cried Sharon.

Suddenly the Arab, Warris, was slipping a gun out of his pocket. Jim got out of the car, making sure the Arab was behind him.

"Sharon. I love you. I am coming back."

"What is this?" She held up the note that came with the earrings.

"That's part of the morning gift."

"What's the other part?"

"I am going to get it."

"I don't believe you, Jim." She was crying, and he held her, and kissed her, and when he couldn't let go, even though he knew he had to let go, he asked for help. It seemed as though there were no end to things he felt he couldn't do that he had to do.

But he did it. He just did it. That was the way things were done. The way to do it was to do it.

He drove out of the parking lot, seeing Sharon start to run after him, and then stop, apparently giving up.

"Will she report us?" asked the Arab, Warris.

"We'll find out, won't we?" said Jim.

"We will never make it," said Warris.

They drove to Ras Pinhas, beyond Capernaum, and then west to the Golan Heights with the car coughing to desperation from the climb.

What surprised Jim was how broad the Golan was. He had thought it was a strip atop a cliff, but it was more like a plain atop a cliff. Suddenly they were stopped by soldiers who warned them to turn back, or they would be driving into Syria. "Thank you," said Jim.

They turned around, and drove a half mile down the road, and then parked the car. Jim opened the trunk and took the bag with the bones, and gave the other with the disk to Warris.

They left the road, trudging across the moist clumps of turned earth for at least a quarter of a mile. Then Jim turned them back toward the Syrian border.

They almost stumbled upon one military post and had to circle it. But what they circled into was some barbed wire. They had no wire cutters, so they had to try to help each other ease through, tearing their clothes and skin.

Then there was nothing for about four hundred yards, and someone called out in Hebrew and they knew they were still on the Israeli side. They stood still for a long while, then continued. What puzzled Jim was why there were no obstacles on this slope, and then he realized he had walked through a minefield. Warris was panting heavily, taking his breath in groans.

In the distance there was a mellow glow. That had to be Damascus. They rested, until Warris was ready to go on. Perhaps Marine training never left, because Jim realized his advantage. He knew this was what traveling at night was, a hope that you got where you were going, and lots of effort for little distance.

Walking became easier as they moved on untilled land, until there was another barbed-wire fence, and a searchlight fixed them, helpless in the dark Golan night.

But the yelling was Arabic. Warris dropped his package and put up his hands. Jim could raise his hands with the light bag of bones.

"They're telling you to drop it."

"I won't drop it. I'll put it down."

"Drop it."

Jim lowered the bag, and a shot went blowing air by his ear.

Jim dropped to the ground with the bag, and another shot was fired and there was more yelling. He could smell the earth.

"Get up. Get up. Get up. They'll kill us if you don't. We made it. We're in Syria."

Warris was yelling something Jim didn't understand. He picked up the name of someone, Abu Silwan, only because Warris was repeating it many times and desperately.

The bags were taken. Jim protested. They belonged to the Catholic Church.

Warris and Jim were taken to an empty farmhouse.

The floor was packed earth and the walls were stone. There had been a fire in the middle of the floor and it smelled of charcoal.

The bags were brought back in by two soldiers, and an officer questioned them, especially about the bones of a person. They were strange bones. Was this a relative? Who was this person who was so valuable that his bones had had to be rescued for reburial? He did not ask about the disk.

"Tell him I represent the Catholic Church. The bones belong to the Church," said Jim.

"No. I will tell him we wait for Abu Silwan himself. Until then, no mystery is resolved."

Warris straightened his back and answered the Syrian officer. The officers left with the bags and they were alone for a day. No one brought them food or water, even though Warris complained that they thirsted.

"Wait, when Abu Silwan comes, we will have water, we will have food."

Toward the next night, they heard the purring engines of several fine cars. They were pulling up near the farmhouse. Doors opened and closed with that muffled sound of fine tooling.

There were conversations outside, low, like plotters in some alley but without the desperation.

"That is Abu Silwan," said Warris. "I told you. He is a friend of mine. He is a good friend of mine. You'll see, priest, everything will be good. You'll see."

The officer was the first one back into the farmhouse. Warris stood up and ran to the man behind him. The man had a little cat's smile, and acknowledged Warris' effusive greeting and hugging with a little smile.

Warris was a stream of explanations, his hands went up and down, he smiled looking for a response on the face of Abu Silwan, but Abu Silwan looked only at Jim.

"You are an American priest?" he said in a soft smooth voice, almost like a whisper.

"I am. I represent Cardinal Pesci's office, Vatican Secretary of State."

"And those bones are . . . ?"

"The property of the Vatican, taken away from Israel by myself."

"Why did you want them away from Israel?"

"You will be doing your own cause a good favor by taking me to the Vatican representative in Damascus. The Vatican has diplomatic relations with Syria." Suddenly Jim realized he might have made a mistake. But the Arabs would have no interest in making this public.

Warris continued to explain, and Abu Silwan laughed. He called in some of his own men, dressed as he was, in tight pants, open silk shirts, and flowered sports jackets. They laughed too.

"They are bringing us something for our thirst."

It was not water but cool champagne, and Jim got dizzy and asked for water, but he was ignored. He noticed a large red can and a hammer were brought to Warris.

Silwan and his men left the farmhouse to continue their partying outside. Warris put the two bags where there had been a fire, and then removed the disk from its plastic carrying case.

"What are you doing?" said Jim.

"It will be good. It will be good," said Warris, but when he put his hand on the hammer, Jim pushed him away. Warris screamed out.

Soldiers came in to hold Jim down as Warris cracked half the disk, mocking the King of the Jews. It shattered with such ease, Jim wondered why he had taken so long to saw off a piece at the lab. It shattered, showing an even, red interior.

And then the poor bones, so worked over, so suffered for in a lifetime, went, so pitiful and delicate under the Arab's hammer. They were piled up, smashed, and piled up again. And from the red can the Arab poured gasoline over them and lit the pile.

Jim screamed that they couldn't do that to Him, but the soldiers held him back, one man to each limb.

"Jesus!" yelled Jim.

And the fire burned away the bones, as Warris gulped from the bottle of wine Abu Silwan had ordered brought in.

He took the bottle to Jim.

"It will be all right. He is out of politics now. They can't use him. No one can use him anymore. Please drink. Don't worry. It is good. It is good."

"What is good?"

"You must understand Abu Silwan is under orders, for whatever reason, to see that nothing interferes with the transfer. That is Russia's interest. But the Palestinian interest is not to see the transfer made because that would split our cause, strengthen Israel. You see? I knew Abu Silwan would understand that. Come, drink," said Warris, and Jim felt the soldiers releasing him on Warris' orders. Warris insisted Jim take the bottle. Warris could wait.

"You see, we Palestinians have our own way of surviving. Abu Silwan must take his orders from Russia. But if I were to destroy the barter skeleton, not he, then he has followed his orders. At the same time, the struggle is served. You see?"

Jim did not answer. He went to the pile of easily burning bones, the fire now charring away the spear mark where the Roman soldier had ended the life, burning away the oxidized iron mark where the spike had held the legs for better humiliation in death. There was no way anyone was going to find those minute marks of thorn punctures now. No way. Gone.

Jim blessed the burning pile with the sign of the cross.

"From ashes to ashes and dust to dust," he said.

"He lives even more now, without the Zionists to disprove him to the Christian world. You've done well, priest."

"I suppose I am supposed to understand you or forgive you, or something. But I don't like you, Warris Abouf," said Jim.

"With apologies, that is not my most pressing concern. I can only say that you do not know me."

When the fires died, Abu Silwan returned, screaming, pointing a finger at Warris, yelling things at the man, who suddenly dissolved to pleading, desperate jelly.

"You give him last rites," said Silwan in English to Jim. "He has betrayed the cause."

Desperately, Warris turned to Jim. "You remember me saying he ordered this. Yes. Yes. You remember! You remember!"

"I can't do anything. I am just a priest."

"You heard me say what he wanted! You heard me say it," said Warris, his bad Hebrew getting worse with the terror.

"Do you want last rites, Warris?" said Jim.

"You heard me. He said it. You heard him. You heard him."

Two men each had an arm of Warris Abouf, and they were taking him out the door. Jim thought he should follow.

"I can't do anything, Warris. Do you want last rites?"

They put Warris against the wall outside, but when he refused to stay there, they grabbed his arms again and held him there while Abu Silwan was given a handgun.

"Priest, give him his last rites. Yes?" said Silwan.

"Warris, say you're sorry, and Jesus will forgive you. He'll forgive you. I know. He will. He will forgive anything. Just say you're sorry."

"I only wanted to go home," screamed Warris.

"Say you're sorry," said Jim.

The men who had the arms of Abouf leaned away, so no blood would splatter on them. Silwan put the barrel of the pistol against Abouf's right eye.

"Wait, wait," yelled Jim. "You've got to let him say he's sorry." He pushed the gun away. He didn't care if he would be shot. Abouf had to say he was sorry. If he said he was sorry, it would be all right.

"Say you're sorry, say you're sorry!" yelled Jim, but apparently Warris understood that as long as he didn't say that, the execution wouldn't go on. And then Jim heard the laughter at the poor man's humiliation, and that's what set him off.

Later, they would tell him he suddenly hugged the Arab and would not let Abu Silwan shoot, saying he would not let him die in shame this time. They were specific on that. They said Jim had kept repeating that this time he was not going to be humiliated. They told him that he had indeed told the man, Warris Abouf, to go meet his God.

They explained, as they delivered Jim to the Vatican Embassy in Damascus, that they used only the force necessary to pry him from the man they had to execute as a traitor.

"I am sorry to say this was the internal business of the Palestinian struggle," said Abu Silwan.

And then Jim remembered they had stopped Warris Abouf from pleading by shooting him in the mouth. And that was why there was so much blood on Jim, when he wasn't bleeding at all.

23

Kaddish

The nun did not speak English, but her smile said everything and she seemed to anticipate by some miracle what Jim would need or even want, whether it was orange juice or just a little walk. She would stay by him as though he had broken a leg or something, when there really wasn't a scratch on him. Everyone said he needed rest. He just wanted to die.

Cardinal Pesci himself had visited his room the first day when he had arrived in Rome, which was the same day he got to Damascus. That was how fast His Eminence had gotten him out of there.

"We thank you for a valiant effort. But really, you should know it was much too complex a situation for you to have created your own solution." That's how Pesci started.

"At least the Israelis won't have leverage, you know," said Jim. He didn't know what was coming. "I think we should have recognized them, but now we don't have to."

"We already did, Father Folan, which is why I am so busy," said His Eminence. He tried to smile. "Everything has worked out."

"You once said you would help me if you could. I know you must know best how the Vatican works. I want a dispensation from my vows. I know the Church is not giving them now. But I want it."

"You don't wish to be a priest anymore?"

"I want to marry someone. I want to marry her within the Church. I want to do it right."

"The Israeli archaeologist?"

"Yes."

"I see," said Cardinal Pesci. "We will talk about that when you feel better."

"I feel better now," said Jim.

"You left through the Golan?"

"Yes. I think I mentioned that in Damascus, to your man."

"Her name was Dr. Golban?"

"Yes."

And then Pesci murdered him with his words:

"James, your woman was killed trying to follow you across the Golan. One of the outposts, I don't even know which, fired on her. She is dead.

"No!" said Jim. "No!"

Cardinal Pesci turned away. "It is a violent place. If you still want your dispensation, we can arrange that, if you still want it."

"Are you sure she's dead? How do you know?"

"How did we know about your affair, Father Folan? That part of the world is more complex than you know. Friends and enemies, enemies and friends, who knows? We are not new to this world. We watch whom we have to watch. She is dead."

After that, all Jim kept hearing was that he needed rest, but he wanted only to die, let it all go and end with a prayer, that this life was the end of all lives.

Because he had killed Sharon. He was at fault. He did it. He had murdered the woman he loved.

She would not have died if she hadn't followed him up to the Golan. She would not have died if he had done what he was instructed to do, and no more.

One afternoon they gave him a clerical collar and a dark suit, and he was taken up for a very special audience on the third floor.

In the elevator, he heard some clerics speaking English. They were talking about the slaughter in the Middle East. Some Christian communities were being wiped out, they heard. Others were being protected by their Muslim neighbors. It still wasn't over and no one knew where it would end.

They must have assumed Jim did not speak English because they ignored him. And he was grateful. What could he tell them? Another slaughter in the Middle East? Did winter follow autumn? Another slaughter, write another line in the history books, and he would bet that only the most learned scholars in a thousand years or so would even remember there was such a thing, because there would be so many other slaughters.to be remembered.

Sharon Golban was dead, and that was the slaughter of all slaughters.

When he met His Holiness he forgot to kneel and kiss the ring, and when he started to do that belatedly, the Holy Father stopped him.

"James," he said, "can you still keep your priestly vows?"

"I don't have anything else, Father," said Jim.

"Then stay with us. Stay here. We need you. We have something for you. Stay here and discover He is risen in your heart."

"I saw the bones, Holy Father. I saw the reports."

"You saw. You saw bones and you saw reports. James, I do not know science other than today's facts are not tomorrow's. I will not put faith in such a thing when I know He is risen. And this is where you know," said His Holiness, putting a finger on Jim's chest, reminding Jim of Mark, the Baptist, who, when the winds blew in from the wilderness, as he and Jim stood above the Kidron Valley, said the only true evidence for Christ was in the heart.

"He is risen, James, and this is where you will find Him," said His Holiness, touching Jim's heart again. "There. There. There, priest. There."

"I wish I could believe."

"Do you think I say it because I need a job?" said His Holiness with a broad grin. "Why do you think I say it? Why?"

"You're the Pope."

"You should believe like a child, but not think like one, James. Father Folan, I believe He is risen because it is so. That what was found in Jerusalem was a test, for whatever reason. We don't know. Give your best friend a chance."

"I think I lost my best friend on the Golan, Holy Father. But I will stay."

"And you will come to see me?"

"When you give me an audience," said Jim. "I wish I could believe, Holy Father. Pray for me."

"You will be custodian of something for us," said His Holiness.

Outside, one of Cardinal Pesci's functionaries was waiting for Jim. Was Father Folan ready to take a little walk outside? he asked.

"Sure," said Jim, and they crossed St. Peter's Square and entered the front like so many tourists, passed the Bernini altar, and then down flights of marble steps until they reached an old metal door, which was open, with a robed priest waiting, a large round key held in front of him. He nodded them through.

They entered a passage with small crypts on either side, and Jim realized he was in part of the catacombs that stretched under St. Peter's and throughout parts of Rome.

Down the passage a man waited by a sealed wooden crate. The man was fairly short and had tufts of white hair, and Jim suddenly recognized Mendel Hirsch.

"Mendel," he said, happy because the last time he saw Mendel, Sharon was alive. She became alive again in that memory.

"Ah, Father Folan," said Mendel Hirsch, shaking his hand warmly.

Cardinal Pesci's man immediately wheeled and walked back along the passage. Mendel signaled Jim to wait before he talked.

Then he said, "I want you to inspect the contents, because you must sign for them."

"What's in there?" asked Jim.

"What you came for."

"That's not the body!"

"You can't tell, looking at the unopened case," said Mendel Hirsch, and he began peeling away the strapping and prying open the case.

"Come, come. You've got to help inspect," said Mendel.

This time Jim saw how bones were packed properly, with a separate box for each hand, each bone pinned by deep cotton. There was the polyvinyl covering on the bones, just like the bones the Arab had smashed.

"You'll understand this. You are supposed to note the very

small indentations on the ribs' right side. It's round,'' said Mendel, looking only at the sheet in front of him.

"The pilum mark," said Jim.

Mendel had more. He had a whole checklist for Jim.

There was even the scraping where jaw met skull. And measurements coinciding with those done precisely by a Dr. William Sproul, a name Mendel had trouble pronouncing.

And then the disk, which matched photographs, one-to-one scale, including a portion sawed off.

Mendel saw Father Folan tap the disk.

"This one is heavier. It is as heavy as I remember. The other one broke too easily. Yes. This is the real one. When did you take it out?"

"The first day your church began negotiations. I wasn't even told until afterwards."

"Why did you people take it out?"

"You saw what happened. We didn't know where trouble would come from, but we were sure it would come. So we protected ourselves."

"The Reb Nechtal went along?"

"He was given a whole graveyard in exchange. Talmudic law requires him to give up the one for the many."

The next was hard beyond belief. Jim felt as though spikes were tearing at his chest. But he got out the words.

"You know, one of your agents was killed because of that trick replacing the body with a phony."

"What do you mean?"

"Sharon Golban. She died chasing me. You should have told her."

"Father Folan, do you think Sharon Golban, an obsessive archaeologist, madly in love with you, is someone we could rely on as an agent? Father Folan, we have done many stupid things in our lifetime, but that was not one of them."

"She wasn't a spy?"

"Father Folan, really. Really."

"You know, it hurts, but it feels better. I am going to pray for her."

"Good," said Mendel, "very good, Father Folan," and he got the signature from Father James Folan, S.J., and wished him well, and then left the lower level with the piece of paper, and left St. Peter's without proper greetings to the proper clerics because he was in a rush. He had to get to the second floor of the Vatican, where His Eminence Almeto Cardinal Pesci broke off a meeting to greet Mendel Hirsch and accept the signed paper.

"Your Eminence," said Mendel.

"Director Hirsch," said Pesci.

They exchanged formal pleasantries for less than a minute because both were busy. The hardest part of his mission was yet to come.

The Vatican needed its man and its secret safe from an endangering love interest. Cardinal Pesci had stressed that such a high price had been paid already for the body, the least Israel could do was to keep its people in place while Pesci made sure the Vatican did the same.

In Jerusalem, Mendel went right to Beit Vagan, and rang the doorbell. A beautiful dark-haired woman, tight with anxiety, answered the bell.

It was Dr. Golban.

"Yes. Yes. Did you hear?" asked Sharon.

"Let me come in, Sharon," said Mendel Hirsch.

"Did you find him? Is he all right?"

"Sharon," said Mendel, "Father Folan tried to escape across the Golan Heights, and we found out this morning that his body was returned to Vatican authorities by the Syrian government."

"No. No. Why? What was he doing on the Golan?"

"Sharon, whatever his reasons were, he had taken the bones and the disk."

"No. Jim doesn't do things like that. What would he do that for?"

"Maybe he thought the negotiations for recognition with the Vatican had something to do with his discovery. I don't know."

"No!" said Sharon.

"I'm sorry," said Mendel Hirsch.

"Can I go to the funeral? Can I share grief with someone?"

"No," said Mendel. "The mistress of a Roman Catholic priest would be a disgrace to family and friends. I am sorry, but that is how they are."

Sharon saw Mendel bow his head and leave. She wanted to run after him to make sure he had said what he had said.

But it was so. She could hardly turn back into the apartment. Jim was there with his things, with the brandy he always liked, three quarters finished. She had reminded herself to get some for him. She wouldn't have to do that now.

All his notes were gone, but he had left those sandals he had bought. They were in the closet, under a duffel bag. She ought to throw them out, right now, she told herself. That is, if she could stop holding them to her chest.

But she couldn't let go.

"Jim," she sobbed, feeling her legs go, falling on the bed. "Jim. Jim."

She didn't know how long she had been on the bed, or how long she had been crying. The person she wanted to share this pain with, the only one she could really share something this deeply painful with, was gone.

She thought of phoning her brother and Rani to share this grief, but when she started to dial, going over the words she would say, she could not control the wracking sobs.

And then she realized her brother and nephew had too much grief of their own. And she knew what she had to do. There had to be prayers for Jim. But who would pray for her Jim? Who would say her prayers for the holy man?

His family certainly wasn't going to want to hear from his mistress.

So the next day she put on her long-sleeved dress and covered her head and went to Mea Shearim to ask a favor of the Reb Nechtal. She took along a translator who knew both Yiddish and English.

And what she said was this:

"I know you think of me as a loose woman. But I also know you had respect for the Gentile who knew the Talmud, the righteous one. He is dead, and I want prayers said for him, Kaddish. I thought you would be the right one to do that. You know what a good man he was."

She heard a quotation from the Reb Nechtal about what it meant to perform services for the good man.

The Reb Nechtal told her grieving was good to do, but when

it passed, she would have life again. And there could be happiness only through living the laws of the Holy of Holies.

"Good Rabbi," she said, "I don't remember when I stopped believing I should be happy. But I once was happy, and it was not according to your laws."

And the translator told her the rabbi answered that then it was not real happiness.

"Oh . . . but it was. It really was," Sharon answered.

24

The Third Day

The cry went through Jerusalem that ''Pilatus will be replaced. Pilatus will be replaced.''

And many said Glaucus would replace him, and that he was even harsher than Pilatus, for Glaucus was known to have said he would keep the Jews in line.

But for one merchant there could be none harsher than Pilatus, the murderer, the butcher.

The merchant's son was being crucified and had hung on the cross two days, as crowds gathered. And when the father begged the guards to let him put some water on his son's lips, the crowd began to chant:

''Water for the boy. Water for the boy.''

Fearing a riot, the officer finished off the young man quickly with a thrust of the spear into the heart, and retreated with his small execution detail to Antonia Fortress to get help. But by the time he returned with a full maniple, the body was gone.

Now, everyone knew the father must be crazed to have stolen a body from a cross, because the punishment for that was also crucifixion. And Roman informers took this back to Antonia Fortress, where it was decided not to pursue the matter, since the man had no following. So crazy was the father that they said he claimed he knew a way to make his son alive again. That certainly was not a man to worry about.

Now, the father had a plan. He took the boy to a storeroom,

hewn out of stone for the safekeeping of valuables. And inside that, he put the boy.

When his wife warned him of the danger of losing everything they owned, he threw a handful of Roman coins in her face to let her know what he thought. His son, Ygal, was everything.

He let her busy herself trying to pick up the coins outside the hewn cave. He had work to do. It was not all lost. Oh yes, they said he was crazy, but they always said that of people who knew things they didn't.

He was lucky Ygal was killed by a lance. That meant there was a chance to bring him back. Careful he was to make the proper words, the words of magic on a clay disk, the magic words which were placed over the rabbi they said had risen.

Come back to life, they said, crucified, finished by a lance stroke and everyone thought he was dead. But he rose again. And why? There could be only one answer. God would not allow anyone called a Jewish king, even in mockery, to be killed in crucifixion. He was showing He was God and not the Roman emperor. And He would do it for Ygal, too.

The father baked, with the magic words, a disk, and put it upon poor Ygal's stomach. And he waited for God to bring him back to life. But on the third day, the body gave off strong odors. And his wife prevailed upon him to seal it off with fresh clay bricks, lest the odors attract attention where no graveyard should have been.

And to make it even more safe, she ordered a great stone put before it. Several times robbers, thinking something valuable was inside, took a great effort to roll the stone aside, and, seeing nothing, they left it there. Eventually, everyone said there was nothing worthwhile in that cave, and no one bothered to move the heavy stone anymore.

Afterword

Father James Folan remained custodian of the body for forty-seven years, until his death, during which time he was called to the bedside of an ailing Pope. And he was asked how he was faring.

"Well, Holy Father, He came to me in my pain, and He bore my burden with me," said Jim. "I just had too much that needed forgiveness and He was the only One who could do it."

"I knew He would," said the Pope.

The Pope died shortly thereafter, and everyone said that there was never so sure a cardinal to become Pope as His Eminence Almeto Cardinal Pesci, most *papabile* of them all, a diplomat for troubled times.

But by some small miracle of Vatican politics, this somehow did not happen, and a simpler, more religious man was elected Pope who guided well the Church for another generation while waiting for the return of the Messiah.

Jim could not forget Sharon and stopped trying. Often he would say Mass for her. He told Jesus that, even though he knew it was wrong, he could not feel it was wrong. All he could do was thank God for the time he knew Sharon and loved her, and all the good things she gave him to remember during that lifetime.

"I'm sorry, Jesus. I just loved her. And I always will."

James Folan died without anyone in the Vatican quite knowing what his function was. And since the old priest had no family or friends to attend the funeral, he died without a friend in the world, they said.

Sharon went on to become head of her department and achieved her prominence with a major dig that proved the exact western line of the eastern fortification of the third level of the lower city of David. This was important, because there were disputes about whether the lower city had a third level.

The report on the find was four hundred pages and had fewer readers than its pages. About fifteen people understood all of it, eight of whom disagreed with it.

As the economy got better, she bought both a new car and an apartment.

She took other lovers, but there was only Jim, and only Jim remained. She was offered marriage but she refused, using the excuse that she could not find her first husband, but she knew she could.

Every year around Passover she went to the Sea of Galilee, alone. She stayed three days and two nights, and then drove back along the coastal plain.

In her last year of life, because she could not take care of herself any longer, she assigned herself to a nursing home. And just before Passover she said she wanted to go to the Sea of Galilee because every year she did that.

The nurses told her she could not go because she would need too much assistance. Besides, they said, the entire world came to Jerusalem at this time of year, what was she doing going to the Sea of Galilee?

And because she was a very old woman, even though she was a respected scholar, they treated this request like some form of senility.

She did not live through Easter Sunday.

And she was buried in Jerusalem.